OLD EARTH

For Vin Di Bona

You have inspired me my entire professional life
and defined the meaning of true friendship.
But this is not just a gift you've given me.
You're the author of a never-ending story of caring—
for your family, for your friends, for your community,
for your personal and professional causes, and for
your industry.
Thank you from the bottom of my heart.

OLD EARTH

GARY GROSSMAN

W☉RLDWIDE.

TORONTO • NEW YORK • LONDON
AMSTERDAM • PARIS • SYDNEY • HAMBURG
STOCKHOLM • ATHENS • TOKYO • MILAN
MADRID • WARSAW • BUDAPEST • AUCKLAND

Recycling programs
for this product may
not exist in your area.

ISBN-13: 978-0-373-28219-7

Old Earth

Copyright © 2015 by Gary Grossman

A Worldwide Library Suspense/August 2016

First published by Diversion Books, A Division of Diversion Publishing Corp.

www.Harlequin.com

Printed in U.S.A.

"Whereof what's past is prologue..."
The Tempest, Act 2, Scene 1
WILLIAM SHAKESPEARE

Principal Contemporary Characters

London

Martin Gruber, *Voyages* magazine publisher

Colin Kavanaugh, *Voyages* magazine editor

Felicia Dunbar, *Voyages* magazine assistant

Marvin, man in the park

Simon Volker, researcher

Leon, Brown's Hotel waiter

Dr. Renee Kritz, Oxford University professor

New Haven, CT

Dr. Quinn McCauley, Yale University paleontologist

Pete DeMeo, Yale University graduate teaching assistant

South Dakota

Dr. Katrina Alpert, University of Cambridge professor

Anna Chohany, Harvard University graduate student

Rich Tamburro, University of Michigan graduate student

Adam Lobel, Penn State University graduate student

Leslie Cohen, Penn State University graduate student

Al Jaffe, University of California, Berkeley graduate student

Tom Trent, Northwestern University graduate student

Carlos Rodriguez, University of Madrid graduate student

Jim Kaplan, director, Makoshika State Park

Franklin, Winston, and Horst, three experts

California

Robert Greene, researcher

Dr. Marli Bellamy, museum director

Italy

Father Jareth Eccleston, priest

Lucia Solera, tourist

Beppe Poppito, Vatican archivist

France

Claude Bovard, spelunker

PROLOGUE

Late July 1601
The countryside
Le Marche, Italy

IF HE HAD turned right, not left, his life would have been different and history would have told another story. But he was left-handed and without thinking, at a fork in an underground cave system, the thirty-seven-year-old professor veered to his dominant side.

Most of his contemporaries regarded caves with utter dread, seeing them as entrances to hell. Not the mathematician, the professor from the University of Pisa. He had heard that the Le Marche region, located in northeast Italy, might provide the perfect laboratory environment to develop his hypothesis that heat has a discrete nature.

To validate his theories, he needed extremes: the summer heat that baked the Appennini Mountains versus the cooler confines of the caves that were said to lie in the hills.

The townspeople and priests who lived in the area believed that the rumored caverns near the town of Genga were portals to hell. The professor would get no help from them. So he invited two noblemen friends from Pisa to accompany him.

Luigi Pino, Roberto Santori, and the professor traveled together reaching Genga on one of the hottest days of an already sweltering summer. For five days they trudged through the hills; exhausting work in heat that couldn't be quantified yet. But that's why the professor, as much a scientist as he was a mathematician, was there.

On the sixth day his friends gave up the quest in favor of eating, and especially drinking, Le Marche's famed Verdicchio—the luscious floral regional wine renowned for centuries. The professor, now alone, hiked through the beautiful hills and valleys blanketed with white asphodel, cyclamen and orchids.

Three days later, the professor found hints of an opening to the caverns—a slight stream of cool air that escaped from behind a boulder. It certainly didn't feel like it was coming from hell.

He carefully removed a thin glass tube from his satchel and placed it on the ground. It measured the length from his wrist to his elbow and had a bulbous top no wider than the circumference of a small hen's egg. At various intervals, he'd drawn hash marks, though they didn't actually stand for any definitive measurement. Not yet.

Next, he methodically took out a small glass cruet, a cork with a hole bored through the center, and a Verdicchio bottle left over from his first dinner in Le Marche now filled with water. He poured the liquid three fingers high into the cruet and inserted the cork at the top.

Time for the first test. While slowly counting to sixty, he warmed the tube by rolling it between the palms of his hands. He gently pushed the end through the cork and down into the cruet.

Water slowly began to rise up the neck. This was not surprising. He had done this much before. Beyond the boulder is where he would truly test his hypothesis.

He chronicled his experiment in a journal, including a sketch of the apparatus and the high point of the water.

After carefully wrapping and returning everything to his satchel, with his bare hands he began to dig at the spot where the cooler air flowed to the outside. Dry dirt fell away around the larger obstruction. After thirty exhausting minutes, he'd cleared an opening around the boulder and was able to crawl forward.

Now he lit a bronze olive oil lamp designed for him by a friend from Firenze—artist and engineer, Bernardo Buontalenti.

The lamp housed a well that would provide fuel for many hours. Its forward-facing high lip shielded the flame from any breeze.

The professor strapped his satchel to his feet and crawled past the big rock. He pushed the lamp forward, looking above and ahead, hoping that the opening he had created would widen. It did.

He wriggled some fifteen body lengths forward and was relieved when he could rise up on all fours. Soon he was able to crouch.

The air was getting cooler, even damp. He decided to take another reading, repeating the process, warming the tube, turning it over and inserting it through the cork and into the cruet. This time he noted that the liquid only rose to roughly three-quarters its previous height.

The scientist was pleased. His apparatus affirmed his theory. The warmer it was, the higher the water would rise. The reverse was true with the cold. He was able to gauge temperature.

Now to venture farther.

Twenty paces beyond he could walk upright. Another thirty paces, and feeling colder himself, he repeated the experiment. The water rose to only half the height of the first reading. Satisfied, he was ready to return to daylight and warmth, however he was also intrigued by the remarkable rock formations in the cave. He felt compelled to continue. The professor walked for two more minutes. That's when he reached the fork.

He automatically took the left spur. Well into this new tunnel, he heard the echo of his footsteps. The walls had widened well beyond arm's length. He lit a second oil lamp. His eyes slowly adjusted to the additional light.

"My God!" he exclaimed. This wasn't the gate to hell. He felt as if he'd just been allowed to gaze upon heaven itself.

How could such beauty exist? he thought. *What words could describe it?* Yet for all the marvels before him, he pressed onward through a grotto so vast that Italy's most magnificent cathedrals might fit within. There were fanciful crystalline hanging rock formations in brilliant shades of green, blue, yellow and orange that resembled icicles kissing their own reflections rising from the cavern floor.

He stopped to document his impressions as best he could, describing the glorious world he had entered. The professor wrote about a dark blue lake, undisturbed by rocks that cut through the surface, and a whimsical landscape that seemed shaped by the Almighty himself.

He no longer felt the cold. *What lay ahead?* With no worry that his lamps would immediately run out, he continued for what seemed an eternity. In some respects it was. For deep in the cavern he saw another passageway that opened into a space more amazing than the last.

Though he couldn't have realized it, this was a defining moment in time. His scientific curiosity now controlled his feet. He inched forward, raising the lamp in his left hand high overhead.

He was a brilliant man, but suddenly he felt small, insignificant. He'd come to the cave to test his heat doctrine suppositions. Now, he struggled for the meaning of things far greater.

This day changed the course of his research. The experience led him to raise infinite questions about how and why things occurred, not only underground, but high above.

The professor from Pisa returned with readings from his *thermoscope* which many would credit him for inventing. But there was much more at work in his mind and his mind's eye; secrets that set the course for what would become a challenging and contentious life for Galileo Galilei.

PART I

ONE

London, England
Present day
Early spring

"*Secretum*," THE OLD man declared.

Martin Gruber lived a life of secrecy, following the path of his predecessor and those in the same position generations and centuries before. Now, after four decades, it was close to the time to pass the secrets on and relinquish the tremendous responsibility.

"*Secretum,*" he stated again.

Colin Kavanaugh listened as he knew he should. This lecture, like all of Gruber's, was conveyed with deliberate intent behind closed doors in the headquarters of *Voyages*, the most well-respected travel magazine in the world. Gruber didn't pause for comment or debate. It was always a diatribe, covering old ground and revealing new ideas. Every word had meaning, even those unsaid between the ellipses.

"Trust no one. Know everything. Have eyes and ears around the world. Put nothing in writing—ever. But read into everything. Follow the leads, yet never leave tracks. Don't allow anyone into your world, but enter everyone else's."

The octogenarian publisher was close to believing that Kavanaugh would make a worthy heir apparent. He was a trusted disciple, though egocentric. *Perhaps*, Gruber thought, *that's what the times demanded.*

"Be guided by the undying belief that *secretum* is what you must live by. *Secrecy*. Faithfully, unquestioningly, and with true devotion of purpose. Your life and your life's work will be shrouded in secrecy."

"Yes, sir, I understand." Kavanaugh relished the day he'd succeed the old man.

"But enough of my pontificating," Gruber said, changing both the subject and mood. "How about lunch?"

"I was hoping you'd ask."

"Good. Today, I have an exquisite mousse foie grås paired with a 2010 Côte de Brouilly Gamay."

"From our May issue," Kavanaugh remarked.

"Yes indeed. Wonderful article and the winery was most appreciative. They sent us a case. I've been anxious to try it with you."

Gruber pressed a button on his phone. "Ms. Dunbar, we're ready. You may send in our delights."

"Certainly, Mr. Gruber."

The voice was obedient and respectful. Kavanaugh had never heard anything but proper business etiquette from Gruber's secretary. Felicia Dunbar was efficient, but not someone he could ultimately live with after he transitioned into the job. Of course, he kept that to himself.

Such was the world that would soon be Colin Kavanaugh's. Aristocratic, formal, civilized. He was eager to publicly helm *Voyages*, reinventing the print and online magazine for younger travel demos. More than that, he believed he was ready to take on the additional burden. The private job. The one that demanded age-old *secretum*.

MARTIN GRUBER GREW up in England, raised to honor civility, duty, and religion. He would be buried in his freshly pressed Brooks Brothers three-piece suit, his Oxford shirt crisply starched, and his handmade Stefano Bemer shoes polished to a mirror-like finish. All his earthly needs would be put in order. What he didn't arrange ahead of time, Felicia Dunbar would complete.

The doctors told him he had two to three months. Gruber took out his pocket watch, wound it in the company of the younger editor of *Voyages*, believing that his physicians didn't know a damned thing.

His thin gray hair and moustache were accented by large black glasses. Although he'd lost a few inches off his former five feet ten inch self, he never added them to his thirty-two inch waist. On the outside Martin Gruber did everything possible to appear fit. Inside, the cancer was progressing. So, if it were a matter of only months, Gruber was going to listen to his cravings because the doctors had nothing interesting to tell him.

"I shall finally indulge in all temptations and excesses we've recommended for our readers, my boy."

Kavanaugh was hardly a boy. Moreover, at forty-four, he was fully nine years older than Gruber was when he assumed the mantle as publisher and *all* that went with it.

Colin Kavanaugh, like Martin Gruber, had studied at King's College in London, and through a religion and philosophy professor, was encouraged to take a special off-campus curriculum taught by teachers from the Pontifical Scots College in Rome. The lessons were not in the catalogue or even sanctioned by the college. Rather, they were quietly offered on an invitation-only basis at a retreat in Bracciano, a small town thirty kilometers northwest of Rome.

The school itself was founded December 5, 1600 by Pope Clement VIII, principally to provide religious education to young Scotsmen, who could not receive a Catholic education because of the laws against Catholics at home. Other than the two times it was shut down—when the French invaded Rome in 1798 and during World War II—it has remained a well-respected institution, renowned for sending priests to Scotland.

However, the special, private program, which carried no course credit or affiliation, provided open-air education in a very closed environment. *Secretum*. It offered a way to screen for potential candidates who could answer a most important calling.

Colin Kavanaugh went to the head of the class. He was diligent, determined, and above all else, someone who exhibited true courage of his convictions. It brought him to the attention of people he'd never met.

Now twenty-two years later, he sat with his boss and mentor, enduring what he hoped would be one of the last of Gruber's harangues and sharing one of the last of his boring meals.

Kavanaugh was six feet tall, bald, trim, and more in tune with today than Gruber's fascination with antiquity. Of course, that would change, too. As publisher, he would have to adjust his habits somewhat, review the worthiness of his friends, and take his obligations to heart. Colin Kavanaugh was still learning what was important and what wasn't, what was worthy of further review and what was destined for the shredder. There was so much to figure out. But he was hungry to take over. Kavanaugh was determined to further contemporize and upgrade the publication and leave *Condé Nast Traveler, National Geographic Traveler* and *Food and Wine* irrelevant in the marketplace. He had the guts and intellect to do it. He loved traveling, spoke four languages, and summered in Rome, wrapping himself in the traditions and rituals.

Indeed, the Catholic Church exerted a strong influence

over Kavanaugh. Early on, his mother had hoped he would become a priest. His father knew otherwise. Colin was devout on Sundays, but he did love his Saturday nights. His annual visits to Rome brought him rewards of both.

However, now Colin Kavanaugh was thinking less of his ongoing affairs and more about the powerful job he would inherit. His mind went back eighteen months to when Martin Gruber told him his plan.

"So, what do you think, my boy?" Gruber had asked across the desk.

"Like I've been hand-picked by God for the best job."

He could still hear Gruber's laugh. It was a hearty, big laugh. Then it abruptly stopped. With chilling authority came a declaration that Colin Kavanaugh only recently understood.

"Oh, not by God. And it's far from the best job. But make no mistake, you should consider it the most important job in the world."

TWO

Spring 1755
Altay Mountains
Southern Siberia, Russia

CLOSE TO RUSSIA's border with Mongolia, China, and Kazakhstan, a rock face rises thirty meters above the Anuy River. This by itself is not unusual. But when the light hits the base correctly, an opening to a cave becomes visible. Today, it is known as Denisova. It contains more history than has ever been reported.

The name is owed to a hermit who lived there in the eighteenth century. Dionisij, or the more anglicized *Denis,* was something of a character. He rarely came out of the shadows, but those who saw him would never forget. He had long, scraggly hair and a filthy, knotted beard. The river provided his food supply, his bath and his toilet, though he fished more than he bathed.

Prior to Dionisij's time, Neolithic herdsmen huddled within the cave, bracing themselves against the cruel Siberian winters, unchanged for thousands of years. They left drawings, evidence that they were there and what they experienced.

Dionisij inhabited the cave's main chamber, away from the wind. It offered him some comfort and a spiritual sense, for atop the high arched ceiling was an opening that shot seemingly holy shafts of sunlight downward.

After his third winter, Dionisij grew tired of digging

through the river ice that was the thickness of two hands. He decided to become more of a hunter than a fisherman. He sharpened his spears as his ancient ancestors had and sat in wait within his lair.

Days and nights went by with no red meat in sight except for a cold fox that was attracted by his fire. It came closer; then, sensing danger, it left. A squirrel tested the opening, but it too was skittish. Finally, a rabbit, brave enough to explore the source of the light and the warmth, ventured further. This would be his dinner.

However, Dionisij's throw went wide. The rabbit dodged, scurried past him and ran deeper into the cave.

Dionisij's hunger fed his quest. He lit a torch from his fire and followed the rabbit. He had no frame of reference of how far he walked, but he was captivated by what he saw.

First, staggering rock formations. Then a lake, a magnificent lake seemingly with no end. He touched the water. It was warm as if God himself had breathed on it.

The hermit continued, forgetting his hunger pangs. He came to another tunnel. It was tight, but navigable. *Why hadn't I explored more before?* the hermit wondered.

He stepped onto what he thought were small rocks. Only they weren't rocks. At least rocks like he'd seen before. He bent down and picked up what looked to be a tiny piece of bone that had hardened to stone. There were other odd things: a jaw or teeth, but maybe not. They, too were hard as rock.

Dionisij couldn't grasp the experience or the significance. Such understanding would not come in his time. However, he took advantage of what it offered: food, warmth, the spoils from placing traps, and bathing in the hot springs-fed lake.

A month later, an old priest, on a full day's walk, arrived at Dionisij's cave with a satchel of dried food and a heavy frock for the hermit. It was a trek he repeated every spring. The priest was surprised to see the hermit looking better than the previous year. He had more color and life, as if food were not a problem.

The hermit, still grateful for the priest's kindness, accepted the gifts then told the white-haired clergy why his stomach was full and his body clean.

The priest listened to Dionisij's story which went far beyond just the artifacts he produced. It reminded him of a conversation he long ago overheard between two cardinals in Rome. They'd whispered about a cave in Italy and the mysteries it revealed.

"Close your ears forever to the words that mistakenly came your way. It is none of your concern," he'd been told under threat of excommunication. "Forget whose lips they came from. Forget everything."

Of course he didn't. Now fifty years later, the exchange came back to him with the belief that his superiors needed to know. He told the hermit to take him inside the cave. Deep inside.

The way was lit by Dionisij's single oil lamp. However, it was the proverbial blind leading the blind, two men tripping over a past they couldn't begin to fathom.

On the walls were crude, ancient cave paintings of primeval hunters bringing down great beasts, and on the cavern floor, hollowed out stone bowls and rocks shaped like teeth. The priest collected some of the finds. Dionisij insisted on holding onto things that he needed to survive. But there was no shortage of relics.

The hermit beckoned him further.

They entered a vast chamber. The priest gasped. Ahead was nothing, or a *nothingness*. He approached slowly with his right hand extended. At the point he thought his hand would disappear into the void, he felt a smooth surface, something that seemed like a wall, carved out from the rocks. Or, he thought, *within it*. Dionisij had worked on it, scraping away layers of stone. So had ancients before him. The wall was flat, completely vertical from base to ceiling. More astounding, even with their two torches, the wall absorbed all light. It was utterly, frighteningly black.

With authoritarian command, summoning God, Jesus and the Holy Mother, the priest ordered the hermit to leave, never to return to the chamber for fear of opening the door to hell.

Dionisij, preferring to stay warm, clean and well-fed, did as he pleased after the clergyman left. But he never got through.

Back at his abbey, the priest wrote a cardinal in Moscow about the discovery. More than a year later, a stranger came to the cave. Thereafter, no one ever saw Dionisij, and the section of the cavern that raised the priest's interest became impassable due to a devastating cave-in.

The story of Denisova Cave might have been lost completely had the priest not committed his observations to his memoirs.

THREE

London
Present day
Late spring

"No 'I THINK,'" Gruber demanded of Kavanaugh. "Never 'I think.' Never! Own what you say. If you don't own it, then it is not ready to be said."

"I am sure." *Am I? Yes, for goddamned sake.* "Our firewalls are secure. No viruses. No intrusions."

Gruber nodded. For all that he knew about history, he also kept current on computer technology…and threats. "Hackers?"

"No sir. We are steps ahead of the Chinese and they're the only ones who have shown interest in us."

"Not the Russians?"

"Well, technically speaking, they're both extremely capable, but we change our protocols daily. We're good." *Damn. The old man's right. I have to dive deeper.*

"So far," Gruber judged. It was not a prediction, but a fact of life.

"Yes, sir and I've added multiple levels of security. Our IT people are subject to thorough background checks. I know who they are, who their families socialize with, and what other jobs they've had," Kavanaugh explained. Whenever anyone leaves, we review everything and make the proper changes as you've insisted. As I insist now."

Kavanaugh cleared his throat, pleased that he was controlling the conversation. "The staff believes we're paranoid of the competition. *Condé Nast* for one. The Travel Channel for another."

"Very good, son." Gruber used the term sparingly. He didn't get close to anyone. But still, like an apprehensive father, he worried that this corporate progeny might not be ready for all that lay ahead.

"And our most valued *reporters*?" The old man placed special emphasis on the word.

"I read their work on multiple levels."

"You will have to recruit and train more. Look at the star pupils coming up. We have a tradition. But beware. In this world of instant communication, people write without thought and hit send without always realizing who they include. Even the best will make a mistake in haste. Our work cannot permit that. Past, present, future. It is all one. No mistakes."

"I understand, Mr. Gruber. You have my assurance."

"Not just your assurance. Your dedication. Your commitment. Your faith."

"Forever. Without question."

Gruber studied his disciple. He had been there himself many years ago, grilled in the same manner, faced with the same scrutiny. *Was I so eager to replace my mentor?* He weighed whether he was seeing the real Kavanaugh with his desire to purely please or his brazen ambition. He hoped it was the former, but he would have to be certain.

"This must be forever ingrained." He wanted Kavanaugh to especially appreciate his next comment. "You will be a guardian without the luxury of failure."

The statement hung in the air. Though Kavanaugh didn't know everything, he had connected enough dots to understand what *fail* could mean.

"I will be ready," Kavanaugh responded with authority. "I *am* ready."

Gruber laughed. "Well, stay ready. Because I'm not so eager to leave this earth. Not quite yet."

Kavanaugh's eyes shifted, a reaction not lost on Martin Gruber. "Sir, I still have a great deal to learn from you and yes, I haven't done enough to protect our hard drives and firewalls. I will do more."

"Well then, on that note, let us toast to how close we both are to a certain kind of ascension."

Gruber slowly rose and walked to an old liquor cabinet at the far end of his office. He opened it and removed a bottle Kavanaugh had never seen before.

"Ah, I have your full attention now. This is indeed special. Though it's not old, the tradition of how we shall drink it is. This is an *Amaro liqueur* made from twenty-three medicinal and aromatic herbs, aged over six months, and crafted by Monte Oliveto Maggiore Benedictine monks."

Gruber poured one brandy snifter two fingers high, then another. He handed Kavanaugh the first glass.

"This blending of herbs and plants originated in the Middle Ages. It promises legendary restorative powers. But first you have to survive the wallop it delivers," he added laughing.

"Take in the scent."

"Lovely," Kavanaugh offered. "Here's to—"

"Ah, no. This is my toast," Gruber interrupted. "To tradition. It is far greater than us."

"To tradition."

They clinked their glasses.

Colin Kavanaugh slowly sipped the Benedictine blend. It warmed his throat, then his whole chest expanded as the monks' combination of herbs, roots, bark, and citrus peel mixed with alcohol and sugar syrup worked its way down.

"Tradition, Colin. You are doing as I did with my mentor, Alexander Dubesque, so many years ago. Before that, glasses of the Monte Oliveto Maggiore Amaro celebrated the passage of overseers for generations, all the way to the beginning of our order and Father Raffaelo."

"And eventually it will be my duty."

Gruber peered into Kavanaugh's eyes and smiled. But behind the smile, the nagging question.

"Tradition." Gruber held his glass of the Amaro against the light of his chandelier. "From *Voyages* and our earlier endeavors, *L'institute de l'adventure* and *LaRosa*. From Rome to Paris, to London. Always maintaining tradition. Always."

He sipped the Amaro and savored the taste. "I'm going to miss this," Gruber said.

"Who's to say there won't be greater rewards in heaven."

"Heaven? You may have a different view of things as you begin to make your mark, my boy."

He refilled his glass showing he was at least going to enjoy it *now*.

"Through it all, through the years, do you know we've only had one rite of passage?"

"No, what is it?" Kavanaugh asked.

"No black robes or candlelight processions marked by Gregorian incantations. No full moon sacrificial bloodletting in ancient abbeys. Not the things of thrillers and pseudo documentaries."

Gruber let the aroma of the drink waft up and fill his nostrils. "No. The only true rite of passage is this."

The old man spoke nostalgically. "Our heralded Monte Oliveto Maggiore Amaro Benedictine is our only tradition. It seals our pledge. In France the commitment was to *Le Sentier*. In Italy, *Il Sentiero*. In our favored Latin, *Autem Semita*."

In Martin Gruber's day, and now as Colin Kavanaugh prepared to take over, the commitment, the mission, and the organization translated simply into English as *The Path,* or the narrow way laid down by continual passage.

Martin Gruber now made himself unequivocally clear. "And, Mr. Kavanaugh, remember, there is only *one* way. Only one *path*. Follow *Autem Semita*."

FOUR

"LOOKS LIKE A solid group," Dr. Quinn McCauley said to his graduate teaching assistant, Pete DeMeo. "Shame you're not coming this year. Look at this photo."

He started to hand his iPad across the desk.

"Don't bother. I know just who you're talking about. The one from Harvard, right?"

McCauley smiled at DeMeo. "Right. Chohany. Just your type. Hell, you could be missing out on the love of your life."

"Got my sights set on finding her in Europe. Besides, you'd hate me if I abandoned you for Boston."

"Spent great years there."

"But these days you're all about sticking to the Yale side of the field."

"So I'm a little bit political."

"And if Harvard gave you a big ass grant and offered tenure?" DeMeo joked.

"Like I said, I'm a little bit political."

McCauley was something of a renegade professor of paleontology studies. He liked to work outside the system, which constantly brought furrowed brows and antipathy from many of his peers. But the media liked him and so did his students. His visibility helped Yale rate within the top

ten best graduate programs in the study of prehistoric life
and evolutionary development. It was a competitive field
and Harvard was their major competition in the northeast.

Yale's Department of Geology and Geophysics faculty
was recognized for its scholarly contributions in the ad-
vancement of earth sciences. Harvard shared international
acclaim, but provided a competitive curriculum in organ-
ismic and evolutionary biology within the Department of
Earth and Planetary Sciences.

It was the scholarly combination that drew McCauley
to both universities. For now, Yale was his home. He basically ate and slept there and looked the part of a college
prof. In fact, the people at the Johnson & Murphy down the
road in Westport loved him. He shopped their store for everything, from loafers and sandals to striped button-down
shirts, slacks, sports jackets, and vests. Everything including his leather zip top briefcase. It fit his academic look,
right down to his black, wavy hair and infectious smile,
made all the more pleasant with his warm, deep voice.

The seven students joining McCauley on this summer's
dig were from a variety of colleges. He liked to cast them
based on their interests and disciplines and how they could
contribute to the whole experience. He personally picked
each of them. The students, alas, weren't the issue now.
He was still trying to decide where to go. There were so
many treasure troves in the west, particularly eastern Montana where students could extract the real crowd pleasers—good old fossilized dinosaur bones. On site, his team
would quickly discover that, in addition to being a brilliant
teacher, McCauley was arguably one of the country's best
archeological safe crackers.

McCauley reviewed the resumes one more time while
DeMeo gave a running commentary. There was Anna Chohany from Harvard, Rich Tamburro from the University

of Michigan, Tom Trent from the University of Chicago, Adam Lobel and Leslie Cohen, both PhD candidates from Penn State, Carlos Rodriguez from the University of Madrid, his only foreign student this year, and Al Jaffe, UC Berkeley.

"Now Jaffe's an interesting guy," DeMeo noted. "A little older. He's a vet. Served two tours in Afghanistan. I don't think he'll have any problem with the accommodations. It may be a step up."

"Yes, a solid group, Pete. Thanks. Send out the acceptances. Tell the dream team they're good to go, but they better be ready to work like crazy."

"Consider it done," DeMeo replied.

DeMeo was a postgrad student, hoping to have a faculty assignment much like his boss. But that's where the similarities ended. McCauley's graduate teaching assistant was a former member of the Yale crewing team, with a winner take-all attitude and a huge sexual appetite. He kept his curly, brown hair short, his body tight, and his personal calendar extremely busy. He lived in black jeans and polo shirts all year long, at least when he wasn't romancing the latest coed.

McCauley stood up, reached for his briefcase, and started for the door. "I'll be at the gym if you need me."

McCauley, had upped his routine to get in shape for the summer. He added weights to his training, jogged, and biked to shave off the New Haven winter pounds. It wasn't as easy at thirty-six as it used to be, but it was more necessary for the dark-haired, six feet one inch, 205 pound former Eagle Scout from Scranton, Pennsylvania.

He'd grown up digging for Susquehannock and Lenape arrowheads in the woods near his home. Now he was digging for deeper, older finds in God's country.

"Oh, and you better tell those pups that they need to get in shape, too!"

McCAULEY TYPICALLY EXHIBITED a flamboyance that was sound-bite worthy when the History Channel, National Geographic Channel, BBC, or Discovery Science needed a handsome go-to expert in the field. He gave the same sense of enthusiasm to his students. Though he talked about being political, he was bad at university politics. He hadn't attracted serious grant money in three years and he wasn't connecting well with the new department chair who was looking to make institutional changes.

Job pressure was building. It didn't help that he had no significant other in his life to take him away from his work.

McCauley liked to say his last girlfriend died one hundred forty million years ago, but reeked of bad breath. However, that wasn't completely true. A few years ago, before he came to Yale from Harvard, he was involved with a grad student who became a Boston attorney. They broke up and now that he was in Connecticut and Katie Kessler moved to Washington where she was working for the Supreme Court, he knew they'd never get back together. More importantly, he heard that she was seriously involved with a Secret Service agent.

So Quinn McCauley threw himself into his work, the ever-punishing "Publish or Perish" treadmill, and his summertime excavations which could dry up if he didn't "win more friends and influence people" in his own department.

There was another issue he had to consider. Science was under siege and evolution was increasingly a hot topic. As a result, fewer checks were being written for anthropological and paleontological work by the government, let alone by corporations or foundations. *The long tail of the dwin-*

dling resources? It seemed like dinosaurs were going to stop making noise even to kids.

How many more years until the virtual end to research? McCauley mused. *Three? Five?* That would put him at roughly the same age as the legendary competing paleontologists Edward Drinker Cope and Othniel Charles Marsh were more than one hundred fifty years ago. True colleagues at first, they named amphibian fossil findings after one another, *Ptyonius marshii and Mosasaurus copeanus*, respectively. However, their relationship fell apart when Cope rushed to publish his work on a new species shipped to his office from Kansas. He called the finding *Elasmosaurus platyurus.* In his haste, he accidentally or mistakenly reversed the position of the head to the tail of the vertebrae. Marsh identified Cope's error and published a correction. This destroyed their relationship and created a scandal in the new field of paleontology that had only been so named decades earlier.

What would be McCauley's bragging rights? As he peddled his exercise bicycle at Yale's Payne Whitney Gym, he wondered if this year's exploration would reinvigorate both his department's support in him and his own belief in himself. And what about his legacy? Would he ever discover his own evolutionary branch that might add true knowledge to the genealogical tree?

Strictly out of frustration, McCauley stopped biking and leaned over the handle bars. He was beginning to think that just wasn't going to happen. That paleontology was just getting old.

Gotta dig out of this hole, he thought.

FIVE

London
Two weeks later

WHOEVER WAS IN charge of *The Path* had the responsibility to pass on the knowledge in the event of something unexpected. Martin Gruber had done so. Now, with the end in sight, he publicly announced his retirement as editor-in-chief of *Voyages*.

He told the staff that Colin Kavanaugh would soon be taking over as publisher. To Kavanaugh, the public statement meant he'd immediately assume more oversight of the magazine and undoubtedly be subject to Gruber's lectures up to the bitter end.

"Colin, come in. Please, please, come in."

It was time for another.

Kavanaugh had been called; no, summoned. He was called when Gruber needed a companion; he was summoned for everything else.

"Good day, Mr. Gruber." Kavanaugh carried galleys under his arm. He placed them on the worktable in the far end of Gruber's office.

So much could be done electronically, but Gruber liked mulling over hard copy. *That'll change.*

"Good day," the old man said.

The nearly forty-year age difference always brought a profound level of formality. It seemed all the more appropriate in the eighteenth century building on Monocle

Street, and all the more correct considering Gruber's failing health.

"Good day, sir."

Martin Gruber slowly stood and walked to the window. He looked down at the people three flights below. *Little people who know little*, he thought for a moment. He drew the heavy, red velvet curtains shut and returned to his austere seventeenth century oak desk.

"Soon this will be yours. Of course, assuming you still want it."

"Without a question."

"Without questioning," Gruber corrected. It was one of his grammatical distinctions. One of many.

"Without questioning."

"You'll tell people this was a desk once used by Pope Clemente IX in the seventeenth century."

"With pride."

"They won't care. But you, as successor must hold to convention. Trust me, the trappings keep you focused. Study everyone. Take interest in them. As Machiavelli warned, 'Keep your friends close and your enemies closer.'"

Kavanaugh frowned.

"Oh, I see I struck a nerve. Yes, you will have enemies. Some in your very midst. Others in the far corners of the world. And the irony of it all is they'll never know they've become your enemy."

"Yes, I understand."

"All accomplished with utmost…" Gruber waited for the younger man to fill in the word.

"Secretum," Kavanaugh replied thinking *Here we go again*. He ran his hand across his scalp, something he did when he was annoyed.

Martin Gruber pressed an app on his smartphone which activated a high frequency audio signal.

"Do you hear that? Of course you don't," Gruber continued. "I've been assured from the security experts you hired—yes, I speak with them, too—that the activated inaudible tone will defeat even the most sophisticated microphone plants and," he laughed, "give any dogs in the neighborhood a terrible headache."

Kavanaugh believed him. The octogenarian was always tinkering; working on making things more secure, more secretive.

"Now sit."

Kavanaugh settled into the only chair facing the historic desk. Gruber cleared his throat, a signal that the rest would become very serious.

"We may only have a few more weeks, Colin."

"Please, sir, don't say that."

"It is the truth. We work in truths. An old man forgets much of his yesterdays, but sees his tomorrows clearly. My vision is not blurred. You are there. I am not."

"Yes, sir," Kavanaugh said. He wished he had come up with a better, more thoughtful reply. But Gruber was looking tired. He studied his mentor. *Thinner today than yesterday. Yes, soon.*

Gruber inhaled fully. It seemed to energize him right before Kavanaugh's eyes.

"Ah, but I have one more edition to put to bed." Gruber was referring to the fall issue on the Caribbean. "Let's get on with the work."

New Haven, CT

McCAULEY GRABBED AN oven-roasted turkey hoagie from the Book Trader Cafe on the Yale University campus and brought it back to his office. He logged onto Pandora's Frank Sinatra channel, always his default when he had important things on his mind. It relaxed him.

Where? Exactly where this year? he thought as he took a satisfying bite of his dinner. He studied a topographical map of Montana with three strategically placed push pins indicating the final areas he was considering. Beside each pin was a yellow sticky note with numbers 1, 2 and 3.

McCauley had put through the paperwork months ago for three potential sites; all offering interesting challenges for his students and the potential for a cool find or two. State park commissions had already given conditional approval for each location. But he still needed to complete the application process. They were due in Billings in just five days.

At the end of last summer, McCauley had flown over the area and found each attractive for different reasons. Site 1, Hell Creek, Montana, was noted for its mudstones and sandstones dating back to the end of the Cretaceous period, with fossils of triceratops, tyrannosaurus, and Ornithomimids. *Interesting.*

Site 2, further east, had real possibilities. It was just outside of Glendive, MT. *Maybe,* he said to himself.

Site 3 was north, part of a prehistoric riverbed and was certain to garner great finds just a few feet down. But he found that less challenging. *No adventure.* He figured there'd be initial excitement, then with the same results week after week—boredom.

McCauley finished chewing another bite, quickly catching a piece of turkey as it dropped out of the bun. He did it instinctively, like the first baseman he'd been in Little League, high school and college. He still had a quick hand and a great throwing arm.

He swallowed the last of his sandwich, studied the map

again and pulled the pin and paper off Site 3. *That makes it easier. Down to two.*

The music on his computer segued from Sinatra to Dean Martin, Dean Martin to Matt Monro, a crooner considered the British Sinatra. The "From Russia With Love" theme broke his concentration.

"Pete!" he shouted. "Need a little help."

DeMeo left his adjoining office and was at McCauley's side in seconds.

"Ready."

"I'm torn between Sites 1 and 2, but drawn more to 2. Give me arguments why we shouldn't go there."

"You want them right now?"

"Yes."

"Site 1 is better. Earth that you can dig and geological footprints evident everywhere. Perfect grazing grounds. And that means perfect remains."

"I know. But the strata at 2 appeals to me."

"Harder. More challenges. Cliffs and valleys. You'll need better equipment. More money."

"Forget the money. If I made my decisions on money, I would have stuck with baseball."

DeMeo had heard the stories about the Red Sox looking at the young McCauley. They even made an offer his junior year at Harvard which he turned down.

"Let's sleep on it for a few days. See what you can come up with." After a pause he added, "And while you're at it, find out why the Brits had this thing about Matt Monro."

London

KAVANAUGH WAS AMAZED at how quickly Gruber was able to shift gears. He would have to master the art as well.

"The St. Lucia photographs are exquisite," he said leaning over Gruber's computer screen. "They capture the beauty of the Grand Pitons." Kavanaugh cycled through the pictures. "Check out this angle. It's extraordinary."

Gruber agreed.

"As I recall, you were there years ago."

"Yes, my boy. It was your first year working directly with me and your calls to the Ladera Hotel were quite intolerable. Am I right?"

Kavanaugh had to laugh. "Of course you are. You didn't get out much after that trip."

"I suppose I became too accustomed to sleeping in my own bed. Unusual for a publisher of a travel magazine." Gruber laughed. "But as you'll see, there are so many other things that will require constant attention."

Gruber recognized the real intent of Kavanaugh's comment. "Ah, but I see you were trying to test me."

"Sir?"

"My memory. You were testing my capacity. Did I remember the trip?"

"I don't know…"

"Oh you were. And rightfully so. You're beginning to understand that *everything* is a test. A test of knowledge. A test of resolve. Tests of commitment and faith. A test of your will."

Kavanaugh stroked his hairless head again.

"But I digress," he continued. "Show me more of the issue that will be dedicated to my memory."

New Haven, CT

McCAULEY WAS REVIEWING his charts. They were anything but exotic, five-star vacation spots. These required the latest in rugged all-weather camping gear: everything from tents to sleeping bags, iridium satphones to walkie-talkies and the basics: backpacks, picks and shovels, bubble wrap, and plastic bags. A lot of plastic bags.

He made notes and then roughed out a draft of an email to his department chair; a formality which he hated.

Dear Dr. Cutler:

Thank you again for your support and the department's underwriting for this summer's field research. I would have written sooner, but I've been putting the final details together on our research expedition. To that point, I am still deciding between two locations in Montana's dinosaur alley based on government satellite photographs and my staff's research. I'll let you know when I come to a final decision. It appears, although I can't be certain, both sites have unique strata that could lead to new discoveries, potentially trapped within Mesozoic to Paleozoic Era layers. If so, we might see remarkable research coming from our work. Of course, I'll file regular reports. Enjoy Nova Scotia.

Respectfully, Quinn McCauley, PhD.

McCauley closed his eyes and shook his head. *No. Too many mights, maybes, and coulds. Besides, he'll never read anything I send from Montana.* He hit delete.

London

"I MUST SAY, we put out a first-class publication," Gruber admitted while reviewing another galley page.

"But, my boy, I think you should have more on Soufrière. After all, the volcanic activity is what people come to see when they're not working on their tans. And considering the Petit and Gros Pitons are the remnants of three-hundred-thousand-year-old lava domes, give our readers a little more meat with their gravy. Always remember the senses. I can still smell the sulphur springs. I've never taken in a nastier whiff of anything, but it doesn't stop tourists from going there. Find a literary way to work it in. 'The anger of the earth,'" he suggested, "'The heat burns all life at the root and the sickly grey tint rises and then disappears against the blue Caribbean sky, proving once again that beauty wins out.' Something like that."

Gruber's prose impressed Kavanaugh. "Sir, if I live to be twice your age I wouldn't have half your writing talent."

Gruber waved off the compliment. "Thank you, but it's wasted on the tourists. They scan the articles, book their trips and lather up with their lotions. During their fifteen minute bus stops, they run in and take cell-phone pictures with that fake clicking sound. Like it's a film camera. Ridiculous. No art to it. Then it's back on the bus. That's travel today. Not like when people really valued the experience."

The conversation, like so many, turned into another diatribe. However, Kavanaugh believed that some of it blurred the lines between the publication of *Voyages* and the work of *Autem Semita*.

"Make sure features contains some subtle theological or historical subtext. Not too much to lose the casual reader; enough to satisfy subscribers interested in a few relevant facts. And why? Because that will keep you on the path. And that is why you are here."

Gruber looked at the galley page again. "But back to the work at hand. The spread is wonderful," Gruber said. "Beautiful pictures. The aerial shots are amazing. Step by step, we get closer to God."

When he was satisfied that Kavanaugh was clear on

all the editorial changes, he invited his associate to take one of the two Louis XIV chairs in his office seating area.

"No, not that one," Gruber stated. "Try mine."

"Oh, I can't, sir."

"It's important for me to see how comfortable you are in it."

"But Mr. Gruber."

"Relax, but you'll still have to listen to me."

"I hope for a long time, sir."

Gruber studied how Kavanaugh sat, how he held himself. He all but peered into his mind. There were more things he had to understand about his heir apparent in the time he had left.

"Time?" Gruber considered the word. "How would you describe *time*, young man?"

"Time. Time is how we measure our lives. It is the space we inhabit as we figure out the manner in which to fill it. We wear time. We breathe time. We run…" Kavanaugh paused, "we run out of it."

"Insightful," Gruber noted. "I prefer to consider Tennessee Williams's view from *The Glass Menagerie*. 'Time is the longest distance between two places.'"

Kavanaugh liked the quote. *The longest distance between two places.*

"And the job, no the duty you're inheriting, is to maintain that critical distance between the two places that we guard. Then and now."

Kavanaugh's pulse quickened. He stroked his scalp again.

"You look anxious."

"Do I? I'm sorry."

"Be patient." Gruber's tone changed. "I'm not going to die on you today."

"Sir, please accept my apologies if I…"

"Accepted. Now tell me what you know that is not between the covers of our next edition."

"Not in the magazine?"

"What our *other* research tells us."

"Thank you," the younger man answered. "Well, the Soufrière cave was abandoned. A little more oil exploration off Grenada. And no one will be able to get back into the mountain in Barbados. So, nothing of any concern."

Gruber's tone abruptly changed. His old eyes bored down on Kavanaugh. "My dear friend," he said without an ounce of warmth, "there is never *nothing* of concern. Never. How can we determine what has value if we don't take everything seriously? We sailed on the Mayflower and survived the gulags. We explored the Antarctic and traveled to the four corners of the globe. Our people have been to the moon, for God's sake. We're always concerned. How we act on that concern is the real issue."

Gruber closed his eyes and lowered his head, a sign that more was coming.

"Satellite telephones. Computers. Even the blasted Internet that we pay hundreds of thousands of pounds to keep secure. Information, Mr. Kavanaugh. I demand information. You must as well. Do I have to live longer in order to train someone else?"

"No, sir."

"Then get a full grasp of it, Mr. Kavanaugh, before it's too late! Out, now. Out of my chair. You're dismissed."

As Kavanaugh left the office, he heard the unmistakable sound of a pill bottle being unscrewed. Martin Gruber was taking more medication. Kavanaugh smiled. The job would be his soon and these egotistical rants would be over.

SIX

THERE WAS NO shortage of boxes, books and piles of paper for McCauley to wade through in his two bedroom apartment. That had to do with the fact that there no reason for McCauley to stay organized. Or more accurately, no one to stay organized for.

After stepping over his work on his way to his lonely bed, he closed his eyes and constructed the summer campsite in his mind. His tent would serve as home and office. Outside there'd be multiple areas to collect, sift, examine, and catalog the inevitable findings. As for sleeping quarters, two per tent: the two women in one, the men in the others. At any rate, it would start out that way. Likewise for the two showers provided by the park. The latrines would be downwind, though that was a bit of a misnomer. The Montana summer would be hot and dry, and with the exception of rolling thunderstorms, relatively windless.

He could predict the routine and prepare for it. His graduate students would come in excited. They'd find *what* and *who* they had in common before deciding whom they'd befriend. They'd listen to him for a few days, then begin to think they know more. He'd settle them down. Some might think about leaving, but they'd all stay. They always did, because by the second or third week, they'd actually find something interesting and it would reinvigorate their sense of purpose.

Hooking up usually hit week three. When partners changed in week five, an uncomfortable silence would fall over the camp. McCauley had the solution for that. A wild night at the bar; laughter, and talk about the sexual and mating habits of the dinosaurs. The detailed descriptions always brought laughter and obliterated the walls that had invariably gone up or the silos where they'd retreated.

The rest of the term would become a pure joy of discovery, growth and understanding. No one returned to grad school the same. Friendships would be forged for life. In some cases, marriages.

McCauley had seen it all over the years. He closed his eyes and focused on each of the students' vitae. He believed that some would eventually make significant contributions to the field of study. Others could become more effective teachers because of the experience. And the remaining students? Still an enigma. They might give it all up or...he didn't know.

London

Colin Kavanaugh couldn't sleep. He kept going over reports he'd recently read. Maybe there was information he hadn't valued correctly. *Damn the old man,* he thought. *He's right.* He vowed to go back, study everything and learn.

SEVEN

April 18, 1913
Universal Colliery
Senghenydd, Wales

IT COULD HAVE been 1713, not 1913, for all that the Welsh town offered. Little had changed for the lives of the citizens except that now they worked in the mines. Since the discovery of coal in the late nineteenth century, the people of Senghenydd and its neighboring areas went to work underground extracting fifty-six million tons of coal each year.

Like most small mining towns in the hills of Wales, Senghenydd was quaint and rural. Nothing bucolic or romantic. The people hungered for work, and the work made them hungry. And the work was grueling. That was life—chosen or inherited. Men were slaves to the bituminous coal, an unforgiving, dangerous employer. Women bore babies, prayed that their husbands would return for dinner, and fed them if they did.

There was also God and country. God, country, and family, to be precise. Those were the tenets most people lived by and voted for. In that order. Their faith couldn't be shaken, no matter how difficult the job was or how devastating a mine disaster might be. They would always return to God, country, and family. The order of things.

The man who drove a 9.5 horsepower Standard Rhyl over the dirt roads through the Aber Valley to the mining office came to preserve such order.

He was two inches taller than six feet, with a Roman square jaw, piercing blue eyes, and jet black, wavy hair. The man hid a muscular build inside a loose-fitting, already dusty gray jacket with matching pants. He knew right where to go. Past the engine and the machine houses. Past the sheds. Nearby was the tipple-tower, a skeletal iron structure that covered the mouth of shaft #1. Soon he'd take the lift down, but first he walked up the metal steps to the single-story, ramshackle field office. The flimsy spring-hinged door snapped shut behind him, creating a loud bang.

"Mornin'," he said.

"Nothin' good about it," replied one of the two men in the room.

The snarky remark came from the forty-five-year-old plump, balding, short, irascible company general manager lazily sitting in the far end of the room. Another man sat at a desk working, perhaps cooking the books. He offered no comment.

"I didn't say there was. Just 'mornin.' I'm Anthony Formichelli, Regional Inspector of Mines. Here to look at things."

The man in front stopped and looked up from charts he was going over. He established eye-contact with the visitor for a fleeting moment, then broke it off.

"Go away," bellowed the man from further back. You fuckin' assholes were just here last week."

"He was scheduled," Formichelli stated.

"And he received ten pounds for doing nothing and going away. One hundred times a miner's day wage."

"Yes. Well, I'm the unscheduled guy. And I'm here."

"Okay how much do you want? Twenty? Don't you people ever think you've gotten enough?"

"I'm not here to take your money, Mr. Dwyer? It is Mr. Dwyer?"

"It is. Wilem Dwyer. If you've not come for sterling what are you here for?"

"Mr. Dwyer, I'm here to examine a portion of your mine."

"You're crazy. None of you guys ever really want to go down. That's what the money's for. So you don't. Not today. Not ever."

"Today is different," Formichelli said in an uncompromising voice.

"Why is that?"

"Because eighty-one died in 1901 and you had another disaster recently with nothing to show for it."

"Coal. We have coal to show for it. That's what we do here. Dig coal out of the damn ground. We get our hands dirty. You guys do it by gratefully taking our payoffs."

"I didn't come for a payoff. We're going downstairs together."

Dwyer decided to be coy. "Look, I get it. You don't want to take it in public. So we do it down there."

"We do what I need to do in your mine."

"For Christ's sake, there's nothing but coal. Fuckin' tons of coal. Save yourself the trip. I'll give you thirty-five!"

"I'll forget about your bribe so long as we go now. If you don't, then I'll see to it that you'll never have the opportunity again. I'm sure someone else would be happy to become General Manager. Like…" Formichelli nodded to the man with his head in his papers, his inside contact he'd met only a week before.

"Okay, okay. The main shaft good enough?"

"As a matter of fact, no. I want to see your new excavation. I believe you call it Lloyd George, the new spur off Central Link."

"How?"

Formichelli didn't let him finish the question.

"It's my job to know."

"Look," Dwyer argued as he reached into a till box. "I'll give you forty-five. How about fifty-five? You go away richer than when you arrived. And alive."

Formichelli pushed his overcoat aside and revealed a sidearm. His hand went to the weapon. "You'll take me all the way to Lloyd George. If you don't…" he glanced over to the other man again. That's where he left the thought.

Dwyer's number two stopped his work. His eyes darted nervously, but his reaction was unseen by his boss.

"We've hardly broken through. Not much to see. Come back in two wccks. We'll start all over," Dwyer said, trying unsuccessfully to get rid of the visitor.

"Today," Formichelli replied. "Now."

Dwyer gave the stranger a long hard look. He was serious. Serious enough to kill.

THE RICKETY MINE shaft elevator started with a jolt.

"Uncomfortable?" Dwyer observed.

"Not at all."

Formichelli had been in coal elevators and deep into caverns, wells and caves throughout Europe and even in America. But Dwyer was right. The rides always gave him the willies.

Through the patchwork metal roof he saw six motor-driven wires attached to the top of the cage. To the sides, guide rails ran the length of the shaft. They kept the car and counterweights from swaying during descending and ascending. It was the coal miner's lifeline. Formichelli would have to trust it.

"Just get us down in one piece," he added.

The ride took six minutes before the elevator stopped

at the foot of the main shaft, Central Link. Like all the tunnels it was named after roads in Cardiff. Dwyer lifted the bar to the elevator gate and said without an ounce of real concern, "Mind your head." The overhead support beams were difficult to see in the spotty lamp light. "You can stand most of the way. But then again, you better be ready to duck some. How's your back?"

"The last thing you need to do is worry about me."

Dwyer was struck by the ominous tone.

They followed the gradual slope downward. At the tunnel's highest, they barely had a few inches of headroom. But it quickly got lower, much lower, making them crouch. That's when they cut far left into the passageway called Lloyd George. The farther they walked, the narrower it got, sometimes barely wide enough for wheelbarrows.

Formichelli had seen how tunnels branched off into networks of rooms where chronically coughing miners, as young as nine, dug, shoveled, and removed the coal by the light of dim electric bulbs, oil lamps, and brass Justrite carbide head lamps.

This was the process every day except on Sundays. The Lord's day.

"Halfway," Dwyer said after twelve minutes. "Need a break?"

"No."

The breeze that had been at their backs from outside air pushing down the main shaft was now gone. The air was stale and full of coal dust. Formichelli wrapped a scarf around his nose and mouth. Dwyer didn't.

After another grueling six minutes they stopped at the end of the electric wing. They lit hand-held lamps now. "The rest of the way we're on our hands and knees. Follow me."

The colliery's chief led the way. Though miners hadn't

extracted any coal from the new vein yet, the air was still heavy with coal dust.

"No other ventilation?" Formichelli asked.

"No," Dwyer said through a phlegm-filled cough. "You'll feel some fresher air, though."

They continued another two minutes through the claustrophobic space, at times on all fours then upright again.

"Here's what you wanted to see," Dwyer said with annoyance. He pointed to the far end of the excavation.

"Where?"

"There," Dwyer said. He brought his lamp closer to the rock. But it wasn't rock. It was a wall. But not a wall. A surface that was there, but wasn't there. A black wall.

"Some sort of metal," Dwyer said trying to sound smart for the company man. "At first, we thought it was silver; a black silver. Now I don't know. Gotta get some work crews down here. Fact of the matter is if it's not coal, and we're in the business of coal, then it's not my job to figure it out."

But it did matter.

"How'd you say you heard about this?" Dwyer said, now curious.

"I didn't."

Formichelli turned in a slow circle, finally settling on the blacker-than-black surface, about eight feet wide and more than ten feet tall. He touched it. Not a spec of dirt.

"What do you think?" the miner asked. "Must have been buffed by millions of years of water, the way a waterfall polishes boulders," Dwyer said.

The visitor continued to glide his fingers along the metal where it met the rock.

The mining manager had had enough. "Can we leave now?"

Formichelli ignored him.

"Like I said up above, no coal. Nothing."

It wasn't *nothing* to Formichelli. He smiled. "Okay, I've seen enough. I can leave now."

The word *I* was different than *we*. Dwyer missed the distinction. He also missed seeing Formichelli remove a knife from his bag and raise it to neck level. Had Dwyer seen it, he wouldn't have been able to defend himself.

Dwyer died without knowing why. That was Formichelli's way.

Now the killer retraced his steps, stopping fifteen meters away. He set the first of the long fuses to the dynamite he'd carried into the tunnel. The length of the fuse would buy him fifteen minutes. On the way back to the lift he lit five more fuses at strategic points.

It wouldn't be the first coal mine explosion in Wales. The newspaper would report that the mine's general manager had died on a survey. The probable cause: an explosion due to a faulty lamp station. Eventually the accident was all but forgotten because of another Universal Colliery explosion barely six months later. That event became the worst in the history of the British Isles. Anthony Formichelli also witnessed that first-hand.

EIGHT

"Insurance certificates are in the yellow file. State and park permits in the green. Your travel is in blue and emergency…"

"I know, I know," McCauley said.

DeMeo grimaced. His boss still hadn't made a final decision on the site, so the graduate teaching assistant had to clear two. That would be the next order of business. "Now please, doc, pay attention."

"I am."

It didn't look like he was. The Yale paleontologist crisscrossed his office, throwing files of his own into a large Fed Ex box. "Keep going."

"The purple file has contacts for your students. Black is for emergencies. Brown has my trip info. I've emailed PDFs of everything so you should have it on your iPhone, iPad, and laptop."

DeMeo mastered organization years ago, a lesson learned at the foot of his mother, a school teacher. She told the young Peter DeMeo that everything comes down to collating and stapling. It was true then. It was true now.

"Got it. Yellow, green, blue. You're yellow, travel is blue, insurance permits green."

"Wrong, wrong, wrong. What about black?" DeMeo asked.

"Black is the color of my true love's hair," McCauley said, citing the traditional Appalachian folk song.

"Wrong again. You have no true love. It's emergency contacts. Actually, I'll put it in a red folder. Just read the damn labels and you'll be okay. And please, don't call me."

"I'll try my best."

"Thank you. Now, can we finally decide where the fuck you're going given you've already lied to the department?"

DeMeo laid out information on the remaining two sites. McCauley read the tab on the top file. *Makoshika State Park History.* He perused DeMeo's extracts, though he didn't have to. He'd passed on the site before. He thought it might be too touristy. But this year? *Makoshika.* The name called out to him. "Makoshika."

"Interesting translation," DeMeo noted.

"Yes. In the language of the Lakota, Dakota and Nakota peoples, it means *bad earth* or *pitiful earth*." He paused for thought. "Bad earth. Yes, bad earth. Maybe this is the year for bad earth."

He considered some of the bullet points in the packet.

- Largest of Montana's state parks
- More than 11,000 acres
- Freshwater shale, sandstone; evidence of mineral rich groundwater
- Carbonized wood
- Interlaced coal
- Smooth agates and towering cap rocks
- Fossilized coral

The file contained eerie photographs that could have been shot on an alien landscape except for the identifiable homegrown vegetation that survived the bad earth. In one direction, knolls rose above the landscape. Another revealed a layered landscape with sedimentary rocks.

The terrain changed with every view: north, south, east, west. Windswept rock formations were punctuated by juniper trees and hearty pines. There were high cliffs and beyond them a rugged desert without all the color variants of other sites. Mostly gray.

The pictures told the story of how erosion shaped the Makoshika geography for three hundred million years.

McCauley saw evidence in the pictures of ancient humid jungles, former lakebeds, and violent seismic shifts that accelerated transformation of the region. But, there was one additional photograph in the file DeMeo had prepared. It made McCauley laugh.

"Oh, this isn't fair."

He held up the photograph of Cottonwood, the eighteen-hole golf course two miles from the center of Glendive, Montana.

"It's considered one of the toughest in the region," DeMeo offered. "Intimidating. Ready for someone who's up to the challenge."

"Makoshika."

"Good, because I already charged a summer club membership on your card."

"What if I'd chosen the other site?"

"You wouldn't. The golf course was the clincher."

"My man! Who's the park director?"

"A guy named Jim Kaplan, Kaplan with a 'K.' I've checked him out. Forty-eight, married, with twin daughters. I think you'll like him. Nothing major published, but he knows his park and he's done his share of digs in the region. University of Kansas grad."

"Does he golf?"

"Now that I don't know, but I'll find out."

"Anything else?"

"Yup. Are you ready for your radio interview tonight?"

"Christ, thank you! I forgot. What time?"

"One in the morning. Set your alarm, doc."

NINE

THE NEWS ENDED. The theme music came up and the late night talk host welcomed listeners to the second hour of his Saturday night broadcast over Boston's fifty thousand-watt powerhouse radio station, WBZ.

"We're back and I have one of my favorite guests on the phone, Dr. Quinn McCauley. He's a leading paleontologist, first from Harvard, now Yale. I'll forgive him for leaving as long as he keeps visiting us. Dare I say, he digs the earth. He actually digs the earth for dinosaur fossils. Every year, he heads out west in search of new discoveries. So pleased you're joining us tonight. How are you, Dr. McCauley?"

"Absolutely fine, thanks, Jordan. Great to be back. But please, it's Quinn."

McCauley had never actually met Jordan Rich, the venerable late night host. These were call-in interviews. Promotion in pajamas. Though it didn't count toward McCauley's scholarly publishing, the exposure on WBZ reached listeners in thirty-three states. The bragging rights were enormous. But so was the enthusiasm of the overnight audiences, who McCauley had no problem holding in awe for hours.

"So, where are you off to this year?"

"Eastern Montana, a dynamic region in the heart of dinosaur country. My team comes from some of the great universities across the country. Harvard, Michigan, University of Chicago, Berkeley, Penn State, and one from Spain. I think it's fair to say we'll have a field day. Or more accurately, if everyone makes it, eight great weeks."

"Do people ever drop out?" Rich asked.

"Rarely. Too much fun. Oh, sometimes, family issues unavoidably come up, but invariably they return before the summer's through. And occasionally there are some who realize the field is not for them. I see it as a real litmus test and a great way to measure dedication and patience. And believe me, our work requires patience. There's nothing quick about what we do. Oh, and it takes good knees."

Jordan Rich laughed.

"And what will you find?"

"What will we find or what do I hope we'll find?" McCauley responded.

"Both. Either," the host replied.

"I expect we'll find a go-to favorite. Tyrannosaurus rex fossils. Always a crowd pleaser. In fact, one of the greatest species was uncovered right where we'll be. But what do I hope for?"

He paused for only a fraction of a second to rev up.

"For me, the best discovery of all is that one or more of the students will become superstars and carry on the work with true desire in a world of slash and burn budgets. That'll help ensure we don't turn into fossils ourselves."

It was a point well worth making; a pitch for new minds to come to the old world.

Rich asked, "In terms of actual scientific discoveries, what's still out there? Are there things we don't yet know?"

"Can a teenager today imagine a life without smartphones, tablets, the cloud? What's around the corner? What devices will we be utilizing tomorrow? They're almost unimaginable. Well, same thing for looking backwards. Say about two hundred, three hundred, four hundred or five hundred million years ago. So, yes, there's a lot out there. I always hope that we'll pitch our shovel in the right spot and come up with something really cool. Then we have to figure out how to put the darned thing together."

McCauley and Rich bantered for another twelve minutes on the character of dinosaurs, what scientists have discerned about their familial relationships, how much they ate, and conversely, how much they likely stank depending upon whether they were meat eaters or vegetarians.

"British scientists have estimated that the sauropods, the dinosaur group which includes the Brontosaurus, produced about five hundred twenty million tons of methane per year. That's enough farting…can I say farting on the air?"

"You have twice, I think you're okay," the host laughed.

"Well, a bit more delicately, they expelled enough methane to warm the climate about eighteen degrees Fahrenheit more than it is today. Let's just say that it's a good thing cave dwellers and the discovery of fire came much later given all the gas in the air. Kaboom!"

With that, Jordan Rich laughed, then led to a commercial break.

Ironically, the first spot was for a local New England Ford dealership selling the all-terrain F-150 SVT *Raptor*.

Two minutes later, they were back into the show. "We'll open up to your calls in a few minutes." Jordan Rich gave the toll-free phone number. "But first, another science lesson. I suppose on the historic timeline, we're the newbies, but the earth itself and other life forms are another matter. Without getting into the religious debate, give us what you scientists see about the history of planet Earth."

"Perfectly positioned, Jordan. I'm not one to disrespect alternate points of view. However I'll tell you what I read."

"What's that?"

"I read the rocks. They have a very old story to tell."

McCauley launched into it.

"The Earth's outer crust, a rocky crust, solidified billions of years ago. But the crust isn't a solid shell. It's broken. I mean it's really broken. Broken into huge chunks, thick rock plates typically 50-to-250 miles thick that constantly drift over the more viscous upper mantle. It can take eons to see the change or seconds to feel it. These plates move sideways and up and down. They bump into one another, exerting dramatic changes in continental shapes and positions. That's why the earth is always changing. Has always changed. Will always change.

"The movement is called plate tectonics. In its most violent motion it creates earthquakes and volcanoes, mountain ranges and deep ocean trenches."

"How fast are these plates moving?" Rich asked.

"Try about a fraction of an inch to four inches a year. Even at that speed, when plates interact, something's going to shake, rattle, roll, split, spurt, or burst. Think of it all in layers. The top is the Earth's major land surfaces, the continental crust, and the oceanic crust, which is thinner, denser, and generally more active than the continental crust. The crust is part of what is called the lithosphere. It's pretty rigid and brittle and is constantly in motion on the top of the viscous, hot upper matter. It's comprised of iron, magnesium, silicon, and calcium. Below that, the lower mantle. Now when two plates try to occupy the same space, the denser oceanic plate pushes under the lighter continental crust.

"As the plate descends, it heats up; then melting mantle mixed with melting oceanic crust rises toward the surface to form a volcano, like in Japan and Mount St. Helens. When two continental plates collide, the collision causes an upward thrust producing mountains like the Himalayas. When there's lateral movement of two plates, stresses build up in fits and starts. When the stress gets too great, it releases quickly. We feel that as an earthquake. The greater the buildup of stress, the bigger the resulting action, the stronger the earthquake. As soon as the earthquake happens, stress starts building up again.

"With all these forces at work, pushing, pulling, colliding, you can begin to see how the earth is ceaselessly, though imperceptibly changing."

"Talk about that."

"My favorite part. For a time it was all fused together. One mega continent comprised of all Earth's land. As a matter of fact, stick around. Computer models tracking continental shift predict they'll come closer together again in another one hundred fifty to two hundred million years, then split apart. Over and over."

"So it never holds in one place?"

"Never. The geologist who first proposed the supercontinent theory, the one way back, was Alfred Wegener. He named it *Pangaea*, Greek for 'all the land.' It wasn't that long ago either."

"When?" asked the WBZ radio host.

"1915.

"No, when did the Pangaea exist?"

"Oh, sorry. 1915 for Wegener's theory. Some three hundred million years ago for Pangaea, but that wasn't even the first supercontinent! Far from it. Go back billions of years earlier for other supercontinents. But Pangaea was significant for the way it rotated and split, then drifted apart during the Middle Jurassic period, first into two smaller supercontinents, Gondwana and Laurasia. Later, by the end of the Cretaceous period, it was beginning to look more like the map we have today."

"And, as you said, it's not over yet."

"Never will be," McCauley said.

"And we came along when?"

"I like to put it this way. Consider 4.6 billion years in terms of the second and minute hands sweeping across sixty minutes on a clock. The earth's crust was formed in one one-hundredth of the first second of the hour. The oldest preserved rocks on the surface occurred at 10:27. The earliest fossil evidence of life, algae cells, shows up at thirteen minutes and bacteria four and a half minutes later. For the very first cells with a nucleus, jump ahead to 40:26. Look how late into the hour we are and we haven't hit multi-celled organisms."

"When did that begin?"

"After the fifty-one minute mark. Fish at 53:15; bugs at almost fifty-five minutes."

"I'm getting the picture."

"It speeds up even more, Jordan. The dinosaurs we've been talking about begin showing up at 57:01 on the hour clock."

"So I have to ask. Humans?"

"Our upright ancestors around 59:58 and the first modern man—59:59.9."

"One tenth of a second ago, Quinn?"

"Converting 4.6 billion years into an hour, yes, just one tenth of one second ago."

TEN

McCAULEY WISHED THAT his teaching assistant was with him for the summer, or even just through orientation. Because DeMeo wasn't, the first job—airport pickup—was all his. Seven students; seven different trips over two days. He didn't look forward to repeating himself and missing the opportunity to run his dog and pony act, or as DeMeo called it, his Dilophosaurus and Pentaceratops act, for everyone at the same time. However, the multiple airport runs actually gave him the opportunity to spend individual time, quality time, with his new students. He'd tailor his group orientation differently based on knowing his cast of characters.

Every greeting started the same. The students landing at Dawson Community Airport, four miles northwest of Glendive, looked around and wondered what planet they'd landed on. Everything was dwarfed by the expanse of Big Sky country. There was no comprehensible scale to the topography.

"Incredible, isn't it?" It was easy from there.

First came Rich Tamburro from the University of Michigan. He had a bright smile and an open face. His long, dark hair almost went to his shoulders, making him look more like a rock star than a rock hound. "You had a hell of a winter in Ann Arbor," McCauley said using the always handy weather fallback.

Tamburro parlayed the discussion into weather patterns during the Cretaceous periods, apparently a specialty of his. McCauley was impressed. He was a great get.

The second trip, he picked up Leslie Cohen, one of two students from Penn State. She was five-seven, with shoulder-length black curly hair and a warm, open smile. She wore shorts, checkered Vans, and a university t-shirt that fit absolutely perfectly. *Attractive,* he thought.

Cohen noted where his eyes traveled. "Dr. McCauley, don't think I'm concerned about getting my nails, dirty. I'm here to dig. I want this to be my life's work."

"Ms. Cohen, you may lead the charge."

"Thanks. I do have a favor to ask, though."

"Sure."

"My boyfriend is due in an hour. He's part of the same program."

"Mr. Lobel?"

She nodded. "Would it be okay to wait for him?"

"Sure."

There wasn't much real food to purchase from the machines in the small single story terminal, so they settled on chips and water. While they waited, Cohen talked about the Penn State paleo program, one of the best in the country. The way things were going for him at Yale, he might need to look for another job.

Adam Lobel arrived on time with a guitar slung over his back. He was close to six feet tall and muscular. However, his red hair and light complexion were going to be a challenge.

"Hope you bought out SPF 50 sunblock," McCauley said shaking his hand.

"Matter of fact, I did. And lots of hats."

McCauley felt Lobel and Cohen seemed to complete each other; a matched pair. But they were still young. Considering the hard work ahead, the summer might be a good test of their relationship.

As they walked to the team vehicle, Cohen said that they'd prefer to bunk together as long as it didn't cause any problems. He could divide them up any way he wanted during the day, but they hoped they'd be able to sleep together at night.

McCauley agreed, but he'd make them pitch their own tent.

Tom Trent, a solid five-feet-ten with short, cropped black hair and deep dark eyebrows, followed later in the day. The Northwestern University PhD candidate got off the plane in a burst of energy. So far, he appeared to be the most serious of the group, offering up his services as camp scribe to catalogue findings and chart progress. McCauley was more than willing to give him the job.

On day two, the first to arrive was Anna Chohany. She had bright brown eyes, light brown hair, a slim, athletic figure and a look that would never grow old. Just as he thought, the Harvard student was definitely DeMeo's kind of woman. But his teaching assistant was off on his own quest.

Chohany carried herself with authority beyond her twenty-six years. From the start she asked detailed, probing questions about their explorations.

Next, the lone international student, Carlos Rodriguez. Rodriguez's wavy blond hair, chiseled face, and steel blue eyes gave him a GQ quality. McCauley expected a thick accent, but the University of Madrid student spoke English fluently. "My mother's from Philadelphia," he explained. "I used to go to summer camp at Sebago Lake in Maine. That's where I picked up my first fossils...and ticks."

"Well, you'll have no shortage of fossils, and the things that bite here rattle first!"

The last to arrive was Al Jaffe, the twenty-eight-year-old micropaleontology PhD student from University of California, Berkeley. The lean and fit former US Army corporal on the GI Bill was the tallest of the team at six-two. He kept his thick, light brown hair just beyond his former regulation length.

"Professor McCauley?" he said bounding through the gate.

Jaffe had a deep authoritative voice and a methodical manner that instantly seemed ingrained from the military or reflective of his own attention to detail.

"That's me, but make it Dr. McCauley for starters."

"Yes, sir."

"Without the sir."

"Yes…" Jaffe caught himself, "Dr. McCauley. Pleased to me you."

McCauley instantly liked him. Jaffe certainly seemed ready to work.

This was the group. They seemed as bright as they get: healthy, inquisitive, and dedicated. Now McCauley hoped they'd stay engaged once the initial excitement wore off and the program moved into its evitable long, hot, boring weeks.

And maybe, just maybe, they'd find something worthwhile and McCauley would get a step closer to tenure.

ELEVEN

COLIN KAVANAUGH ENTERED the code to the security system outside Room Ten. Ten was on the fifth floor and bore no relation to the way the other twenty-two offices were numbered. The office required special access. General staff members were told it was where serious market research was conducted. Inquiring minds never learned anything from those who worked in Ten. They never mixed with the rest of the staff. Never.

Kavanaugh had spent a year working in the office. He earned his way in.

Now as the door swung open, Kavanaugh remembered the day he truly distinguished himself to Martin Gruber, the day he figured out the real reason the room was numbered *Ten*. This was before he was assigned to the space.

"Sir, I'm Colin Kavanaugh," he began after waiting forty-five minutes to see the publisher.

Without looking up, Gruber said, "I know who you are. I don't understand why you're here. You have a supervisor."

"Yes, Mr. Gruber, but I felt this was worthy to bring directly to you. The significance of Ten."

Gruber raised his eyes. "Pray tell."

Kavanaugh smiled. "Precisely. The Bible, sir."

"Oh?"

"Ten. It has so many meanings in numerology. Considering the secrecy you bestow upon the room, it fits perfectly. Absolutely perfectly."

Gruber studied the man. He motioned for Kavanaugh to continue.

"Ten. Ten Commandments. But more than that. There are a total of 603 commandments. Add the ten that God gave Moses atop Mount Sinai, there are 613. Six plus one plus three equals ten. There's more. John 3:16, the thesis of the Bible, adds up to another ten. Noah was the tenth patriarch prior to the Flood. God says he will not destroy Sodom and Gomorrah if ten righteous people step forward. We have ten God-given appendages on our hands; another ten on our feet."

Gruber's silence only encouraged him.

"Jesus performed thirty-seven miracles. Three and seven. Ten again. He quotes Deuteronomy forty-six times, more than any other book. Ten! And in the original Greek, Jesus uses the word 'fulfill' ten times in each Gospel."

Colin Kavanaugh caught his breath. "Mr. Gruber, ten is a fulfillment of a duty. You recruited me for a reason. A duty. I believe it's time you told me what that duty is."

Gruber smiled. He followed that with something totally unexpected. Martin Gruber stood up and offered his hand to the young man. "Mr. Kavanaugh, have a seat. Indeed, it is time for us to chat."

The entire episode played out in Kavanaugh's mind. He surveyed the room and wondered if anyone else had ever displayed such insight. Gruber never told him, though he was eager to find out.

Everyone worked diligently. The people pored through their individual assignments at their own computer workstations. Five read English language newspapers from Great Britain, Canada, Australia and the U.S. They also reviewed *The International Herald Tribune*. Five others perused the same paper's websites. Another five wore headphones, monitoring radio broadcasts in various languages. Another five multi-lingual researchers listened to podcasts in Mandarin, German, French, Spanish, Russian, Japanese, and Swedish, among other languages. They also reviewed all emails and correspondence from *Voyages'* writers around the world.

This was the routine. Seven days a week, around the clock. They'd read, listen, research, and when necessary, write evaluations that would go upstairs—to Martin Gruber. The evaluations were based on strict parameters and gut reactions. Everything was considered important. Success was never reported. That's not to say that the results of their work didn't make the news later. When that happened it was never discussed up the hierarchical chain of command, and certainly never down.

Secretum

Kavanaugh looked over the staff. No one took notice. They didn't fraternize with one another. They were paid well not to. Only two new people had joined the team in the past five years. No one heard from those who retired. They were given mortgage-free off-shore homes with enough money to more than comfortably live out their years and the assurance that they'd have lifetime subscriptions to *Voyages.* The underwriting was there as long as they continued to fulfill their obligation: their vow of silence about the true nature of their career.

Colin Kavanaugh had argued for, and successfully introduced, critically needed twenty-first century upgrades. The night staff was added at his insistence. Researchers were now assigned to review Twitter, Instagram, and other newer voices in the social media space based on a series of complex algorithms also recommended by Kavanaugh. Another ten trainees were being vetted.

Kavanaugh's efforts helped provide greater, quicker and more definitive research; research that wasn't intended for the pages of *Voyages*. This was special information culled from the field, from the media, and from the Internet; information that ultimately made it to Martin Gruber's desk. A desk that soon would belong to Colin Kavanaugh.

TWELVE

Makoshika State Park, MT
The next day

"WHAT DO WE know about where we are, people?" McCauley asked his full team. They were assembled for an early morning orientation under the food tent, each in a folding chair facing McCauley who stood next to a five by seven foot dry erase board set on an easel.

The professor drew a big question mark on the board. "Anyone?"

He wrote the name Makoshika on the board.

There were a few whispers. Nothing more. The group hadn't begun to gel yet.

"Look around. Kind of mysterious and eerie. The Native Americans called it Makoshika. Translation—*bad earth* or *pitiful earth*. Why?"

Still no answers.

"You'll find out soon enough. But here's a little history for you. The Sioux and their ancestors who lived here were humbled by the quiet. It was, in their experience, truly pitiful, unforgiving. Hot in the summer, freezing in the winter. Some of which you'll experience. But it wasn't always this way. You're sitting on what used to be a humid lowland tropical swamp. As humid as Florida is today. Maybe more so. And then?"

"It got a lot colder," one of the men said. It was Tom Trent from Northwestern.

"Thank you, Mr. Trent. Big time colder," McCauley underscored. "With tons of ice reshaping the terrain."

The Yale professor surveyed the group. "Okay, anything else about Mah-KO-shi-kuh?" he said with intentional emphasis.

"Montana's state dinosaur is the duck-billed hadrosaur," said Leslie Cohen.

"Planning on finding one yourself, Ms. Cohen?"

"Love to. Where do you think, Dr. McCauley?"

"Dig your heels into the ground. Your hadrosaur might be right under you. You never know. It could be your invitation to a formal Penrose dinner."

This brought applause. The Penrose Medal was the Geological Society of America's highest honor. However, it would take more than one exceptional fossil to merit the prestigious award.

"Ah, my group lives," McCauley said. "And now welcome to home for the next six weeks. Look around. It doesn't get any better than this. I mean it. This is as good as it gets."

The students scanned the foreboding terrain. To some, it appeared prehistoric; to others, post-apocalyptic.

"So, back to my question. This time with answers. What do we know about where we are?"

"It's God-awful hot," said UC Berkeley's Al Jaffe.

"Tell me something I don't know," McCauley responded.

"That will be difficult, you're the professor," the Harvard woman offered under her breath.

"It's Ms. Chohany, right?"

"Yes, Dr. McCauley."

"I imagine that if you display that attitude defending your dissertation it will be a very short session."

"Yes," she said sheepishly. "It would."

McCauley liked attitude, but he figured he needed to establish lines of authority first.

"Then enlighten us, professionally."

"Well, we're in the heart of the mother lode of archeological and paleontological sites. There have been more than nineteen thousand digs in the immediate area. This is the home to one of the most famous T. rex—"

"No abbreviations," McCauley interrupted. "These creatures deserve our respect."

"...one of the most famous Tyrannosaurus rex fossils ever unearthed..." she said, thinking *fuck you*. "...nearly ninety percent complete."

"Ever or in the area?"

"In Montana," the University of Michigan's Rich Tamburro interjected.

McCauley nodded. "And its name?"

"*Her* name," Chohany declared. "It's a *she*. Sue."

Quinn McCauley was actually pleased that personalities were beginning to emerge with spirit. He needed to gauge their strengths and weaknesses. So far he was seeing clear distinctions from three of his students; Chohany being the strongest.

"And do you know where Sue was discovered? Let's hear from the so far silent Penn Stater, Mr. Lobel and our representative from Madrid, Mr. Rodriguez."

"Well, right here, on former Sioux land," Lobel replied.

"And how long ago? Again, to you Mr. Lobel."

"Sixty million years. Sixty-million-ish."

Leslie Cohen, Adam Lobel's girlfriend, cringed.

"More accurately."

"Sixty-seven?" he asked.

"Look it up," McCauley stated. "What else do we know about Sue?"

"She had awfully huge hips," Tamburro joked. "About

twelve feet wide. She was forty-two feet long. A big, big woman. Not the kind you'd want to get mad."

"Sue was born mad," McCauley corrected. "And you've all done well for any eighth grade general science student who could type Tyrannosaurus rex into Google. Who's got more?"

"I do," Carlos Rodriguez offered. "Sue is really just one of many on the tyrannosaur family tree. We happen to know more about tyrannosaur genera than any other classification of dinosaurs, even more than some other groups of living organisms. They range from Sue's build right down to others about one-hundredth the size. And some of her cousins go back a good one hundred million years earlier."

"Thank you, Mr. Rodriguez. And welcome. And to everyone, congratulations. You're up to ninth grade. Now show me I made seven good decisions about my choices for this team. Mr. Jaffe, aside from digging up the fossilized bones, what are we finding?"

"Finding? We haven't started yet."

"Oh yes, we have. Everyone get up and walk around." McCauley was opening their eyes to what they hadn't seen.

Chohany stood and headed fifty yards south. She saw a canyon and a drop she calculated at nearly three hundred feet. She gasped at the natural beauty. Magnificently colored sedimentary layers, every inch representing eons with history ready to be unlocked. All exquisite. There were reddish-brown layers of stone laced with orange, yellow, and green where the irons and other trace metals had oxidized.

The others came back with similar reactions and descriptions of more minerals and colors.

"Okay, now that you've done a site survey, give us some geological forensics about this place."

"I'd say these rocks were formed when water carried particles of sand down a river delta. There used to be a sea here and streams would have fed it."

"Did you deduce that or read it on the park website, Mr. Trent?"

"One hundred percent observation. Look at the slope of the strata. The signs are all there."

"You're right, but there are larger rocks within the shale," McCauley noted. "Anyone?"

Chohany spoke again. "Well, if the streams dried up or slowed down, the heavier rocks would have settled to the bottom." She pointed to an area she'd seen. "And then as things speeded up again, other particles would have been trapped creating bands of sandstone, each representing distinct geological periods."

"Very good," the teacher said. "Now, let's get to what this can mean for us. What good can come from all this work beyond tagging some fossils?"

The team didn't seem to understand the question.

"I'll try it another way. Are there any breakthroughs you can report? The things that get journal attention? Your ticket to tenure." McCauley laughed at his own comment. However, he looked around, hoping for more in the way of a response. "Mr. Jaffe, show us how bright you are."

"Well, on the medical side, cancer research has benefited from paleontological discoveries."

"Welcome to tenth grade." This was an answer he hadn't expected. "Go on."

"Molecular paleontologists have actually extracted hardy, fibrous protein collagen from a Tyrannosaurus rex thighbone found in the Hell Creek Formation. Other researchers discovered soft tissue in," he paused, "may I please just say T. rex, Dr. McCauley?"

Quinn McCauley laughed. "Only because you're on a roll."

"Well, pathologists and mass spectrometry experts at Harvard sequenced peptide fragments which produced evidence that T. rex was actually a BFUC."

"A what?" Leslie Cohen asked.

"A 'B-F-U-C.'" Jaffe spelled out the letters. "Big Fat Ugly Chicken."

Everyone snickered.

"And what does that have to do with the price of eggs?" McCauley asked.

"Molecular evidence that can be extracted from fossils is a door opener," Jaffe continued. "We see links between extinct species and modern day animals. Animals like us. The study is leading to more understanding about tumor growth. From just a minute amount of material they've been able to work on ways to sequence *oncoproteins* with the hopes of ultimately determining why an individual gets cancer."

"Wow, I had no idea," Leslie Cohen said.

"There's a lot of wow beneath us and we haven't even"—McCauley smiled at where he was going—"scratched the surface."

This was the ice-breaker the group needed. They all laughed.

"Okay, okay, okay," he said settling them down. "So now we're ready to get back to my initial question. What do we know about where we are?" He looked around trying to see who would put all the pieces together.

"We're at the beginning of finding answers," Anna Chohany said without hesitation.

"Correct, Ms. Chohany. Absolutely correct."

MCCAULEY HAD SELECTED his summer companions on their resumes, the passion in their letters, their recommendations and his teaching assistant's recommendations. One-hundred twenty had not made it. Seven did. The seven best. Different personalities, all dressed the same—for the heat, the dirt, and the work.

Clothing *de rigueur* was a white or light gray t-shirt, shorts, white socks and a Panama hat or baseball cap. No expensive watches. No fingernail or toenail polish on the women. They wore laced-up leather work boots which protected them from cuts and bruises, sprained ankles, or worse.

"Time for a site survey. We'll initially work in basically one hundred square yards. But it's not what you see that matters. It's what's below. So let's walk and talk."

Now they were clicking as a group and displaying their individuality. Chohany distinguished herself as a great pick, willing to get out in front. Tamburro's acerbic personality was emerging. Al Jaffe was smart as a whip and someone to lean on. Leslie Cohen and Adam Lobel were clearly a couple, with Cohen being the driver. Trent was still quiet, but he looked like a dedicated worker who would undoubtedly help everyone. Rodriguez, the Spaniard, was an unknown quantity.

Jaffe walked closest to McCauley. He took a series of photographs with his iPhone.

"The first time I did a dig, my site director told me to save my film for later," McCauley said.

"Later?"

McCauley laughed. "Film. It used to be expensive." He stopped and turned around facing his team.

"Okay, listen up. Look around. You've got a clear view of some sixty miles. And wherever you dig, it'll be almost impossible not to come up with something. Dinosaur Alley is one of the world's most impressive burial grounds.

Maybe that's another reason to call it pitiful. But now let's see where your $200,000 in tuition is going."

"Try upwards of three hundred," Tamburro joked. "Adding on the cost of a PhD without a full ride, which I don't have, and…"

"Right. So, Mr. Tamburro, give us a history lesson *Jeopardy*-style. The answer is *3.8 to 3.9 billion years old.*"

"What are the oldest rocks on Earth?"

"Correct, but…"

"I'm not finished. Some sedimentary rocks include embedded minerals that are as old as 4.1 to 4.2 billion years. These are relatively rare, but they've been excavated at sites around the globe from Africa to Asia, Australia, Greenland and North America."

"Very good. Next answer—three isotopes of lead that are contained in meteorite samples."

"I know," shouted Leslie Cohen. "What's the best measure for determining Earth's age?"

"Take it further, Ms. Cohen."

"Well, the baseline comes from critical estimates of when common pool matter was formed and then uniformly distributed in the solar system. Over eons, pronounced changes in the isotopes occurred. Computing these changes against the uranium-to-lead ratio gives us the ability to determine how much time has passed since galactic pool matter became separated."

Cohen stuck her tongue out at her boyfriend. The others laughed.

"Very, very good. Double Jeopardy, where everything doubles. Are you ready?"

"Yes, Dr. McCauley," said Tamburro.

"Yes, doctor," smirked Chohany.

"The answer is, *They think you're crazy!*"

"Got it!" Six of the seven yelled in unison. Rodriguez was trying to figure it out.

McCauley held up his hands, not certain whom to go to. "Looks like a tie, so, ladies first."

"Ms. Cohen?"

"Easy. Young Earthers."

"Incorrectly stated."

"Who are Young Earthers?" Al Jaffe said.

The group laughed.

"No laughing gang. They're serious about their beliefs, so no editorializing for now."

"I'll do my best," Jaffe offered. "Well, according to them, smarty pants scientists…"

"Snarky."

"Sorry, Dr. McCauley. *Many* scientists maintain that Earth, as a whole, has to be as old as any of its parts. If we were to light birthday candles, we'd have about 4.55 billion, about the same number, give or take 1%, we'd place on the solar system's cake. But Young Earthers or Ultra-Creationists base their beliefs in strict biblical interpretations and by the rate at which rivers deposit metals into the oceans. They claim that the true age of the oceans and therefore Earth is merely, I don't know, more or less six or seven thousand years."

"Theology over geology?" McCauley asked. "Isn't there room for both?"

"Science demands strict testing. Religion requires strict beliefs," Jaffe continued taking the middle of the road.

"And we'll never be able to resolve the interpretation of the word *day*," Lobel said. "Twenty-four hours or eons?"

"It's not open to interpretation," Cohen shot back.

"Then how come this debate doesn't go away?" Mc-Cauley proposed. The professor encouraged the argument and recognized that they would no more solve the question now than anyone on a college campus or church pulpit had before.

Trent said, "It's all part of a political agenda." He was showing his stripes. "Lots of different kinds of politics. Government, the church, even academia. They're singing the chorus led by others. And who knows who else is out there in the shadows pulling strings?"

McCauley had the distinct impression that Chohany suddenly broke her eye contact.

THIRTEEN

October 1, 1632
Firenze, Italy

"GALILEO GALILEI?" the priest asked barely able to hide his nervousness in the home of the famed scientist.

The sixty-eight-year-old Galileo was unmistakable as he stooped before the priest in the anteroom. His twisted white beard flowed to collar length. A receding hairline pushed almost halfway back across his scalp. Galileo wore loose-fitting pants and a thick, gray shirt with a ruffled, dirty-white collar that was pulled up over his neck to keep him warm. He looked old and certainly in ill health, but it was the scientist's piercing brownish black eyes that warned the priest to measure his words carefully.

"Yes, and what is the occasion of your unscheduled visit?"

"By order of his Eminence, Pope Urban VIII, you are hereby ordered to present yourself to the Supreme Sacred Congregation of the Roman and Universal Inquisition at the Holy Office."

"With what authority do you present such contrivance?" Galileo defiantly demanded.

"I am the Inquisitor of Florence," the local priest, half Galileo's age, affirmed.

"You?" Galileo hazarded a throaty, phlegm-filled laugh.

"You are compelled to comply."

"And the charges against me?"

"They are here."

The Inquisitor handed Galileo a document. The ailing scientist read the official declaration from the Vatican Inquisition. The principal charge referred back to 1616 when the church's Index of Forbidden Books censored the works of Copernicus. At that time, Jesuit cardinal Robert Bellarmine instructed Galileo never to hold or defend the opinion that the Earth moved. Galileo agreed but arguably only loosely complied.

"I have a certificate signed by Cardinal Bellarmine that states I have no such restriction other than any applied under the edict of 1616."

"Which, according to the charges, you violated. I suggest you find it." The priest felt empowered and fully in control now. "Though such a paper should bring you little consolation."

"This is how they come to me?" Galileo looked up to the heavens. He sighed heavily. "I would request that any proceedings against me, no matter how fabricated, be settled here."

"His Holiness requests your presence in Rome."

"But, as you can see, I am in ill health. An extended trip to Rome will take its toll." Galileo coughed, not just for effect. He was sick.

His request was denied. In late January, 1633, Galileo began an arduous journey to Rome in the dead of winter. Twenty-three days later, two days before his sixty-ninth birthday, weakened by crippling sciatic pain, he took up residency in the Florentine embassy. Over the next four months, he tried to get his strength back to endure the private hearings and public humiliation. As he prepared, Galileo feared for what the Inquisitors would conclude from his writing given their strict Biblical interpretations, and what they might find if they explored further. He was certain the punishment would be death.

FOURTEEN

Makoshika State Park, MT

THE DISCUSSION FROM earlier in the day continued around a campfire.

McCauley used the time to better understand his team, their individual abilities and personal perspectives, and whether they could also listen and work well with others. It was good information for him and a character building exercise for them.

"Play the devil's advocate now," McCauley said.

"I'm not sure the devil needs an advocate," Al Jaffe chided.

The gang laughed.

"Okay, okay. Got me," McCauley acknowledged. "What I want are arguments in the affirmative that the earth is under ten thousand years old. And as you do, remember, you're representing the view of nearly fifty percent of the country. Who's first?"

The crackling wood in the fire pit didn't drown anyone out because no one volunteered. McCauley could read the faces in the glow of the flames. This was going to be harder than he thought.

"I'll kick it off with an assumption: Evolution cannot be observed. Therefore it doesn't exist."

It worked. Anna Chohany jumped right in. "But fossils—"

"Fossils? There aren't any transitional fossils," the professor quickly countered. "If the ancestor of today's horse, supposedly *Miohippus,* evolved from *Mesohippus,* where are its fossils? And again, don't argue against the proposition, speak in favor that since evolution cannot be observed in real time, it does not exist."

"All right, though there are ways to support evolution under the microscope," Adam Lobel offered.

"Nope. Stick with the argument."

Leslie Cohen raised her hand ready to join the conversation, but Lobel held the floor.

"There's the erosion of Niagara Falls. I could argue that it absolutely lines up with the timeline of a few thousand years since the flood. It proves we live on a young Earth because its erosion is consistent with biblical fact."

"Not a lot of support, but it would make a strong sermon," McCauley noted. "Give me more detailed thought that debunks *deep time*, the long-held view of evolutionists."

Cohen put her hand down.

"Can I try again?" Lobel asked.

McCauley laughed. "Okay, sure. Back to the gentleman from Penn State."

"The Grand Canyon. It was cut by the receding waters after the flood."

"The Flood?" Trent asked.

"THE Flood," Lobel responded. "The Noah's Ark flood."

"Got it, but to do so, the water would have had to rush through five times the speed of sound." Trent was highly sarcastic.

"Whoa. I said no counterarguments. Not yet," McCauley proclaimed. "Only positions that speak to our inhabiting a young earth."

Anna Chohany was ready again. "Where are the geologic columns of recognizable soil layers? If deep time was correct, with two hundred million years of life on earth, there should be an overabundance of evidence in fossilized soil formation." Role playing, the Harvard grad student sounded indignant. "There isn't any!"

Al Jaffe stood up. "Ladies and gentlemen, both the Royal Greenwich Observatory and the U.S. Naval Observatory have made exacting measurements that show our sun is shrinking at a rate of roughly five feet per hour. Moreover, records of a dwindling number of solar eclipses over the last four centuries reinforce the shrinkage. A smaller sun by the year, fewer opportunities for the heavenly phenomena to occur. Even the most zealous evolutionists would have to deduce that if the sun existed millions of years ago, it would have been so *ginormous* that it would have cooked the earth and no species could have lived here. Ergo, young Earth."

His argument brought a round of applause.

"Nice job, Mr. Jaffe. Deeper reasoning. You may sit down now."

"There are other astronomical arguments. Anyone? Mr. Tamburro?"

"Well," he started slowly. "This wasn't going to be my example, but I can go with it. Up there." He pointed to the crescent moon. "Consider the rate the moon accumulates meteoritic dust. If it were really billions of years old, that layer should be a mile deep. NASA was concerned about that when they sent the Apollo astronauts to the moon. They worried that they'd sink into dust. But there was very little, which to them proved that the moon, like the Earth, is young."

"Hadn't considered that," McCauley said, complimenting him. "Let's go back to Leslie. Looks like you've been thinking something through."

"I have. It's about the spin down rate of the earth."

"The what?" Rodriguez asked.

"The spin down rate," she repeated. "Atomic clocks

have measured the earth's rate of rotation for the past three decades to billionths of a second. They've found that the earth is slowing down almost a second a year. If the earth were as old as the evolutionists claim, its initial spin rate would have been so fast that the earth would have been a different shape. Therefore it is not billions, only thousands of years old."

"Wow, that was good!" Cohen's boyfriend, Adam Lobel, said. "Very good. Now how about this? It's absolutely improbable for life forms, as complex as they are, to develop by chance. It's like saying that a tornado could rip through a junkyard and create an Alfa Romeo or a Boeing 777. Improbable? No, impossible. There's intelligent design to it all. There's a creator."

It was the first mention of a higher force by anyone in the group. It was followed by complete silence.

McCauley let the quiet settle in. Then he spoke just above a whisper.

"We're not going to change people's minds. Young Earthers base their evidence on their own set of facts and their faith. Again, they maintain that since evolutionary phenomena can't be observed in motion, they doesn't exist. That since evolution doesn't explain things like the Big Bang, it is therefore false. That scientists disagree on its veracity. And most importantly, new species do suddenly appear through intelligent design. They claim we are evidence of that.

"Certainly many of the arguments are deeply held, unshakable beliefs by everyday people, your own clergy, dedicated fathers and mothers, teachers, police officers, librarians, computer experts, perhaps members of your families."

This brought some nods.

"They're also propagandized and exploited for political and financial reasons by those in government and media personalities who preach through their own commercial pulpits. The views become valuable political capital for lobbyists and corporations. So, we must work hard to patiently separate argument from beliefs."

"That's impossible," Jaffe complained.

"Your impossibility is someone else's faith."

"And their faith negates the possible. X is the age of the earth and they claim that A is evidence of it."

"Basically."

"Then conversely, *not A* is evidence against their X. But they won't consider that," he added.

"No they don't because they don't *believe* it," McCauley offered. "Belief is different from consideration. They hold intelligent design near and dear. So while you may chalk up Young Earthers' arguments to pseudo-science, absurd 'uniformitarianism,' unsupported assumptions, false dilemmas, affirming a consequence or invoking miraculous violations of physics, you cannot sway basic religious belief. We can refute them and challenge data mining, but when it comes down to fundamental convictions, we'll have no more luck turning *them* around than they will *us*."

"So what's the point of what we do, Dr. McCauley?" Leslie Cohen seemed to speak for her colleagues. "What's the chance of making a significant new find? Who's to say there is anything new to discover, that there's nothing remarkable right here?"

Quinn McCauley smiled. Leslie Cohen had just stepped into what he liked to describe as *intellectual quicksand*.

McCauley paced, which made it look like he was thinking. But he knew exactly what to say. He didn't want to embarrass her. That could humiliate the young woman and destroy the team building that was so important for the full summer experience.

"All fair questions, Leslie," he finally said. "But how

about if I flip it around. What if we're all standing atop something remarkable? Groundbreaking? Astounding? Right here. This very spot." He pointed straight down. "But we're exploring over there a thousand feet away."

"Bad luck," Leslie replied, taking McCauley's bait.

"There's an expression."

"I'm sure there is," Jaffe called out.

"Really. It's been used and misused by a wide variety of people—for laying down scientific theories and for strictly political reasons. You can find examples from astronomer Carl Sagan to Secretary of Defense Donald Rumsfeld, and a slew of others. Anyone?" He waited a few seconds before picking up the point. "That's okay. I'm happy to share it. It's simple. The absence of evidence is not evidence of absence."

McCauley saw recognition on some of the faces. Others were working through the circular phrasing.

"I know. It's hard on the ear. Let me give it to you again. The absence of evidence," he paused, "is not evidence of absence."

Now it registered across the board.

"Someone want to take a stab at it?"

Carlos Rodriguez raised his hand. "Mathematically, if you look for X, but don't find it, it doesn't mean X doesn't exist."

"Excellent. Now practical examples."

Chohany spoke up next. "Rumsfeld was making the case that just because the U.N. didn't find WMD in Iraq it didn't rule out the possibility that they had them."

McCauley nodded approvingly and saw that Rich Tamburro had another idea.

"Take life like us on other planets. We haven't found any yet, but that can't suggest that we won't ever. I suppose that was Sagan's argument."

It was going well. Now to see if the young woman who proposed the question was following the line of thinking. "Ms. Cohen?" he asked.

"Dinosaurs," she admitted. "New species, new genus. We won't know until we find them."

"Very good," McCauley said. "There is an actual probability theory in support of the proposition. If I had the whiteboard up, it would be easier. So, consider yourself spared from classroom pedagogy."

McCauley heard an "amen" and "thank goodness."

"Just trust me," he continued, "it weighs probability against events in the favor of evidence. In our realm, Young Earthers and creationists might assert that the lack of some fossils disprove evolution. But specific proof may be missing because fossilization is not a democratic process. It has not occurred with every specimen or species."

McCauley stopped again and let the thought truly sink in.

"Remember," he continued, "there's still so much to learn about our planet. Just a few years ago, the world's longest canyon was discovered below two miles of ice in Greenland. It's been there for some four million years but invisible until ice-penetrating radar hit it during airplane flyovers. It's still buried under two miles of ice, but we now know it's twice as long and twice as wide as the Grand Canyon even though it can't be explored."

"The absence of evidence is not evidence of absence," Cohen said.

"Absolutely," McCauley proclaimed. His lesson had penetrated. "And since we're here to dig for evidence, I think it's time to call it a night. We start tomorrow."

MCCAULEY WAS LOOKING over the last embers of the campfire when he heard footsteps and someone call his name.

"Dr. McCauley?"

"That's me."

"Hi, I'm Jim Kaplan. I look over this place."

"Mr. Kaplan, great to meet you. I've heard all about you. Thanks for coming by."

"We're going to get along famously if you call me by the name my golfing buddies do. It's Kappy."

This made the Yale professor very happy. "Kappy it is. And I'm Quinn."

"Like 'The Mighty Quinn?'"

"Not so mighty, and certainly not an Eskimo, but you know your music."

"Manfred Mann. 1968." Kappy laughed. "It comes from years listening to Cousin Brucie on SiriusXM."

"We're definitely going to get along, Kappy. How about saying hello to my team, then we can knock down a scotch in my tent."

THAT NIGHT THEY talked dinosaurs and music. Kappy gave McCauley a primer on the park. The teacher had read much of it, but hearing about the geological history from someone filled with such passion reinforced McCauley's decision to come to Makoshika.

"We're the largest state park in Montana. More than 11,500 acres. I challenge you to find a better ancient burial ground. They call it badlands. I think we should be promoting the park as the world's great lands."

"I like the ring of that," McCauley said. He offered up his half-filled plastic cup with a wonderful twelve-year-old Glenlivet Scotch. Kappy met his toast. They laughed at the dull thud the cups made.

"Did you know there are a number of stories about the origin of the toast?" McCauley asked.

"Oh?"

"Yes. The first is owed to the Greek gods. As they drank their wine or other fermented delights they could appreciate the brilliant color by holding it up to a candle or the sun, which they controlled. They could take in the most pleasing of aromas. The could touch the velvety liquid and they could savor the flavors as they drank to their hearts' content. But there was nothing for the ear, so...."

"Ping!" Kappy concluded. "They clinked their glasses."

"So the mythology goes."

"The other story?"

"Well, from Greece to Rome. The priests also enjoyed their libations. But it was not always considered in the best of form. So, they created a good reason to justify their more serious drinking. They told parishioners that by bringing their glasses together and creating the distinctive, high-pitched musical tone, the devil would be chased away. What better justification to get drunk than to scare off the devil?"

"Gotta love it. Yes, seems the Church has always been able to invent parables to explain away a great deal of things."

"I suppose that's what makes history so interesting," McCauley said. He spoke from his comfort zone. His undergraduate degree was history with an emphasis on the world since 1914. Ironically, paleontology—even earlier history—came to him later.

"I like to believe it also makes for more enlightenment, not less. Out here, it's Native American culture that leads to a certain open-mindedness," Kappy commented. "You'll hear your fair share of stories the more time you spend in the badlands. They had a way of seeing and interpreting things spiritually and quite naturally."

"What would you recommend?"

"Look up, look down, look everywhere. You're going to

want to take your team along Kinney Coulee Trail, about four miles south of the entrance. The terrain's rougher than the basic loops, but the rock formations are amazing. You've been to Bryce Canyon?"

"Sure have."

"Well, we've got examples of similar windblown formations in isolation: sculptured spiral statues painted in earth's most lively colors. Positively beautiful."

"There's a half-mile loop off the Cap Rock Nature Trail. The walk is one of my favorites. It begins on Cains Coulee Road. You'll catch great views of our natural rock bridge. The formation still astounds me. Also, take Diane Gabriel Trail up the line a bit. It loops through a prairie section. About midway you'll see a duck-billed dinosaur fossil embedded in a cliff. It's a real crowd pleaser."

"I've seen pictures," McCauley replied.

"Nothing compared to the real thing. But all you'll really need to do is stand anywhere in the park and turn 360. The topography changes everywhere you look. Microclimates and ancient water sources have carved out the most unbelievable landscapes, a feast for artists' and photographers' eyes. Pure gold for us. You'll feel a solitude that's indescribable."

"The Lakota used to put their ears to the ground, listening for the footsteps of their direct ancestors and even those who came before them. It's all legend, of course, but who's to really say? There's so much we don't understand."

"That's why we've come to your backyard, Kappy." He raised his cup for another thud. "We're going to have a great time and you're welcome to join us whenever you'd like. But let's get something equally important on the books."

"Oh?"

"I've come equipped and we need to set a date."

He walked to the end of his tent and lifted a black tarp that had covered a shipping skid. In addition to backpacks, canned food, digging tools and rain gear, Kappy saw McCauley's prize possession: his Callaway golf clubs, bought used on eBay.

"When do we play?" he asked.

FIFTEEN

Makoshika State Park, MT
Three weeks into the dig

THE SIMPLE TRUTH was that the process hadn't changed since the time of Cope and Marsh or even years earlier. You had to dig. The treasures were usually lower. Exhaustingly lower. Depressingly lower. Sometimes unforgivably lower. And, as McCauley had pointed out, no matter how far you dug, you had to be in the right place. Modern equipment made some searching easier, but luck still played a heavy hand.

It was a percentages game. For most people in the field, it was completely and utterly a game of failure. You were simply a few feet off. You stopped too soon. The weather was too hot or too cold to go on. Your support staff gave up. You lost your funding. Your bones ached. You grew too old to continue…or to care. However, there were still extraordinary things to uncover.

"The earth has all the time in the world," McCauley explained. "We don't have such luxury. So gang, get your backs into it more."

It was hot, and work was tedious, exactly what Dr. Quinn McCauley had promised. He'd chosen a spot nearly two miles off the beaten path, far from the park entrance where the tourists stopped to gaze at the famed dinosaur cemetery and well beyond the main road that led up to Makoshika State Park. With the exception of jet contrails during the day and satellites sweeping past in the night sky, contemporary time hardly existed. It was the perfect environment to explore the past.

WELL INTO THEIR first week, the students were enthusiastic and already an effective team. McCauley's prompting helped shape their camaraderie, but each wanted to be the first to find something really noteworthy.

The closest layers bore sloths and horses. The mammoths were deeper. Then the dinosaurs. There was evidence of the ancient ocean with shells literally photographed in time by sediment and silt.

"Fossilization is Mother Earth's three-dimensional photographic record," he casually noted around one of the evening campfires. "You surely have the picture. Some animals sank into mud and sand after their death. If scavengers didn't immediately raid the carcasses, layers of sediment eventually covered the remains. Under the right combination of heat, pressure, chemical reactions and time, the harder parts of the creatures—bones and teeth—*could* become fossils. But it was far from automatic."

His students knew this to a great extent, but the rest was a powerful lesson.

"Most animals never fossilized. They just decayed; disappeared from earth's record and, the missing fossil record, forever lost, is far, far larger than the remaining, existing fossil record waiting to be found. That in itself is staggering. What we will *never* know is greater than what we will *ever* find."

"Be patient gang," McCauley implored through the second and third weeks. "You're in one of the richest dinosaur graveyards in the world, but only a small percentage of the genera that ever lived makes it to the scrapbook. For paleontologists, it's like randomly spinning the tumblers of a giant safe. Most of the time they don't click. But, when all the numbers fall into place, the door can open to untold treasures…or another vault."

Not that McCauley had ever found the combination to anything really remarkable himself.

"HEY, DR. MCCAULEY, your TA, Pete, is on your phone," yelled Rich Tamburro from the base camp tent.

McCauley had left his cell there while barbequing the team's chicken dinner. By the time Tamburro brought him the cell, the line was dead. Service in the park was spotty. Not surprisingly McCauley couldn't get DeMeo back.

"No go?" Tamburro asked.

"Nope. Probably checking to see if there's anything to report." *Nothing major so far*, he thought.

The students might disagree. Tamburro and his digging partner Anna Chohany uncovered Triceratops fossils. Lobel and Cohen worked a nearby gully and came up with evidence of an Edmontosaurus. Rodriguez, Trent and Jaffe working together found dinosaur gizzard stones. These were smooth, egg-sized rocks which looked like they had been polished by a tumbler. But the process that resulted in the glass-like quality was actually something quite natural and amazing: the dinosaurs' own digestive system. They'd used stones to grind up food in their gizzards. Of course, the finds would have to be confirmed. However, each discovery prompted McCauley to push his students further.

Over dinner he did just that.

"You want to make history, you have to beat history," he said. "It's full of tricks. Keep reading the rocks; the slope of the strata. Feel the winds and the directions they blow. Look for signs of streams and where they could have made twists and turns through the ages. Follow the leads. And work harder."

These were important lessons. Wind and water erosion constantly changed the landscape, reshaping the cap rocks, sandstone knobs and freshwater shale. Scrubs, grasses and more than one hundred forty species of wildflowers conspired with the land to mask clues. Pine and juniper roots dug into the earth and spread in all directions creating more barriers to exploration.

The next day

"FINALLY," MCCAULEY PROCLAIMED when he reconnected with his teaching assistant.

"Hi, boss. How's it going?"

"Pretty well. They're all engaged. How are your travels?"

"Good. Taking trains some of the time. Renting motorcycles occasionally. Meeting cool people."

"Cool or hot?"

He laughed. "So far they're cool and, well, some of them cold. But I'm having a great time anyway," DeMeo said honestly. "Think you'll come up with anything?"

McCauley turned his back on his students. "I can only hope. But I'm already thinking about moving to a new area. We could use some bigger challenges."

"Like what?"

"Still looking around. There are some formations down the valley that might be interesting. Remember last year in South Dakota?"

"Oh yeah," Pete DeMeo recalled. Careful excavation of sandstone revealed some interesting finds for the students. They weren't worthy of a scholastic journal account, but it led to a rewarding summer program.

"Well, that's what I'm hoping for."

"Good luck, boss."

"Thanks."

"You still have my itinerary?"

"Yup, somewhere."

"Well if you find it, don't call. Oh, and did you get a text about your visitor?"

"No, who?" McCauley asked.

"Someone from Cambridge. The department wrote me maybe thinking I was with you."

"Cambridge, Massachusetts—Harvard?" McCauley asked.

"The other Cambridge. The original one. Cambridge University. University of Cambridge. However they say it."

"Fuck." McCauley knew what that meant.

"The department *invited* someone on your behalf…"

"To spy."

"They call it an evaluation," DeMeo offered.

"Same difference. Bureaucratic shit."

"I'm sorry. I wish I could have…"

"It's not you, Pete. I wish they'd just leave me alone." McCauley swore to himself. "Well, who do I have the pleasure of babysitting and for how long?"

"Just have a last name. Alpert. Some Brit. And at least five days."

"Five days too many. Starting when?"

"What's today?" DeMeo asked.

"Tuesday."

"Tomorrow. Maybe sooner."

"Oh shit! I'm going to call the chair and make his vacation miserable!"

"Wouldn't do that. I think they held off sending word until the last minute."

"Intentionally."

"You think?" It was a sarcastic comment for certain. "Suck it up. Before you know it, it'll be over. You'll be fine."

"I won't be fine. I'm taking off for golf this afternoon at Cottonwood with the park director. After that I promised myself a nice hot bath in town, not a soaking from the department." McCauley was truly frustrated.

"Like I said, suck it up and play nice."

"Easy for you to say. While you're exposing yourself to every beauty in Europe, I'll be under some bloody academic's microscope."

"Be a good boy. And like I said, do me a favor, don't call. I might get lucky yet with some French or Italian babe who wants to try on an American for size. Consider me out of cell-phone range for the next month."

"Okay, have a good time and for God's sake, be careful tooling around."

"I will. Take care, boss."

McCauley hung up, cursed his department and wondered whether he'd even be able to keep his mind on his golf game now.

London
The same time

MARTIN GRUBER'S THOUGHTS were focused on taking it slow as he walked with Colin Kavanaugh to Kensington Gardens, one of the seven Royal Parks of London.

"Beautiful isn't it, young man? It makes you pause and want to take in your surroundings."

Kavanaugh didn't see it. Nor did he really care.

Two different men; two different approaches to life. The old man wanting to hold onto the moment; his successor ready to race through it.

"I know you're wondering where we're going," Gruber said. "It's up ahead."

He transferred a folded newspaper from his right hand to under his left arm making it easier to point to a specific park bench with his umbrella. The umbrella was a needless accessory in the cloudless sky. Nevertheless, it completed Gruber's presentation.

Of course, everything Gruber said or did had purpose. Kavanaugh was about to find out what today's walk was about.

They ended up at a park bench under a maple shade tree. Another bench backed up to theirs. Gruber rested his umbrella against the seat and marveled at the park. They had a clear view of the greenery and the Long Water that separated Kensington from Hyde Park.

"I've always enjoyed coming here. Do you know why?"

"No, sir."

Gruber tapped Kavanaugh's thigh in a fatherly manner. "Why this is the park where J.M. Barrie conceived Peter Pan. It was the setting of his first novel, a prelude to his Neverland stories. There's a statue of Peter Pan over near the water. Erected in 1912. You've never noticed it?"

"No, I'm afraid not."

"A shame. We did a story about it a few years ago. Remember?"

"I think it was before my time, Mr. Gruber."

"Oh, perhaps memories are failing me," Gruber sighed. "Do have archives pull it for you. It's a truly wonderful article. After all, Peter Pan holds such charm. I suppose if I had had children, I would have read it to them."

"I'm sure you would have."

Gruber drifted into what seemed like another reflection. "So much to see. So very much."

Suddenly, as if a switch had been thrown, his voice

changed. It became deeper, stronger, and direct. No longer living in the past, he commanded Kavanaugh's attention.

"There is so much to see, and yet you must learn how to see, but not be seen yourself. How to hide in plain sight."

"Sir?"

"How many people took notice of an old man walking at half speed accompanied by a younger business associate? Who noticed us?"

"Well, nobody I think."

"Not completely accurate. People saw us, but took little notice. They were watching the children with the balloons. They turned to the bobby's whistle as we crossed the street. The car horn that followed. The birds in flight. That's what caught everyone's attention. Not us. Not today. In fact, I've hardly ever been seen, though this is part of my regular routine, as it will be yours."

Gruber continued, "Who cares about you if you show no interest in return? You insert yourself into a habitual schedule and blend in. You become the person no one really sees. You become invisible."

Gruber was getting to his real point.

"You just sit and settle in. Spread out so no one joins you. Discourage any eye contact by not having any, yet see everything."

Kavanaugh tried. He stayed too long on a woman pushing a stroller and a young boy watching a squirrel climb a tree.

"Ah, it's not so easy, is it? You're lingering. You have to appear like you're taking in a wide view. However, you're actually recording every detail. It takes practice. Soon it will become natural and when that happens you are ready to do your work."

Gruber casually removed his pocket watch. It was 16:52 hours.

"Like now."

At precisely that moment a man sat down on the bench behind them.

"And then you wait for the proper things to be said."

"Peanuts?" the man said.

Still talking only to Kavanaugh, Gruber said, "He'll always start with a food reference. Alphabetical. A-Z. Then you start all over again. We're up to 'P'. Thankfully *peanuts* are easy. By agreement, we skip Q, X, Y and Z.

"Your reply is always the same. 'No thank you.'"

The man continued. "Are you sure? They come from a great place."

"Now," Gruber continued, "the second level of a security check. The correct response always is a reference to a location in the most recent issue of *Voyages*."

Gruber leaned back and said to the stranger, "Oh? Pray tell, where?"

"A little stand in Boston's Quincy Market."

"This is how we make contact. And this is where. No other acknowledgement is needed. No other confirmation. No glances. No pleasantries. You spend two more minutes. Maybe three. No more. It is the same whomever you meet. And whomever you meet will always act in the same manner. I invented a name for our contacts. My personal homage. Perhaps you'll figure it out one day.

"Mr. Marvin." The man pushed back in his bench. "Meet Mr. Kavanaugh. Soon he will be your contact."

"I wish you an easy passing," the man said. "Should it not be so and you require my assistance, I will take care of your needs."

"Thank you, Mr. Marvin. I'm prepared to let nature take its course."

Gruber checked his watch again. 16:54. "Two minutes. Time to go, my boy."

The young man rose first. He helped Gruber to his feet. Gruber recovered his umbrella and used it to point the way out, a different direction. "This is the way you will always return. Routine."

It wasn't until they were out of the park that Kavanaugh realized that Gruber had left his newspaper on the park bench. When he brought it up, he learned why. It contained information from the field.

Glendive, MT
Later that night

"Dr. McCauley. Dr. McCauley."

He thought he heard his name in a dream. It had to be a dream because McCauley had treated himself to a night in the lap of luxury—by Glendive standards. After a few hours of friendly, but exhausting golf with Jim Kaplan, he checked into the GuestHouse Inn and Suites on North Merrill Avenue, soaked in a bathtub for the first time in months, and fell asleep on the bed only half dry. It was just as he wanted. Seclusion. No calls, no conversations. Restful sleep.

Restful until...

He heard a knock in his dream. Then scenes later, which amounted to barely seconds, another knock accompanied by, "Dr. Quinn McCauley?"

He stirred, but remained asleep until a louder knock.

"Dr. McCauley, I'm sorry to bother you, but please let me in."

It was a woman's voice. He rubbed his eyes and checked the clock display on the nightstand. 11:30 P.M. "Go away. I don't need housekeeping."

"It's not housekeeping, Dr. McCauley. Open the door."

"I'm sleeping."

"No you're not. You're talking to me."

McCauley detected an accent. British and distinctly out of place in Glendive.

"Really, go away. Whoever you are, we can talk in the morning."

"I think not," came the reply.

McCauley sat up. "And why's that?" he asked without an ounce of courtesy.

"Because I'm here."

"And I'm supposed to care?" He was now sitting upright on his bed.

"Yes you are. We have an appointment. Dr. Alpert. Do you recall?"

McCauley's mind raced. "Appointment?"

"Yes, your university cleared it. You did get word. Right?"

Oh shit, he said to himself.

McCauley turned on the light. "Give me a second." He reached for his jeans and shirt, which he'd thrown over the back of a chair. "You sure this can't wait until tomorrow. I did want to get a good night's sleep."

"So I heard when I went to your base camp where I thought you'd be."

"Aren't you a day early?"

"Yes, but if you don't open the door soon, I'll be on time," she said with all proper authority.

McCauley stumbled over his golf clubs which were leaning against the foot of the bed. "Shit!" he yelled.

"Excuse me?" the woman said.

"Nothing. Nothing."

He picked up the clubs, set them aside, unlatched the lock and opened the door to reveal a beautiful brunette with hazel eyes, striking dark eyebrows and a beguiling smile.

"There, that wasn't so difficult, was it?" she said.

He stood quite awkwardly, three inches taller than her.

"Two things. First, aren't you going to invite me in?"

"Ah, well…" He looked around at the mess in his room he'd managed to create in a short time. "Yes. And second?"

"You might want to button your shirt and zip up."

In his haste, he was two buttons off and just a little bit exposed.

"Sorry."

The tenured Cambridge professor breezed into the room. He caught a whiff of her perfume; a smoky fragrance that brought him fully to his senses.

"And about the room. This is as good as it gets on my salary." He was referring to the décor. The mess was something else entirely: computer printouts in piles, maps on the floor, and dirty shoes on the corner of the bed.

She glanced at the only chair available and moaned. "Mind if I…?"

"Here, I can do that."

It was too late. With two fingers, she gingerly removed his underpants from the only chair in the room and put them over the doorknob. Next, the uninvited guest sat down as if she owned the room.

McCauley was plainly embarrassed. If he was supposed to make a good, professional first impression, he was surely failing.

"How about we go out?" he said.

"Good idea. I'm famished."

"There's a restaurant down South Kendrick."

"The Melting Pot," she volunteered.

"Yes, how do you know?"

"Research, Dr. McCauley. You know what that is."

He didn't like how this was going.

"Wait. What did you say your name was?"

"Still is. Dr. Alpert. Dr. Katrina Alpert."

"Dr. Alpert," he replied. "Dr. *Katrina* Alpert."

"Yes. Still the same one from a second ago."

It came to him: *The Cambridge professor from the Invertebrate Paleontology Department whose crowning achievement was Leonardo,* he thought. *And definitely not DiCaprio.*

Alpert's Leonardo was a bit older, and *Jurassic Park* would have been his only starring movie, though he didn't make the cut for accuracy's sake. Leonardo was a Brachylophosaurus who walked the earth seventy-six million years ago during the Cretaceous period, some one hundred million years later. Now, Leonardo—Dr. Alpert's Leonardo—was considered by the Guinness Book as the best-preserved dinosaur ever found. And for Dr. Alpert, she was just returning to his—Leonardo's—and her stomping grounds: Montana.

McCauley knew this and a lot more about the distinguished Dr. Katrina Alpert, probably as much as she knew about him and his work. The two scientists could have much to talk about if attitude didn't get in the way. *Let's find out.*

"I read your latest article on Leonardo." He paused. "Very *interesting.*"

"Interesting?" She picked up on the word. "That's what people say when they don't like something and they won't admit it. Or, if they have nothing worthwhile to say. How does this apply to your usage?"

"Ah, point taken. Your findings were undeniably remarkable, doctor. But detail in your account was lacking from a Yale perspective. So in fact, I found it very 'interesting,' yet academically insufficient."

"Well, since you raise the issue of academics, you've certainly taken some liberties naming your finds."

"Not names, doctor. Nicknames. Like Leonardo."

"Acknowledging a great artist, a scientist, a thinker, a visionary. Not a..."

"A member of the Baseball Hall of Fame?" he volunteered.

"Clearly not."

"You have your heroes, I have mine, Dr. Alpert."

McCauley liked to name his finds after great Red Sox players. He took digital pictures of his finds, printed and cropped them to baseball card size, added stats on the back and had handouts for whoever wanted them. There was a meat-eating Sauronitholestes named Yaz and a slow moving Allosaurus, suitably dubbed Tiant. Neither challenged Leonardo for attention, but McCauley viewed paleontology as a science and a sport. He was one to pitch in.

"Each to their own," she said dismissively.

"Look, Dr. Alpert..."

"You could call me Katrina," she said.

"Dr. Alpert," he replied, keeping it formal, "as I understand it, you're here to report on me; to determine if I meet certain academic standards."

"Not certain standards. Specific ones, Dr. McCauley."

"Okay, *if* I meet specific ones. Perhaps yours, with *if* being French for *fucked*."

Alpert laughed. "No, actually, *baisé* and *foutu* are French for fucked," she said like a teacher correcting a student.

"Thank you, Dr. Alpert. I'm obviously not as well-versed in romance languages as you."

"There's always Rosetta Stone."

Another day he might have laughed. Not today.

"I'll put it on my credit card just as soon as my department reimburses me for all the other incidentals I've had to pick up outside the budget. Or, are you reviewing expenses in addition to evaluating me?" It was his sharpest comment. He wasn't finished. "I'm sure you'll look very good to my department, especially if you can help them slash and burn my allocations. You'll also effectively keep one of your competitors out of the journals by ending my annual expeditions. So, if you don't mind, let's keep this purely professional. I'm dealing with enough extinct species without becoming one myself."

Alpert took it all in and smiled. "Ground rules established, Dr. McCauley." She decided they both needed to clear the charged air. "But I have a suggestion. How about we skip going out and start fresh in the morning? I'll meet you at the site after breakfast. Okay?"

"That's the best idea yet."

"Good."

Alpert stood ready to say goodbye when McCauley suddenly realized she'd traveled all day and probably needed a hotel room.

"Wait, where are you staying?"

"I've taken care of that. Two rooms down." She turned to the door, delicately removed his underwear and returned it to the chair. "Well, at least one question is answered," she said coyly.

"What's that?"

"Briefs, not boxers. Goodnight, Dr. McCauley."

SIXTEEN

The next morning

McCAULEY RETURNED TO base camp early at four thirty. Earlier than normal waking time. Earlier, he hoped than Dr. Katrina Alpert's waking time. Even with the interruption from the interloper he felt renewed with a good night's sleep.

His team began to rise at 6:30. By 7:15 everyone was wolfing down scrambled eggs, toast and coffee, prepared this day by Jaffe and Rodriguez. Once they finished cleaning up—a shared job—they took to the valley and spread out while McCauley hiked even further into the park. He liked the way the morning shadows played tricks with the rocks, creating very relatable images from a human standpoint: A face that looked like a Sioux chief. Lincoln in his top hat. A galloping horse. The things that gave birth to legends and tall tales.

The Yale professor also studied the strata, hoping something special would call out to him. It was now 8:25.

One thing caught his eye. *Another shadow? A sound?* McCauley stopped and strained to bring the impressions into focus.

He peered at a section of rock he calculated to be about thirty feet above the valley floor, maybe fifty yards away.

He saw some movement. *A coyote? Maybe a bobcat or a deer,* he thought. "No," he said aloud. Then he hoped it wasn't a mountain lion. He was alone and certain they were indigenous to the area. But if so, he needed to make sure his people were safe. He didn't have a gun, which was probably a mistake.

It's moving again. McCauley continued to walk, carefully closing the distance. At fifteen feet from the cliff he slowly bent down and groped for something to throw; all of this done silently. A few steps more, while keeping his eyes on the target, he put his hand on a rock about the size and weight of a hardball. Getting up just as slowly, he stretched his arm back, pivoted his body ever so much to the left, narrowed his focus to the area above hidden by shadows, and threw the projectile like he belonged on the Red Sox starting lineup.

It was a difficult throw but it scored a hit directly. Suddenly, a flurry of noise filled the morning air as a family of huge birds took flight.

"Jesus!" he gasped. McCauley immediately recognized the birds as turkey vultures by their dark reddish brown featherless heads and the way they soared with their wings raised in a V.

The birds, very distant cousins of the animals that the students had come to uncover and discover, flew high above the cliffs. McCauley figured they were sharing a morning feast in their nests set within the shady rocks. He knew that while other vultures could kill their prey, the turkey vulture couldn't. Its claws were too weak to grip live animals, so they scavenged.

Ultimately, it wasn't the birds that intrigued him. They migrated to the region every year. It was where they were nesting. He ventured forward recalling the Lakota people's legends about the great thunderbirds depicted in their petroglyphs. Perhaps their drawings were born from finding fossils of a pterosaur in their own time.

McCauley's pulse quickened as he carefully scaled the

cliff. His arms and shoulders ached from yesterday's golfing, but he paced himself, finding the proper footing and places to hold. A final long reach brought him to a ledge where he was able to stand. Four careful steps laterally, McCauley was at the opening where they birds had nested.

This is stupid, he thought. Still he was curious enough to enter.

"Hello," he said. His voice trailed off without even an echo.

He spoke louder. "Hello." There was a faint return.

"Hello!" McCauley now yelled.

He heard a hello, but it didn't sound like his echo. It was higher pitched, and the direction was off.

"Hello!" he called out at the top of his lungs.

"Hello!"

It was a woman's voice. Definitely a woman and not from the cave.

McCauley held onto rock that jutted out and turned his body. He looked around, then downward.

"Jesus!" he exclaimed. He saw Dr. Alpert at the base of the cliff. "Don't you ever just announce yourself quietly?"

"Like the scorpion said to the frog, *'It's just my nature.'*"

"Right. After the scorpion bit the nice frog that had just given him a lift to the middle of the river. Remember, they both sank and died."

"Whoops, bad metaphor." She smiled. "I believe you were saying hello to nothing in particular."

"Yes I was. And if you keep quiet I'll be able to make a scientific observation."

"Well, don't let me stop you," she shouted back.

"Later."

"Me later or whatever you were going to do later?"

"Try both." He climbed down, brushed himself off and

began to walk away. McCauley was not happy. It was going no better than the night before.

"Whoa," she said, doubling her pace to catch up. "Dr. McCauley, please."

He stopped, but kept his back to her. Once by his side she picked up where she left off.

"I'd really appreciate it if you'd make this easier. I've come a long way to…"

"To spy. To judge," he said staring her down.

"To evaluate, doctor. And so far I've seen you with golf clubs in a cushy motel room rather than on a cot at your camp like everyone else. Today, you're off gallivanting, not supervising your students. I just…"

"Came the wrong day," he interrupted. "How about I give you a call when we discover something worthy of an academician of your stature?"

"I'm a scientist like, you, Dr. McCauley."

"Well, at last a positive acknowledgment. Will that appear in your evaluation?"

"It will. And if you want to know the truth, I had a really nice summer trip planned. But my dean handed me a ticket to Montana. If you think I'm happy about this, you're mistaken. I expected time at the ocean."

"You're a few million years late."

"What?"

He gave a sweeping motion across the landscape. "Back in the day, there used to be a great inland sea right here. Perfect for kicking back, putting on a bikini, and soaking in the rays."

Alpert automatically made sure all the buttons were fastened on her loose white cotton shirt and she was otherwise put together properly. Proper was the right term and the right British term. Her hair was pulled back into a ponytail.

She wore perfectly pressed khaki shorts, a white cotton button-down shirt and work boots with a high sheen polish.

He continued walking. She kept pace with him now.

"Dr. McCauley, I've read your file. I know your work. You could probably teach until the dinosaurs inhabit the earth again. At issue is your research output. You haven't made any significant contributions in years. You know that as well as I do. Your department is, shall I say, rethinking your ability to attract serious research funds."

He stopped again and squarely faced her. "So this is really all about my ability as a rainmaker?"

"Well," she stuttered, as if thinking about the possibility. "No, the quality of your research. Like everything else, money is attracted to success. Washington, London, Tokyo, Beijing, Yale. It's all the same."

"Right," he replied sarcastically.

"Look, I'm not comfortable with my role any more than you are at being held accountable."

"So what should we do, Dr. Alpert?"

"We could start over. Let's have a real conversation instead of sparring like Mothra and Godzilla."

"They're not dinosaurs, doctor."

"And neither are you, Dr. McCauley."

MINUTES LATER, THEY were back at base camp. McCauley had waved off his grad students who wanted to know what was happening. At this point he couldn't objectively or fairly explain.

He held the tent flap open for his visitor, set two folding chairs around a bridge table next to his cot and said, "Let the inquisition begin. Water?" he offered reaching into a small refrigerator powered by a gas generator.

"No thank you."

He grabbed one for himself. "Can the condemned man have one?"

She laughed. "Help yourself."

They began to discuss a wide range of issues, avoiding anything personal. The talk moved from recent lackluster government interest to how fewer and fewer corporations and foundations backed paleontological work, and onto the pressure research institutions faced. The deeper the conversation, the more McCauley began to see that Dr. Katrina Alpert was not so different from him. She'd spent years in the field before finally deciding to create a comprehensive dinosaur database going back two hundred years, something sorely missing and uniquely fundable.

"I figured it was where the money was," she admitted. "And I went for it."

The dialogue served to reset their relationship which made them both feel better.

After forty-five minutes Alpert ran out of questions. McCauley had one. "So what's next?"

"I'd like to check out of the motel. Think you can find someplace for me to bunk?"

"Really, with us?"

"Yes."

"There's room in the women's tent."

"That was what I had in mind. Okay then?"

"Okay, Dr. Alpert."

"You could try Katrina."

"Not sure I'm ready to do that."

"I'd rather be seen as a team member instead of hit man."

McCauley smiled. He liked that idea a whole lot better, but he just wasn't sure about her yet.

WHILE ALPERT RETURNED to her motel, McCauley spent time with his grad students, examining their cache of fossils that would make them happy but still wouldn't add to the greater good. Nonetheless, it was important to give them positive feedback to encourage them. More than anything else, he was a great teacher and mentor.

Ninety minutes later, and without telling anyone where he was headed, McCauley returned to the area that had sparked his curiosity. Once up, he crawled through the entrance. It was stinky and sticky, making the on-ground excavations a pleasure by comparison. Four feet into the darkness, he yelled, "Hello" at medium volume. This time his voice echoed back. He wondered why it was always "Hello," as if someone was going to say, "Yes, I'm here. I've been waiting for you. Where the hell have you been all these years?" And when it wasn't hello, people just tended to yell "Echo." That was his next call.

"Echo," This was at the top of his lungs.

This return astounded him. "Echo" bounced off the rock walls changing volume and pitch. With it, the legends of the badlands came to mind again. Lakota storytellers had recounted tales of ancient creatures that roamed the earth and ruled the skies eons before Lewis and Clark explored the area, or discovered a dinosaur skeleton near the Missouri River. *How did they know? Faint echoes of the past in the winds?*

McCauley crawled further and sat up. He took out his iPhone, engaged the flashlight app and saw what looked to be a faded cave painting on the wall.

Lakota.

He turned off the flashlight, switched to camera, aimed at the rock and took a flash picture.

"Jesus! Are you trying to blind me?"

"Holy shit!" he exclaimed. He turned to the silhouetted form of Dr. Alpert, backlit well inside the cave entrance. "There you go again!"

"Sorry, just looking for you."

"How the hell?" he asked.

"Hey, this isn't my first rodeo," she said, substituting a western drawl for her British accent.

"Alright, but can you back out carefully now?"

"Why?"

"Because I need more than an iPhone picture or flashlight app."

"It's just a cave," she said.

"Probably," McCauley answered. "But you never know. It could be my vindication?"

"You wish," she joked.

Once on solid ground she saw how disgusting they both looked. "This is why I got out of the field."

"I'll introduce you to the badland's best friend."

"What's that?"

"The hose. It's cold, but it'll wash off most of the crap. Maybe now you'll understand why I wanted a tub at the El Centro!"

"Trust me, that's off the evaluation."

McCauley was finally feeling a bit more comfortable with Dr. Alpert. "Come on, let's clean up."

Back with the others McCauley clapped his hands to get everyone's attention.

"Gentlemen. Ladies," he said. "A few things. Gather around."

The team converged.

"Time to formally introduce you to Dr. Katrina Alpert. She's sticking with us for…"

He wasn't sure. "How long, doctor?"

"Maybe a week, give or take a few days. But please, treat me like one of the team. Nothing special."

"Believe me, we have nothing special here," Jaffe said for the group.

"No Marriott points," added Chohany.

Alpert laughed. "So I heard."

"Dr. Alpert is from the very prestigious Cambridge University. So show some respect."

"Doc, she smells," Jaffe joked.

"So will the rest of you. I found a cave down the line. We got a few feet in and this is what we look like coming out. But there was a Native American cave painting. There might be more. Who's up for checking it out for a day or so? You never know."

"Excuse me, Dr. McCauley, but didn't Dr. Alpert come to check you out?" Jaffe asked.

"As a matter of fact, yes. But this way we'll keep her busy and maybe she'll forget."

"No chance," Alpert joked.

"Seriously, I'm beginning to think she's a good egg. She traded in a summer vacation for a trip back in time with the likes of us. Consider her a friend…after she hoses down, of course. Then, who's up for a ride into town?"

"Why?" Leslie Cohen asked.

"Shopping. We're going to need a whole helluva lot of extra equipment, and"—looking at Alpert and himself—"a lot of tarp."

MCCAULEY SPREAD MORE than $1,400 over his three credit cards. The cashier at Ranch and Farm Ace Hardware Store on Harmon Street in Glendive couldn't have been happier.

The biggest expense was a National Parks approved DuroMaxXP4400E four gallon gas generator. The power source would feed portable lights and fans for hours. Also on the shopping list, four two-story First Alert metal folding ladders, hard hats for everyone, twenty high beam flashlights with extra batteries, ten twenty-five foot extension cords, five fuse protected power strips, fifteen electric lights with clips, and three hundred feet of rope.

"Okay, two more stops before we call it a day." McCauley drove to a liquor store on South Merrill and Reynolds Market over on West Bell.

Finished with the errands, McCauley finally provided a hint of what was going on. "Okay, I think we've got enough to get a good ways in."

"Tell us more about this cave," Chohany said showing increased interest.

"It's actually not all that unusual. Over near Billings, Pictograph Cave State Park has more than one hundred rock paintings, the oldest dating back to two thousand years ago. Scientists have pulled out thirty thousand artifacts from stone tools and weapons, but the artwork holds the clue to understanding how natives lived, hunted and survived."

"That's all well and good, Dr. McCauley," Rodriguez offered. "But I've seen far older pictographs in my country. I came here to find dinosaurs."

"We all did. I'm hoping the cave will let us go further and maybe deeper into the past than we otherwise would."

He recounted the Native American legends of the thunderbirds and dinosaur-like monsters, which, as incredible as they sounded, foretold actual discoveries that wouldn't come for centuries. "You can read about it on other cave walls across the state. So, maybe we'll find something that gets us closer to the dinosaurs we all seek through fossils embedded in the cave walls."

McCauley had them fired up. The team was eager to start.

"We'll begin with first light tomorrow. Tonight, a cookout and beer."

Cheers broke out.

FACING AN EARLY MORNING, the students hunkered down by 10:00 P.M. They were all up seven hours later. Considering their SUV would not get them to the valley floor, they divvied up the equipment. What they couldn't carry in their backpacks went into old-fashioned wagons which Mc-Cauley had picked up at local thrift shops the first week.

By 6:45 A.M. they were below the site.

"The first thing we'll have to do is get the turkey vultures out," he said. "Who's good at *Angry Birds*?"

It actually took a dozen rocks to get the entrance clear. The next problem was to make sure they didn't return. That required some of the team's clothes and straw and twine they'd gotten from the hardware store. The result was a very comical scarecrow to be sure, dressed in a red bra, black briefs, a cowboy hat, and high-heeled shoes Leslie had no idea why she brought. To a turkey vulture that lacked a sense of humor or fashion sense, it looked threatening enough.

McCauley was first up, scaling the rock with one of the folding ladders stuffed in his backpack. Once above, he carefully secured the ladder to a rock with grappling hooks and lowered the rungs to the team below. Then he tossed down a rope. Tamburro attached the scarecrow. McCauley hauled it up.

"Okay gang, now the rest of the gear."

The generator and five gas cans remained on the ground under a large picnic table umbrella. They plugged in the extension cords and power strips and fed them up by rope. Lights, shovels, picks, hardhats, and tarp followed.

Then it was time for the first four students. They'd drawn straws. Chohany, Tamburro, Jaffe, and Trent comprised the lead team, along with McCauley and Alpert. The students kept their backpacks relatively light as they climbed the metal links. Each carried more bottled water, walkie-talkies, first aid kits, digital cameras, painter masks, and gloves.

"Ready to see what we've got?"

A resounding, "Yes!"

McCauley called to Lobel below. "Fire up!" The generator began to rumble. Rodriguez checked the power, flicked the circuit breaker, and the first light turned on. Chohany acted as photographer and quickly clicked off six pictures.

Tamburro automatically shouted the way McCauley had before. He chose *echo* instead of *hello*.

"Tom and Al, start laying down the tarp. Might not need it further in, but the bird shit is awful right here. Masks and gloves, everyone."

The plastic helped. It took some of the grossness out of the initial ten feet. But not all of it.

"Disgusting," Chohany complained.

Fifteen feet in, the cave floor was not as bad. They stopped and tapped a hook into the rock and hung a second light.

So far, the only good part was the cooler air that flowed from deeper within. Dr. Alpert wished she'd had a thermometer to see how quickly the temperature was going down while her blood pressure was going up. This clearly wasn't her line of work.

SEVENTEEN

April 12, 1633
Palace of the Holy Office
Rome, Italy

GALILEO WAS NOW sequestered in the Dominican Convent of Santa Maria sopra Minerva in the Piazza Minerva, the site of the hearings. Here he was afforded far more comforts than any other prisoner in the long and brutal history of the Inquisition. Instead of serving time in a basement dungeon, he was considered a guest; a most special guest whose conviction without torture would benefit the Church more.

Chronic bad health still plagued him. Failing sight, persistent discomfort from arthritis and ongoing sciatic nerve pain continued to break his spirit. Still he hoped he could square his views of science with their theology through lithe rationalization.

Galileo had written about controversial things: the way of the world and the way he saw the solar system. Scientific fact to the learned and enlightened; sacrilegious postulates to many in the Church.

He had allies and enemies. The Collegio Romano had honored him for his astronomical discoveries. The Inquisition declared that his views violated Scripture.

Investigators dug back into twenty-year-old, self-incriminating correspondence the accused had written to University of Pisa colleagues and twisted his more recent publications into damning testimony.

Galileo Galilei's observations of the earth, moon, planets, and the sun, his arguments about tidal motion, his *Discourse on Comets* which disputed Jesuit views, his position on sunspots printed in *The Assayer* and his *Dialogue Concerning the Two Chief World Systems* were beyond the pale for Pope Urban VIII and his cardinals.

Galileo now stood before his accusers as a heretic. They were clergymen, but he saw no mercy in their eyes.

"As you face us on this first day of your testimony, Galileo Galilei, be of sound mind that you have taken a formal oath," stated Fr. Carlo Sinceri, the Proctor Fiscal of the Holy Office. "You are compelled to tell the truth before this court of Inquisition for now and for all time."

The court was comprised of the sternest looking men he had ever faced. Chief among them, Father Vincenzo Maculano da Firenzuola, Commissioner General—the lead prosecutor.

Galileo nodded. "I do so agree."

"Do you wish to offer an opening statement in your defense?" Sinceri said, bearing down on the old scientist.

"I do. I view this as an enlightened opportunity to discuss my writings and stated *opinion* of the sun's stability and the earth's motion. It was decreed by the Holy Congregation of the Index that this opinion is repugnant to Holy Scripture and is admitted to only as supposition. I wish to discuss that."

"And since you so freely embrace the word *opinion*, has your opinion changed with time?" Sinceri demanded.

"Yes, Your Eminence. I have been thinking continuously and directly about the interrogations that have preceded this session. Accordingly, and with true forethought, I reread my *Dialogue*, which over the last three years I had not even looked at. I wanted to check very carefully whether, against my purest intention, through my over-

sight, there might have fallen from my pen not only something enabling readers or superiors to infer a defect of
disobedience on my part, but also other details through
which one might think of me as a transgressor of the orders
of the Holy Church. Being at liberty, through the generous
approval of superiors, I started to read it with the greatest
concentration and to examine it in the most detailed manner. Not having seen it for so long, I found it almost a new
book by another author."

Galileo shut his eyes in an attempt to hide his inner
thoughts.

"Now I freely confess that it appeared to me in several
places to be written in such a way that a reader, not aware
of my intention, would have had reason to form the opinion
that the arguments for the false side, which I intended to
confute, were so stated as to be capable of convincing because of their strength, rather than being easy to answer."

With that statement, Galileo admitted his guilt before
Papal authority, though in a qualified manner. For the sake
of the Inquisition he was repentant and humiliated. To himself, he had lied before God. Eternal punishment would
come, not for his beliefs, but his recantations.

Father Maculano nodded with utmost satisfaction and
excused the Church scribe.

Galileo watched the secretary leave. *Will they sentence
me to death here and now?*

Maculano leaned across the table, projecting his supreme authority. "A very good position to take. Skillful.
I would expect nothing less from a mathematician who
seeks to equal things. But now in camera, without notes
taken for which we shall deny, let us discuss the past, the
present and the future, of which there is likely little for
you. The number of those days is yet to be decided. It is

in God's hands. But the past holds much interest for us. A most interesting past—truth be told."

The priest stared cruelly.

Galileo recognized where this was going. He had attempted to cover his steps. Apparently he hadn't succeeded.

EIGHTEEN

Montana
Present day

It took a moment for everyone's eyes to adjust through the smartphone camera flashes. As they popped, shadows appeared and disappeared. Quartz, mica schist and other crystalline metamorphic rocks sparkled and shimmered, then faded. Small creatures froze mid-flight, then scurried off.

Seconds later, they understood why Quinn McCauley had been so curious about the cave. It offered pure wonder and excitement. A long tunnel into nothingness lay ahead. What could be more inviting?

"Okay, enough gawking gang. We do this carefully. Last time I read your bios, none of you were seasoned spelunkers."

"Nor you, doc," Cohen countered.

"Damned straight. So it's inch by inch, one step at a time. We lay lights out every ten feet and we never go beyond the last light we put up. If you're not comfortable, you stop and leave…with a partner. Not alone. You never go off by yourself. Understood?"

He received unanimous consent.

"Mr. Tamburro, you're principally a geologist, correct?" McCauley asked.

"That I am."

"Anyone else with comparable credentials?"

"I ultimately plan on going for a second degree in geology," Chohany stated.

"Okay, you partner up with Rich. Mr. Tamburro you are hereby appointed CEO and president of all things rocky. The stability of the walls. The strength of the ground. The safety of the passage. The two of you—rope together. We'll be holding the slack, and there will be very little. Al and Tom, they don't call it a lifeline for nothing. Gloves on and grab the line. You hold them. Dig your feet into the ground or brace yourself."

"Are you sure this is a good idea?" Dr. Alpert looked worried.

"We explore a little farther. If nothing looks good, we stop. If it feels dangerous, we leave. But let's see. Okay?"

There was nervous affirmation.

"Just in case, anyone know *Help!* in Lakota?" Tamburro asked as he tied the rope around his waist.

For the record it was *anáuŋkičikšiŋpi*.

THE FIRST MINUTES were slow going. They made certain that lifelines were attached correctly and that the electrical wiring and lights were out of tripping range. Every step was measured and documented.

Twenty feet in, Tamburro held them up. "Stop!" He put his arm out, preventing Chohany from taking another step.

"What?" she didn't see what was ahead.

Tamburro pointed down.

"Do...not...move," he said. "Doc, we need more light here."

"Coming."

McCauley caught up. Alpert remained behind. Tamburro shined his flashlight into what appeared to be a hole large enough to fall through. "Tunnel stops and there's this drop," he said.

"Got it," McCauley acknowledged. To everyone else he added, "Make sure you hold the line, guys. Looks like it's a good fifteen feet. We'll need a ladder and more lights."

"I'll get the stuff," Trent said.

"Not alone. Wait. We'll do this in an organized manner."

Meanwhile, Chohany examined the tunnel walls short of the hole. Something caught her attention directly above the opening. "Hey Dr. McCauley, check out the chisel marks up there. Native Americans did this. But why?"

McCauley raised his flashlight to a petroglyph on the cave ceiling. It appeared to represent a meandering map with a figure of a tribesman against a deep dark tunnel. It was less crude, more illustrative than most ancient cave drawings, and for that reason intriguing. He took a series of photographs and cursed the fact that Pete DeMeo was away and couldn't do some basic research back at school.

With a decision point ahead, McCauley ordered everyone out. They'd break for lunch, take stock of their supplies, then explore further if possible, switching out Trent and Jaffe for Rodriguez and Cohen.

During the hour break, Tamburro went online, researching the indigenous tribes and looking at other examples of cave art. Basic styles were similar, but the depictions were different. He couldn't find anything like it on museum, library, or tribal websites. "Love to get more detail on the petroglyphs, doc," he said. "It's not our field, but someone's going to know how to read them."

Following lunch, it took twenty minutes for them to return to the point where they'd stopped. Tamburro lowered the ladder down the hole. Rodriguez took care securing it safely.

"Sure you want to go down?" McCauley asked. "I should go first."

"Nah. Let me get the lay of the land. I'll be fine."

Suddenly insurance issues were hitting McCauley. This was beyond the normal scope of the work. He'd make some calls later.

Tamburro slowly descended.

"Clear," he called reaching the bottom, or the newest bottom. He shined his flashlight ahead. "Looks stable. Come on."

While the others climbed down the collapsible ladder, Tamburro continued exploring. He spotted another vivid ancient petroglyph. Chohany was standing by his side as he was taking a picture.

"Check this out."

"Jesus. Weird."

Now McCauley was with them. The professor took a series of pictures himself. Wide and tight.

"What do you think, doc?" Chohany asked.

"Well, conventional wisdom says these Indian drawings are depicting some legend. But I have no idea what they represent."

He examined the petroglyph again. Holding the light and looking closer he saw more detail, vibrant colors, and...

"Look." He adjusted the lamp and stood only inches from the drawing. "Like the others, this just seems to dead end. More of what they've explored here, rather than serving as a chronicle of life outside."

Chohany and Tamburro moved closer. Alpert, Cohen and Rodriguez were also crowding around.

"Says to me they reached the end of their journey. The dark sections probably represent the awareness or presence of death," Cohen whispered.

"I'm not so sure," McCauley responded. "The Lakota

generally believed that death was a liberating experience, with the spirit lifted to the sky. There's nothing *sky* about this."

"Then any idea what it represents?" Dr. Alpert asked.

McCauley paused as Chohany took more photographs. "It seems like they were doing what Anna is right now."

The team looked confused.

"Creating their own kind of picture of what they saw."

NINETEEN

The English Tea Room, Brown's Hotel
London
The same day

"I HAVE TO CONFESS, I'm going to miss this, too." Martin Gruber admitted as he savored a fine Jing, one of the many Brown's served from the assortment of the world's finest family-owned tea gardens.

Colin Kavanaugh chuckled, but quietly. Gruber had tutored him about the importance of maintaining the image of a distinguished British editor. Taking proper afternoon tea at Brown's English Tea Room was Gruber's favorite part of the job.

Kavanaugh had no such tradition. Perhaps, he thought, he should begin one, though he considered such habitual activities a waste of time.

Gruber sensed what his protégé was thinking. He was dressed for the part in a tailored three-piece black pin-striped suit. But he wore it like a costume.

"Not for you?"

"I don't know," Kavanaugh said, surprised he so easily telegraphed his reaction.

"It's all right. It's a bit stuffy. But this *will* be your table. You'll sit here, maintain a dignified image, meet with writers and even members of Parliament. Smile and relax. You'll never complain and you will, as a gentleman, never speak of money."

Kavanaugh had heard it all before but he nonetheless agreed as if it were the first time.

"Fortunately, money will not be a problem for you. Our financial resources extend far beyond the print revenue or online ads. However, you are never to discuss that point with staff. Never. If there is a legal problem of any type, immediately refer it to our counselors." He smiled an artful smile. "They have special connections."

Gruber caught himself. "There I go again, getting off topic. I was waxing philosophical on Brown's tea."

"It doesn't interfere with your day?"

"Quite the opposite. It is an essential part of my day. I get work done and often simply sit back and relax. Speaking of relaxing, you'll have to learn how. That will not be easy for you. You're eager to jump in and multitask. I suppose that is a quality of your generation. Certainly not mine."

"Oh, you should see what fifteen-year-olds are doing now," Kavanaugh told the older man. "They make my head spin with their multi-tasking and second and third screens."

"Ah, but their attention span suffers because of it. And that is what you must work on. Focus and patience. Time to consider things that have come to pass and things to come. That's one of the reasons I'm introducing you to tea at Brown's. In years past there were other establishments in different countries. In each, there were corner tables like this where our predecessors would also sit facing out to meet, observe, calculate, and…relax." Gruber had given extra emphasis to the last point again. "If you don't learn to lighten up, the weight that you carry on your shoulders will crush you."

"That sounds like a mixed metaphor, Mr. Gruber."

"Alright. You may rewrite it any way you wish. But take the advice."

"To tell you the truth, it's not the environment, Mr. Gruber. It's the tea. I…"

"Let me tell you the difference between tea and your coffee, Colin. You sip tea, you gulp coffee. You take your time with tea, your coffee speeds you up. Tea, like wine, offers something for the ages. Coffee is pedestrian; a bitter gift from the New World. There are tea sommeliers. Your coffee shop has baristas. You drink tea in fine china. You bring your Starbucks to the office in cardboard cups. One is refined. The other, undefined."

Kavanaugh was tiring of these discussions. *Please God, take him now.*

"Have I lost you again?"

"No, no, no, sir. Just thinking about what you're saying."

Gruber laughed. "No, you weren't. You were pondering how much longer you'd be enduring my interminable diatribes. And I don't blame you one bit. My irascible secretary will have none of it either. Considering I never married, I suppose I'm taking it out on you."

"It's all been…"

"Boring. I know." He reached across the table and patted Kavanaugh's arm. "But there is a point to all of this." He raised his cup of tea and sighed. "I have no real faith that there's an afterlife or what it shall be. Heaven? Hell? For me, heaven would be right at this very table, listening to the world's most beautiful music on Brown's baby grand, and delighting on the delicate scones, sandwiches and pastries without fear of adding inches to my waist. All of that would be heaven without complaint. Hell? All the same, right here, but instead of being greeted by the experienced staff, there's only the devil. He's plum out of tea.

And he's only serving coffee in a paper cup." He paused for impact. "For eternity."

Kavanaugh nodded. "Heaven it is. Deservedly so."

Gruber shook his head. "Let us talk about a decision," he whispered. "It is yours to make."

The senior executive bent down and removed a file folder from the briefcase beside his foot. He had no concern that anyone would see or hear. They sat at his reserved corner table in privacy.

"Read this." He passed the file across the restaurant table.

Kavanaugh opened it and read the single page summary from abroad. Kavanaugh read it once, then again. He began to form a question, but Gruber put a finger to his lips.

"We'll talk more about it later."

"Why wasn't this sent to me first?" Kavanaugh insisted. "I would have…"

"There are still some things that come right to me. Only me. You will insist on the same, but not until…"

Kavanaugh filled in the thought almost cruelly. "Your passing."

Gruber didn't mind the comment. It was the eagerness. "Read it again. It is the kind of problem that you will have to deal with not just effectively, but exhibiting proper discretion. Not all challenges require the same action. Learn that, you will succeed…" Martin Gruber left the rest of the equation unsaid.

TWENTY

Makoshika State Park, MT
Base camp

"Slow down!" McCauley called.

Enthusiasm was one thing; recklessness another. McCauley was insistent. "Slow down, Rich."

"I'm okay," Tamburro replied. He was in the lead about twenty yards ahead in the gradually sloping tunnel. The lifeline was still around him with rope also attached to Anna Chohany and anchored by the team that followed.

"Maybe, but wait."

"Okay." That comment was followed by a discouraging, "Damn."

Chohany, caught up. "What's the problem?"

Tamburro shined his flashlight at rocks that blocked the way. "Oh, no," she said.

"Yup," Tamburro stated. "End of the line. Looks like a collapse."

Now McCauley, Alpert and the others were upon them.

"What's up?" the professor asked.

"We're fucked."

McCauley assessed the obstruction. "Set up two lights facing this mess on either side of the walls. Let's see what we have here."

Rodriguez attached the wiring and the lights. He had two left.

"Hey, how's…going…'n th… ?" Tom Trent's walkie-talkie transmission from outside broke up. "Haven't check…while."

"Say again?" McCauley's reply was equally poor on the other end.

"Are…okay?"

McCauley responded in shorter blasts. "Ok. Blocked tunnel. Repeat. Blocked tunnel."

"Copy that."

"Hang on."

With Rodriguez's lights in place, McCauley felt around the debris. Some crumbled to his touch. Then he moved to the right side of the tunnel and ran his fingers against the wall.

"I think this was a natural rock slide and if the petroglyphs were essentially Native American maps, the tunnel continues beyond it."

He groped around more. "Mostly loose rock. We might be able to dig through it.

Again, they didn't have all the equipment they needed, but there was enough to start: one folding shovel with an axe and two picks.

"Let's do this methodically. Rich and I can cut away from the top. Dr. Alpert and Carlos, you can spread out the dirt behind us. Nothing high. Everyone, wear your masks. Keep the dust out of your lungs. If we don't get anywhere in the next hour, we'll call it quits. Leslie, have Tom come up with more water. I think we'll need it."

THE LOOSEST DIRT easily fell away. After forty minutes, they'd cleared two feet of the rock, about three feet high, enough to crawl forward. That's when McCauley's pick hit hard rock.

"Shit," he said.

"What is it?" Katrina Alpert asked.

"Another damned boulder."

RICH TAMBURRO JOINED McCauley in the cramped space. "Give it another tap, Rich," McCauley said. "Not too hard. But dead center."

The Michigan student, on his side, complied. McCauley was sandwiched next to him.

McCauley cocked his ear to the sound. "Again." The paleontologist pointed. "Right there."

Tamburro tapped again. "What?"

"Don't know. Move over. I want to hear."

That was easier said than done given the tight quarters. Behind them were Chohany and Rodriguez, ready to pull them out if any dirt and rock above gave way. Alpert was on all fours trying to look in as well.

McCauley struck the boulder with his pick. *The sound,* he thought. It didn't sound right.

He placed his left ear against the rock, closed his eyes in case any stone splintered off. *Again.* His eyes popped open.

"That. Did you hear that?"

"Yes. The unmistakable sound of a hammer hitting solid rock," Tamburro joked.

McCauley rolled on his back and lifted his head. "Half right."

"Huh?"

"Listen."

McCauley hit the rock wall to his right. It produced a dull, flat thud. Then he hit the rock in front of them again. It created more of an open sound. McCauley repeated the action and rolled onto his back.

"And?" he asked, ever the teacher.

"Thinner." McCauley explained. "One more time."

McCauley tapped again.

"Or hollow, like a huge geode. Probably easier to roll in and…"

"Out," Tamburro said. "Did the Lakota put it there?"

"We'll explore that question tomorrow. Enough for today." McCauley motioned for Tamburro to inch back. "It's getting late and we need a better plan."

He explained the same thing to the others in the cave and then added, "Time to clean up and head to town."

"Celebration?" Rodriguez asked.

"No, just more shopping and some heavy drinking."

TAMBURRO RETURNED FROM the camp shower with only a towel wrapped around his waist. "It's all yours."

Anna Chohany wore only a bathrobe herself. She was typing quickly on her laptop.

"All yours," he said again, letting his towel drop down. He was trying to engage Anna. They had not so quietly begun to see each other a few weeks into the summer.

"Uh huh." Chohany continued to type.

"Before someone else takes it," he added.

"Uh huh," she said again. "In a sec." She finished by moving the cursor up to the send command. "There."

Chohany quickly closed down her computer and turned around to see her boyfriend completely naked.

"Now, what could possibly be on your mind?" she asked.

It was abundantly obvious.

"All mine?"

"You bet."

"Good. Then it will also be mine when I get back," Chohany said, brushing past him.

"But?"

"Shower."

"Okay, but then no more computer," he replied. "And we'll have to make it quick. Doc wants to leave soon."

Anna Chohany had already decided she was going to stay at the base camp.

TWENTY-ONE

Glendive, MT
Late afternoon

THE TEAM PILED into the Chevy Tahoe for the bumpy off-road ride into town. The first stop was the hardware store. Once loaded up with more supplies, space became much tighter. But it was a short drive to early dinner at Maddhatters Bar.

For a half hour they just drank. The local hangout had a great assortment of craft beer. Then came an hour of potato skins and shrimp appetizers. Compared to their meager cooking around the campfire, it tasted like Wolfgang Puck himself had been in the Glendive kitchen. Over their steak dinner came free-wheeling conversation, made all the looser by the liquor they consumed.

London

IT WAS LATE and Kavanaugh was tired, but Gruber was on one of his rants. Kavanaugh wondered if it was the Amaro they were drinking or if the old man was racing against time himself, knowing he was the slower of the two.

"Again. Tell me again." Martin Gruber demanded.

For weeks on end he believed Gruber was losing control of his faculties. Nonetheless, he responded with the directive drummed into him.

"We have a tremendous responsibility, sir. On one hand,

there is chaos. On the other hand, there is order. We help maintain the order."

"Help? Help?" Gruber shouted.

It was a slip on Kavanaugh's part.

"We maintain order."

"Yes! It is never *help*. We do. We simply do. With determination. Unknown to anyone but those we trust. A sworn duty you have accepted and will faithfully abide as if your life depended upon it."

Gruber paused for barely a moment. "Because it will."

Gruber never talked about anyone who left *Autem Semita*. *The Path*. Maybe now was the time to press the issue.

"Mr. Gruber, you've spoken of the men who preceded you. They held the job…"

"Not a job. Your job is *Voyages*. Your slips of the tongue are most concerning."

"You have no need for concern, sir."

"At this point, I would hope not. Your question?"

Now Kavanaugh was reluctant to ask. He considered another way into the problem, taking himself out of any hypothetical.

"There are, of course, those who must not have lived up to their responsibility. What if that…"

Gruber explained.

Maddhatters
Glendive, MT

"WHAT I DON'T get is how the actual record can be denied," Tom Trent said.

They had returned to one of their first discussions, the age of the earth.

"It's not like it's an unsolved mystery for God's sake."

"Interesting choice of words," Katrina Alpert noted.

"Well, yes. For God's sake…for our sake. We can have our beliefs, but we can't deny the facts."

London

"THE RELATIONSHIP IS for life," Gruber said. "Once you are fully committed, you enter a holy marriage."

"God's work." Kavanaugh said.

"Man's work. We help God stay right where he belongs."

Montana

"IT'S STILL AMAZING to me that people come with their own set of facts," Al Jaffe exclaimed.

"They do," interjected McCauley. "And successfully. Special interest groups have even blocked the distribution of some publications in national parks that support evolution."

"You have a troubled country," offered the befuddled Spanish student.

"Conflicted," Alpert added.

Lobel jumped in. "Who needs a meteor this time? Ignorance could destroy intelligent life on earth."

"Again, think about your words," McCauley implored. "Not ignorance. Faith."

"Supported by?" Lobel shot back.

"Well, that is the point of delineation," McCauley concluded. "Considering our argument, two deities. Religion and business. Or, better put, the business of religion."

McCauley passed the conversation to Katrina. "Dr. Alpert, your thoughts?"

The Cambridge professor wasn't used to this kind of intellectual free-for-all, but her respect for Quinn was growing.

London

"THE WORLD IN balance is a better world," Gruber continued. "There are those who would prefer that civilization as we know it fall apart. We won't let that happen. We never have."

Glendive, MT

"OKAY, TAKE NOAH'S ARK. And the flood," Alpert said.

"The Russell Crowe movie?" Trent offered.

"Ah, more the original text," she added. "But, for the sake of argument, open it up to the millions of species. How would you say Noah got them all on the ark?"

"Good question, people," McCauley noted. "Stay with this and try to understand, because you will have to stand up to the positions held by others. And you'll have to do it reasonably and with reason—in your research, in your departments, and certainly, when you go on the road for speaking engagements. Trust me," he turned to Katrina Alpert. "You have to develop a thick skin and realize not everyone with a different opinion is out to destroy you."

"Just your credibility," Tamburro interjected.

"Maybe," McCauley continued. "So, to Dr. Alpert's question?"

"Well, he didn't take two of each species," Leslie Cohen volunteered. "He took two of each *genus*. Not every species of dog, but two dogs. Not every kind of ant, but two ants."

"But creationists claim that man and dinosaurs walked hand in claw," Lobel said. His reference brought a needed chuckle. "Aside from the fact that they didn't, how would they have gotten onboard?"

"Can I try this one?" Jaffe asked.

"Go for it," Katrina replied.

"Well, go to the Bible. There are descriptions of 'behemoths' and 'leviathan" which lived with man from the beginning, and they fit dinosaurs more closely than any other animals."

"You sound like you support the point of view," interrupted Lobel.

"Well, in this argument, yes. And if Noah took only one pair of dinosaurs on the ark, it easily explains how and why the others died. They drowned in the flood."

"Maybe you haven't noticed, but dinosaurs could be incredibly big," Tom Trent stated.

"Good point," Dr. Alpert said. "Dr. McCauley? Care to weigh in?"

She felt confident he'd have the right answer, and he obviously liked the way she had re-framed the discussion.

"Happy to. Actually, as you all know the average dinosaur was no bigger than sheep. That alone makes for an easier boat ride. But even better, what if Noah picked a pair of babies? Their growth spurts were likely to be after they were five or six. So, yes, while some dinosaurs were behemoths, they *grew* to that size. They weren't born that way."

Katrina Alpert smiled. "Hey, would you take a fierce man-eating dog or a puppy on your ship?"

"A puppy," Cohen easily answered.

"And so would Noah. Puppies and baby dinosaurs."

London

GRUBER'S BREATHING SOUNDED SHALLOWER. The once robust publisher now delivered his thoughts in shorter sentences, all designed to fit into his diminished capacity. But, everything he said still had power. Power because of who he was. Power because of the legacy and power because of the resources at his command, which included the muscle to manipulate thought.

Montana

"TAKE THE MEASUREMENT of a cubit. How big?" McCauley asked.

"One point five feet. Basically the distance between the fingertips and the elbow. That's what's generally accepted," Jaffe said.

"What if you're wrong, Al? What if translations were imprecise?"

The younger man nodded. He realized he had accepted dogma as truth. But McCauley insisted that his students look beyond simple explanations for answers that would define the position.

"What if a cubit was really more like eight, nine, or ten feet? Wouldn't Noah's Ark be bigger? A lot bigger?"

"A lot," Jaffe agreed.

McCauley extended the hypothesis. "So that would mean that instead of fitting on a boat some four hundred and fifty feet long by seventy-five feet wide by forty-five feet high, as Genesis claims, the ark could have been a great deal larger."

Jaffe put his hands a foot apart as if holding a small ship. Then he moved them apart creating a space ten times bigger. "Maybe 4,500 feet long," he exclaimed. "Nearly a mile. You'd sure get a helluva lot of creatures booked on that sailing."

London

"HAVE YOU EVER thought of a cruise, Mr. Gruber? Maybe the ocean air could help."

"I've never found the idea of a burial at sea appealing."

"That's not what I meant." Kavanaugh tried to sound sincere.

"No cruise. I will die at my desk or in my bed. I am prepared to accept my future. I ask the same of you. Are you, my boy? Are you?"

Kavanaugh was amazed how Gruber could so quickly pivot on a word and turn a discussion around. He'd have to do better himself. *There really are things to learn from the old man*, he thought.

"I am, sir." Kavanaugh framed it as a promise more than a casual reply. He felt that Gruber needed assurance. If he equivocated, then Gruber would somehow find another replacement. Colin Kavanaugh would not let that happen. Not for Martin Gruber, not for his teachers at the seminary years earlier. Not for his own commitment to *The Path*.

Montana

LESLIE COHEN JUMPED deeper into history. "Come on, there are unadulterated facts. The Big Bang occurred fourteen-plus billion years ago. The earth is 4.5 to 4.6 billion years old. It took early forms of life a couple of billion years more to emerge. Way before the dinosaurs came and went. Way, way, way before our ancestral hominids yelled 'fire' around 100,000 years ago. Hell, dinosaur fossils I uncovered this week could be carbon dated back some sixty-five million years."

"But believers in a Young Earth claim the planet is only five, six, maybe seven thousand years old," McCauley countered again. "Same bones, just different conclusions."

"What about natural selection?" Rodriguez proposed. "The food chain. We look at carnage of natural selection

and see it as the process of adaptation. One species survives, another doesn't. *Speciation*."

"And?" McCauley challenged.

"And what?"

"And the answer is simply survival, not evolution. The
good make it. The bad don't. In this universe of thought,
science and creationism coexist. It's a powerful argument
backed by powerful people."

London

"AND ARE YOU PREPARED?"

"You have prepared me, Mr. Gruber."

"I have taught you. But are you prepared? They are two
different questions."

"They are two questions with one answer. You have
taught me. I am prepared."

Montana

TRENT SLAMMED HIS bottle on the table. "People have been
trying to reconcile this for ages. And no one will ever
succeed!" He was letting emotion get the better of him.
"Hell, modern geology goes back to Steno." He was referring to Nicolas Steno, a Dutch cleric who published
a treatise of fossils in 1669. Steno proposed the principles of rock strata formation. He claimed that fossils in
the sedimentary rocks were the remains of animals that
died in the Noachian Deluge—a flood, not necessarily
the Flood, but maybe.

Trent summarized the history for the group explaining
that the opinion gained traction with support from En-
glishman Thomas Burnet in his 1691 publication, *A Sacred Theory of the Earth,* in John Woodward's 1695 book

An Essay Toward a Natural Theory of the Earth, and William Whiston's *A New Theory of the Earth*, which was published a year later.

"Very interesting, Mr. Trent. How about Comte Buffon?" Katrina Alpert asked.

No one recognized the name.

"Good person to add to the discussion. In the mid-eighteenth century, Buffon sparked to the notion of evolution. Like Darwin, he was a naturalist. He wrote *Natural History*, maybe the first real argument in favor of variation of the species."

"And what happened to him?"

"He was slapped down, discredited and belittled by theologians at the Sorbonne in Paris."

London

"THOUGH IT'S NOT in any record, our work goes as far back as the debates on evolution. And earlier. You recall the recantation of Comte Buffon, Mr. Kavanaugh?"

"I'm familiar with it," the younger man replied.

"Become completely conversant with it. Study his denial. It established the fundamental response for years to come." Gruber now quoted from memory: "'I declare,' said Buffon, 'that I had no intention to contradict the text of Scripture, that I believe most firmly all therein related about creation, both as to order of time and matter of fact. I abandon everything in my book respecting the formation of the earth, and generally all which may be contrary to the narrative of Moses.'"

Kavanaugh was surprised by the retraction, but it reminded him of another, more famous example.

Montana

"SOUNDS FAMILIAR," COHEN OBSERVED.

"Certainly not the first to cave to theological arguments," Dr. Alpert added. "Perhaps he did so in order to quietly live out his life and continue his work." She took another sip of the local brew. "Sometimes you do what you have to do."

"Like Buffon, you will face obstructionists," McCauley stated. "Religious, political, corporate, academic. They'll question your hypotheses. They'll reject your proposals. They'll dismiss your research. They'll pull your grants. They'll shove every 'saurous up your sore ass and test you to kingdom come. They push paper, but they don't get their own hands dirty. They stay inside while you're out baking in the sun. They live in the present. You make the past relevant. They say *no* and don't even consider *maybe*. But I do have something to hang your hat on. The rejoinder of all rejoinders. Get this fundamental down and you're set for life."

Alpert didn't know where McCauley was going.

"Here's to the great British paleontologist—well, not really, but he sure said things right. William Shakespeare."

They laughed.

"Come on raise your glasses. Do it."

They complied.

"To William Shakespeare who put it best. 'Past is prologue.'"

Tamburro reacted first. "Past is prologue!"

"Past is prologue!" the team responded bringing their glasses together. "Past is prologue," they said again.

Dr. Katrina Alpert smiled. Maybe for the first time in years, she felt she'd come to the right place.

WHILE THEY WERE drinking the time away, Anna Chohany was in the cave, scraping away dirt around the boulder. She wore a hard hat. Her beam illuminated the way ahead, and ahead was a narrow crawl space.

Chohany was in good shape. But she was not experienced as a caver, which she realized an instant later.

No one was there to hear her scream as she fell twelve feet into complete darkness.

TWENTY-TWO

Makoshika State Park, MT
Ninety minutes later

TAMBURRO RODE SHOTGUN on the way back and dialed through stations on the AM radio. He settled on a powerhouse signal out of Kalispell, MT broadcasting the national late night show, "Coast to Coast AM."

"Cool," he said. I love this guy. The host was interviewing a guest about curious satellite photographs of the moon. Shapes that could be things. Things that could be relics. It was a favorite topic of the show. "Dr. McCauley, you do shows like this. You should get on it."

"What?" McCauley wasn't really paying attention. His team was wasted. They were falling asleep into one another in the second and third rows of his Tahoe. McCauley concentrated on driving.

"A little bit of ooga booga, a lot of paranormal stuff, UFO's and the like. They're talking about secret sites in the South Pole designed to control the weather."

"Conspiracy crap," McCauley said.

At that moment, the host doubled down on that very point, speculating that the cover-up went as high as the White House.

"Definitely pushes the limits. But seriously, you'd be a good guest."

"No I wouldn't. Way too *out there* for me."

"Naw, listen," Tamburro said.

The guest, Robert Greene, was a regular. The question to him was simple. "What's the government hiding?"

Greene ran with the answer, talking about what he'd gleaned from his Freedom of Information Act requests and his own website. No smoking guns, but enough to build a few hours of conspiratorial talk.

Greene was engaging and entertaining. He easily moved from recent rumors to long held views. He sprinkled it with references to black ops, the Pentagon, and a money trail that seemed to disappear in the South Pole snow.

It was impossible not to get caught up in the conversation; virtually a radio reality show with over-the-top characters and suppositions that could neither be proven nor disproven.

"See, you're into it," Tamburro said.

AT BASE CAMP everyone said good night and went to their respective tents. Rich Tamburro slipped away from what Chohany called "the boys' tent." He crossed the grounds and pulled the flap back on her tent expecting to find his new girlfriend sound asleep. She wasn't in her cot or, when he checked, in the lav. *I know where she is,* he thought. They had a special place where they made love under the stars.

It was dark, very dark. A moonless night. Tamburro picked up a high intensity flashlight and set out for Anna at their rendezvous spot.

"Hey, Anna," he called out at moderate volume. He expected to hear her answer softly; alluringly. No response. He aimed the light into the immediate area. Nothing. He widened the field. Still nothing.

"Anna." He said louder. "Anna!"

The call brought Leslie Cohen and Dr. Alpert. "What's up?" Cohen asked.

"Just looking for Anna. She must have strolled off. Probably nothing. See you in the morning."

"K, goodnight."

"No," Alpert said sensing concern. "Try again."

Tamburro aimed his beam further into the darkness. His voice more urgent. "Anna!"

McCauley emerged from his tent wearing only his Bermuda shorts and sandals. He double-timed over to Tamburro. "Problem, Rich?"

"Well, I can't find Anna." He didn't stop to explain. "Anna!"

One by one, the others made their way.

"Hey, what's going on?" Jaffe asked.

McCauley interrupted. "Everyone. Splash cold water on your faces and get your flashlights."

"Why?"

"Just do it. Now."

Quinn McCauley returned to his tent to put on a shirt and change into sneakers.

Within minutes, eight beams of light cut through the pitch black sky. Eight voices called out from an area now spreading over fifty square yards.

McCauley caught up with Tamburro.

"She said she was just going to read." Tamburro's tone showed real fear.

McCauley looked back at the supply hut and quickly ordered, "Come with me."

They ran at top speed and barged into the tent that housed all their daily supplies. After a quick inventory McCauley identified what was missing: rope, lights and shovels.

"Christ!" he exclaimed. McCauley summoned the team. "Grab everything we just bought and more flashlights! And the first aid kit! Anyone who doesn't feel good enough, tell me now." He cursed the fact that he allowed everyone to drink so much.

"What?" asked Trent.

"We're going to the cave."

"Why?"

"Do it!"

McCauley had a bad feeling. *It was dangerous enough to explore during the day. But at night? And alone?*

The cave

McCAULEY RAN AHEAD, hoping he wasn't going to find the lights on at the cliff site, praying that Chohany wasn't there. He stumbled over a few rocks, steadied himself and came around a sandstone spire at the base of the valley.

"Jesus Christ!"

The generator was on and the lights high above illuminated the cave entrance.

Rich Tamburro had the same reaction when he pulled up behind McCauley. "Oh no! What was she thinking?"

"Not thinking."

McCauley caught his breath. "Okay, we have to do this carefully. Let's get everyone together and divvy up duties."

"Right."

A few minutes later, McCauley circled the team for instructions. "Here's how we're going to do this," McCauley stated. "Rich and I will take the lead. Carlos and Al behind us. Leslie, come up, but stay posted at the cave entrance. Dr. Alpert, Tom, and Adam, you're here, but be ready to call for help. We'll check in with Leslie every two minutes on the walkie-talkies. Leslie keeps the three of you posted.

"I'm going with you," Alpert argued.

"No," McCauley replied.

"Yes, and that's final."

"No! And that's final."

She grabbed a hard hat and begin walking toward the ladder. "All right," he said calling to her. "But stick close to me." It sounded silly considering she was already ahead.

"Ready?" McCauley asked.

"Ready," they replied in unison.

One by one they climbed the cold metal rungs. They checked their gear at the top, tested communications and reviewed the plan again.

"She's definitely in here," McCauley said. "The lights are fired up way down the line."

"I just don't understand why, Dr. McCauley." Rich Tamburro was confused and concerned.

"Stay focused. Here we go."

After taking a few steps in McCauley yelled, "Anna! Anna Chohany!" No response. "Too many twists and turns. Rich, you call. She might respond better to your voice."

He shouted her name. All they heard were his echoes.

At the first two-minute mark, Jaffe transmitted that they were okay. Leslie Cohen relayed the message. They did the same thing at the second check-in just before they climbed down the interior ladder.

"Anna!" Tamburro continued to yell.

Eight minutes in, McCauley held his arm out for everyone to stop. "Quiet. We're making too much noise ourselves." Once it was stone cold silent, the professor signaled Tamburro to go again.

"Anna! Can you hear me?"

Still no response.

"Anna! For God's sake. It's Rich!"

At twelve minutes, they were close to the spot where they'd stopped hours earlier. McCauley examined the dirt. More was piled up. "Look," he exclaimed. "She dug around the rock."

The professor shined his light. "I'm going ahead. Hold onto my legs."

"Got you."

McCauley crawled forward through the loose dirt. Three feet in his fingers were no longer grasping the ground. There was nothing. "Whoa. Hold on!" he called back.

Tamburro grabbed hard, "What? What's the matter?"

McCauley now aimed his flashlight down. He thought he saw something, but he wasn't sure. He looked again. Leaning over as far as he could he listened and turned off his flashlight. That's when his heart sank.

"Anna," he said.

After a half-minute, McCauley asked to be pulled out.

"Is she there?" Tamburro pleaded.

"There's a drop just beyond the opening."

"But did you see her?"

"No, but there's a little light. It has to be her flashlight. She must have fallen. I would have too if you hadn't been holding on."

"I'm going down." Tamburro started toward the crawl space.

"Wait, Rich."

"No, I'm going."

"No. I'm responsible," McCauley said. "It's my fault and it's my job."

"Dr. McCauley's right," Alpert said. "He should go." She walked over to him and looked in his eyes. "But you better be careful."

McCauley nodded. "I will, thank you." He turned to Tamburro. "Harness me up. I'll go in feetfirst this time. Looks like I'll need fifteen feet of line or more."

He described the next steps. Once down, he'd search for Chohany and determine her condition. He had gauze and bandages, a splint, water, and mild painkillers. "If she's okay, we'll raise her. If not, get the paramedics."

Tamburro concurred.

Jaffe alerted Cohen. Lobel ran back to their campsite to find blankets they could use to carry Anna back.

McCauley attached the rope around his stomach and shoulders in a way that would support him, but not cut into his flesh. He went in backwards flat on his stomach wishing he'd never found the cave.

London
Morning, The same time

GRUBER NOTED KAVANAUGH'S EAGERNESS. *Too eager?*

"Years ago, before all the instant reporting, the talk shows, everything going viral, we could contain. Today it is harder. My work was harder. Yours will be even harder, but you will not be alone."

"When will I know about the others? Who they are? Where they are?"

"Soon."

"Not now?"

"Soon." Gruber was cold and emphatic.

"But how can I—"

Gruber cut him off. "When I decide."

Martin Gruber studied his prodigy. Perhaps he had moved him along too quickly. Perhaps it was just the difference in younger people today.

He thought back to his own training. *It was so long ago.* He remembered how the old man in his time, an easier time, worked with him. *Had I come to this point in my training with the same intense zeal?* He laughed to himself. *Of course.*

Gruber decided the time had come to reveal the remaining secrets to Colin Kavanaugh and begin the final test of will. In every generation only a few would be permitted access. Would the younger man remain true to *The Path*, as Martin Gruber had done? He would have to find out.

Gruber pressed a button under his desk. The overheads dimmed and a warm blue light grew visible from hidden floor boards. Kavanaugh was quite surprised that he never noticed the array. Gruber was right. *I have to pay more attention.*

"The regular lighting is too harsh on the old documents," the old man stated. He kept his back to Kavanaugh as he slid open a portion of the rich wood behind the great desk. Kavanaugh had always taken it as just wall. *Another oversight.*

A shiny metallic plate soon reflected the bluish tint. Gruber placed his hand firmly on the center. After twenty seconds, the color of the metal changed from silver to gold. Gruber lifted his hand, but the impression remained.

"It's a touch pad. It will read your handprint as well," Gruber said softly. "It's been programmed for months in the event of my death. But you see I'm still very much alive, so I get to share one of the high tech toys even I know how to use."

Gruber did not say that the technician who installed the pad had a rather unfortunate sailing accident on a trip he'd won, a trip he never remembered signing up for.

The plate, actually a screen, switched from Gruber's handprint to a touch screen with numbers and symbols. Kavanaugh recognized the symbols; ancient runes that dated back to the Vikings.

"The combination will be yours. But first you will read. Remember how Latin was one of the job qualifications?"

"Yes, sir. I never really needed it."

"You will shortly."

When Gruber finished inputting the code, the whole screen slid to the side and the wall behind it rose to the ceiling, revealing another room, no more than ten by ten meters. It was a combination of old and new, classic and antiseptic at the same time. Solid metal walls and a traditional black and white checkerboard floor.

"Walk where I walk." Gruber began a step-by-step pattern, ultimately in the sign of a cross.

"Really?"

"Don't make all my years with you go to waste with one misstep."

It was all the warning Kavanaugh needed. Little pen-sized tubes in the wall and ceiling seemed to track his every move.

At the far end of the room was an area composed of black tiles large enough to stand on.

Gruber placed his hand on another wall touch screen that appeared as soon as he stepped on the forwardmost white tile. Soon, a pedestal rose from the floor with an ancient cast iron safe atop. "Even with all the high tech possibilities, I'm still a traditionalist. I like a good old combination lock. It'll be up to you if you want to make a change."

Martin Gruber carefully turned the dial, saying the combination aloud. Kavanaugh instantly memorized it.

Gruber completed his turn of the tumbler and the safe clicked open. As it did, the room light changed to the same blue as in Gruber's office.

Two items were inside the safe: a pair of white cloth gloves and an old parchment document. Gruber put on one glove and handed the other to Kavanaugh. "You must only handle the document with the gloves. Put one on. I'll take the other and hand the paper to you. Then you'll put on the second glove. Never touch it directly. It must never be exposed to natural light or leave this room."

Kavanaugh was caught up in excitement. *What could be so worth all of this security and precaution?*

"And now, a test of your Latin."

Kavanaugh took the pages and the second glove. He breathed deeply and began to read slowly, methodically, religiously. At the top of the first page was a salutation to Pope Urban VIII, which placed it at more than four hundred years old. *"Eminentissimo sanctum tuum, anno Domini MDCI de spelunca repertum...magnus et terribilis..."*

His Latin didn't fail him. *"Your Holy Eminence, in the year of our Lord, 1601 a great and terrible discovery was made..."*

The cave

MCCAULEY FELT HIS way down a space no more than three feet wide. The sides were rough and the air was getting colder. It was dangerous with a rope. *Without?* "Slowly," he said again. He groped for places to hold onto as he descended, cursing the fact that he forgot gloves.

"More...more." He concentrated on not getting cut.

Rich Tamburro was above him. He shone his flashlight down which helped give Quinn the sense that he was not alone in space.

During the process, they missed their scheduled check-in. Jaffe's walkie-talkie crackled. Leslie was trying to reach them. However, he didn't dare take his hands off the lifeline. Not yet.

"Almost," McCauley said. He extended his toes in anticipation. But it wasn't the ground he felt. It was emptiness. He had nothing to hold onto. His feet were not on the ground. He dangled in midair.

He looked up at Tamburro. "Any more line?"

"A little."

"Slowly then."

The end went from Jaffe to Tamburro, who held on tight. With all the rope out, McCauley was still not on the ground.

"That's it?"

"Yes,"

"Damn." He misjudged the drop.

McCauley looked up. "You're going to have to let go. I've got about three more feet."

"Wait." Tamburro turned his head back and asked Dr. Alpert to call for more line. They'd need it to secure and haul Anna, if that was even possible.

"Okay, Dr. McCauley. Say when."

McCauley took a deep breath. "When."

A second later, McCauley hit the ground hard.

"I'm standing," he said. As he adjusted his position, his foot rubbed against something hard. It wasn't a rock. He shined his light down. It was Anna Chohany's head.

Gruber's Office

KAVANAUGH REVIEWED THE parchment first for language. He read the three pages again to put precise meaning to individual words and the full context. Then he read it a third time, asking himself if there could be any other possible interpretation than what he had considered.

Although Kavanaugh didn't know it, Martin Gruber had reacted the very same way when he first read the letter written by Father Vincenzo Maculano da Firenzuola in 1633. It was the secret directive that led to the establishment of an organization that would be known as *Autem Semita.*

The cave

"SHE'S HERE AND ALIVE," McCauley yelled. He instinctively held her hand and felt Anna's fingers tighten around his.

McCauley gave her water and assessed her condition. Possible concussion, broken arm. Cracked or bruised ribs. He was most worried about her neck and back.

McCauley knelt and checked her breathing. It was labored.

"Listen, it's not going to be easy, but we have to get you back up. Rich's just up above. He's looking right down. Rich, say hi."

"Hey, Anna. You're going to be okay. We'll get you out."

She opened her eyes.

McCauley talked to her softly.

"Can you move your toes and legs?"

He shined the flashlight to see.

"Good girl."

"Now can you roll from side to side?"

She showed some movement, but it was difficult. But most importantly, Anna Chohany wasn't paralyzed.

An hour later, the Harvard student was strapped to a county medevac helicopter gurney and on her way to Glendive Medical Center. The paramedics were ready to start the IV drip.

"No, no!" she screamed.

Chohany dug her cell phone out of a pocket and struggled to compose a text. It was full of auto corrects, but she got the point across. She hit send. "Okay, now," she said. "Pile on the painkillers."

TWENTY-THREE

Glendive Medical Center, MT
The next day

"HOW ARE YOU FEELING?"

"Stupid," Anna Chohany told Rich Tamburro.

"Not too bad considering it could have been worse."

It looked worse. She was hooked up to an IV and a heart monitor. Her right arm was in a cast, her neck in a brace. That's all he could see on top of the covers.

"Good thing you have such a hard head."

"Yeah, but not such a hard body. Sorry. And a body that's out of commission. Even more sorry."

Chohany was lucky to be alive. In addition to McCauley's amateur diagnosis in the cave, she had a dislocated shoulder and two fractured ribs.

"So we'll catch up after your rehab," Tamburro said while holding her hand.

"Right. You know I am sorry."

"It's okay."

"I should have been more careful."

"You should have never gone in by yourself," he argued.

Chohany looked away.

"We're a team. What were you thinking?"

"I don't know," she answered. "I can't really say."

"Hell, you ruined a summer of great sex. That's for damned sure." He caught himself laughing.

It hurt her too much to laugh. Besides, she was thinking of something else.

"Listen, Rich. Will you keep me up to date on every-. thing?"

"Of course, hon."

"I mean really. Pictures. Everything." She squeezed his hand and locked on his eyes again. "Like I'm still there. Emails and calls every day. Okay?"

"Okay."

"Promise?"

"I promise."

The cave
Later

CHOHANY HAD OPENED up the route to the new shaft, but she never saw where it led. Dr. Quinn McCauley and his team did.

A new tunnel angled downward, far beyond the distance their extension cords reached. Far beyond the range of the walkie-talkies. Far into the obscure past told through Native American cave paintings, more of which appeared to plot a direction.

"What do you think?" Katrina Alpert asked.

"I really don't know."

The plan was to stay only an hour-and-a-half. That meant turning back at the forty-minute mark. They had ten more minutes. And yet...

"Getting chillier," Jaffe noted.

McCauley's phone app showed that the temperature had dropped to fifty-three degrees. More interestingly, the sound of their footsteps had changed—like the tunnel was opening up.

They needed additional electrical lights and longer extension cords. But even with the lights they had, they could see that they were entering a magnificent cavern. Yet unlike others formed by wind, water and violent geological episodes, this appeared different. The walls were shiny and smooth as if perfectly polished igneous rock. And further up, there was another tunnel, also smooth and reflective, but smaller and much more claustrophobic.

"WE CAN'T RUSH through this," Quinn McCauley said to his dejected team an hour later at base camp. "There's a great deal we don't understand."

"Like everything," Leslie Cohen said.

"Well, yes. So let's look at this like the research scientists we are. Put our findings into identifiable categories: geological factors, seismic patterns, whatever we can deduce. Adjust for millennial cycles in climate change and how that might have influenced where and how people took shelter. Don't make anything up or jump to conclusions. Through this we should come to see the expected in the unexpected; answers we can trust."

The team was already a fan of Dr. McCauley. Now Katrina Alpert was impressed.

"I can add some insight," she said. Katrina reached down for a handful of the dirt. "Volcanoes make for smooth rocks. Smooth rocks reflect light." She found one on the ground; black, shiny, smooth. "Is this from the same geological period?"

"Relatively so." Cohen chose both.

"You're right. It is and it isn't. Could be millions of years apart from the cavern. But where's the rest?"

"The natives picked them up for weapons and carving food. That's expected," Rodriguez declared.

"Yes and why?"

"Need. It made life easier."

"Okay, so reasoning backwards from the unexpected will provide us with credible answers in every case?" Tamburro asked.

"That's right," Dr. Alpert responded.

"I'm not so sure this time," McCauley added.

BACK IN THE CAVE, the team moved slowly. "Did I mention I don't like fun houses?" Alpert whispered to McCauley.

"Not to me. We've only had a few conversations," McCauley replied. "I don't recall discussing that."

"Well, put it on your list."

"Right to the top," he said as they crawled uncomfortably through the cavern. "But you sounded like you were really into it back there."

"I think I was lying. And you?"

"That I was born to work in the sunshine. Not in enclosed dark places."

At that moment his flashlight flickered and off. "Damn." He tapped it twice. It came back, but only intermittently.

"Quinn!" she said, "My flashlight's on the fritz…"

"Mine, too. Give me a sec. I'll change up the batteries, then I'll do yours."

He unscrewed his flashlight, found replacements in his backpack, swapped them out and pressed the button.

"Dammit," he said. "Same problem."

By now, the others were catching up and also complaining. All their flashlights were acting up.

TWENTY-FOUR

London
The next day

"MR. KAVANAUGH." MARTIN Gruber's assistant Felicia Dunbar was noted for her brevity on the phone. However, this was more clipped than normal.

"Yes."

"Mr. Kavanaugh, please come up to Mr. Gruber's office."

Good, he said to himself. He urgently wanted to discuss information he gleaned from Ten. "Be right there."

Following Gruber's procedure for carrying sensitive papers through the building, Kavanaugh locked the report in his attaché case. One important lesson had stuck.

Three minutes later he was at Dunbar's desk. Gruber's door was closed.

"I'm ready?"

"Mr. Kavanaugh..."

"Yes?"

"Mr. Gruber is not here. He collapsed at his home today."

"Is he all right?"

"Mr. Gruber died thirty minutes ago," she stated. "On the way to the hospital."

"Oh my God!" Words failed him, but his thoughts didn't. He'd actually been waiting for the end, hopefully not too obviously. Gruber had been pestering him with lessons for years. The last few months were almost intolerable. *Do this. Think that. Don't question. Pay attention. No mistakes. Listen. Learn. Obey.* He'd had enough of the old man's endless diatribes. He'd been ready to take the reins, no *take control*, seemingly forever. But he would have to mask his enthusiasm and proceed respectfully.

"Ms. Dunbar, I will expect your complete cooperation and faithful assistance through this difficult period."

"Just as Mr. Gruber instructed, Mr. Kavanaugh."

Bitch, he thought. *Show some goddamned respect for me.*

"The first thing you will need to do is read a letter Mr. Gruber left for you. My instructions were to give it to you upon his death. Please come with me." She stood at attention.

It wasn't a question and there was definite attitude. Kavanaugh would deal with the fifty-eight-year-old secretary later. Now he continued to project grief and sorrow.

"Of course, Ms. Dunbar. But give me a moment."

Kavanaugh excused himself to the men's room closest to Gruber's office. Soon he'd have his own private bathroom. Such things meant something to him. He splashed cold water on his face and rubbed his eyes until they became bloodshot. He loosened his tie and slumped his shoulders creating the perfect look to bring back into Dunbar's office and then into Gruber's inner chamber.

A few writers for *Voyages* saw him leave the bathroom. They'd report that he looked positively shaken. Soon they'd put two and two together and word would spread that the inevitable had happened. This would help him when it came time to bring the staff together; both the general editorial team and the others who only worked in Ten.

"Ms. Dunbar, I'm so sorry." Kavanaugh said returning. "I just needed to…"

She didn't let him finish. "This way."

The secretary led him into Martin Gruber's office. The curtains were drawn. It felt cold, and in fact, dead.

"The envelope is on the table at the sitting area. His wishes were quite specific. You are to read it there. Do not sit at his desk until I pack up his personal possessions."

Kavanaugh stopped and peered down at Dunbar. He had a significant height advantage, yet she exuded greater stature in the situation, which he hated. He decided this was going to be a defining moment for him.

"Ms. Dunbar, I will pick up the envelope and I will read it at what is now *my* desk. You may remove whatever you must after I am through. That is the way it's going to be on this most difficult day and every day forward."

"Mr. Kavanaugh," she replied, "the office is certainly yours. Rest assured, Mr. Gruber left me an envelope as well. In it, very specific procedures to help you through the transition and beyond. I will be doing that."

And *beyond.* Colin Kavanaugh did not like the sound of that at all.

"Thank you, Ms. Dunbar," he replied with a more conciliatory tone. Inwardly he was determined to rid himself of the witch. "You may leave now." Kavanaugh picked up the envelope and walked to *his* new desk. Without another word he sat in the chair that still held the mold of Martin Gruber's ass.

The letter was in Gruber's own hand. Three pages long. Instantly ponderous and full of the same tone Kavanaugh had come to despise.

Congratulations, young man. The job is finally yours. You may feel it's long overdue. You probably wondered when, or if, I'd actually depart. At last that time has come. However, even though I am no longer there to quiz you, the greatest tests of your life are still ahead. Will you have the moral fibre to do what must be done, to decide, to lead, to implement? It, of course, is no longer what I believe. You must now prove it to yourself. Prove it to Autem Semita. Prove it to God Almighty.

More lectures. The importance of everything had been drummed into his head every way. Kavanaugh knew it all. He believed in *The Path* and the absolute responsibility he inherited. It's just that Colin Kavanaugh was ready to do it on his own. New times called for new solutions. And a new boss to call the shots.

You will live your duty. It remains a nagging internal voice when you fall asleep and when you awaken. It is your wife and mistress, but not your friend. And if you fail, you fail more than yourself. You fail history. You change things that cannot be unchanged.

Three full pages. More rambling advice. Nothing Kavanaugh hadn't been told to his face time and time again.

Kavanaugh now waited for Dunbar to leave. The rest he would do without interruption.

Thirty minutes later, she finally went through her exit ritual: pushing her chair straight in, locking her drawers, making sure everything was in its place on her desktop, removing her purse from the closet, and taking perfectly measured steps to the door.

Once gone, Kavanaugh began his real search—through Gruber's desk and the hidden compartments behind the false backs.

For more than a year he wanted to find out what was in there.

Secretum, he thought. Now, he was going to learn it all.

PART II

TWENTY-FIVE

The cave

MCCAULEY COUNTED ON life's standard frames of references. The sun rises and sets. Sixty seconds to a minute. Sixty minutes to an hour. Twenty-four hours in a day. The earth beneath stays where it's supposed to, except during earthquakes. And baseball has nine innings.

But there was no frame of reference for the teacher and students who returned to the cave, especially as their eyes widened to the perplexing sight now lit by their newly purchased propane lamps.

"What is this?" Alpert asked.

"Dr. Quinn?" Leslie Cohen needed reassurance.

"I…." Rich Tamburro couldn't get past the pronoun.

Tom Trent was speechless.

It was as if everyone was waiting for Quinn McCauley to explain things.

"What the hell?" Katrina Alpert mouthed, but hardly articulated.

"Everyone take a deep breath. Lanterns in front. Slowly now." McCauley remained calm and authoritative.

Ten steps forward he said, "Okay, stop." He raised his light and examined the wall ahead of them, first closely… only inches away, then from two feet, and ten feet back. It was as if it wasn't there, concealed by the blackest black he'd ever seen.

"Jesus," Tamburro proclaimed. "I can't see it."

"It's absorbing all the light," McCauley said.

Jaffe came forward and touched the surface. "Smooth. Metallic. No sign of corrosion. Gold, silver, iron, galvanized steel would all show corrosion. This doesn't feel like there's any."

Next, Dr. Alpert touched the surface. She looked at her hands in the light and rubbed her thumb against her forefinger. "And no dust. This place is very well maintained. A lot cleaner than your motel room," she directed to McCauley.

"What was that?" Jaffe asked with keen interest.

"Nothing," McCauley quickly stated. "Can we stay focused on our observations?"

"Corporate?" Tamburro offered.

Jaffe disagreed. "Military."

"Military?" Alpert repeated.

"That's what I'm leaning toward, too," McCauley said. "Left over from the Cold War."

Katrina Alpert looked at her hand again. "With a full-time maid to dust?"

THE NATURAL THING to do was to take pictures. Leslie Cohen was the first to try.

"My cell's not acting right. Can't hold the charge. It's going on and off."

Rich Tamburro found the same on his. In fact, none of their phones fired up long enough to shoot any pictures.

"Something in here is neutralizing the circuits," Jaffe concluded. "Anyone up on electrical anomalies?"

"Not me," said Cohen. "I stop at about Brachiosaurous."

"Beats me," Lobel said.

"Anyone else?"

No takers.

"Okay time for another plan," McCauley began.

"Is that Plan B or C, now?" Alpert asked.

"Okay, who has some thoughts?" McCauley was opening up discussion around the evening campfire. "Like who the hell would build such a facility in the middle of nowhere?"

Tamburro started with the *Twilight Zone* theme.

"Gonna need more than that."

"Okay, then it's like Area 51," he continued. "We uncovercd a secret facility."

"Yeah, like maybe one the government just forgot about," Lobel proposed. "How else can you explain the electrostatic *thingy* that also zaps dust away. Love that patent!"

"The government doesn't just forget about places like this," McCauley argued.

"Then ancient aliens," Tom Trent interjected. "Wouldn't that be something! A ragtag team of paleontologists discover proof of ancient aliens. Talk about irony."

"Someone do a Google search on super light absorbent materials," McCauley proposed. "Okay?"

"Super absorbent? Like Bounty?" Trent joked.

"Yes, but Bounty for light," he replied.

They continued to speculate, with no basis on which to hang any real theory. Jaffe was the only one not throwing out ideas. He was on his computer.

During a lull in the discussion Tamburro saddled over to McCauley.

"Doc, I have an idea."

"What's that?"

"The other night when we were listening to the radio on the way back from town...."

"Yes."

"The guy being interviewed...."

"The conspiracy nut?"

"That guy. I think he might have some insight."

"In made-up shit."

"Getting government documents released through the Freedom of Information Act more than anyone else. That's for real. He's been at it for years. You won't have to tell him much, but I think you might gather some intel."

"And my dear spy," McCauley whispered and smiled to Alpert who sat out of earshot, "tells my chair I'm relying on crackpots as experts. Just great."

Tamburro laughed. "You won't be the first professor to be accused of that. Just talk to him."

"He's a quack."

"He researches stuff. So do you. He goes on late night talk radio. So do you."

McCauley threw his hands up in frustration. Dr. Alpert caught the gesture and joined the conversation.

Dr. Alpert caught this part of the exchange. "Do what?"

"Toss my career in the toilet. Doesn't matter."

"It's worth a shot," Tamburro said ignoring McCauley's comment and Alpert's question.

"I'll think about. That's as far as I'll go now."

"Just engage him a little. Nothing specific. Keep the lid on it."

"Engage who?" Alpert asked.

McCauley waved her off just as Jaffe yelled, "Got it!" He turned back to the conversation and looked up from his computer.

"Doc was right. A British company invented a thing called *Vantablack*. Made from carbon nanotubes, whatever the fuck they are. It absorbs all but .035 percent of visual light. Set a new world record."

"A new record for doing what?" Rodriguez showed more interest.

"I guess the amount of light it could absorb. Here, it says there are vast applications in photography and telescopes. Better ways to focus primary light sources and block out others. *Vantablack* is so dark the human eye can't grasp what it's seeing." Jaffe paused. "Sound familiar?"

"Sure does," Lobel said excitedly. "Did we stumble onto a beta test?"

"Or a practical application?" Tamburro added.

"I don't think so," McCauley offered. "They've got labs for stuff like that. Why would a British company be doing anything in a cave here in Montana?"

The team members looked at one another for an answer.

"Not a company," Leslie Cohen quietly offered. "Like you were saying before, it's government. I've read about places like this. CDC or nuclear waste facilities. They lock the door and throw away the keys. We shouldn't be messing with it."

"Thank you. Back to my point," Tamburro interrupted.

McCauley turned to the student. "I said…"

"Right," Tamburro backed down.

"Look, it's clearly out of our area," Trent interjected. "I'm with Leslie. We shouldn't be messing with it."

"I don't know."

Dr. Alpert's comment came as a surprise, particularly to McCauley. "Maybe one more trip?"

McCauley was taken by her enthusiasm. She shrugged and added, "For the sake of scientific curiosity. What do you say, Dr. McCauley? Up for an adventure?"

TWENTY-SIX

London
Early the next day

KAVANAUGH EAGERLY EVALUATED Ten's latest summaries. The developments would surely be his first true test of will. He needed to know more.

Kavanaugh flew up the stairs to quiz the principal in Ten who was compiling the ever-expanding file. He was tall and blond, with an air of danger lurking within. Not the kind of person who would be attracted to a life indoors doing research. But he was in his mid-fifties and likely happy to have job stability.

"Get your coffee and come with me. We have to talk." The man followed without objection. They went to the rooftop deck and sat at a table under a shade umbrella.

Kavanaugh didn't even know the researcher's last name or how he'd lost his index finger on his left hand. He'd have to find out, make him feel needed, and stress how much he would rely on him.

"Simon, I want you to clear your desk of all your general searches to exclusively focus on this."

Simon—Volker was his last name—didn't say thank you. He was not that kind of man. A nod was enough.

"Done. I'll move up one of the night team."

"Good. Now tell me what you have," Kavanaugh insisted.

Kavanaugh listened to a report that greatly troubled

him. He decided he had to act. The prospects actually excited him.

Late afternoon

COLIN KAVANAUGH BELIEVED he had the resolve to do whatever was necessary. The only problem—there was no glory other than what he could feel himself. No bragging rights. No accolades. No tributes. He wondered how others had dealt with such invisibility. He never thought to ask Gruber. Living a double life. A life of secrecy suddenly took on more meaning. *To never have anyone really know.* This was going to be hard to live with.

The thoughts continued to consume him at Martin Gruber's funeral. Aside from Dunbar, seven colleagues from *Voyages* and the old waiter from Brown's, few mourners came to pay their last respects at the Brompton Cemetery Chapel in the Borough of Kensington and Chelsea. In final interment, Martin Gruber would be joining royalty, scientists, explorers, artists and statesmen, though Colin Kavanaugh most enjoyed that the sanctuary was used in the James Bond movie, *GoldenEye.*

Kavanaugh ignored the platitudes in the priest's sermon. Surely he had no real idea who he was burying. Kavanaugh also dismissed the visible displays of sorrow from his associates. He wrote it off as employees wanting to make sure that they were seen mourning by their new boss. And the waiter? Leon. His appearance puzzled him.

When the service was over, Kavanaugh politely lingered, thanked the clueless clergyman, and noticed that the waiter was making slow passage to talk to him. Kavanaugh extended his hand and spoke first.

"It's nice of you to come."

"Mr. Gruber was kind to me over the many years I

served him," the sixty-eight-year-old man replied. "Rest assured, I'll *serve* you just as if Mr. Gruber was seated right there. Your table will always be available."

Kavanaugh struggled to understand the comment. *Your* table, not *a table*.

"Thank you," Kavanaugh replied. He really wondered if he even wanted to continue the ritual.

"I can expect to see you this week."

Kavanaugh now felt unsure if Leon had proposed a question or made a statement. "Excuse me," he said. "I must talk to Mr. Gruber's assistant."

Kavanaugh quickly excused himself and cut across the lawn to intercept Dunbar.

"Ms. Dunbar, all things considered, I'd like you to take the rest of the week off to collect your thoughts."

"That won't be necessary," she said as coldly as anything she ever stated. "We have a great deal to consider. I'll be in tomorrow at the normal time."

"Thank you, Ms. Dunbar, but that won't be necessary."

"Yes it is, Mr. Kavanaugh. Yes it is."

TWENTY-SEVEN

Glendive, MT
The same day

THE CHECKOUT CLERK at the hardware store must have thought the now familiar group of fossil hunters was planning on lighting up the whole park. They purchased ten more gas lamps and an equal number of fuel canisters. McCauley put it on his credit cards again, without a thought about the air miles he was accumulating. Just before paying, he spotted something he hadn't seen in years.

"How much are these?"

The teenager on the register scanned one. $17.50.

He saw another two on the shelf. "Any more?"

"That's it. Nobody uses them these days."

"We sure will. I'll take them all."

"Hey, buddy, what's that?"

The park director was shopping and overheard the exchange at the counter.

"Oh hi, Kappy. More supplies."

Kaplan saw all of the equipment piled into five shopping carts. "Planning on working all night?"

"Making the best of our time," McCauley said keeping his response brief.

"Well, keep me posted. Any new discovery helps the tourist traffic."

"You bet."

"See you at the links again."

"Sure thing. I'll give you a shout."

With that, McCauley joined the others pushing their shopping carts, which now included the last of the store's disposable film cameras.

The next morning

THE ADDITIONAL LAMPS didn't shed any more light on the questions that needed to be answered. Once again they were stopped and stumped at the wall.

At least the mechanical wind-up cameras allowed them to take pictures since their cell phones and SLRs weren't reliable.

What they couldn't see because of the super black, they could feel. McCauley ran his hand across the surface. It was broken up by some rock and then exposed again a few feet further down a cavern corridor.

"I'm not so sure," he began.

"About?" Alpert asked.

"Timing. This doesn't feel like it was embedded into the rock. It seems like the rocks formed or fell around it."

"Earthquakes? Natural shifting," she explained. "After it was installed."

"Yes, but recently? Here, give me your hand."

McCauley guided Alpert's hand along the smooth, metallic super black wall. When she came to rock, she felt changes in vertical layers and stopped.

"Bring your light closer," she said.

McCauley tipped the lamp toward her.

Alpert nodded.

"What?" Tom Trent asked.

McCauley knew. He looked at Alpert just as surprised.

"Am I missing something?" Trent said more emphatically.

"Strata," Alpert stated. "Eons of fused strata. Typical of earth changing over time. A long time. Say millions of years."

McCAULEY CLICKED ANOTHER picture and then asked for a pick. He wedged it between the wall and a section of the rock and pushed hard. It loosened an area, but not enough to dislodge any rock. He struck the pick in hard above the first spot and put his shoulder against the handle. It loosened more dirt, allowing him to wedge the end in further. With the next effort, a three-foot portion of stone fell to the ground.

"More light!"

Alpert brought hers closer, as did Jaffe. More *nothing*. More of the super black wall which absorbed all their light.

"It's buried behind this," McCauley exclaimed.

He reached further. It was smooth for inches, and then he felt an indentation in the surface. First one, then another, and even more angling downward. They all felt the same, about an inch wide and a quarter of an inch deep.

"Help me clear more rock. Now!"

TWENTY-EIGHT

That evening

RICH PULLED THE flap back on McCauley's tent.

"Gotta a minute, doc?"

"Sure. Hey, how's Anna doing?"

"Okay. She's not a happy camper, but she wants her computer. That's a good sign. I keep her in the loop, which she loves."

"Nice going. I'll try to stop over tomorrow," McCauley said.

"She'd like that."

"So, what's up Rich?"

"You'll probably want to toss me out of the tent, but I really think you should call Robert Greene."

"Him again. The conspiracy nut."

"Yeah. We may have stepped into a secret government project or some hidden black ops facility. You said as much yourself. Or it belongs to a private corp that was testing something. Even scarier, a CDC research lab, which I hope to God it isn't."

Some of the newer possibilities Tamburro raised had also occurred to McCauley. Clearly he needed help, especially if the CDC was involved. He could go to Kappy, but that didn't seem prudent.

"What if we do more research first?" McCauley asked.

"To tell you the truth, I have. Not much comes up except coal mine accidents. Just call."

Tamburro handed McCauley a sheet with the phone number. "Mind if I stick around?"

"I have to call now?"

"Right now. In front of me."

"Okay, okay."

At that moment, Alpert walked into McCauley's tent.

"Room for another?"

"Sure. You can witness the beginning of the end of my career."

"Oh?" she asked.

Tamburro explained.

"Just call," Alpert implored.

McCauley punched in the number on his cell.

"Speaker," Tamburro insisted.

The professor activated the speaker function. On the fifth ring the call went to voice mail.

"Apparently I don't know you well enough to give you my cell, so leave your name at the beep and if, after investigating *you* a bit, and I'm so inclined, I'll call you back. If you don't hear from me, don't bother calling again. We'll never be talking."

McCauley shrugged his shoulders and thought, *What an asshole!*

"So here comes the beep. Make it quick. I'm busy."

Not knowing how much time he had, McCauley jumped right in. "Hello, Mr. Greene. My name is Quinn McCauley. I'm a paleontologist working at a site in Montana. We, ah...."

Alpert gave him a speed up sign.

"We found something..." he took a beat, "...interesting."

Interesting took Katrina back to her discussion with McCauley. It was a safety word.

"And I'd like to talk to you about it confidentially." He gave his number, said thank you and ended the message.

"What's the chance he'll call back?" Alpert asked.

"Oh, he'll call," Tamburro said. "The operative words were 'interesting' and 'confidentially.' Too good to ignore. He'll call back all right."

McCAULEY'S PHONE RANG at an ungodly hour. He was in such a deep sleep he almost missed the call.

"Hello," McCauley said finally answering.

"Is this Dr. McCauley?" the male voice replied.

"Yes." Quinn struggled to find his watch to check the time. 3 A.M. *Jesus.* "Who's this?"

"Robert Greene. You called me earlier."

"A lot earlier, Mr. Greene."

"Oh. I'm sorry. I wasn't looking at the time." He laughed. "Guess I'm too much of a night owl. If this isn't good, we can talk tomorrow. But it'll probably be way late again."

"No, no," McCauley said as he gathered his thoughts. "Now's okay."

"I've looked you up on LinkedIn, on the Yale website, and a few other places I have access to, Dr. McCauley. Read your bios and a paper you wrote on dinosaur communal behavior in the Jurassic period."

"Thanks. You're probably the fifth person to get through it."

"Actually, I didn't finish it. Made some of the government reports look dry. But I have to ask, anything more than theory?"

"Just theory."

"Pictures would have helped."

"Academia. They weigh the ink."

"Really? Pictures tell so much more."

"Look, next time I'm in my time machine I'll be sure to bring my camera."

"Now you're speaking my language."

"I'm not really the science fiction type," McCauley said.

"Not even *Jurassic Park*?"

"Well, of course. Got my undergraduate degree from Harvard. That's where Crichton went."

"There's hope for you yet. So what did you find that was *interesting* and we needed to have a *confidential* talk?"

McCauley smiled. Tamburro had been absolutely correct.

"I'm not really sure," McCauley admitted. "Some of my colleagues recommended I get in touch with you, but quite honestly..."

"Here I go again," Greene interrupted. "You don't believe I'm for real."

"I was trying to put it more delicately."

"You don't have to. The only thing I'll say in my own defense is I'm a researcher not a rumormonger. Like you, I look for things no one else has found. Most days there's nothing. And then there are the times when it's all worthwhile. I think it's safe to say you recently had a good day, but you don't know how to explain it."

Greene waited for an answer.

"Dr. McCauley?"

"I'm here."

"Am I correct?"

There was another long pause.

"Okay. I take it I am. That means you might want my help," Greene said breaking the silence again.

Quinn McCauley thought hard.

"When?"

TWENTY-NINE

The cave

THEY RETURNED AGAIN with better tools. The more rock they cut away, the greater the mystery.

Soon they had a fifteen foot wide portion of the smooth, sleek wall. Yet, no matter how much light they aimed, they still couldn't see it. The smooth surface simply absorbed all the light, reflecting none back.

"Blacker than black," Jaffe said.

McCauley was more interested in what he was feeling than what they couldn't see: the indentations. The wall was riddled with them.

He felt with his fingertips, then with the palm of his hands. "I can't quite get it, but it feels like there's a design to them."

"A design?" Alpert responded.

"Here. Feel." He took Dr. Alpert's hand and blindly moved it across the wall.

"I don't know," she said. "It's just random depressions."

"Slide your hand down. There's more."

She closed her eyes to focus her concentration.

"Wait, Yes. They begin to spread out," she noted.

"Okay, let's switch." McCauley now reached in and tried to get a picture in his mind's eye. It was hard. "Damn," he complained. "Wish I could do a rubbing. No chalk or pencil."

"We have dirt," Alpert said. She scooped some and

let it flow through her fingers. "And I have a few sheets of paper."

"You're better than a Boy Scout," he joked.

"I should hope so."

McCauley pressed the paper against the surface and rubbed dirt in, making a virtual negative of a portion of the pattern. He felt one small dimple at the top of the design. Below it, more, in a still indeterminate pattern. Soon he began counting the indentations aloud as he felt groups of the dents and visualized where they were.

One by one, he handed the 8.5 x 11 inch papers back to Alpert. It took five pages in all.

It didn't look like much. Putting the rubbings in her backpack she said, "We'll have to see this in better light." McCauley stepped away. He was onto something.

"Okay. Your turn again. Come back in here and close your eyes. Get a sense of the larger picture as you feel the wall. Tell me what you *see*," he said to Alpert.

Katrina started again. It took her a few tries to come to a blind observation. "A pattern, but I don't get exactly what it is." She began to count just as McCauley had.

"Aloud."

As she counted out, McCauley wrote the numbers down.

"I still don't see anything," she said.

"Come on, Dr. Alpert. Think."

She started all over again. The other students watched in wonder. McCauley was seeing it come together on paper as she called out the seemingly random numbers.

Suddenly she stopped. "A…a…pyramid."

LATER THAT AFTERNOON, Quinn was on Expedia looking into airfares. At first, he thought he'd go it alone, but he realized he needed a counterbalance. *Tamburro? No. He should stay with Chohany. Jaffe? Maybe.* Then he considered another possibility. He'd put Jaffe in charge of the site and ask Katrina Alpert to join him. If nothing else, in the short time that he'd known her, McCauley was impressed that she didn't hold anything back. *Worth a try.*

McCauley found her in the mess tent pouring a cup of coffee.

"I've decided to take Tamburro's recommendation."

She wasn't sure what that was.

"To go meet the conspiracy nut we heard on the radio. What do you think?"

"Conspiracy nut?"

"Well, it's a label. I suppose he does some credible research. I just thought that under the circumstances…"

"Unusual circumstances," she replied.

"Completely unusual."

"Given that, what the hell. I say go."

McCauley was actually surprised.

"You do?"

"Sure. Go. I can help here."

"Thank you, but I thought," he began to fumble, "I thought that maybe I needed someone to tag along to keep me sane. You've been doing a good job of that since you joined up. So, I figured you should be the voice of reason. What do you say?"

"Really?"

"Really."

Now she was surprised.

"Where?" Alpert asked.

"Bakersfield, California."

"Never heard of it."

"Well, apparently it just hasn't made your bucket list yet. It's north of Los Angeles by an hour or so. Pack for a few nights."

"Promise me no underwear on doorknobs?"

"I'll do better than that. Separate rooms."

"Oh, you got that right, mister."

"Then you're up for it?"

"Wouldn't miss it for the world."

"Great, because we've got a plane out of Glendive at four fifty-two. First, I'm going to run into town to see if I can get the pictures printed up. We might need them."

· THIRTY

THE TEENAGE BOY working the cash register at the CVS put the film through the processor and the finished prints into the sleeves without comment. McCauley thanked him. He didn't look at the pictures until he returned to his SUV. There, he open up the sleeves. The electronic part of the camera, the flash, hadn't worked. But his decision to buy the disposable cameras was still rewarded.

During the first leg, McCauley removed a sheet of paper from his Johnson & Murphy shoulder bag.

"What's this?" Dr. Alpert asked, scanning the sheet.

"A sketch of what you felt in the cave."

Now, with McCauley's handwritten scribbling, the pyramid had indeed taken shape, but with far greater impact. Not just a pyramid, but a pyramid of numbers. Very familiar numbers.

Bakersfield, CA
The next day

THE INTRODUCTION AT the door had been cordial and quick. Greene, actually awake at mid-day, invited the two paleontologists into his home. He was in his early thirties, about two hundred pounds, five-eight, with short military length black hair, and an open moon face. This was not the look of a conspiracy theorist or whatever McCauley had imagined a conspiracy theorist to be.

His mid-century house was another thing. It was lacking in all amenities. If there was furniture to be found, it was under boxes that lined every hallway, the living and dining rooms, and, McCauley presumed, the bedrooms and bathrooms.

"So nice of you to come all this way," Greene said as he led them through his maze. "You have to understand I get the weirdest calls from people all over the world. That's why my phone message sounds the way it does." Greene was positively apologetic. "It's designed to discourage people. Most I don't even answer. I mean, who would want to talk to *them*?"

Greene's stock went up in McCauley's estimation. "I understand. We have some of the same in our world."

"*The Lost World*," Greene declared.

"Excuse me?" Katrina was confused.

"*The Lost World*. One of the classic dinosaur movies." She still didn't get the reference.

"Michael Rennie, you know, he played Klaatu in *The Day the Earth Stood Still*. Claude Rains, Fernando Lamas. David Hedison. And," he turned to McCauley, "my heart be still, a very hot and young Jill St. John."

McCauley nodded yes, though Greene wasn't sure if it was because of the reference to Jill St. John or the movie. So he went on…and on.

"1960, based on Arthur Conan Doyle's novel. He also wrote Sherlock Holmes."

Katrina was trying to keep up, but it was difficult.

"Explorers investigate a mysterious mountain in Venezuela. They get past the cannibals, only to have to contend with man-eating plants and then giant spiders. But it's the dinosaurs that make it so cool. Well, not dinosaurs in any sense you know. The budget was so low that the director, Irwin Allen, used lizards instead of models or stop motion. *The Lost World*—you should see it sometime."

"Matter of fact, I have," McCauley volunteered. "And the 1920s original. The effects are actually better. And there's *Lost Continent* from the '50s, but that's not even worth talking about."

"Well, I guess I've met my match. Sorry. Sometimes I get wound up pretty tightly."

Quinn McCauley smiled. He just bonded with Robert Greene and they hadn't even gotten to the reason for the visit. "Not a problem."

"How about coffee?"

"Sure," McCauley replied.

"Tea?" Alpert asked.

"Got both." He led them through the obstacle course he called home on the way to the kitchen. While the water was heating, they chatted about more dinosaur films. With their drinks in hand, Greene took them into his office which contained three computers and blacked out windows.

"Welcome to World Headquarters. Doesn't look like much."

Alpert agreed. "Definitely not."

Greene laughed. "Doesn't need to. The picture I use on my website is a fake created in Pååhotoshop. It's my dream office."

"I thought you're all about the truth?"

"Oh, I am, Dr. McCauley. Read the small print. It's just below the photo. A disclaimer with the warning, even pictures lie."

"Very cool," McCauley said.

Katrina kicked him.

"What's that for?"

"I thought you wanted me to be your reality check."

"Ah, good cop, bad cop?" Greene said picking up on the exchange.

"Simply trying to keep skepticism in tow," she added.

"Well, if it's any consolation," Greene continued, "that's what I'm all about. Information is king. That's what I request from the government. That's what I deliver online. No speculation. Documents, records, transcripts. All facts, or at the very least, what isn't blacked out on the way for public consumption. Once in hand, I give it the contextual wrapping. Then, I plug it into appropriate webisodes, video links, podcasts I've appeared on, and my Internet radio show. Impressive, huh?"

McCauley had to agree. "Before I talked with you I thought it was primarily going to be paranormal stuff. But hell, when I looked at your site, you've got more on Iraq, Vietnam, and Voting Rights issues than UFOs and ghosts."

"Thank you, Dr. McCauley. I take that as high praise. You're not quite accurate on the balance, but I'll accept the compliment. Now to your questions. I need a little more than what you gave me on the phone. Bullet points will do for a start. Actually, depending upon whether the government is involved, less is even best. Okay?"

"Okay."

McCauley looked for a place where they could settle. Greene removed two storage boxes from a couch opposite his desk. He stacked them higher atop others. "Sit, sit. What can you tell me?"

"In general terms, we're camped at one of Montana's richest dinosaur locations. But after nearly halfway through our time, our work wasn't leading to anything out of the ordinary. Not that it necessarily ever does. But I don't want my students to get too bored, especially early on. So I checked out a valley with a deeper geological footprint by a few million years. Before moving everyone down, I spotted something up a cliff."

Greene listened intently.

"On its own, it wasn't unusual, but I was curious. I climbed up about thirty feet and found an entrance to a cave."

"Getting interesting now."

"Well, as you can imagine it was dark."

"Caves are."

"And I realized I needed help and supplies."

"What kind of supplies?"

"Lights, extension cords, a generator. I pulled the team together. We bought out a hardware store, hooked things up, and started to explore…" McCauley glanced over to Dr. Alpert for approval. *So far, so good.* "…fairly far in."

"And…?"

"And we saw Native American petroglyphs. Not at all unusual for the Sioux and their immediate relatives. But the drawings didn't document their tribal life. They depicted a specific route through the cave."

"To where?" Greene logically asked.

Suddenly, McCauley wished he'd said less. "I don't know, it's hard to say."

"Try."

"Well, the cave drawings were like maps through corridors and halls. At the end was a wall or maybe a door."

"Sounds religious. Doors often represent openings to other experiences; spiritual worlds beyond their dominion."

"Well, it was more than that," McCauley offered.

"Oh?"

"A specific wall, but very hard to describe."

"Go on." Greene leaned into the conversation.

"A wall. Definitely a wall. Smooth and metallic—"

"Interesting."

"… That reflected no light. The blackest black imaginable. It literally absorbed all the light from our lamps."

Greene picked up on the word lamps. "Lamps, not flashlights?"

"Right. The electrical was unreliable, so we switched to portable lamps. The most curious thing is the black itself. One of my students went online and found a company that developed a similar substance?"

"Similar, not this particular one?" Greene asked.

"Not the same. At least we don't think so." McCauley did not elaborate. "But its properties could also soak up all light."

McCauley waited for a response. After a long pause he prompted Greene for one. "Well?"

"Cool."

"Cool? That's the best you've got?" he complained.

"I'm sorry. But it is cool. It's also got me stymied. Tell me more."

They did. McCauley and Alpert explained how they cut away more rock and felt around the polished surface.

"We took pictures, but of course, you can't really see anything," McCauley explained. He shared some of the photos. Greene saw what he meant. There was the rock, then nothing; as if he was peering into a black hole.

"And this," he taped the black area, "was behind the rocks?"

"Yes, buried," McCauley answered.

"What else?"

McCauley had told Alpert that he didn't know whether he'd show Greene the pyramid design. Now he wondered if he should. He tipped his head to his backpack. Alpert read his doubt and spread her hands apart, indicating her own uncertainty.

"Okay, what's going on doctors?"

"We're deciding," Alpert said.

"I suggest you get your act together otherwise I can't help you. You probably think I'm some crackpot; but the truth is, I may be able to point you in the right direction. That's assuming you want to go there. But unless you come clean...."

"There is more," McCauley interrupted. "After we chipped away at the rock," he pointed to the photograph, "we found a section of the wall that had some indentations; dimples grouped, then separated. They formed a pattern."

He reached into his backpack and handed Greene the page he'd shown Alpert on the plane.

"This. The numbers are mine, but they represent individual groups of indentations we felt."

At first, Robert Greene only saw the pyramid shape. Then he focused on the order of things.

$$
\begin{array}{c}
1 \\
1\ 2 \\
1\ 2\ 3 \\
1\ 2\ 3\ 4 \\
1\ 4\ 3\ 2\ 5 \\
1\ 4\ 3\ 2\ 5\ 6 \\
1\ 4\ 3\ 2\ 5\ 6\ 7 \\
1\ 4\ 7\ 6\ 5\ 2\ 3\ 8
\end{array}
$$

He recognized it that could have gone on far longer. But what was there was more than enough.

"You see it?" McCauley asked.

"Of course I do. It's a prime pyramid."

THIRTY-ONE

"This was on the metal wall buried *behind* the rock?" Greene asked.

"Yes," McCauley said. "Any thoughts?"

"I'd love to see it myself."

"Other than that."

"Well, I'm fascinated by a couple of things. First of all, the black composite." Greene now admitted that he'd also read about *vanta*, which stood for vertically aligned carbon nanotube arrays. But as far as he knew, it was a substance so far only grown on sheets of aluminum foil, not manufactured into solid metal walls.

"I'd say you stumbled onto a secret facility."

"But the petroglyphs?"

"Well, Dr. McCauley, that does argue against that notion, unless they were put there to throw someone."

"If that's the case, it worked!" Katrina noted.

"What else?" McCauley asked.

"Back to the prime pyramid. Now, I'm no mathematician, but it was a favorite subject of mine. I've got respect for numbers. And it's been said that primes are virtually the atoms of arithmetic. The basic tool that we're using to reach across the galaxies; a universal language for the entire universe. It's the code that gives sense to the things we otherwise don't understand. Besides, they fascinate the hell out of me.

"Take the pyramid itself. The magic is in each row, starting with the first. The number one—the first prime number. Like the other primes, it has no positive divisors other than one and itself. Same for 3, 5, 7, 11, 13, 17, 19, 23, on and up to a number that hasn't even been calculated yet."

"But not all the numbers in the pyramid are primes," Katrina said.

"That's the beauty of the thing," Greene continued. "But they work to make primes. Any two numbers next to each other on any row add up to a prime. Perfection itself. So perfect, it's found in nature."

"How so?" she wondered.

"Many. My favorite example are the cicadas."

"The what?"

"Oh, right, you're British. They're bugs that are pretty much indigenous to North America, much less so in England. They have a life cycle where they emerge every thirteen years or seventeen years. In between, *nada*. Then, and only then, on that schedule, those noisy little buggers take over. Thirteen and seventeen are both indivisible and that very fact gives cicadas a leg up on their predators which might appear in six year cycles. They win mathematically."

"Incredible." McCauley was impressed.

"Incredible when you consider they cracked an evolutionary code that must go back millions of years. They evolved through primes. It became their key to survival."

"So back to the prime pyramid. Who put it there?" McCauley said.

"I have no idea. But let me give you something else to think about."

Quinn and Katrina were completely engaged.

Greene turned to his computer and typed in Arecibo. Dozens of references came up. Greene clicked on the radio telescope in Puerto Rico.

"Now I can really talk more authoritatively about this."

He began to explain, concluding with an astonishing experiment. "They're sending messages to other galaxies from here. How are they doing it?" Greene asked rhetorically.

"Prime numbers?"

"Precisely, Dr. McCauley. Radioing primes that, if and when received, may be arranged in a vertical column to create a picture. Like the rudimentary computer images on those Nano Pets that were the rage with kids years ago."

Greene clicked on the actual image of the Arecibo transmission. It depicted the atomic numbers of hydrogen, carbon, nitrogen, oxygen and phosphorous, the basic constructs of life on Earth. It included DNA information, a block image of a human with the approximate height, a layout of our solar system and most importantly the position of Earth. "It's the human race in prime numbers for all the universe to see. The announcement of *here we are*."

"Here we are," McCauley repeated.

"Yes," Greene said. "Here we are. Now how about I share some pretty wacked stories with you?"

"About prime numbers?" Dr. Alpert asked.

"Put that question aside for now."

"Okay."

"You'll find them on my website. Clearly, you don't have to believe all of it or, for that matter, any of it. But too often we assume we know everything there is to know."

"I don't necessarily agree," Katrina said. She smiled at McCauley. He understood.

"Well good, because it would be pretty small-minded if we did. Every day science invents new tools and then discovers old stuff that's been around since the dawn of time. We just didn't have the means to see it. Forwards and backwards. It doesn't matter which direction we look. There's always the unknown."

Greene had their attention. "Let's look at your work.

You only explore what is, in fact, an infinitesimal part of the earth; a virtually microscopic section within the fifth of the planet that isn't water. And simply because you find Barney and a few of his friends from year to year, does that mean you've struck the mother lode? Given the great ancient continental shift, can you even imagine what there is to discover in the world's seas?"

It was a staggering thought. Greene was correct, in the field of paleontology, the ground beneath the oceans was quite literally *untapped*.

"And look up," Greene continued. "Our ancestors viewed the stars forever; with dread and wonder, giving flight to dreams. But it wasn't until Galileo set his telescope to true focal points and challenged prevailing dogma that we began to think the unthinkable or imagine the unimaginable. Galileo, doctors. And, Dr. McCauley, because I've heard podcasts of your radio interviews—yes, I found them—I know you recognize that on earth's evolutionary clock, that was barely a fraction of a second ago."

THIRTY-TWO

April 30, 1633
Rome, Italy

FATHER MACULANO WAS opining about something in his chambers. Or maybe he was building up to another holier than thou bluster. Either way, Galileo wasn't listening. He was living his life in chapters he never wrote.

His childhood in Pisa. His itchy first-growth beard. His father's insistence that he go to the university. His mother reading to him from the Bible. The ideas he wrote down on whatever was in reach: school notebooks, the back of used envelopes, condensation on early morning windows, even dirt.

The purest of pleasures for Galileo was expanding on a notion, proving a supposition or developing the means to explore it further.

He remembered his friends growing up, who tried to keep pace with him intellectually, and his colleagues who followed such safe, conservative paths. His thoughts went to his children and the hard lives they were leading, and on to his wife and the strain his controversial research had brought her.

Most of all, Galileo recalled his temporal victories over the church and his undeniable belief that time was the thing he least understood for reasons stated and unstated.

"And so it will be," Maculano concluded.

The priest's icy tone brought Galileo back into the conversation.

"And there are no words that will appeal to you, your eminence? I have been a good man. I've lived a pious life. My daughters are in a convent."

"You bore them out of wedlock. Who would marry Galileo's bastards? Their prayer remains their only salvation. It surely won't be yours."

"My son has been legitimized and is married."

"Perhaps he shall somehow escape the sins of the father who committed his blasphemy to print."

"They were observations. Postulates. I was paid in tribute for the work."

"Yes, by Pope Paul V. Paul, who introduced you to Cardinal Francesco Mari del Monte. Another who showered you with accolades. What did he say, 'If we were still living under the ancient Republic of Rome, I verily believe that there would be a column on the Capital erected in Galileo's honor.' You shall never hear such things again."

Maculano walked to his desk and picked up a book. "You acted as if there were no boundaries to the privileges granted you," he said. "Your words are swords that strike the heart of His Holiness."

"This Pope," Galileo argued, "Urban."

"And as cardinal he favored you. He extolled your virtues. Didn't he describe you as a great man, *whose fame shines in the heavens and...*'"

Galileo helped him with the quote. "'*...goes on earth far and wide.*' Yes, he was a friend. As was Pope Paul V."

"Pity that you didn't hold your tongue. Urban simply suggested you take an approach that would have allowed you to privately hold your Copernican views without precisely claiming them as truth. A proposal as it were. It would have been easy, but the Galileo Galilei ego said *no* to a compromise on any terms. The Pope sought a re-framing of your position. You fail to do so even in these private conversations.

"You denied Urban a solution that would have most of all benefited you." Maculano's eyes widened. His nostrils flared. "You betrayed an ally who has risen to greatness. And in greatness, he will see to it that you shrink and shrivel into a speck of cosmic dust that the finest glass in your telescope will not see. He will never forgive you, Galileo. Never."

Galileo's hands shook. His face was drawn. None of the fire and fight that had driven the scientist throughout his life was evident.

"You and your few supporters are defeated. What's worse, you've been discredited. You're guilty of vanity. You ran to Rome to win support, which for a time worked in your favor. Yet you had to ridicule opponents and make enemies of the most powerful people."

"People who became the most powerful."

"Your mistake," the inquisitor demanded. "Your grave mistake. Your life, as you knew it, is over."

Galileo stood. The full weight of the church was on him as he walked to a narrow window at the priest's third floor chamber. He peered into the night sky. A crescent moon was rising. A moon he knew to circle the earth, and the earth to revolve around the sun. He feared he'd never put his eye on his telescope again or his mind to the other great discoveries that lay in waiting in the universe.

"Your writing, Galileo. Your own writing spells guilt. *'Philosophy is written in that great book which ever lies before our eyes—I mean the universe.'* In that single sentence you demonstrated irreverence to God Almighty. You defamed the Book of the Lord in favor of your own publication. Never has the Church seen such impiety."

"You are excellent at quoting only portions," Galileo said, still looking outside. "There is more."

"That further damns *you*!" the priest charged.

"I sought to propose the Pythagorean standpoint that truth can be found in mathematics and science, in numbers and the order of things," Galileo weakly countered.

"There is only one order. God's."

"But the Jesuits themselves are modern-minded humanists, friends of science and discovery."

"And where are they now that you are imprisoned?"

Galileo turned away from the moon, which also seemed to abandon him as it began to disappear behind the magnificent Basilica Dome.

"Will you permit me a modest argument, if only as an academic exercise?"

"You may babble to your heart's content or to the point I become bored."

"Your Eminence, can we accept that the fundamental scientific methodology I employed, if put forth by others, could have led to similar conclusions about the nature of the earth and the planets in relation to the sun?" This was Galileo's test of Maculano's intellect.

The priest considered the point. "Quite likely," he admitted. "Another scientist performing corresponding research *might* reach a comparable," he returned to his role, "and equally heretical position."

"If you were a scientist, might the same be true of you?" Galileo asked.

"Ah, you would make a fine judge yourself."

"I believe that while you have the best interests of the Church, you harbor the curiosity of a man of science—with the mind of an inquirer more than an inquisitor."

"Galileo Galilei!" Maculano shouted, "there is nothing in my activities that would suggest such things."

"Yes there is," Galileo said summoning all his strength. "You visited the Le Marche cave yourself! Tell me what you *think* you saw?"

THIRTY-THREE

Robert Greene's residence
Bakersfield, CA
Present day

"Oh, of course, I have my wild theories," Greene continued. "That's what they love to hear in interviews—my go-to talking points. Crowd pleasers. Beyond that, I have things I keep to myself. If and when I feel confident to go public, I do. I'm just another guy searching for some truths. But believe me, there are some things better left where you found them."

"You make it seem like you have to wade through conspiracies to get to anything factual," McCauley observed.

"Welcome to my world."

"Thanks a lot," McCauley added. "But I interrupted."

"Yes, you did. So back to my stories, which overlap with earth science or fiction. Your choice. Science says that Earth's oldest rocks are about 3.8 to 3.9 billion years old. Since Earth itself has to be older than its oldest rocks, we can likely place *terra firma's* age at 4.6 billion. Yet there are those who claim, validated by their interpretation of the Bible, the earth is just ten thousand years old or less."

"We know all about them," McCauley replied. "The Young Earthers."

"I avoid the label and I'm particularly bad in head-to-head debates with them, especially when I deep dive into ancient civilizations."

"Like the Mayans?"

"Much, much, much more ancient than Mayan culture, Dr. Alpert. Ever hear of the Mu or Lemuria?"

The guests nodded no.

"The Rama Empire?"

Another no.

"The Osirian civilization?"

Once more, no.

"Ah, you have to listen to me more on the air or my podcasts."

They laughed.

"Atlantis, for sure."

"For sure," McCauley said.

"Well, there are those who quite convincingly maintain that the first civilizations arose, not thousands of years ago, but tens of thousands. The first, seventy-eight thousand years ago on a giant continent called Mu or Lemuria. Believers in its existence argue that education was its hallmark, but it, like other civilizations to follow, was destroyed by massive earthquakes. Believable?"

"Questionable," was McCauley's reply.

"I'll state it all as fact, if only to piss you off. When Mu sank, water rushed into the Pacific basin leaving small islands in the Atlantic high and dry to form the continent of Atlantis. I'm sure you've heard the characterizations about their technology."

"A few," Katrina acknowledged.

"Fantastic. Phenomenal. Does evidence exist to prove or disprove? Not really, or for the fun of it, let's agree, not yet. The same for the other great empires that are said to have existed. The Uiger civilization in the Gobi Desert, the Aroi Sun Kingdom of the Pacific, Tiahuanaco in South America, and of course, the Mayans. But these are simply the appetizers in the smorgasbord of unexplained facts, some of which actually have *me* scratching *my* head."

"Like what?" McCauley felt he hadn't gotten the information he sought.

"Like ancient artifacts. Really, really old ones."

"How old?"

Greene carefully studied McCauley and Alpert.

"Really old. Based on the work of some Australian geologists—you might know about them…"

"Afraid not," McCauley stated.

"Well, no matter. They analyzed zircons found deep in the outback and postulated that the Earth may have had all the conditions to support life, oh say, maybe two hundred to three hundred million years ago."

Kensington Park
London

"THERE ARE CHALLENGES, but not insurmountable ones," explained Marvin, the man who passed the code word test. He sat in the bench that backed Kavanaugh's.

"How will it be done?"

"Mr. Gruber never needed to know."

"Well, Gruber is gone." He ran his right hand over his scalp and checked his pocket watch.

"Let me put it another way, Mr. Kavanaugh." The man leaned back, close enough that Kavanaugh wouldn't misunderstand the meaning of his next remark. "Mr. Gruber never needed to know because that was the rule well before him and it will remain the rule well after you."

Suddenly, Kavanaugh felt he was being treated more like a functionary, not the one in control. He didn't like it.

"With all due respect," Kavanaugh said in an equally

flat tone, "this is a new day. And if you don't want to follow my directives, then I'll find someone who will."

The immediate silence was satisfying. Kavanaugh rejoiced with the notion that he had stood his ground and apparently won. He left without looking back. The new age of *Autem Semita* had begun. He was forging his own path.

Bakersfield, CA

"I'LL TRY ANOTHER way into all this," Greene decided. "Let's go back to when more than ninety percent of life was wiped out in a geological blink of an eye—sixty-five thousand years ago. Ninety percent! So fast that it destabilized the biosphere before animals and plants could adapt. The record is in the rocks—evidence that speaks to the quick increase in carbon levels."

McCauley and Dr. Alpert could have recited the history as well, but they'd never heard it delivered with such electricity, like a Ted Talk on steroids.

"It was followed by widespread ocean acidification. The earth's temperatures increased seventeen to eighteen degrees Fahrenheit.

"That was just one of at least five extinctions. Five. We're well on our way to a sixth with mass extinction on a scale that rivals the death of your beloved dinosaurs. Facts, doctors. Species are dying at a bewildering rate. The oceans are rising. The air is getting thicker with crap. It all has an impact on the ecosystem."

Greene let out a long breath. "Sorry. I'll get off my high horse and back to some stuff you'll really hate."

"What?" McCauley asked.

"The stuff that keeps talk shows calling."

Greene stood and searched for files. He pulled one from a cabinet, another from a pile on the floor, and two from his desk. He looked around, apparently for more. "One sec," he said. Greene went to the kitchen, opened his refrigerator and removed more files.

"The refrigerator?" Alpert asked.

"Yup. Some that are too hot to keep out," he joked. "Not really, I stuck them in there while I was getting dinner one night. Never took them out. Now's a good time."

Greene returned and handed over the first of many photographs. McCauley took the first.

"It's a picture of a vase found in a Massachusetts quarry in 1851."

"Intricate. More like a candleholder."

"Well, maybe. Who knows? It was embedded in a rock." Greene paused. "Would you like to know how old researchers claim it is?"

"The rock or the vase?" McCauley said.

"Well, considering the vase is inside the stone, both!"

"What?"

"Look again. Inside the stone. Try 534 million years old."

McCauley laughed. "Impossible."

"Here's another." Greene handed Alpert the second photograph. McCauley slid closer on the already crowded leather couch.

"This is from the Chernogorodskiy mines in Russia. See the rail-shaped piece of aluminum machinery? It was discovered in a piece of coal. Again, *in a piece of coal*. The metal was dated to the time of the coal's formation— three hundred million years ago."

McCauley laughed again. "By whom, the Moscow Ballet?"

Greene ignored the snarky comment. "Another." It was a drawing, not a photograph, of a semi-ovoid device. "This came from a French coal mine in the 1880s. Workers broke open a block of rock and *voilà*—a metallic tube. Put a sixty-five million year sticker on it."

"You said it. It's just a drawing. A sketch," McCauley argued.

"Yes, quite accurately a drawing. A photograph of a drawing, though in a sense, wouldn't Native American petroglyphs be considered sketches?"

"I'll give you that one," McCauley admitted.

"Okay class. I have more. Check this out. A human handprint."

They examined the photo of a stone with a human hand spread out next to it.

"It's a fossil uncovered in limestone. One hundred ten million years old. And here, a fossilized human finger discovered in the Canadian arctic. Again, one hundred ten million years ago. Another fossilized hand from Bogota, Columbia. One hundred thirty million years old. And this footprint, found in a shale deposit near Delta, Utah."

"Three hundred up to six hundred million years old," McCauley proclaimed.

"Jesus, you're familiar with this?" Alpert asked.

"No way, I just know my Utah shale."

"I saved the best for last."

Greene pulled one more photo from his refrigerator files.

"They call this a Klerksdorp sphere. It was excavated from a mine near Ottosdal, South Africa. It's not one of a kind, either. Miners have been digging them up for decades."

The object was oval with three parallel lines which ran across the entire circumference. "Two types have been found. One solid bluish with flecks of white, the other, hollow. Both were recovered with pyrophyllite."

"That can't be," McCauley insisted.

"Why?"

"Why? Because pyrophyllite dates back to Precambrian."

"So?"

Dr. Alpert now jumped in. "Precambrian is the oldest of the planet's geological ages and covers the largest span of time in earth's history. Roughly eighty-eight percent. It began with the planet's formation 4.5 to 4.6 billion years ago and continued through the emergence of complex multi-celled life forms billions of years later."

"Its record is evident through different layers of sedimentary rock, laid one on top of another over eons," she continued by heart. "There was almost no oxygen until 2.4 billion years ago when oxygen was released from the oceans through photosynthesis of cyanobacteria. It wasn't breathable until some eight hundred million years ago. That's when complex organisms began to emerge. And yes, there are fossilized remains of early plants and animals within the sediments. But a man-made metal sphere?"

Greene let the question settle, then simply added, "Who said *man*-made?"

PARKED DIAGONALLY ACROSS the street and three homes down from Greene's ranch house sat a rented black Lincoln Navigator. The driver kept the motor idling and the air conditioning blasting to keep the interior cool. He had a straight in view of the subject's house and all the comings and goings. The driver, a dedicated man, had already emailed out the first photographs from his Wi-Fi capable Canon digital/video camera. Now he just waited.

This was a relatively easy job, with no fingerprints to clean up or trails to cover for the retired SAS officer and ex-Halliburton security chief. His assignments came in encrypted messages. Deadly boring or adrenalin pounding, it was all the same. He didn't ask what or why. Money took the question mark out of everything. He was a veteran and, unlike the firm he worked for, he didn't have to be a believer.

THIRTY-FOUR

"NOW YOUR TURN, doctors. I'm sure you didn't come all this way to listen to me go on and on about something you could have seen online."

McCauley stood. "Mr. Greene, I want to thank you. You've been very generous with your time. It's been entertaining to say the least. But ancient aliens are not going to cut it for us. They're great for your audiences, but not for me."

"Excuse me. My fault. I didn't make myself clear," Greene offered. "Give me a few more minutes to explain. Maybe I can get beyond your discomfort."

"A few minutes," Katrina said agreeing with McCauley that Greene was beginning to sound too far-fetched.

"Thank you," the researcher responded. "Maybe this will help. What is not mankind is not necessarily alien."

"Say that again," McCauley implored.

"What is not mankind is not necessarily alien. And the reverse as well. Not alien does not have to be human in the developmental terms as we know it."

McCauley stopped and gazed past Greene and all his boxes, beyond his house and all the way to the cave system. "I'm not sure I get where you're going." He paused to consider an interpretation. "Are you suggesting that accounts of ancient civilizations *may,* and let's keep it at *may,* have existed on earth with some degree of technological know-how?"

"Sticking to the narrow confines of your comfort zone,

Dr. McCauley, I really don't have any scientific fact to support that. That said, I'm not a scientist. I merely research and discuss what I come across. Anyone can do it. The fact is, no one else has to the same extent."

"But you believe those pictures are authentic?" Alpert injected. "The artifacts and fossils and—"

Greene interrupted Alpert.

"Reports. Research. You could have done a Google search and come up with the same thing. Can I stand behind any of them? Hell, I get the government to release loads of documents. Does that mean what *they* wrote is true? Was an FBI investigator covering his butt? An Air Force pilot citing a UFO encounter as an excuse for a poor decision he made in the air? Are the dates of relics from Russia, South America and Asia to be taken as credible when respected scientists haven't laid their fingers on them?

"I have great stories and fabulous photographs. The largest download of previously classified documents anywhere in the country. But validity?" Greene shrugged his shoulders. "Beats the hell out of me."

"Then, with all due respect, what the fuck are you talking about?" Quinn McCauley couldn't have been more direct.

"You stood in front of a metallic wall you couldn't see and felt a prime pyramid that doesn't make any sense. And yet you question things that I bring up that are equally confounding. Again, why do we assume we know everything there is to know?" He paused. "Why do we do what we do? To see if we'll ever be lucky enough to uncover a *something* that no one else has discovered, hoping to add to a greater wealth of knowledge," Greene continued. "Proving a theory we've long held or just being surprised by a big old aha!"

"You are by far one of the oddest people I've ever met," McCauley said. "But you're right."

Greene smiled. "I have an idea. Give me a few minutes."

Greene went to work on his desktop and began printing out a number of pages.

"Here you go," he said after a few minutes. "I can't guarantee you'll have any success, but nothing ventured…"

"What is it?" McCauley asked as he scanned the papers.

"Articles on people who might be able to fill in some blanks. Then again, they may just shut you down or worse send you down a deeper rabbit hole than even I've done. Oh, what the hell. I like you. You're a nice couple—"

"We're not a—" Katrina quickly cut in.

"A nice couple of academics."

"Oh," she replied, somewhat embarrassed.

"So," he said leaning over and pointing to the papers, "start with this guy. Gene Krein. He's a TV producer who does a show for Nat Geo called *World's Greatest Coverups Uncovered*."

"Really?" Alpert asked incredulously. "A TV producer?"

"Believe it or not, they can do worthwhile research."

"I bet." It was Alpert's retort. "Does it show up in their programs?"

"Well," Greene acknowledged, "that's another thing entirely. But I've worked with Krein. Worth a try."

"More?"

"Yes. A retired archeologist/historian somewhere in New England. He must be pretty old by now. Not sure where, but I've read his work. DeCoursey Fales. He used to teach in Boston. Emerson College. Imagine a teacher with that name? I love it. I understand he made some cool discoveries years ago. Here's his picture. It might lead to something."

"Maybe *he* should call the TV producer." Alpert offered.

"You tell him when you meet. I also think you should talk to this old French spelunker. Bovard." Greene handed them a picture and contact information. "If anyone knows caves he does. I've never met him, but I know his work."

Greene checked his watch. "Okay, I have to wrap this up. I've got a live webcast tonight and I'm way behind on my homework."

"But you've got another," Alpert noted. Greene held more printouts.

Greene gave it some thought. "Well, yes. I'm just not sure."

"Why?" she asked.

"I met him at a convention."

Given Greene's following, this worried her. "What kind of convention?"

"Ah, *sciency.*"

"Sciency?" Alpert responded. She didn't like the sound of that either.

"Well, maybe more science fiction. But don't get me wrong. He's the real deal." Greene turned back to his computer, quickly found an article and printed it out.

"Area 51? *Star Wars?*" McCauley said.

"Actually *Star Trek.*"

"Further into the abyss," McCauley complained under his breath.

Greene heard him.

"No, really. A lot of PhDs go to these things. You'd be surprised. There's real enthusiasm for research at these things."

"And a lot of people dressing up. What's he wear?" McCauley asked completely sarcastically.

"Oh, I'm so glad you asked." He handed McCauley the article. "A black jacket and a collar. He's a Vatican priest."

THIRTY-FIVE

May 10, 1633
Rome, Italy

"ASSUREDLY, WE CAN all reflect on the meaning of time," Galileo argued. "It is not ours to control any more than the truth. You may do what you want with me now, but it's temporal only to us; a pyrrhic victory for you and those who sit in judgment of science."

Father Vincenzo Maculano sat silently. His fellow inquisitors had left, as had the Vatican scribe. Just two men now, continuing to explore a most uncommon ground.

"Tell me Father, how did you find out?" Galileo asked.

The inquisitor smiled. "Quite simply. Your coterie."

"My coterie? I don't understand?"

"The thinker doesn't think?" Maculano declared. "Are you so old that you have forgotten your friends Pino and Santori?"

THIRTY-SIX

Bakersfield, CA

"FATHER ECCLESTON. JARED ECCLESTON. A Paulist. He does his research through an agency called The STOQ Project. STOQ for Science, Theology and the Ontological Quest."

"Ontological?" McCauley was unfamiliar with the term.

"Metaphysics focusing on the nature and relations of being; the essence of being."

"Oh, that ontological," McCauley joked.

"Don't worry, Dr. McCauley. I had to look it up myself," Greene admitted. "STOQ embraces chemistry, earth and environment sciences, botany, genetics, molecular biology, biochemistry, and neuroscience. But Father Eccleston also crosses over into astronomy. Kind of a Brother Astronomer. Pretty incredible turnaround for the church that made an example of Galileo."

"I guess." McCauley said not really knowing.

"Just promise me that if you figure out more, you'll give me a call. I'm dying to know."

"WHAT DO YOU THINK?" an anxious Katrina Alpert asked as they left Greene's house.

"Wait," McCauley said. "The hundred foot rule."

"The what?"

"One hundred feet. Sorry, I guess it would be more like thirty meters. Thirty meters before you talk about a house you're going to buy after you see it. Thirty meters before you discuss a job interview after you've left. Breathing room, doctor."

"Got it."

Their rental car, a Ford Fiesta was parked in front. The short walk gave McCauley only a moment to think. But even that was cut short when he noticed something.

"Keep walking to the car," he whispered, "but casually look up the street." We passed that SUV, the black one, when we got here. The engine was running. It's still running."

She saw it, though couldn't identify it by make and model. It was just big to her. "So?"

"So, that's a long time to be sitting outside on a residential street."

"My goodness, is the good doctor showing a paranoid streak?"

"Not paranoid, observant."

In the car, they buckled and slowly rolled forward. When they passed the SUV, which McCauley ID'd as a Lincoln Navigator, he glanced at the driver.

"Jesus," he said.

"Come on," she replied without concern. "It's hot, he's sitting in air conditioning, probably waiting for someone."

"Right. Us."

"Is he following?"

McCauley checked his rearview mirror. "No."

"Then…"

"He might have been waiting for us to leave."

Alpert didn't believe it.

At the first intersection off Greene's street, Meadowlane Avenue, McCauley began to meander through the suburban neighborhood.

"Where are you going?" Katrina asked. "Your freeway is the other way."

"Circling back around. I want to see if the Navigator is gone."

"Really, Quinn?"

He looped around Valley Springs Avenue, onto Mountain View Street and back to Meadowlane. As they drove down the street, McCauley was relieved that the SUV was gone.

"Okay smarty pants. See, no problem."

"You're right."

McCauley pulled a three-point turn at the end and drove by Greene's house, feeling particularly stupid that he'd been so suspicious.

At that moment, a near-ear-shattering blast pierced the silence and a shock wave fiercely pitched the Fiesta to the right. McCauley grabbed the wheel with both hands. The back of their rental took the full impact, spinning the car around. The rear window imploded.

Katrina screamed.

"Christ!" McCauley slammed on the brakes to look back.

"What?" she screamed.

McCauley knew. Fire belched from the ruins of what used to be Robert Greene's house.

THIRTY-SEVEN

McCAULEY WAS FLYING through stop signs. Alpert was struggling to hold onto her cell phone and enter a number through the high speed turns and bumps.

"What are you doing?" he shouted.

"Calling the police," Alpert cried.

"And say what?"

"A bomb blew up a house where we were, but we didn't do it. We're paleontologists visiting…"

"Good approach Dr. Alpert. And when they ask what the hell's a paleontologist and then you explain we just popped in on one of the nation's leading conspiracy quacks…what then?"

"For God's sake, Quinn. We can't just run."

"We can and we will until we're safe. Then we get help."

"At least slow down. Okay?"

McCauley nodded and let up on the gas. One block. Two blocks. It was clear. He took a deep breath. It felt like the first one in minutes.

"I think"—he glanced over to his passenger side mirror, then to his rear view mirror—"we're…" He was about to say clear. But they weren't.

McCauley hit the accelerator hard. "Shit!"

Alpert quickly looked around. McCauley flashed his left thumb backwards. "Behind us!"

"Oh my God!" she exclaimed. She saw the SUV coming up fast in her side mirror.

"You're right. Call 911! Now!" he shouted.

Alpert dialed too quickly, missing the right numbers.

"… Catching up!"

They were quickly approaching a stop sign at South Real Road and Alum.

"Hold on!"

McCauley avoided the stop, cut the corner across a lawn, and headed left down Alum.

Katrina dialed again, correctly, and waited for a 911 operator to pick up.

McCauley made another sharp left onto Sweet Water at almost double the speed limit. The force threw Alpert against her door. She dropped the phone.

"Dammit!"

The phone fell between her seat and the door. As she fumbled to find it, McCauley had to speed up even more.

"Careful!"

"Got the phone?"

"Not yet," she cried out. "What about yours?"

"In my left front pocket. Can't get to it. Will try."

McCauley checked the mirrors. He lost the SUV on the quick turn. He slowed down which allowed Katrina to lean over. She groped for the phone, extending her fingers under the seat. "It's down…"

Suddenly McCauley swerved left, just clearing a school bus that came to a stop ahead of them.

"Can you please drive straight for a few seconds?"

"I'll do my best. This isn't quite what I'm used to." He made a slower right onto Rocky Road Avenue, and another onto April Street. He was now lost in the middle of a meandering bedroom community.

Katrina touched the phone with her index finger, inching it toward her feet.

"Almost."

"Oh fuck!" McCauley declared.

The SUV crossed an intersection ahead of him.

"Hold on!"

McCauley made a sharp U-turn and accelerated, once more slamming Alpert into her seat. He turned right past a row of homes, and right again. As he passed single story houses he peered across the lawns. The SUV was barreling down a parallel street. Now it was a race.

Each vehicle ignored three stop signs as they tore through the neighborhood. Nearly losing control, McCauley careened right, back onto South Real Road. The SUV was in his rearview mirror less than a block behind.

"Forget the phone. Go to the GPS. Get the map up!"

The screen was on climate.

McCauley tried to point but couldn't take his hand off the steering wheel. "Should be upper left or right, to the side of the screen."

She took in the display and pressed the map function. "Got it."

The screen changed to a fairly tight view.

McCauley checked his rearview mirror and floored the car again. "Good. Now find a minus icon."

"Where?"

He quickly turned away. A woman started crossing the street holding a young girl's hand. McCauley hit the horn, swerved to the left and flew by the mother and child.

"You might not need to find the phone after all."

"Why?"

"The woman I nearly hit is already calling the cops."

He watched as the SUV similarly raced around the pedestrian with even less caution.

"Did you find the minus sign?"

"Not yet."

"Lower right. It's usually on the lower right of the screen. On the monitor."

"There!" she said.

"Press it until the view widens enough to show the highway. We need 99. Find us a way fast."

She tapped the icon once. Not wide enough. She pressed it again and again, which took the screen from the default five hundred foot view to about a quarter mile.

"It's in the other direction!"

"Get us there!"

"Okay, sharp left on Planz. Coming up in a block. Wait. No, there's a dead end first. The next one. Then a right on Akers, another right on…"

"One at a time."

"Okay, okay. Coming up."

The black Navigator was closing fast. The only advantage McCauley had was the knowledge of where and when he was going to turn. It might be enough to throw off his pursuer until they could have the protection of more traffic.

The straightaway on Planz gave Katrina time to re-locate the cell phone under her seat and continue to move it forward.

"He's gaining on us." The SUV was barely six car lengths behind.

They were silent for a few blocks, not that there was anything to say. Also, Alpert was concentrating on retrieving the phone.

Come on, she silently mouthed. *Come on.*

The Ford Fiesta hit a pothole. McCauley struggled to control the car. A few inches deeper and he'd have blown out the tire. The SUV careened around it giving McCauley a little more lead. But that disappeared in seconds. McCauley was now honking fiercely before every intersection. It helped him avoid two collisions, but he missed the turn onto Akers.

"Yes!" Alpert exclaimed. She grabbed the phone, brought it up to her lap and dialed.

"What's next? I couldn't turn."

"Go down, no that won't work…left on Stine Road. Next big left. Up there!"

The traffic light was with him, not with the SUV. But the pursuer blasted through nonetheless.

"Next left on White Lane. Another main street ahead." She repeated the route. "White Lane. Make a left. Then the right on a big cross street, Wible. The freeway is off Wible, but another left turn against traffic.

"Ok and call the police now!"

"Willingly!" Connected, she explained, "Hello, please just listen to me, We're in a blue Ford Fiesta, pursued at high speed by a crazy driver in a black SUV who's trying to run us off the road." She'd taken McCauley's advice and kept it to the basics. "Right now we're on"—she checked the screen—"Stine. He wants to—"

At that instant the SUV rammed their car. It took all of McCauley's wits to maintain control, but the phone flew out of Alpert's hand and hit the windshield. It bounced back and caught her right cheek.

"Where's that turn?" McCauley yelled.

Alpert ignored the pain. Her eyes shifted from the screen to the road. Getting her bearings, she shouted, "There!" She pointed straight ahead and to the left.

"Brace yourself. He's going to hit us again. Then I'm taking that turn as fast as I can."

McCauley was more prepared for the next slam. He held the wheel straight. The impact propelled them ahead again. At the last possible moment, he tapped the brake, slowing just enough to control the car through the turn. It was too fast and too late for the SUV to make the same move and he continued straight across Stine, missing White.

"Two big blocks," Alpert called out.

McCauley's hands gripped the steering wheel in the most harrowing white knuckle driving of his life. He raced through the orange light at Wible Road and made a fast cut to the on-ramp of 99, entering at sixty-eight mph and speeding up to ninety on the highway.

"We're clear."

Less than a mile down the road they heard sirens wailing.

"This might be a good time to slow down," she said.

"You think?" He said it like a joke. Katrina laughed nervously.

A minute later the Bakersfield Police cruiser was signaling them to pull over. Quinn complied. The fact that their rear bumper and trunk were smashed and the window had been blown out should certainly help their case. But they still had a lot to explain.

THIRTY-EIGHT

Kern County Sheriff's Department
Bakersfield, CA

NOW AN ENTIRELY new problem: the local police.

The Kern County Sheriff's Department had 575 authorized deputy sheriffs who patrolled Bakersfield and county streets, held down the substations, detective units and court services and ran the special investigations units. If there was an understanding officer with a sympathetic manner in the ranks, he or she had the day off. Dr. Quinn McCauley and Dr. Katrina Alpert were being questioned by an intimidating pair, Sgt. Buck Todd and Sgt. Judy Tenant. They looked like a real match. Two five-eight blonds. Short hair. Chiseled faces.

McCauley was surprised they needed separate bodies. *They could have been Siamese twins, and saved the department the cost of a uniform,* he thought.

"You heard my call to 911," Alpert stated.

"And the calls from the people you just about killed, the cars you nearly hit, and then there's the school bus," Todd glowered. He hovered over McCauley and Alpert, seated on an uncomfortable bench in a holding cell. "You're damned lucky to be alive. Here on out, I'm not so sure."

"Didn't anyone say we were being chased?" Katrina said sharply.

"Excuse me, Miss Alpert?" Tenant interrupted.

"It's Dr. Alpert," she shot back.

McCauley tapped her arm, an indication to dial back.

"May I explain again?" McCauley offered.

"You can explain," Sgt. Tenant said, "all the way to the arraignment."

"Someone will confirm that an SUV was chasing us. For Christ's sake, he rammed us! Just look at our car."

"Could've come that way." Todd argued weakly.

McCauley now realized these officers were neither detectives nor skilled investigators. They were the missing link.

"There's got to be wreckage along the route. We were driving for our lives. This man had just blown up a house and…"

This opened the door to a longer conversation, which had started when they'd been arrested on Highway 99.

"And why where you there, Doc-tor Mac-Cauley," Tenant said stretching out his name with deliberate disrespect.

"Shouldn't we have a lawyer?" Alpert whispered.

"A lawyer? People claiming innocence need a lawyer?" Todd asked.

Quinn decided to reply.

"We were discussing a research project that might have been in his field."

"Then you left and minutes later his house blew up." Tenant continued her sarcastic tone. "A little odd wouldn't you say?"

"I can't say. But that same SUV was there when we arrived and when we left."

"And this mysterious vehicle which we haven't seen. It chased *you* through the streets of Bakersfield? Do you think we're idiots?" Todd demanded. "Why would he do that?"

"Because we could identify his car…and him!"

"So in full view he tried to run you off the road," the female officer said incredulously.

"More than that, Sgt. Tenant," McCauley said. "He tried to kill us."

AN HOUR LATER, Todd returned to the holding cell. "Looks like you both have an angel on your side," he said unlocking the door. "Follow me."

They passed through two secure doors and entered the lobby. There, standing in the corner with the most recent *National Enquirer* in his hands, was a very much alive...

"Greene!" McCauley exclaimed.

"In the flesh."

It was too good to be true. Alpert ran over and hugged him. McCauley followed with a good strong handshake. Sgt. Todd held back. Tenant was at the door looking on in disgust.

"How?" Alpert asked.

Greene turned his back on the officer and gestured for them to come closer.

"Let's just say I have my own early warning systems. After you left, I watched this guy approach the door with a backpack. He left it without ringing the bell. That didn't require a PhD on my part. I scrambled down my basement stairs and into a bomb shelter I built years ago. The blast-proof room wouldn't have saved me from a direct nuclear hit, but it did me well a minute later."

Now he whispered. "So take your get-out-of-jail card and split town. That bomb was for me." He paused, took a breath and continued, "Because of you. You're onto something. I don't want to know any more unless we're live on the radio and I'm surrounded by big fucking bodyguards. Now get."

"What about you?" Alpert asked compassionately.

"I've got plans. Hell, I'll go on the air tonight talking about it from some remote location."

"Without…" McCauley didn't have to finish the question.

"Without mentioning you. There are enough conspiracies to hang this on."

"But all your archives?" Quinn asked.

"Copies. I've got copies of everything. Plus my website is in the cloud." Greene laughed. "When the insurance settles, I suspect I'll have some cash for the first time in years. That'll undoubtedly make me the subject of somebody else's conspiracy theory which, of course, will lead to more appearances. All of it, great publicity. I'll just have to roll out a new book to take advantage of it. Maybe I'll dedicate it to you."

"No thanks. But you're not concerned they'll come back?" Alpert was seriously concerned.

"Naw. I'll start deflecting it with a report of some black op. And that much is true."

"What if the insurance doesn't pony up?" McCauley asked.

"That's the best of it. Just let them try. I've got some disturbing documents on their business practices after Hurricane Cassandra that they're not going to want to see on the news. They'll know exactly what I'm talking about. All I'll need to mention is New England."

McCauley and Alpert both laughed. They hugged their newest and oddest best friend and settled up with the Kern County Sheriffs, neither of whom smiled.

THIRTY-NINE

THE HOUR DRIVE and the alone time provided the opportunity for Quinn and Katrina to talk about their lives and the twists and turns that got them to Interstate 5 heading south to Los Angles.

"Two siblings," McCauley answered when asked about his family. "An older sister and a younger brother. Both followed our parent's careers. Like my dad, Zach's a school principal, now at Moeller High in Cincinnati. Sasha is a city councillor in Scranton, like my mother was years ago."

"Are they married?"

"Yup. I'm the holdout."

"Why?" Katrina asked unashamedly. *What the fuck,* she thought. *A few hours ago we were running for our lives.*

"I suppose I've been waiting for the right one to knock on my door."

Katrina smiled inwardly. *A reference? An inference?*

"And your history?" he asked.

"Not so fast. I want to hear more about you."

"Alright, why not?" he replied. "I had a shot at a career as a ball player."

"That's a career?"

"Baseball? Absolutely! Especially if you make it to the majors."

"You were that good?"

"Well, that's something I didn't really put to a full test. But if I had and been successful, I'd probably be retired by now and running a car dealership. 'Come on down to

Quinn's and check out the fins!'" He laughed. "But, looking down the line early on, it wasn't what I wanted. So I went for my PhD in a related field."

"Paleontology is related to baseball?"

"No, but teamwork is."

She was seeing the real Quinn McCauley and liking him. Maybe more than she would admit.

"But enough of you," she said avoiding the possibility of addressing her own feelings. "Want to hear my story?"

"Yes."

"Okay, you choose which is right."

"What?" McCauley responded.

"A game. See if you can correctly determine who I am and where I came from."

"I'll try."

"Okay, here we go."

"Give me a second." She stopped to think or to bluff. He didn't know which.

"A. I was born in North London, the daughter of a sometimes fill-in sessions guitar player for the Kinks. You know the rock band."

McCauley did.

"Of course, I came along well after their '60s hits. My father actually had a real affinity for engineering. He gave up the dream of going further in music—I guess, kind of like you with baseball—he went to college and founded one of the first computer companies in England. Dad made a ton of money, met my mother at his company, and she started rolling out babies. Four of us. My three brothers and me. I'm number three. That's usually the one that's trouble. We grew up in Cambridge and I've never left. That's choice A."

"Okay, not sure, though congratulations for knowing one of your country's greatest R&B crossover bands. What's B?"

"B is sadder and still difficult for me talk about. My mum was married to a British soldier who was killed defending the Falklands against Argentina. She struggled for years, got remarried to a local insurance agent, but I always felt her heart was with her first husband, not my dad. It caused problems through the years and they finally divorced six years ago."

"Sisters or brothers?"

"Oh, yes. My identical twin sister Nicole. She's older by four minutes."

"Another you. I can't imagine."

Katrina hit him in the arm. "Shut up and listen."

"I'm listening."

"My mother's proudest moment was seeing us both graduate from university with PhDs Nicole's is in molecular biology. And mine, well, you know. Nicky's married with a second child on the way."

Katrina gave McCauley a confident smile. "What do you think?"

"Plausible, uplifting at the end. Do you have a C?"

"Of course. You'll love C. My father is a member of Parliament. The House of Commons. He used his influence to get me into Cambridge and ultimately secure an appointment. My mother was a food columnist for *News of the World* in London until Murdoch shut it down after the wiretapping scandal. Now she's got a food blog and a regular spot on the BBC. We can watch her on the channel website."

"Siblings?"

"One. Younger. Jake. He's a fashion photographer."

"Married?" Quinn asked.

"No, but he gets laid a lot."

McCauley laughed while keeping his eye on the road. "I bet."

"So, Dr. McCauley. Which is it? A, B, or C?"

After debating the possibilities, judging her delivery, and considering the finer points of history, McCauley chose correctly.

FORTY

Interstate 5

HALFWAY TO Los Angeles, Katrina fell asleep. It had been a long, life-threatening, exhausting day. He was sufficiently worried for their well-being as well as the students under his care. They all faced danger. He didn't know from whom, but the *why* was becoming increasingly evident.

About an hour out of LA, just beyond the section on the I-5 known as The Grapevine, a memory triggered. Years ago he'd seen a History Channel documentary about a British World War II officer with a unique talent. *Maybe. Just maybe.*

He decided to call Al Jaffe and talk through a plan.

Minutes later

"HOLY, SHIT!" WAS all Jaffe could muster when McCauley explained.

"Now listen carefully, Al. I need your help, just yours. No one else. Nothing illegal to worry about, but it's vitally important you don't tell anyone. Are you up for it?"

Jaffe had never been asked to fulfill such a request. "I guess…"

"Al, this is for everyone's safety. Please. Immediately. I'm trusting you."

"What about Rich?"

"No. Only you."

McCauley's real reason for not including Rich Tamburro was his growing suspicion about Anna Chohany. *Why did she go into the cave that night?*

McCauley didn't share his reason for keeping it from Tamburro, but he'd have to explain it somehow. That would require more thought.

"Okay. What should I do?" Jaffe asked.

"First, tell everyone we'll be back in a day. We're working on travel plans now. But they have to stay clear of the new site."

"Got it."

"Finish cataloguing what everyone's working on. Trent's a speedster at that. Move him into even higher gear. Then box up and get ready to break camp."

"We're leaving?"

"We may have to."

"They'll want to know why."

"Potential gas in the caves."

"Really, Dr. McCauley?"

McCauley ignored the question.

"The next thing—listen carefully—look up a man named Jasper Maskelyne. You'll easily find him on the Internet. I want you to check out an operation he executed during World War II." McCauley explained more. "Okay?"

"Can do," Jaffe said with true excitement.

"Any concerns about going solo?"

"Nope."

"Good. Now pass the word to pack up. And good luck."

JAFFE PULLED EVERYONE together under the home base tent.

"Doc called. He's driving down to LA from Bakersfield. They met Greene and based on what he learned, we have to stay clear of the cave."

"Why?" Lobel asked.

"Well, apparently there's an issue with gas. Or the possibility there could be."

"Gas?" asked Cohen.

"Something to do with similar facilities. Yes, we may have stumbled across a sophisticated monitoring station through a separate entrance."

"That shuts down electronics?" Cohen continued.

"Doc said *sophisticated*. We need to read it as a warning."

"This is fucked," Carlos complained.

Leslie Cohen added, "If there's an issue with gas, I'm outta here."

"We all might be going?"

"What?" Trent asked.

"Dr. McCauley will fill us in tomorrow. For now, let's do what he said."

The team broke up. Al Jaffe went to McCauley's tent for privacy. There he Googled the British officer named Maskelyne.

McCAULEY MADE ANOTHER strategic call on the way to LA.

"Hi, Rich. How's Anna doing?"

"Okay. Disappointed and a little depressed that she's not out with us."

"I'm sure. Give her my best. I know it's not easy."

"Hey, neither is searching for one-hundred-million-year-old bones no one else has discovered," he joked. "What's up?"

"Rich, I wouldn't ask you to do this if I didn't consider it terribly important."

"What?

"Be careful what you tell Anna from here on out."

"Why?" He raised his voice, immediately sensitive to criticism.

"Because…" McCauley stopped short, concerned how best to frame his misgivings, considering Tamburro's romantic relationship with Chohany. "It's hard to explain. I'll do better when we get back."

"You can't just drop that bomb and leave it like that. Why?"

McCauley gave an answer with as much conviction as possible. "We've been advised to keep this under wraps for now."

"I get that," Tamburro said, "but Anna just wants to know."

"Of course. But there are two other reasons." The first was a lie. "We don't want to worry her and there's the chance, probably unintentionally, she told someone what we blundered into."

"Impossible."

"I said *probably unintentionally*, Rich. And I have no reason to think otherwise, but remember, she was the one who went into the tunnel on her own. You have to wonder why, too."

Tamburro considered the point. "And the second reason?"

"Well, there was a problem." McCauley told Tamburro about the attack on Greene.

The young man was appalled and defensive. "And you think Anna… ?"

"I never said that."

"Bullshit. You implied. That's enough."

"Look, Rich, I'm sure you're right. But we're feeling a little edgy right now and I'm thinking about everyone's welfare. Including Anna's."

They hung up. In spite of his indignation, Tamburro began to wonder why Anna had struck out on her own.

KATRINA ALPERT CALLED the television producer Greene mentioned. The conversation didn't go far. It was short and frustrating.

"Felt like the third degree from the receptionist."

"Do you think you'll get a call back?" McCauley asked.

"Doubtful."

Alpert was correct. The message went unanswered through check-in at The Sportsman's Lodge in Studio City and dinner at The Daily Grill on Ventura Boulevard.

They returned to the legendary San Fernando Valley hotel, worn out, yet more alert and aware of their surroundings. McCauley worked out how they should survey the environment and signal each other if they saw anything out of the ordinary. Now everything and everyone was suspect: The man sitting alone in the lobby with a newspaper. *Was he reading or watching them?* The woman on her cell in the corner. *Was she reporting to someone on their whereabouts?* The security guard who seemed to take an active interest in them. *Had some cash turned him into an informer?*

"Keep talking and walking," McCauley said.

"Take my hand," she added.

That wasn't hard at all. It eased the anxiety they both felt. Two minutes later, they were still hand in hand as they exited the elevator. They continued to walk to Katrina's room, next to and adjoining Quinn's.

This is where it became awkward. He released her hand.

"Well, here we are."

"Yes. Here we are."

They sounded like bumbling high school students on a first date. Thirty seconds of uncomfortable silence didn't improve the situation.

Finally, McCauley said, "I think we should call it a night."

"Right. It's been a long day. I've got a few emails to send if I can even keep my eyes open."

"Same here."

"Well, good night," he said.

"Good night."

"Will you be okay?"

"Sure. You?" Katrina asked in return.

"Yup. But make sure you double lock."

"Will do."

"I'll leave my door unlocked though, just in case."

"Just in case."

FORTY-ONE

FELICIA DUNBAR HAD summoned Kavanaugh to her outer office, another breach of protocol that infuriated him like everything she did. "Mr. Kavanaugh, you have an appointment at Brown's in an hour."

"No I don't," he shot back to the contemptible assistant he'd inherited.

"It's the regular date that Mr. Gruber always kept and you're…"

"Ms. Dunbar, apparently I need to remind you that Mr. Gruber is no longer with us, you may put his calendar away. I'll keep my own."

She straightened up in her office chair, which served to eliminate all the folds in her expensive gray jacket. Kavanaugh really had no idea who she was, where she came from, whether she was single or married, or how she lived. All he knew was what he saw in her body language, which he despised.

"Another thing," Kavanaugh continued, "I've been thinking that it would be best to make some changes here at the magazine. I'm sure you can understand that I need to have my own team."

"Oh," she said, removing her reading glasses. She

folded the frames and put them on her desk in the exact place where they always were.

"You faithfully served Mr. Gruber for years. No one can question your devotion. I assure you I'll review your file and provide you with a more than adequate severance package and a letter of recommendation."

She listened to him showing no emotion.

"You obviously had a strong working relationship with Mr. Gruber. Those bonds are hard to break. I understand. I hope you recognize my position."

Still no response.

"I'm sure we can tidy this up amicably by the end of the week." Kavanaugh smiled insincerely.

"Thank you for your offer, Mr. Kavanaugh," Dunbar finally replied. "However, proper arrangements have already been made." She matched his callous smile. "My *path* has been set for years."

Kavanaugh felt the lingering presence of Martin Gruber from his grave. *Will he ever go away?*

He prepared to leave, but Dunbar began the conversation again. "As I stated, Mr. Kavanaugh, you have an appointment at Brown's. Eighteen-thirty sharp. Your regular table."

"I'll be there," he replied with open hostility.

Although he didn't watch, he just knew that she'd picked up her glasses again, rolled closer to the computer and got back to the job she wasn't going to leave on his account.

Los Angeles, CA
The same time

QUINN AND KATRINA drove to the TV production company office a few miles away on Lankershim Blvd. They were there by 10:15 A.M., without a meeting scheduled.

Alpert took the lead with the receptionist.

"I'm Dr. Katrina Alpert from Cambridge University in England. This is Dr. Quinn McCauley from Yale. We're both paleontologists. I left a message yesterday for Mr. Krein. Since we're on a tight research time frame, we do *need* to see him this morning. Can you let him know? We won't take much time, but it's *urgent*."

She had stressed two words in particular: *need* and *urgent*.

Alpert wasn't certain if she was addressing the same person she'd spoken to on the phone, so she added more. "Oh, and please mention that Robert Greene said it was very important that we get together."

"Once again, you are?"

McCauley looked away totally frustrated. The young redhead had just fulfilled his stereotypical image of a Hollywood airhead.

Alpert slowly repeated their names.

"Please take a seat, Dr. Al-bert," she said immediately underscoring McCauley's impression.

"It's Al*pert*. Doctors Alpert and McCauley. We're," she decided not to say paleontologists again. "We're dinosaur scientists."

"I'll try Mr. Krein's assistant," the young woman said.

"Thank you," Katrina said.

They waited ten minutes, mostly watching the receptionist text between calls. Finally, another woman, barely a few years older, came through the doors. She had black hair with red streaks and wore a short navy blue skirt, a yellow button-down linen shirt and two inch heels.

"Dr. Al-bert?" She automatically addressed McCauley.

"Yes," Katrina said offering her hand. "It's Dr. Al*pert*." She stressed the correction. "And Dr. McCauley."

"I'm Autumn, Gene's assistant."

"Autumn?" Katrina tried to stifle a laugh. "Very pretty name." *Very LA.* "Nice to meet you."

"Thank you. But I'm sorry to say Gene can't fit you in today. He's in edit hell with network notes."

McCauley quickly deduced that Autumn was the gate-keeper and Krein was dodging them. He was about to respond, but Katrina beat him.

"Excuse me? What does that mean?"

Autumn seemed surprised by the question. *Everyone knew what network notes were, didn't they?* "Sorry, he's dealing with changes from the network."

Katrina smirked. She raised her finger to make a point. Autumn cut her off.

"He can't leave the edit bay." Her eyes darted. Now she acted more stressed than surprised. "And he's really under the gun."

Under the gun? McCauley thought it was an interesting choice of words. However, he responded tactfully. "Of course, we understand. We'll only take ten minutes. Robert Greene said Mr. Krein—ah, Gene—was the best person in television to meet." He decided to throw in some bait. "We're onto something that he will be *very* interested in hearing."

"Well, we have a website portal where you can pitch your ideas."

Shit! That didn't work.

"Listen, I apologize if I don't have the TV jargon down, but this isn't about pitching or submitting, or whatever you call it." McCauley gave up the niceties. "I can't emphasize strongly enough that we need to speak with Mr. Krein. Ten minutes, that's all. Ten minutes."

Autumn was unprepared and inexperienced for an escalating situation. She lost her composure.

"He can't possibly see you. You have to leave. Goodbye."

She turned on her heels and spoke sharply to the receptionist. McCauley and Alpert easily overheard her say, "If they don't leave immediately, call the North Hollywood police."

"What the…?" Katrina whispered much too loudly. "I can't believe it!"

"Believe it. Krein obviously heard about Greene," McCauley said as they cleared the door. "And he's scared."

"Well, join the club," she added.

The English Tea Room, Brown's Hotel
London

COLIN KAVANAUGH WAS led to the regular table. Like clockwork, Gruber's waiter appeared.

"Good day to you, Mr. Kavanaugh. So pleased to see you."

"Thank you, ah…" Kavanaugh hesitated, trying to remember the waiter's name.

"Leon, Mr. Kavanaugh. Not a problem."

"Thank you, Leon."

"Of course. And may I add that it's a pleasure to see you carrying on an important tradition."

"Yes. Tradition is important."

"Then I will assume you'll be in more frequently?"

"As often as possible."

"More than that, Mr. Kavanaugh." Leon leaned forward and quietly repeated, "More than that."

The comment stung as sharply as those of his assistant.

Leon straightened to a proper waiter's posture. "Now, will it be an Earl Grey, sir?"

"That will be fine, Leon," Kavanaugh managed.

"I also suggest you try the plain scones with clotted

cream and the strawberry preserves. They're delicious and among Mr. Gruber's favorites."

"Yes."

"And as an old teacher of mine once said, let a word to the wise be sufficient, sir."

"And that would be?" he snapped.

"Mr. Kavanaugh, you walk in the footsteps of your esteemed predecessor and those before him. You are part of an organization, not the organization."

The construction of the statement, like the other things he'd heard that day, was unmistakable. *A warning.*

"Leon."

"Yes, sir."

Kavanaugh motioned with his finger to come closer. Now within earshot he continued. "Who are you?"

Leon pulled back and gave a proper smile. "Why, just another servant, sir. Nothing more, nothing less, though perhaps with a *soupçon* of grace you won't see elsewhere," he chuckled. "I'm simply a lifelong, loyal employee."

Anyone who might have overheard the response would have considered it merely the comment of an appropriately devoted Brown's waiter. But no one heard. The standard *Voyages* table was separate from the others in the austere tea room.

"And, if I may, I would recommend a nice walk in the park after your tea."

North Hollywood, CA
The same time

"Now what?" Katrina said as they got into their distressed Fiesta.

"And where?" McCauley clamped his eyes shut in thought. "We need to track down the archeologist teacher."

"Start driving to the airport. I'll look him up. Remember the guy's name?"

"How could I forget a college history professor with the name DeCoursey Fales?"

It did seem unbelievable, but Katrina's Internet search proved him right. She read as they drove. "Here it is. Dr. DeCoursey Fales, archeologist and professor of history at Emerson College, Boston. Noted for his in-depth study of a single two-feet high Athenian black-figured vase from sixth century BC, considered the most important find of its kind, discovered in a tomb at Vulci, an ancient Etruscan town in northern Italy."

"Aren't there caves in that region? Big ones?" McCauley asked.

"I think you're right. There's more." She paraphrased now. "The vase is decorated with some two hundred mythological figures including Achilles and Ajax. Apparently a real historic and cultural treasure." Katrina looked up. "So he could very well have...."

McCauley completed the sentence. "Discovered something else." He merged onto the 101 Freeway West for the first leg to LAX with renewed excitement. "Let's go find Professor Fales."

Katrina returned to the Google homepage and clicked on a *New York Times* abstract. "Uh oh."

"What?"

"I think I know where the good professor is. But we won't be able to speak to him. He died in 2000."

He slammed his hand on the steering wheel and sped up. "Damn! Two dead ends."

"I'll check on his publications as long as you don't start driving like we're back in Bakersfield again," she only half-joked. "And I'll see about the spelunker and the priest."

"Yeah, right. I can only <u>imagine,</u>" McCauley said.

Fifteen minutes later, they ground to a halt on Interstate 405, the quickest way to LAX when traffic moved, which was rare. Right now, it didn't matter much. McCauley and Alpert had no idea where they were going.

Kensington Gardens
London
The same time

As KAVANAUGH STROLLED to the park bench, he decided to project a better attitude, at least publicly. He noted that someone was already seated in the bench that abutted his.

After a short time, some of which Kavanaugh used to feed peanuts to the squirrels, he initiated the password routine.

"Usually things go well," the man who went by the name Marvin quietly said. "This time, *we* moved too quickly."

Kavanaugh felt the *we* was aimed at him. He rubbed his scalp with one hand and with the other, threw more peanuts at the squirrels. Then, emphasizing the word his own way, he responded, "Well, *we* need to fix this!"

Marvin chuckled, "An arrangement is already in progress."

"Since this is the first operation on my watch, I especially welcome your help. I would like the details, however. Details meaning more than cursory overview. I'm sure you understand."

Kavanaugh expected Marvin to reply. He didn't.

Kavanaugh shifted slightly and tossed the remaining

peanuts on the grass. This allowed him to glance over his shoulder.

His companion was gone.

FORTY-TWO

Glendive Medical Center, MT

"How ya feeling sweetheart?" Tamburro asked Chohany.

"Embarrassed. Ridiculous. Stupid. Out of it."

She was, and so far Anna, as McCauley suggested, wasn't opening up.

"Doctors say you might be out in a few days."

"Hope so."

"The best thing now is for you to get more rest," Tamburro replied.

"Can't wait to get back," she said. "What's the latest on the dig and the cave?"

"Not sure."

"What kind of answer is that?"

"We're waiting for Dr. McCauley to come back tomorrow. But we might be shutting it down."

This was more than he wanted to reveal.

"Really? Why?"

"Too dangerous. Potential pockets of gas."

"Come on, Rich. You told me it was amazing and when Leslie visited she couldn't stop talking about…"

"The doc got word that it's off limits," he said.

"You're holding out on me."

He was.

"Nope. We might move to another site. Not sure yet. I guess there are some insurance issues considering what happened."

Guilt could work, he thought. He hoped.

"I'm sorry," she offered.

Rich Tamburro moved closer to her. "It's okay. Look, we met each other. I consider it a great summer."

"Thanks." She sighed deeply. "Maybe I'll get a little sleep. Wanna lie down with me?"

TWENTY MINUTES LATER, Rich Tamburro rolled off the bed and tiptoed around the room. Anna's phone was on the nightstand, but he didn't want to be too obvious. After a moment, he reached into his pocket to look at his cell. He swore under his breath, suggesting—in case she were actually awake—that his battery was dead. Tamburro casually picked up her cell and turned away. He knew her password, and although he felt guilty, he checked her email and texts. What he saw made him exhale slowly.

Tamburro thought hard about what to do next. With his back to her, he created screenshots of three texts and immediately forwarded them to his phone. There were more, but he heard Anna stir so he deleted the screenshots from her camera and the texts he'd sent.

"Hey, what gives?" she asked, apparently waking up. "Come back to bed."

She watched Rich return the phone to the nightstand. "Hope it was okay. My battery was dead. Trying to reach Jaffe."

"No problem," she replied, fully aware that he was stumbling through an explanation. "Let me check on *your* battery right now."

"But…?"

"There are always ways, sweetheart."

It took him awhile. There were other things now on his mind.

Hertz Rental Car office
Los Angeles International Airport
Later

"Doc, I THINK you were right," Tamburro said. He began to describe Anna's text messages, but McCauley was simultaneously listening to the Hertz salesperson closing out his rental agreement.

"I'm sorry, sir. Same issue," the rental agent stated. She was a fifty-something African American woman with a pleasant smile and a reassuring tone.

"Hold on a sec, Rich."

"This card was declined, too," the agent said. "Do you have another we can try?"

"Yes, sure." McCauley handed her a third.

"Thank you. No worries."

While she ran the charge for the car, McCauley jumped back on the phone.

"Still there? Rich?"

"Yup," Tamburro said. "Just saw Anna at the hospital. Heading to the parking lot now."

The woman shook her head again.

"Damn. Hold on again, Rich. I've got a problem with my cards. Must have maxed out when we bought all the stuff."

McCauley got Katrina's attention. "Can you talk to Rich? I've gotta deal with the account."

"Sure," she said.

McCauley handed over the phone.

"Hi, Rich. It's Katrina. What's up?"

McCauley apologized. Once again, the Hertz representative said, "No worries." But she wasn't the one who needed to come up with a solution.

"I think your system doesn't like my cards," he said fumbling through his wallet. His Bank of America and

Chase debit cards and a Citibank credit card were all declined. He retrieved an American Express Jet Blue card. "Let's try this one."

"Okay," she pleasantly offered.

She swiped the credit card once. Then again. "Dr. McCauley, do you have any another means of paying? This card was also declined."

McCauley, completely frustrated, looked for Katrina. She was still on the call, obviously engrossed in the conversation.

McCauley addressed the Hertz sales woman again. "I… I…" he stammered as he fumbled through his wallet. "One more left." It was an American Express departmental credit card, his emergency backup. "Okay," he sheepishly offered, "this better work."

The woman swiped the card. This clearly wasn't her first time through such difficulties. Her training taught her to keep the customer calm.

That wasn't necessary. "The charge went through, Dr. McCauley. Everything's good." She returned the card with the receipt for $794.00 which included the $500 deductible for the damage.

After the paperwork was printed and signed she directed him to the airport shuttle kiosk. "The bus stops at all the terminals. Out the sliding doors and at the curb. I hope you'll have a good day."

McCauley looked over to Alpert who was still on the phone and pacing.

"I think I'm about to find out."

ALPERT PRESSED END and handed the phone back to McCauley.

"More," she said.

"More what?"

"More problems?"

"Same here," he added. "You first."

"Outside. Your hundred-foot rule."

They pulled their rolling suitcases, walked past the shuttle bus stop into the parking area, and settled on a bench out of earshot of other customers.

"Rich found texts on Anna's phone while she was sleeping. They were to an international number. He's forwarding them."

"And?"

"You were right. She was leaking information."

"To whom?"

"No name, but multiple texts," Katrina continued.

"Go on."

"The cave, the tunnel, the drawings and whatever else she learned from Rich and Leslie, too, even after she fell."

"Christ!" McCauley exclaimed.

"She described it as something inexplicable. Something technical."

"When?"

Alpert knew the next revelation wasn't going to go down easily. "Here's the worst of it. Before she went to the hospital and after."

McCauley ran his hand through his hair.

"It gets worse," she continued.

"How?"

"A text from the other day said we were heading to see Greene in Bakersfield."

Glendive Medical Center, MT
The same time

ANNA CHOHANY SENT another text. Like the others, it wasn't answered. She had a phone number to call in case there was something absolutely urgent. She'd been told to use it only once. After that it would be disconnected. This was the time to try.

Anna caught the attention of a nurse and asked her to close her door. Once alone, she dialed.

On the fourth ring a man with a deep, monotone, but friendly voice answered.

"Yes, Anna."

Chohany was surprised that she was addressed so personally and informally.

"I sent a text a few minutes ago."

"I have it. Is there something else we need to know?"

The *we* threw her. She never really thought about a *we* or much about the research organization that had contacted her right after she was accepted for the summer dig. There was competitive money in the field—from museums, universities and even pharmaceuticals. Based on the little she gathered and the $12,500 she'd been given, she figured no harm, no foul. It would have been, had it not been for her accident.

"I... I don't know."

"Anna, what is it you want to tell me? It's all right."

Chohany was a back channel, one of many that covered explorations around the globe. She'd be surprised to find out how extensive a network there was and how long it had been around. Most of the time it led to nothing. But not here. Not now. Anna Chohany's reporting had put into motion the kind of concern that Martin Gruber and his predecessors had operated on for centuries and Colin Kavanaugh seized on now.

The voice on the phone sounded reassuring, so she told him what Rich Tamburro had done.

FORTY-THREE

TWO MEN SPOKE cryptically on the sat phone. One was in London walking through Kensington Park, the other in a vacant hangar at the abandoned Glasgow AFB, seventeen miles north of the town of Glasgow in eastern Montana.

The facility, activated in 1957, had been home to the 467th Fighter Group and a base for Air Defense Command interceptors. In 1960, at the height of the Cold War, operations were transferred to the Strategic Air Command which tasked B-52C and B-52D bombers.

The wing was inactivated in February, 1963 and the airport was shut down in 1968 for five years.

In 1973, Glasgow was rehabilitated, intended as an Army Safeguard Anti-Ballistic Missile depot. But, the construction was never completed. The base closed again in 1976.

Today it offered the perfect place for work to go unobserved.

"Run through the schedule," the man in London instructed. They'd never met the caller, but they recognized the voice and the clipped delivery. So would Colin Kavanaugh from his conversations on the park bench.

"The talent is in place. We're on time. Thirty-six hours away from curtain."

"Are we feeling any pressure from the stars?"

"None. We aim to please. The backers will enjoy a successful opening night."

Nothing else would be gained through a longer conversation. It was said without saying it. The mission, strike target, payload and deployment were all moving forward as planned. He'd report the basics to Kavanaugh when they next met.

Outside the LAX Hertz office

"It can't be connected," Katrina declared.

"Can and is. The bombing, the chase and now they shut down my bank accounts. Ten to one, yours are also frozen," he explained.

"Who?"

"Whoever they are, they're very powerful. If these people have access to my credit cards and have Chohany on their payroll, I can't imagine what they're capable of."

"They'll kill us."

"No they won't," McCauley said, simply because it was the thing to say.

"Jesus, McCauley. What the hell am I even doing here? I was supposed to be sunning myself in Belize or at the least evaluating some wild ass dinosaur doc who had no real discoveries to his credit. Now—" she stopped, realizing what she'd said. "I'm sorry Quinn. I didn't mean that."

"It's all right."

"No, it's not. And honestly, it was total bullshit. I'm just scared."

Dr. Alpert broke down.

McCauley took her into his arms. Though he didn't say it, he was actually relieved. Until this moment, he didn't completely know if he could trust her.

KATRINA PULLED HERSELF together and walked back inside the Hertz office. She casually inserted her debit card into the ATM. It was declined. She turned around and mouthed a definitive, *No* to McCauley who stood across the lobby.

"Try another," McCauley implored. Four more credit cards; two from Citibank, one Barclays, and one American Express. Four more declined.

She rejoined McCauley. "What are we going to do?" she asked.

"I've got 250 dollars and my Yale card. But it's only a matter of time before that gets shut down. What about you?"

She checked her wallet. "I have 440 US dollars and 300 in British pounds. We sure can't buy airline tickets with cash."

"Right, but it's good for a cab downtown to the Los Angeles County Natural History Museum."

"What for?

"To see a friend."

Museum of Natural History
Los Angeles, CA

THE RIDE FROM Hertz was ninety-five dollars; with tip, $115. That left McCauley with only $135. He hoped his unannounced visit would pay off.

"Ever been here?" he asked Katrina.

"No. Remember, I've got the Natural History Museum in London. Hard to top that."

"Oh, I think you'll be impressed," he offered.

"Do they have a children's program where you can sleep with the dinosaurs?" she asked. "I've taken friends' kids to the London program."

"Don't know if they do. They have a knockout exhibit

with three Tyrannosaurus rex showing their growth spurts. There's a two-year-old baby, a thirteen-year-old juvenile, and a fully-grown seventeen-year-old that's seventy percent complete. They named it Thomas."

"How cute. Like the engine."

"Like a thirty-four foot long, 7,000 pound engine that tore through Southeastern Montana," he replied.

McCauley automatically looked around to see if they were being followed. He'd done the same thing during the cab drive. It looked safe now; however he wanted to speed them along. He took Katrina's hand. "Let's hope my friend *fondly* remembers me."

"Why *fondly*?"

"I gave her an incredibly hard time when I was a teaching assistant at Harvard. Probably harder than anyone I've ever had. But I saw great potential and I drove her in her studies, on an expedition, and right through her PhD."

"Sounds like an evolutionary tale."

"Yes. She's now curator and director of the Dinosaur Institute."

"Maybe you should go in alone. I mean, that way you two can get caught up."

McCauley closed his eyes and let out a chuckle.

"Oh, no. You're coming with me. Dr. Marli Bellamy is way tougher than Thomas ever was. When I said, 'fondly,' I meant that I hope she'll take pity on us and not bite my head off since I gave her such a hard time."

"MARLI, GREAT TO see you!" Quinn exclaimed the moment Dr. Bellamy greeted them in Dinosaur Hall.

"Not a problem. Well, not yet. Depends," said the museum's resident paleontologist. She was a beautiful, statuesque brunette with a pronounced New England Brahmin accent. She could have passed for a young Katherine Hepburn, especially in her black pantsuit, white blouse and red scarf.

"You've done a great job here," McCauley continued. "I've read about your new exhibits and how you've increased membership and traffic. Impressive in this day and age."

"Well, fortunately, some kids still get excited about dinosaurs. But it's a struggle. So, throughout the year we run all night dino-snoozes, patterned after what London's done."

Katrina gave McCauley a smart-ass grin.

"What?" Dr. Bellamy said, gauging Katrina's obvious reaction.

McCauley jumped back in, wrestling control. "Dr. Bellamy, meet Dr. Alpert, from Cambridge University. She was just filling me in on the program in England."

The women exchanged handshakes.

"Nice to meet you. You wouldn't be Dr. Katrina Alpert?"

"Yes."

"I've read your work on the South Africa expeditions. Very impressive." Bellamy turned to McCauley. "And I see you've upped the company you keep."

"Thank you, Marli."

Katrina mouthed the word *fondly* as a joke.

"Want a tour?"

"Sure. We can walk and talk."

For the next ten minutes they toured the fourteen thousand square foot space known as Dinosaur Hall. The LA Natural History Museum, under Dr. Bellamy's supervision, had expanded the collection of fossils and dinosaurs. Marli Bellamy had lived up to her potential.

"So, can I assume you haven't come to tell me you're finally giving me the grade I deserved?"

"You assume right."

"What a shame. You robbed me."

"You didn't deserve an A."

"Maybe so," Bellamy laughed. "You made me work for everything."

"That was my job. But maybe I have a way for you to earn that grade after all."

"Oh?"

"We need five thousand dollars," he said without hesitation. "Call it a loan."

"What?" Bellamy exclaimed.

"Ten thousand," Katrina interrupted. "We'll need ten thousand dollars."

"Why?"

Even McCauley was surprised.

"There are two of us," she whispered, hitting him on his side.

"How about we explain in your office?"

Glasgow AFB, MT
The same time

MONEY WAS NO issue for the three men at the abandoned Air Force base. All the resources necessary had been deposited in their accounts. Moreover, they were on schedule, each working on separate parts of the mission.

Three men. Hardcore military types with three different accents. They all went by first names only. Not their own. They were motivated by two things—duty and money. Though in the privacy of their own thoughts, it was probably only one.

Franklin, Winston, and Conrad. An American, a Brit, and a German. They'd worked together before. Mostly in silence, as they did now. It's what they preferred, what the rules required. They only spoke to get the job done.

Franklin, the American, did not discuss the last assignment he'd remotely overseen. To his mind it had been botched by an aide. The target survived and two collateral subjects got in the way. Without orders, his field man pursued them until it was necessary to break off. Franklin was pissed, but he couldn't be in two places at the same time. He figured he'd have opportunity to clean up the mess, if and when the order came.

The American stood six foot five. He'd been trained by the Marines and went rogue after being approached by a recruiter who offered a much more lucrative life without a tax bite.

Winston had a somewhat different story. He'd been an SAS officer who concluded that his country, like much of Europe, was losing its cultural identity and religious heritage to Muslim immigrants. When the offer came to the prematurely graying special forces operative, he jumped at the opportunity. Of the three, he was more inclined to truly believe in the cause.

Conrad was the shortest, the angriest, and possibly the deadliest of the bunch. Five-seven, scarred and bald. He wasn't pretty to look at, and he didn't care. He couldn't even remember how many people he'd killed: men and women, politicians, spies, clergy, explorers, reporters, former partners. They were all the same. Nothing to get weepy about. Merely assignments and targets.

This unholy alliance teamed, as they'd done before, to re-configure a private Cessna 150 for a new purpose. Franklin had bought it from a pilot in Prescott, AZ two days earlier and flown it to the retired Air Force landing strip.

Winston came to the site in a Winnebago he'd rented

in Denver. Along the way he stopped at various hardware stores and Walmarts, purchasing everything on his specific shopping list.

Conrad had the more difficult job. He was in charge of delivering the package that the Cessna would soon carry. For his part, he had to drive extremely carefully and not raise suspicion. For a man with a short temper and deadly intent, he was extremely cautious.

They were a day-and-a-half away from finishing. It went without saying that with only one pass, everything would have to work.

Los Angeles Natural History Museum

"Do I LOOK like the bank?" Bellamy said sitting behind her desk. She motioned for her uninvited and now seemingly broke guests to sit in the twin high back chairs that faced her.

McCauley nodded in the affirmative. "As a matter of fact."

"You son of a bitch, Quinn McCauley."

"Allow me to explain to Dr. Alpert. Marli is filthy rich."

"Quinn!" Bellamy exclaimed.

"Old family money and new personal causes make for a remarkable philanthropist," he continued. "None better."

"Okay, okay," she said. "Flattery doesn't mean you're going to get a dime."

"Not a dime, Dr. Bellamy," Katrina said. "We're in trouble and we need cash. A lot."

McCauley started to speak up.

"No, not you, Quinn." Marli focused on Katrina. "I like this woman. Go on."

"It's serious," she admitted.

"How serious?"

"Very. Our credit and debit cards have been cancelled. No, co-opted, hacked. And we have to get back to Montana. God only knows where we'll go from there. Quinn said you were the only person he could trust."

Marli laughed. "I'm also the only person he knows in LA. But tell me why."

"You don't want to know. Not really. Let's just say we uncovered something that's caused a little stir."

McCauley shivered at the understatement. "Trust us, Marli, less is best."

"What the hell did you find?" Bellamy asked not letting up. "A new species? The Holy Grail?"

"Neither," McCauley laughed. He ran through the high points, describing the discovery in general and the questions they had. Then they got to the bombing at Greene's.

"That was you?" she exclaimed. "I heard about it on the news."

"That's us," Alpert offered lightly.

"See, you're better off not knowing more, Marli. If anyone asks, you never even saw us."

Dr. Bellamy looked at a picture on her desk. It was her graduation photo from Harvard, a graduation that Quinn McCauley had a big hand in. After a half minute she stood.

"Will you excuse me? I've got to make a bank run. In the meantime, grab something in the commissary," she smiled, "if you can afford it."

FORTY-FOUR

Los Angeles Natural History Museum
An hour later

THE CHOICES WERE LIMITED. Six-plus hours out of LAX, Burbank or Ontario and four flights to get back to Glendive's Dawson Community Airport, or…

"I'm booking you on a private jet out of Van Nuys," Marli said.

"No you're not," McCauley argued.

"Yes I am. Based on the nothing you've shared, better you don't mingle with the riffraff."

"But the expense?" he said.

"Mark up my transcript to an A+," the former student responded. "I'll call us even."

She counted out the cash. "Here's your money. In 50s and 100s. But you're going to need some plastic. I can give you…"

"No. Nothing with your name on it. We'll pick up some pre-paid credit cards at a 7-11 or a few supermarkets."

Katrina was impressed.

"Can we get a cab downstairs?"

"Yes, but no. I'm driving and I'll book the plane on the way." Marli checked her watch. "It's 1:30 now. We should get you out no later than four or five."

"How far is Van Nuys?"

"It's in the Valley. If there's no traffic, which there shouldn't be at this hour, it'll be about forty minutes.

"I don't know how to thank you," Katrina said.

"Just take care of Quinn, will you? I have a soft spot for endangered species."

THEY TOOK OFF at 4:45 in a Citation 5. The winds were with them and the captain said they'd land at 8:25 P.M. Mountain Time. A few hours later, Quinn and Katrina cleared arrival. They were met by Al Jaffe who had gotten McCauley's text from one of his new phones.

"How was the flight?"

"Bumpy," Katrina quickly complained. "Small plane. Not my favorite. And I always worry about them crashing."

FORTY-FIVE

Glasgow AFB, MT

WINSTON REVIEWED THE photographs he'd tacked up on the hangar wall. He had no doubt he'd programmed the right coordinates into the GPS, but real-time corrections were inevitable. It would have been far easier if the mission could have been accomplished with a military drone.

A simple commercial observational drone, such as the Puma AE, about the size of an adult golden eagle wouldn't cut it. They needed military strength. But what they had in the works had been field-proven and effective. Moreover, it offered a good cover story.

Franklin guaranteed the Cessna would be flying in another day. Winston was finalizing his guidance system strap-ons. Conrad had to wait for them to finish before he brought the most critical part of the assignment onboard—the payload.

They worked with light and electricity from the Winnebago. It was not particularly hard, but extremely precise. Except for Conrad's contributions and Franklin's flying, the rest could have been accomplished by very smart high school robotics students and a teacher with deniability.

FORTY-SIX

Makoshika State Park, MT

JAFFE LED MCCAULEY alone to the site. The professor looked across the landscape.

"Damn! Good work, Al. No mistaking it. Better than I could have imagined."

"It didn't take much, doc. You pointed me in the right direction. Have to say, I found it exciting."

"What about the others?"

"Busy with, what do they say, their own knitting."

"That's what they say."

"Doc, what do you think?"

"In all honesty?"

"Honesty would be good."

McCauley scanned the valley from where they entered to the far end. "The best thing we can do is bug out."

"No argument from me."

"But while we're here, do me a favor, Al. Take a couple of pictures." He pointed. "There, there, and there."

"Cell okay?"

"Perfect. Couple of wide shots."

Jaffe snapped the first shot which showed the cliff, the ladder leading up to an opening, the generators on the ground, and the power cables. He took another, turning the camera sideways, which he liked better.

"Any videos? I can do those, too."

"Why not? Hold the shot for about twenty seconds."

"K. Wanna be in the videos?"

McCauley considered it, then thought better of the idea. "Nah. Just the landscape."

"Give me a bit. I'll have it all." He walked around and got everything McCauley wanted. A few minutes later Jaffe was back at his supervisor's side.

"Want me to send these to you?"

"Yes, but first, someone else."

"Who?"

"Anna. Include a nice cheery message," McCauley said. "No reason she shouldn't have a few souvenirs."

"Souvenirs?"

McCauley explained why.

Jaffe understood. "Okay, what's next?"

"Team powwow."

"Here?"

"No, we'll steer clear of this area. Back at base camp. Say in an hour."

Jaffe trekked back. McCauley remained in the valley sorting through the possibilities. After one more look, he headed on to join the others.

"Well, gang," McCauley began as everyone was gathered. "Three things. First, great work while we were gone. You did magnificently. I'm truly proud of everyone, which leads me to my second point. It's been a terrific, and shall I say a surprising summer. We might not have all the fossils we'd expected, but we sure have one helluva story, which brings me to the third point. It's a story that you'll have to keep quiet. Really quiet. Like nobody gets to know. Military quiet. You can only guess what that means. They're clamping down on us."

"They? Who's they?" Cohen asked.

"Folks who have a stake in the installation." He thought that was innocuous enough.

"And you learned that in one day?" Trent wondered suspiciously.

"Let's just say it became abundantly clear."

Now McCauley gave them a warning that had come to him during the flight to Glendive. He believed it would serve to keep things under wraps. "Considering most of you are on federal loans," he said, "I wouldn't recommend doing anything to jeopardize things."

This caught students off guard. "Really?" said Leslie. "But…"

"It's the best advice I can give you."

"Did anyone threaten that?" Lobel wondered.

"They didn't have to."

At least that part was true, McCauley thought.

"And there's actually a fourth point."

The team, relaxing on their folding chairs, leaned forward.

"We're going home."

The questions came faster. McCauley was ready. Alpert stood by his side.

Lobel: "Can't we move to another location?"

"No, it's best that we leave immediately. Actually, not best. We have to."

Jaffe: "We're just leaving the cave as it is?"

"That's correct."

Trent: "Who's going to tell my department that we shut down three weeks short?"

"I will."

Cohen: "I think it's been an unusual summer. What's the chance we come back next year?"

This broke the tension. McCauley was quite relieved.

"Great! Thank you, Leslie."

McCauley looked around. They were all exceptional students. Surely the news was disappointing. However, breaking camp was for their own good.

"Gang, I'm sorry," he said lowering his voice. "I really share your frustration, but I have a responsibility. To you, to my employer, to your schools and departments. We got more than halfway through the time. It's not what I wanted, but you can consider it a success."

McCauley hadn't sold them yet. He'd have to do better.

"Naturally, you feel you're just beginning to break through and don't have much to report back home or to your advisors. But remember, we came across something exciting. The only problem is we can't talk about it. Certainly not right now."

"But it's our discovery, Dr. McCauley," Tom Trent said for the group. "That's good enough for me. And I've catalogued some great fossils. I'm up for coming back next year."

"Great attitude," Katrina added. McCauley looked to Katrina for reinforcement. She gave him a nod in the affirmative.

"So what the hell did we find?" Leslie Cohen asked the question most wanting to be answered. "Some Strategic Air Command mountain base like in…what was that old movie with Matthew Broderick?"

"War Games," Lobel said.

"Yeah, like *War Games*?"

"Maybe," McCauley said. "But it was my mistake for even looking into it; even worse for dragging all of you along."

"That's what we're supposed to do," Cohen offered. "We're scientists."

"Yes, but this got out of hand."

With the exception of Al Jaffe, Rich Tamburro knew

more than the others. But the pieces he put together played into the story McCauley proposed.

"Okay, folks, so we'll box up the fossil finds, write some good scholarly papers, and then wait for the doc to tell us when we can go public. In the meantime, I agree. We go home. We don't email about this. We don't tweet. We don't tell anyone. I certainly don't want to jeopardize my loans."

"Thank you, Rich." McCauley crossed over to Tamburro and hugged him. Then he smiled and turned to everyone. "We sure as hell stepped into something. I don't normally believe in bad guys in black helicopters, but this is as close as I want to be. So let's back out quietly."

Everyone agreed.

"Okay. Here's the drill. Tomorrow we'll break camp and by dinnertime check into the GuestHouse Inn. I'll get you all out on planes the day after and take care of shipping everything out. Rich, you'll check on Anna and see if she can be discharged. If so, make sure she gets where she's going."

"My pleasure."

"I'm sure it is," Leslie said. "Give her a kiss for me."

"From all of us," Rodriguez added.

"A few more things, everyone," McCauley continued. "We have cash for your expenses and we'll figure a time to regroup. I promise I'll keep you posted on when, if ever, you can discuss this wild experience. Believe me, for now you'll just want to walk away."

FORTY-SEVEN

Glasgow AFB, MT

FRANKLIN CHECKED OUT the cockpit. He'd be piloting the first leg of the flight. A remote control take-off was not something they had the time to prepare. Though the cameras and GPS would be sending back data, the operation required a human at the stick before the systems could be handed over to the remote guidance system.

"Any issue on the coordinates?" he asked.

"None at all," Winston proclaimed. "Believe it or not, I got ground photographs a few minutes ago. I'll print them out and match them to the onboard cameras. We'll do a visual in." He wiped the sweat from his forehead. "I'm glad we moved the curtain to dawn. Much easier than relying on infrared. Much."

For the next few hours, the men worked independently; silently. They were not a tight unit prone to personal camaraderie or team loyalty. No high fives. No *see you next time.* If ordered, each easily could, and would, put a bullet in another's head. They focused on the job, testing the relays, charging the batteries, reviewing the charts. It was a clear case of the devil's in the details.

FORTY-EIGHT

Glendive, MT
The next night

MCCAULEY'S TEAM WAS grateful for the baths and privacy at the GuestHouse Inn. They were equally happy with the blowout at Maddhatters, covered—though they didn't know it—by Dr. Marli Bellamy's generosity. The next day they'd be on their way home, earlier than expected, without a reasonable way to explain it.

McCauley gave Katrina an unmistakably non-sexual hug at the motel door. "Goodnight," he said.

"Goodnight," she replied, feeling the desire for more.

Neither immediately let go of one another.

"Early morning," he replied awkwardly.

"Guess so," Katrina replied.

"Goodnight then."

"Right. Good night."

They turned and walked to their own rooms more, each aware of the footsteps getting further away.

Glasgow AFB, MT

FRANKLIN TOOK OFF in the dark at 3:45 A.M. Winston had left three hours earlier and was already at his radio safe point. Conrad was on his last hour cleaning up, scrubbing the staging area for finger and footprints, DNA traces, and tire tracks in the dirt. For extra measure, he made the old hangar look like it had been used as a shooting gallery by local kids. He left spent BB's, broken bottles, and ragged targets everywhere. For extra measure, he smashed mostly empty beer bottles he'd pulled from dumpsters outside Billings' bars and tossed disgusting moldy fast food into the mix. Should any investigators dust for prints, they'd be sent on a wild goose chase for years.

GuestHouse Inn

McCAULEY TRIED AGAIN to close his eyes, but he couldn't relax enough to sleep. His mind raced through recent events. He tried to sort and catalogue them as if they were paleontological finds. Everything came back to the prime pyramid.

McCauley got out of bed and sat naked at the desk in his hotel room. He ran his index finger over the impressions on the page; the rubbings he'd made. *Indentations, not actual numbers.*

They'd made the leap to prime numbers, but he still wondered why it had been done this way.

Then McCauley thought about what Greene had said. *The radio telescope in Puerto Rico.*

Oh my, God!

Above the Montana Badlands
Early morning

FRANKLIN WAS ON COURSE. Right speed, right altitude. His gloved hands held the throttle. The flight was smooth so far. Thermals that could affect the flight weren't going to be an issue at this hour. He looked over the console. The displays were all lit with the green bulbs that Winston had installed, indicating that he was within ground communication range.

He checked his watch. *Sixty seconds.* Next, a final look at the GPS. *On the prescribed flight path.* Franklin pressed the *P* key on an onboard iPad. The green lights blinked three times and then went to a solid green again. He repeated the command three more times, entering the rest of the code with an *A, T* and *H.*

Thirty seconds.

Franklin opened the port door, unbuckled his safety belt and gave the cockpit GPS a last glance. He counted down to himself. *10...9...8...7...6...5.* At four, he leaned out. The Cessna was now on autopilot, but he didn't want to throw off the attitude or the altitude. His departure would be quick. *2...1.*

On ground

WINSTON SUCCESSFULLY ACQUIRED control of the Cessna. There was nothing else to do for another thirty-five minutes.

From his point of view and experience, the operation was amazingly simple. The principal guidance required a jerry-rigged radio control transmitter that connected to the plane's receiver and wired through amplifiers and actuators. This controlled the pitch, yaw, and roll of the plane and the throttles. Radio control, or RC commands came from his fully charged iPad to receivers on the plane. As a redundancy, he had backup on the same frequency.

The RC transmitters were tuned to the Amateur 6 meter band, utilizing amplifiers, available through the open market, principally eBay, Craigslist, and local hobby shops. Their range was limited, but enough: thirty to forty miles at the most.

Franklin had brought the plane close enough. Now, if he'd followed the schedule correctly, the pilot would be gently floating to the ground. To be sure, Winston pitched the plane slightly lower which immediately registered on his laptop screen. Satisfied he had complete control, he returned the Cessna to its mission profile.

The real operational brain was the plane's internal GPS tracker. It sent the Cessna's position to the control site— Winston's Winnebago—via another amateur radio link operating on the two meter VHF band. Inside amateur circles, this has been known as APRS for Automatic Position Reporting System. Winston was able to accurately track the position, velocity and altitude on an app.

He also had two eyes in the sky reporting back. Ham analog UHF video links fed back a semi-wide angle cockpit view for general assistance in remotely flying the aircraft. This gave him perspective of how the Cessna lined up with the horizon. The second camera provided a longer, forward field of view, key to the terminal guidance phase to target.

Glendive

ONE MORE LOOK *inside the cave. One more,* McCauley thought. His heart was racing as he drove in the dark toward the entrance of Makoshika State Park. He was more excited than ever to touch the wall again; to *see* if his *feelings* were right. One more. He had to.

The Badlands

FRANKLIN DEFTLY MANEUVERED his parachute to his landing zone—an abandoned ranch southwest of Glendive. This was an easy descent. He settled down fifty yards from the car that Winston had rented and left forty-eight hours earlier.

If anyone had seen him, his story would square with someone bailing out before a crash. But, at this hour, there weren't any witnesses.

He gathered up his parachute, stuffed it in a backpack in the car's trunk and drove to Interstate 94. The man known for now as Franklin wouldn't stop until he got to Bismarck, ND.

Fifteen miles away

THE CESSNA UNDER Winston's ground control was literally a large drone, cruising at 120 knots; on time and on target. A dawn glow was emerging low in the eastern sky. Soon, that light would allow the forward facing cockpit camera to see.

He checked his watch. 0448 hrs; 4:48 A.M. In one minute he should hear the plane. Ninety seconds later, he'd slowly bank the Cessna from a southern heading to west-southwest. Then eight minutes to burn off altitude and...

Glendive

MCCAULEY HEADED WEST into the darkness. In his rearview mirror he could see the sky brightening. Soon there would be enough light to cast long shadows and reveal haunting shapes created by the geological monuments that defined Makoshika State Park. This wasn't bad earth. McCauley saw extraordinary beauty in the land, evidence of the world as it had been and where it was going. The ultimate message he wanted to impart to his students was that for now it was ours. And like the dinosaurs, we're merely leaving footprints, only smaller. *The earth has it all over us*, he thought. *Makoshika State Park is the proof. Old, yet ever evolving.*

FORTY-NINE

May 10, 1633
Rome, Italy

GALILEO STRUGGLED TO his feet. *Thinking.* Thinking hard. The sixty-nine-year-old fixed a cold hard stare on his adversary, Father Vincenzo Maculano.

"Of course I remember Pino and Satori. We traveled together from Pisa. They were sponsors, patrons."

"For a time you were inseparable; and they were infinitely insufferable with too much wine," Maculano noted.

"That could be said of anyone."

"Yes, I suppose it could."

"Besides, we lost touch after."

"And so you did, but they continued to talk of your travels together. The camaraderie and conquests, your experiments and your *discovery*."

Galileo's eyes widened. Indeed, the finding had haunted him, too.

"Remember how your dear friends drank, smoked and fornicated? When inebriated, which they increasingly became, they talked at the top of their lungs about their sexual peccadilloes, their free access to the rich and powerful, and one remarkable exploration with you. They gossiped with anyone who would share a drink with them; particularly if they didn't have to pay. How do I know? Seventeen years ago my secretary was at a table next to theirs in Pisa. Though he tried at first to ignore them, it was impossible. Then he stopped trying. They bragged about their friend, the great Galileo Galilei and how they sponsored his early research."

"They gave me little other than earaches."

The priest laughed heartily. "Yes, I can believe that. But, when the conversation was relayed to me, I thought I should meet these talkative aristocrats and determine if there was an ounce of truth in anything they had to say.

"We met on a lovely October night at a villa in Tuscany. I had coached up from Rome and they were so impressed. I suggested they might one day dine at the Vatican. We talked about what wines they would bring and how they embraced the true word of God."

Maculano laughed again. Galileo imagined Pino and Santori tripping over one another for attention.

"As we drained bottles of *Vin Trebbiano*, I led them from one exaggeration of theirs to another until we got to what was so amazing it had to be true."

Galileo listened without comment.

"They talked of a trip you'd taken together to Le Marche. They bragged in great detail with such enthusiasm about your findings. You should be proud how they represented you."

"They were not with me!" Galileo shouted.

"Oh, but they said they were. They spent hours on it. With vivid descriptions."

"They tired of hiking. They didn't want to get their hands dirty. They saw nothing of what I did."

"Ah, but what a story they still told. Eventually, enough blasphemy that I had no other choice but to invite them to the Vatican. Though they dined here, it was less than succulent servings. Let's say your accommodations are far superior."

Galileo's shoulders sank. "You arrested them?"

"Quite so. But I'm not through. In prison, we delineated what they claimed they did versus what was truly your achievement. You should have heard the boasts at first. It was as if they were by your side as you took your experiments into the mountain. Then, under some, shall we say *persuasive techniques* they recanted. They admitted, just as you suggest, it was you and you alone, who ventured forth that day in 1601; ventured forth into the cave. It was you, Galileo, who saw what I then had to see for myself."

Maculano brought his voice down. "Pity, too, they never went with you. They would have been amazed."

"Pino and Satori?" Galileo quietly asked.

"Alas, they expired under the strain."

"You executed them."

"They failed to survive the final interview."

"Why? You saw they were lying. I actually told them very little."

"But they knew enough. And even a little is far too dangerous."

FIFTY

Montana

THE TIMING WAS PERFECT. The rising sun began to give the target definition. The onboard cameras sent back clear video to Winston's tablet. He made a few minor midair corrections. The Cessna nosed down, gained speed, and banked to the right ever so slightly. Another few degrees lower. Another three minutes.

MCCAULEY HAD PARKED the car as close to the cave entrance as possible. Now, on foot, he trudged toward the cliff, completely awake and refreshed in the cool morning air. It heightened his senses. The only thing that interrupted his thoughts was the sound of a distant airplane which seemed to be floating in with the west-to-east breeze. He didn't think Dawson Community Airport had any traffic at this hour. But that wouldn't necessarily stop a small plane from landing.

WINSTON WAS ALWAYS disappointed that he could never see the final split second—the culmination of the planning, the preparation, and the delivery of the package.

The package was C4, wired inside the Cessna 421B to dual redundant impact detonators, set to explode two one hundredths of a second after plowing into the cave entrance. The onboard aviation fuel would add extra bang.

THE LOW RUMBLE of the twin engines increased. McCauley stopped in the flats short of the rock wall and peered over his shoulder. The wingtip lights of the airplane appeared to be angling toward the park. Toward him.

The lights grew brighter. The engines louder. The plane was speeding up and bearing down on a deadly trajectory.

Pull up! he wanted to say. But there was no time.

McCauley instinctively dove to the ground as it flew right overhead. *Flew* wasn't even the right term. He knew the plane was going to crash.

He could feel the wash of the propellers. It was that close.

McCauley quickly crawled behind a boulder on the valley floor. A second later a massive explosion boomed, then echoed against the cliffs. The sound was instantly followed by a shock wave with a burning heat and a stench that engulfed the entire area. Then rocks blew past him. Without coverage from the boulder McCauley knew he would have been killed.

When the dust settled, he peered out from behind his cover. But Quinn McCauley didn't need to see the precise location of the impact. He knew.

PART III

FIFTY-ONE

Montana

WINSTON DROVE SOUTH. Franklin headed west. Conrad north. They wouldn't see one another until next called, or not at all. There were no thank-you emails or letters of commendation. All the thanks they needed were handled by wire transfers.

Makoshika State Park, MT

MCCAULEY ROAMED THE site with his jacket covering his mouth and nose. Metal was strewn below the cliff and the area reeked of burning oil, plastic, and rubber. He saw a portion of the fuselage wedged into rock thirty feet up. The airplane had plowed directly into the spot where the team's lights, cables and equipment had been—*like hitting a bulls eye on a target*, he thought.

No one could have survived, he reasoned.

A half hour later, he was still walking the ground when a stern voice shouted, "Hey, you! What are you doing here?"

McCauley turned to see a local police officer sweeping the area with a bright flashlight.

"I'm… I'm Dr. Quinn McCauley. I was in charge of a graduate student dig here. Right up there." He pointed to crash site. "Thank God we started packing up yesterday and didn't hit the site early today."

"Damn lucky," the officer said. McCauley figured the she was in her late twenties, and had never witnessed anything like this. For that matter, neither had he. Well, not exactly.

Typically, Glendive was quiet. Aside from the dinosaur discoveries, little put them on the map. This surely would for a few days. "Damn lucky," she said again.

"May I see some identification?"

"Certainly," McCauley pulled his license and Yale ID from his wallet.

The Glendive cop shined her flashlight on the cards and then onto McCauley. She did not return the IDs.

"And what did you say you were doing here?"

"I've been working with my students for the past month. We started breaking camp and…"

"Why are you here now?" she demanded.

"I'm sorry. We moved to a motel in town last night. I couldn't sleep and since we're usually up by this time anyway, I came over see if we left anything behind."

"Did you?"

"Up there. But it's all gone now. Like you said, we're damned lucky."

"Luckier than whoever was flying."

"For sure," McCauley said. "Look, we should call Jim Kaplan, the park director."

"He's already on the way," the officer said.

"Is it okay if I stay then?"

"No. Return to your car and wait there."

"And my ID?" McCauley held his hand out expecting his license to be returned.

"I'll hold onto them until I speak with Mr. Kaplan. Under the circumstances…" She didn't need to complete the sentence.

London
The same time

THE RESEARCHER ON the America desk in Room Ten was surfing her Internet news sources in the normal manner when a story popped up on the *USA Today* website. It was a simple alert, but it had enough key words that she flagged it for further review.

> July 28, 5:18 AM MST: Billings, MDT
> The Montana State Highway Patrol reports that an aircraft, possibly civilian, crashed into a mountain in eastern Montana early this morning near the city of Glendive. The exact crash site has not been determined, but police indicate it was away from populated areas, within Makoshika State Park, popularly known as Dinosaur Alley. Investigators from the National Transportation Safety Board have been notified. There is no information on the origin or destination of the flight or whether there are survivors.

The seminary graduate who had taken special courses in Italy marked it Category Five and passed it on to Simon Volker.

Makoshika State Park, MT

JIM KAPLAN VOUCHED for McCauley. But the officer still insisted on getting a complete statement, which took another thirty minutes.

"I guess it must have seemed a little coincidental to her," Kaplan said as they prepared to say goodbye. "I wouldn't worry."

"Worry? I can tell you a lot about worry. I'm just happy none of us were here when that plane hit."

"You were. And you sure dodged the bullet, buddy. What were you doing right up there anyway? You guys usually dig in the flats."

"I decided to get off the beaten path. I thought we were onto something. I was wrong."

"You made that decision just in time."

GuestHouse Inn
Glendive, MT
8:30 A.M.

EVERYONE HAD CHECKED out as planned and assembled in the coffee shop, with the exception of Rich Tamburro. Jaffe reminded Dr. McCauley who joined them after gathering his things, that Tamburro had driven to the hospital to check on Anna.

The students were discussing the topic that was sweeping through Glendive this morning: the freak plane crash at Makoshika State Park.

McCauley described what he'd seen and how the area of the park was now closed off.

They were more than grateful that they'd left. They were also doubtful that it was an accident.

Lobel murmured to Cohen in a voice not meant to be completely quiet, "Looks like the government closed it down permanently." No one could disagree. McCauley and Alpert certainly didn't try. They'd been prepared and left at the right time.

McCauley felt there'd be inevitable follow-up questions from the NTSB. He hadn't decided what he'd tell the federal investigators.

For his students, it had been a challenging summer.

Now it was over, or so he hoped. They were finishing up their breakfasts when Rich Tamburro burst in.

"Anna's gone!" he exclaimed.

"What?" The reaction came as a chorus rather than a single comment.

"I went to see her at the hospital. She discharged herself at six."

"Well, maybe they needed to get her out," Katrina explained.

"Without calling me?"

McCauley signaled for Tamburro to go outside.

"No text?"

"No doc. No text, no email, no call. And she hasn't answered any either. Now you got me thinking she was in way over her head."

FIFTY-TWO

New Haven, CT
The next day

"How much do we have left?" Katrina asked softly.

The cab driver had certainly heard that before from airport-returning passengers. He waited for the response.

"We're doing okay. Even after covering the airfares, we've still got almost...," McCauley caught the driver's interest in the rearview mirror, "...enough." He whispered *seventy-five hundred* into her ear. "Plus, I might be able to get another ATM card from the bank, too," he hoped more than believed.

"I wouldn't count on it."

She instinctively looked over her shoulder to see if they were being followed. *Not here. Not yet.*

Minutes later they were in McCauley's office. "Welcome to home away from home," he said opening the door.

"Fit for a professor," Katrina observed. She walked in. "Bigger than mine." A few books caught her eye. Some she had, some she didn't. There were fossils, all of which she could identify, a few awards and citations, and stacks of magazines.

She took a seat on a worn fabric couch under a window and paged through an old issue of *Scientific American* while Quinn listened to his phone messages. He largely ignored them, pressing the delete button, swearing every now and then, and writing nothing down.

"Uh-oh," he said, "I half expected this."

"What?" Katrina asked.

"An NTSB investigator."

Alpert looked up from an article on gravitational waves detected in South Pole experiments. It supported the theory that the universe inflated rapidly—very rapidly—at one trillionth of a trillionth of a trillionth of a second after the Big Bang ten billion to twenty billion years ago. In that single moment, space expanded faster than the speed of light, doubling in size ninety times.

Katrina felt that things were moving at the same pace now.

"You going to call?"

"Not if we didn't stop in my office yet. Which I don't think we've done," he said slyly. "Do you?"

She got what he was saying. "That's only going to work for a while."

"All we need is awhile."

Voyages *Room Ten*
London
The same time

"THIS CAME UP. Take a look," Simon stated.

Kavanaugh bent over and read an itinerary on the computer screen. It chronicled a trail that led McCauley and Alpert from Glendive to New Haven. "How'd you get this?"

"An airline database."

"I didn't think they gave out this sort of information."

"They don't," Simon Volker declared smugly.

"So what are they up to?"

"I'd say they're doing exactly what we are. Putting pieces together."

"That's not good," Kavanaugh surmised.

"No, sir, it's not."

"Use whatever means you need to keep track of them."

"Yes, sir."

Colin Kavanaugh excused himself for what was becoming his regularly scheduled meetings at tea time, followed by a walk in the park and a conversation with the grimmest of the grim reapers. It was time to really find out how things worked in the field.

FIFTY-THREE

"DAMMIT! I DON'T even know where to go," McCauley admitted. They were heading west on the Connecticut Turnpike.

Katrina gave the situation some thought. "London. I say we go to London."

"London?"

"Yes, and don't tell me you didn't think of Europe either. I saw you grab your passport."

"Observant."

"Just not blind."

"Why London?"

"I have a friend who's an Oxford European history professor. Worth seeing if she'll have some insight. And we can hide out with her. From there we can reach out to the cave explorer and do whatever we need to do…"

The rest of the thought, unspoken, was *to stay alive.*

McCauley nodded. "Okay. South is New York. If we turn around we can fly Boston to Heathrow. But I vote for North and Canada. We can fly out of Montreal. It's about seven hours away. Game?"

"Game."

En route, Katrina found some leads to the French spelunker, Claude Bovard. She read a story of his explorations in China's super caves, carved out over six hundred million years. Maybe he'd have a clue.

FIFTY-FOUR

Canonbury, England
The next day

"OH, MY GOD! I don't believe it," Renee Kritz exclaimed. She hadn't seen Katrina Alpert in more than three years. Now, one of her best friends was at her brownstone doorstep with an American.

Kritz lived on a cobblestoned street lined with gable-roofed houses in the quaint north London neighborhood of Canonbury. It has a rich history and over the centuries, notable residents included Thomas Cromwell, Sir Francis Bacon, George Orwell and in recent years, Keira Knightley.

Quinn instantly liked Renee. She was five feet four, a dirty blonde with an engaging sense of humor, quite in contrast to the three advanced degrees she held in theology, history, and anthropology. Anyone who called her Dr. Kritz could have been referring to any of the disciplines. She was the perfect friend for Katrina and the perfect person to trust.

After they cleared the dishes from dinner and switched from the complex French burgundy to an Italian late harvest dessert wine, the conversation turned to the subject of Quinn and Katrina.

"So, how long have you known one another?"

They laughed and simultaneously said, "Let's see, a

week? More? Not sure with the time differences. The travel keeps throwing me off," Katrina admitted.

She explained what her assignment was and her first impressions of McCauley. Next she deferred to Quinn.

"We've actually been through a great deal in a short time," he said. "You might call it explosive."

They had agreed on the London flight that Katrina would handle the initial explanation. She took Renee through the events from their first exploration of the cave to the meeting, the discussion with Greene, the subsequent chase through Bakersfield, and the *attack,* as she now described it, at the site.

Kritz was particularly intrigued by the photographs McCauley produced—which actually showed very little. She examined them once, then again, each time without comment. On the third review she stopped and tapped a picture which best captured the rock against the blackness "This."

"Yes?" Katrina asked. "What about it?"

"Reminds me of…."

McCauley encouraged her. "Reminds you of what?"

Kritz shook her head. "Can't pinpoint it. But I think I've seen a picture like it before." Suddenly she changed her mind. "No, not a photograph, a sketch…possibly in a book."

"A sketch?"

Her friend tried to recall. "I think."

"But you're not sure?" McCauley added.

"Well, not completely. I can't place it or…"

"Renee," Katrina said, "it's very important."

"I understand. I'm just not sure."

It was a frustrating answer, but it was something.

"Was it in a scientific journal?" Katrina asked.

"No, it reminds me of…" Kritz searched her memory. "Maybe it was in…" She thought more. "Describe it."

"Like you see here. Just totally black, but with a high gloss to the touch. You can feel it, but you can't see it. Weirdest thing I've ever encountered."

"Got it." Kritz looked for answers in the ceiling and around the room. Nothing immediately came to her. "Maybe it was in an old book."

"How old?" Katrina followed up. Her heart was racing.

"I don't know. Old."

"More specific?"

"I'm trying to remember. Archival old."

Kritz taped the photographs again.

"Maybe something from the 1800s. I'll give it more thought. Maybe it'll come to me."

They sat silently for minutes. Kritz broke the silence with a different thought.

"I can't speculate on what you have seen," Kritz volunteered. "I can talk about who may be after you."

"How?" Quinn wondered.

"Deduction."

Katrina and Quinn were ready to listen to any theory, plausible or incredible.

"I'll start with the basic truth. You discovered a secret."

"No argument there," McCauley agreed.

"So, let's make a list of whose secret it could be."

"Good idea," he acknowledged.

Kritz went to her desk for a yellow pad.

"Okay, don't bother explaining why, just list what comes to mind." She handed them the pad and a pencil.

"Like?" Katrina said needing some prompting.

"Like big and small; obvious and outlandish."

"I still don't get it."

"Come on. Think paranoid, Katrina. Who's after you?"

McCauley took a stab at creating the list. He called them off as he wrote.

US Government Army
Air Force
CDC

Katrina understood now. She added her own thoughts.

Research Corporations
Think Tanks
CIA
NSA

"Can I be honest with you?"
"Please," Katrina and Quinn both said.
"Too ordinary."
"But you said obvious," Katrina replied.
"I did. But go outrageous."
Kritz rose again and went to her bookshelf. She pulled a number of volumes while her guests threw out additional guesses.

Halliburton
Black Ops
Area 51 guys

"More!" Renee implored.

A rogue corporation
Aliens

"Okay, now based on what you *think* could be possible, eliminate those that don't meet that test," she said from the other room.
Katrina took the pencil from Quinn. She had no idea what to cross out.

Renee returned with a set of books. She put them on the table, examined their list and picked up another pencil. "At this point, there's no logic, only supposition. So here's what I'd remove." Renee proceeded to cross off *everything*.

"Oh, shit," McCauley proclaimed. Then, "Sorry for my language."

"It's okay," Kritz said. "I'll explain." She pointed to each. "Too new, too new, too new," she said thirteen times. On the final, "aliens," she exclaimed, "Wouldn't that be fun. But no."

Katrina posed the natural follow up. "Then who? Or what?"

"Well, I'd go for something more unusual. And we should reframe the question. To my thinking, ignore what you've found. Think about this as a cover-up."

Katrina didn't follow.

Kritz cleared her throat. "Whoever is after you is real. They may not have created it…whatever *it* is. But they're trying to keep your discovery from the public. Actually, more than that, from public scrutiny. Their goal is to protect, not expose. And that, my dear friends, brings us to secret societies."

She dropped eight books squarely on the dining room table.

"What kind of secret society?" McCauley asked. "Like Skull and Bones? Bilderberg? Freemasons? And what the heck is that religious sect?"

"Which one? There are so many," Kritz replied.

"You know."

"The Illuminati?"

"Right. Them," he said. "What about them?"

"Come on, that's not the real world," Katrina argued.

Kritz disagreed. "Debatable, but, I'd say we should go beyond the usual suspects."

"So who?" Quinn wondered.

"Well, the trouble with secret societies, really secret ones, is that they are secret. I did a master's thesis on them and after I ran through a litany of organizations, my faculty advisor came back with the stupidest comment in the history of the world."

"I'll bite," Quinn said. "What?"

"'Admirable research, but I haven't heard of half of these.' What an ass!" she added. "But instead of calling him out I politely stated, 'That's why they're *secret* societies.'"

Quinn laughed. He knew the type all too well.

"Where do we go from here?" Katrina asked, returning to the subject at hand.

"Don't know. In the meantime, what's your next step?"

"Well, we've got a couple more people to track down. One is a French explorer named Bovard," McCauley explained.

"I've heard of him. He did some research with National Geographic. The other?"

"A Vatican scientist."

"Oh?"

"Why *oh*?"

"It ups the stakes. Who recommended you look there?"

"The guy we met in California. The one whose house was blown up."

Kritz nodded. "And he pointed you to Rome?"

"Yes. Is that meaningful?"

"Not sure. But there's something about Rome and the Church that takes me back to that sketch again. Damn."

"So what's in the books?" McCauley asked.

"A lot of crap and maybe some gold, but let's read." Kritz slid a book to each of them.

"Since you just mentioned the Church, let's start with

this one." She opened the brown leather cover and leafed through to the title page and copyright. "The author was an American minister, Peter Rosen. It's pretty rare. Here. Enjoy *The Catholic Church and Secret Societies*."

"But you said…" Katrina started to say.

"Not the usual suspects," Kritz interrupted. "It's for background."

"Okay, let's have at it," McCauley stated.

"The reverend opens quoting a note written by Pope Leo XIII to a cardinal. '*Christ is the Teacher and The Example of all sanctity and to His standard must all those conform who wish for eternal life.*' Standard stuff. However, the book takes an interesting look at how secret societies began to flourish in the US on university campuses, through men's groups, and some religious organizations that could find something to hang their hats on and get their membership cards stamped.

"But Reverend Rosen also gives us the common denominators we may be looking for. Here." Kritz began to read from Chapter 1.

> *By a secret society was formerly meant a society which was known to exist, but whose members and places of meetings were not publicly known. Today we understand it to be a society with secrets, having a ritual demanding an oath of allegiance and secrecy, prescribing ceremonies of a religious character, such as the use of the Bible, either by extracts therefrom, or by its being placed on an altar within the lodge room.*

Kritz stopped to make an observation. "The key takeaway from the passage is that *a secret society is a society with secrets*; keeping something secret that they hold dear and making certain anyone else who learns about it will not use the secret. Follow?"

Quinn and Katrina nodded.

"Further in the chapter, *'Most of all ranks in public and private life belong to secret societies. The character of many of these people is such that it is sufficient proof in itself that the final aims and object of these societies are not understood by them.'*"

"What does that mean?" Katrina asked. "Is the church…?"

"Not the church. The society. It means they're vulnerable. Secret societies may exist under the radar, but they have a public face somewhere and since they're run by people, they'll ultimately make human mistakes. Or at least, you'd hope so."

FIFTY-FIVE

June 21, 1633
Rome

GALILEO FULLY RECOGNIZED it was not just the Church he faced. Father Maculano was charged with a goal greater than defending the faith. He was protecting the institution.

"You believe that science justifies your vaulted intellectual pursuits; that your ideas are as limitless as the skies. They are not. We live with laws of the state and our firmly held Canon Laws. When it comes to standing up to you, Galileo Galilei, they are one and the same. You are a threat; a threat that cannot be permitted an audience or a place in history."

"I'm merely a thinker with no political power."

The priest grasped the point. "A thinker? *Thinking* is the root of political power—proposed by Plato, redefined by Aristotle, and reinterpreted by heretics and outcasts ever since. *Thinking* leads to the organization of apostates who espouse the secular rather than the holy. We can't afford thinkers, Galileo. We cultivate followers and believers. And so, by your own admission you are a thinker?"

"I am."

"Then your guilt is solidified."

"It isn't the Holy Inquisition that judges me or seeks to purge the name of Galileo Galilei from history. You represent something else."

"The Inquisition suffices for our purposes. And our decision will serve all purposes."

Galileo sat again and rested his head in his hand.

"Perhaps your head hurts from all your thinking. It should. Your thoughts do the work for me."

"Thoughts, observations, intellectual pursuits. I have no arrows in a quiver; no knives in a sheath."

"Words that undermine faith are equally dangerous weapons. You are well-armed with those," Maculano resumed. "So is research that threatens how things ought to be."

Galileo considered his next words carefully. He spoke slowly and with conviction.

"I did not understand what I had come across. My interest was in my experiments. Though I somewhat described it to my two friends, I did so as a fantastic story. Bedtime tales and fodder to pass the time away."

"But what you discovered was real. As real for me as it was for you. It set the course for your greatest work. It pointed you to the stars and the heavens. But did you see God through your lens or his great deeds? No, only something that would challenge him."

Galileo, weakened by argument, years and pain, lowered his head.

"Alas, dear Galileo, the cave is sealed and so is your fate. You see, I am a man who understands what needs to be done. And others are in accord. What was there represents chaos. I will not permit chaos to undermine order."

FIFTY-SIX

Voyages *office*
London

THE ONE THING Gruber never hinted at was a hierarchy above even him. Now, with people flexing their muscles at seemingly every level, including the secretarial, Kavanaugh questioned the structure he inherited.

Gruber, you left this place totally dysfunctional with outdated tools. All your boring lectures and you couldn't tell me if anything is on automatic or not. Who else is out there? That's got to change. Colin Kavanaugh was determined to lead the organization into the future.

With that thought, he dove into the latest reports from the field. Something new intrigued him: the phone history of the Yale paleontologist's graduate teaching assistant. There were calls to him from phone numbers that hadn't shown up before. *That's another thing*, he said to himself, *we have to do better trolling for metadata.*

He decided to dial a number on the hacked call log to see who would answer. He had a strong suspicion already.

Kritz's apartment
The same time

"MISTAKES?" MCCAULEY ASKED.

Kritz was about to respond, but she was interrupted by McCauley's phone ringing.

Quinn was surprised. Katrina had the same reaction. *A call on that phone, particularly at this late hour?*

The phone continued to ring.

"Who?"

"Probably Pete," he said. But the screen read "No caller ID." He shook his head. "No, not Pete."

"Aren't you going to answer it?" Katrina asked.

"I don't think so."

"Could be a wrong number?" Renee offered. "Then again…"

The ringing stopped. He was happy he hadn't recorded a message.

"Tell us more about secret societies," he said.

Voyages *office*
Minutes later

COLIN KAVANAUGH REALLY didn't expect anyone to answer, especially if his theory was right. He had another idea. He dialed DeMeo, who had been tracked to Italy.

On the third ring he heard a tired, "Hello."

Kavanaugh hadn't really considered what to say. He would have had the same problem if someone had answered before. So he fell back onto a natural default. He hung up, but not before he made a decision that would define his leadership over Gruber's.

FIFTY-SEVEN

London
The next day

"'MORNING. POUR YOURSELF some coffee," Kritz said to Quinn, who was the first to join her for breakfast. "I racked my brain last night over that damned sketch. I'm not certain, but I seem to think I saw it on a library shelf in a Russian studies section. At least that's my vague recollection. Anyway, it's a place to start."

"Where?"

"Oxford. Years ago."

McCauley knew from his own work that in an instant, a memory could take him back to a dig he hadn't visited in years. Calling it to mind, he'd see where specific rocks laid and the color of the dirt. Rich details. Maybe Renee was beginning to have that same kind of recollection.

Katrina joined the conversation. While Kritz caught her up, McCauley called Pete DeMeo.

"Where are you, buddy?" McCauley asked when his teaching assistant answered.

"Getting in touch with my Catholic roots. Exploring Rome. Are you still driving around in my car?"

"Well, not exactly. It's parked."

"Where?"

"Montreal Airport."

"You're in Canada?" DeMeo asked.

McCauley took a deep breath. "Ah, no. London, in fact. Things have changed even since the last time I called."

"I guess."

"And where are you?"

"In Firenze. It's a beautiful day. I'm having a cappuccino outside watching life stroll by. Gorgeous life." He smiled at a young brunette carrying bags from a shoe store in one hand and clothes in another. "Deciding who my future wife will be."

"Up for any research?"

"What do you think I'm doing?"

"For me," McCauley said.

"Not really." He caught another woman's eye.

"But could you be?"

"Well, maybe if it doesn't interfere. What's up?"

McCauley told him about the Vatican scientist. "Dr. Alpert and I can make it to Rome, but it would be helpful if you could do some legwork."

DeMeo laughed to himself. He thought he was doing just that now.

"Can you check out the project where he works?"

He gave DeMeo the only information he had on Father Eccleston. DeMeo had the same initial reaction McCauley and Alpert had had.

"A priest?"

"Yup. Works with a thing named STOQ."

"What should I say if I find him?"

"Not much. Just that an acquaintance of his recommended we meet about a discovery we've made."

"Urgent?"

"Yes."

"Why?"

McCauley finally told his teaching assistant what had happened.

"Christ!" DeMeo was no longer focused on the eye candy walking by. "You're in way over your head. Don't you think you should get some real help?"

"We're hoping Eccleston will be that."

"I mean people with badges who carry guns. That kind of help."

"Not sure whom to trust right now, Pete. Please?"

"Okay, I reach this priest. Then what? You wave his cross in front of the next bad guys to come your way? For God's sake, boss, go back home and lock all your doors."

Pete DeMeo got Quinn McCauley to do something the paleontologist should have done earlier. Think about what he'd gotten himself into.

"I wish I could, but I can't. I'm excited about things again. The way I haven't felt in years. I don't know where it's going take me. But, maybe this is the discovery I've been looking to make all my life."

He stopped. Another thought rushed forward. It wasn't only what he'd gotten himself into. Others were deeply involved.

"Oh my God," McCauley proclaimed.

"What?"

"I'm putting you at risk now along with Katrina, Marli Bellamy, Greene, the students…"

"Don't worry about me," DeMeo interrupted. "I'll get you your Vatican priest. After that, have your talk and call it a day."

Quinn McCauley knew his assistant was right, but he couldn't stop now. He could, however, go it alone.

"Thanks, Pete. See what you can find out, but no entanglements yourself. And look over your shoulder. Be…" He was about to say *careful* when Renee Kritz called from the other room.

"I think I remember where I saw the sketch!"

FIFTY-EIGHT

Oxford University
That afternoon

HISTORICALLY, EACH OF the Oxford Colleges had its own archives and libraries. They reached as far back as the twelfth century. In recent years, the shelves, stacks and volumes have been brought together into one home, the Bodleian Library. Now, the Bodley or even the more abbreviated Bod serves as the principal research library of the University of Oxford. It contains more than eleven million entries. The only library in Great Britain that eclipses the Bod is the British Library. Until the British Museum was founded in 1753, the Bodleian was, for all intents and purposes, the national library of England. It has been the repository of histories and mysteries, scientific journals and science fiction, biographies of the famous and the infamous, today's newspapers and yesterday's fairy tales. The Bod is where Renee Kritz took Quinn McCauley and Katrina Alpert.

For the better part of the first hour, Kritz went shelf-to-shelf in the Russian history and anthropology section, looking for anything that might jog her memory.

"Not here," she said.

"What about this aisle?" Katrina asked not once, but five times as they walked through the Bod's collection.

"Not here," she kept reporting. "Or here...or here," was the constant, discouraging response.

McCauley began his own search. After another hour, Renee and Katrina caught up to him. "This isn't working," Kritz admitted. "I could have sworn it was in a book in this section of the library. I thought maybe the size of the book or the color of the binding might jump out, but so far…"

"It's okay," Katrina said. "Take your time."

"Now I'm not even sure if we're in the right part of the Bod or the right library."

"All right, let's look in general anthropology."

"Or archeology," Renee added as an afterthought.

They renewed the search. At the two-and-a-half hour mark they took another break, this time for tea and sandwiches in the commissary. The Oxford scholar was clearly frustrated.

"I'm sorry. I thought it would be easier. You know how when you take notes you remember where something specific is on a page even weeks or months later?"

"Try years," McCauley answered.

"The good thing is I can literally see *where* it was on the shelf. Third of the way up, right side. The row is another thing. Might have black binding, gray lettering. I can't really recall."

McCauley nodded. *Just like digging for dinosaur bones.* "Maybe you're not taking into consideration how many new books have been added since you saw it last," he noted. "It's probably not in the same place. You sure you don't remember the author?"

"Positive."

"Then we simply keep looking."

Two hours later, Renee threw up her hands. "I'm sorry. I give up."

"You can't," Katrina implored.

"My knees ache from bending. I've got a headache as big as Big Ben. It's useless."

"I'll give it another hour," McCauley said. "The two of you take a break."

McCauley decided to act on Kritz's first impression again. He returned to the Russian anthropology section. Aisle after aisle opened up to him in the immense space. The lighting was never right for close-up examination at different levels and his knees were also feeling the stress. Nonetheless, he kept looking for a book he didn't know by appearance, name, or location.

After forty-five minutes, McCauley stood in front of a shelf he'd passed quickly earlier in the day. By now everything looked the same. He was tired and frustrated and about to give up himself when…

He focused on a thick tattered black book with Cyrillic block lettering in gray. He removed it from the shelf. On the leather cover, a worn etching of a haggard old man. McCauley carefully paged through what appeared to be a chronicle with sketches of the same man, as weathered as a Siberian winter, with a beard as long as time.

McCauley sat on the floor, catching the ambient light from the window. He gathered the book was the account of a recluse who lived above the Anuy River…in a cave.

He couldn't read Cyrillic, but impressions and thoughts jumped out that suggested the work was written and sketched by someone in the church.

McCauley stopped on page 273. His eyes widened. He felt like his heart skipped a beat. And then he did something he'd never done before. Dr. Quinn McCauley stole a library book.

MCCAULEY FOUND THE two women outside, sitting on a bench.

"Have you ever been in a bookstore, not knowing what

you wanted to read, and suddenly it seems like a book picks *you* out rather than the other way around."

"Well, yes," Katrina said.

"Then care to take a guess what happened inside?"

"You found it?"

"No, Dr. Kritz."

Her smile faded.

"It found me," McCauley said. "By accident, like books do."

"Let's go get it," Kritz said. She stood ready to trudge into the Bod.

"No need," McCauley said. He knocked on the left breast of his jacket. It made a thud.

"You didn't?" Katrina exclaimed.

"I did. Trust me, we don't want any of our names on the loan out."

Understanding, Katrina said, "Okay, let's see."

"Not here." McCauley motioned for them to walk back to the parking lot. "Someplace quiet where we can all look at it."

Back at Kritz's home, McCauley opened the book to page 273.

"That's it!" Kritz declared.

He laid the photograph from the disposal camera right under the sketch.

"My God, it's so close to what we—" Katrina began.

"Shot," Quinn interrupted. "Yes."

Two representations of virtually the same thing discovered a half a world and centuries apart. The photograph looked like it was taken of the sketch; the sketch a representation of the photo: A wall of rock framing utter blackness.

McCauley gathered his thoughts. "We can sure rule out NASA, the NSA, a black ops site, or anything contemporary."

"Who then?" Katrina asked.

"Based solely on the author and what I remember about the work, it's the memoir of an old Roman Catholic priest in Tsarist Russia," Kritz offered. "He was like Alexis DeTocqueville, traveling and writing about his observations; relaying his experiences. We should get someone to do translations, though."

"No," McCauley said. "No one else."

"What about Google translates?" she replied.

"It'll be hard without a Cyrillic or Russian keyboard with all the different characters."

"I think I can load that on your computer," Alpert volunteered.

"Okay. Worth a try. But focus on the chapter with the sketch," he responded. "What else?"

"Well, I'm more intrigued that there's a church connection," Kritz noted.

"But if it's the same, how can this exist now and in Dionisij's day?"

"One thing at a time," McCauley proposed. "Start with who might keep secrets such as this?"

They struggled with the answer.

"Not who," Katrina finally said. "It's bigger than who. It takes influence and power and money. A lot of money. An institution that's been around for a long time."

"A monarchy?" Renee proposed based on her studies.

"Back to the church?" Kritz added. "Or a business." She paused considering her own idea. "What businesses have been around for hundreds of years?"

Kritz proposed a few. "Railroads, oil, mining."

"Publishing?" McCauley added. "Whatever it is, there's a sophisticated operation behind it."

"Rules out publishing," Kritz grumbled.

FIFTY-NINE

DeMeo had driven his motorcycle to Rome. He spent the morning trying to track down Father Jareth Eccleston. The best he could get, which wasn't much, was that the priest was out of town; returning in a few days. So in lieu of waiting, DeMeo booked himself a Vatican tour.

"Good thing we passed up the waiting line for the fast track tickets."

DeMeo turned to see a slender blonde, beautiful beyond all belief.

"I'd say," DeMeo responded. She wore a knee-length black skirt, a dark blue blouse and a simple pearl necklace. He noticed her when she joined the tour late. It was impossible not to.

"The wait for the regular tour was going to be a couple of hours," she said. "So I'm glad I found this one. Did I miss much?"

The woman had a soft Italian accent, sexy, yet with an easy, natural quality. DeMeo was partial to blondes, always had been. To add to the allure, she had deep blue eyes and inviting lips.

"Just prelims from the guide."

DeMeo thought for a moment then asked *one* of the things on his mind.

"Do I really look so American you knew to speak English?"

"It's an English language tour, silly man."

DeMeo laughed a little too loudly.

"Excuse me?" said the tour guide, a very serious sixty-three-year-old former religious history teacher.

"I'm sorry," DeMeo offered.

"It was me," the young woman interrupted. *"Mea culpa."*

"Are you with us?"

"Yes, a little late," she responded.

The guide gave her an insincere smile and continued. "As I was saying, the Vatican has the most celebrated and priceless art collection in all Europe. Of course, when we come to the Sistine Chapel at the end of our tour, you'll recognize Michelangelo's expression of the grand design in his brilliant work. But as we walk through the Candelabra Gallery, the Gallery of the Tapestries, and throughout the Vatican, I'll point out the great talents including Raphael, Botticelli, and Bernini; all beloved by the popes.

"We'll stop at key locations for pictures and questions. But stay together. If you wander off, you might not be able to catch up and you'll miss important explanations. We'll pace ourselves with ample time for rest throughout the next three hours."

"Three hours?" the blonde said under her breath. She saddled up to Pete. "You may have to carry me."

DeMeo smiled at the thought and wondered if she was just being friendly or coming on to him. It felt like the latter.

They strolled from Vatican Square through the *Fontana della Pigna* Courtyard, named for the oversized pinecone in the middle found in the Roman Baths of Agrippa, then onto the Gallery of Maps. The gallery was actually a 120-meter tunnel with displays of the spiritual and geographical maps that defined Italy through the ages.

DeMeo asked a probing work question when they entered the Vatican Library.

"I understand the Vatican conducts a great many scientific studies in astronomy and earth sciences. Do they house all the research here?"

The tour guide wasn't ready to take questions, but it was a good one.

"There are many places where research is conducted and stored. We have an astronomical center at the Pope's summer home outside of Rome and in the United States. Earth sciences are conducted around the globe. Much of the accumulated research is archived here, managed by a dedicated library staff and experts in their fields. However, you bring up a very interesting topic. While many view the Church as dogmatic, Vatican scientists are enlightened investigators seeking the truth, wherever it takes them. We are long past the age of the Inquisition. Our research and works that span the globe are among the millions of volumes in the Vatican library. I hope that answers your question."

"Yes," DeMeo said.

As the twelve-person tour approached the Gallery of Tapestries, the woman who joined the tour late dared a whisper to DeMeo. "So, you're probably wondering what I'm doing on this English language tour?"

"Am I?" DeMeo replied.

"Of course you are," she said as seductively as allowed in the Vatican. "I'm working on my masters in comparative religion with a minor in English."

"Ah. *Multo buona.*"

"Very good," she replied.

The tour guide shot them a look again.

"How about we grab a coffee later and stay on Madame Mussolini's good side for now?" she proposed.

"Absolutely," DeMeo said. *Abso-fucking-lutely,* he thought.

Agustarello Restaurant
That evening

IF THINGS WERE to run their normal course, DeMeo would finish dinner and take Lucia Solera to bed. She was making such overtures apparent.

Solera playfully fed him pasta, rubbed his leg with her foot, and touched his thigh. He felt a stirring, but held back. The blonde picked up on his reluctance. She poured DeMeo a third glass of the house Chianti and cooed, "I would have thought we had no language barriers."

"What do you mean?"

"Oh come, silly man. Can't you read the universal language for 'I find you attractive?' We're having a romantic dinner in Rome, we've shared *rigatoni con la pajata* from the same fork and spoon, and I want to make love with you."

"Ah, yes, I was able to translate. It's just that..." He was trying to remain focused.

"What? Have I come on too fast?" She straightened up. "Oh, you're in a relationship."

"Well, no."

Lucia smiled seductively, nibbled his ear and whispered, "Well then, we're in the most romantic city in the world and I've already undressed you with my eyes, so we're more than halfway there."

DeMeo wished he'd never taken McCauley's phone call and thought about the dangers he encountered. His boss aroused concern. Lucia Solera was arousing something else entirely, and right now she was becoming the more persuasive.

"I can't," he said.

She slumped back in her chair frustrated. Her pouting only lasted a moment. Then she smiled. "Okay. You sleep on it." Solera patted his crotch. "We'll discuss this again tomorrow."

DeMeo's eyes widened. "You don't even have my number."

"Oh yes I do." She leaned forward and kissed him passionately. He couldn't resist.

When they separated he had to laugh. "Not that number. My phone number."

Solera took out a bright red lipstick from her purse, seductively twisted it open and handed it to DeMeo. "Oh," she said almost as an afterthought. "You need something to write on." With that, she hiked up her dress with her right hand.

She got his phone number. He got the message which thoroughly trumped McCauley's advice.

"Sure you want to stop there tonight?"

SIXTY

London

RENEE KRITZ SPENT the day cleaning up the translations at her office while Quinn and Katrina finally rested from their travels. That evening, the Oxford professor put a stack of papers on her dining room table and said, "Give these a look."

"Anything promising?" Katrina asked.

"Well, there's Russian history and anthropological goodies for me. You'll have to decide on the rest."

This brought McCauley to the floor so he could read the printouts more easily.

"I've translated some of the priest's account which is interesting in itself and pulled more recent information on the cave based on what was in the book. It's called Denisova Cave, named for a hermit who lived there in the last half of the nineteenth century. Dionisij in Russian; anglicized as Denis. He was also referred to as Saint Denis."

"Saint?" Alpert asked. Her mind went to the obvious place.

"Not really. Not a Church saint. Probably more for the way he lived. But it came up in the priest's memoirs," Kritz explained. "Here's the skinny from other sources. The Denisova Cave is in the Bashelaksky Range of the Altai Mountains. That's Siberia, along the border of the Altai Republic, 150 km south of Barnaul."

McCauley stopped. "No clue where that is. Got a map?"

"I'll get one in a sec. But look at this. Something I pulled from the Internet." She continued to read and paraphrase, "The cave has sparked significant interest and local lore. Known to area villagers as *Aju-Tasch* or Bear Rock—you'll especially love this—it's produced bone fragments of the Denisova hominine; the 'X-woman' dating back to 40,000 Before Present (BP). She wasn't precisely Homo sapiens. Perhaps a subspecies or another extinct hominid species."

"Amazing," Katrina commented.

"There's more. From a paleoanthropological standpoint, the portions of the cave that have been excavated have produced twenty different layers of remains dating back some 300,000 years. Findings include now extinct animals, fifty bird species, large mammals and reptiles. Lots to chew on, or at least there was for X-woman and her clan. And apparently the Neanderthals who followed developed the implements to work with, in particular, Mousterian and Levallois flint tools and weapons. This represented a real step forward in shaping and scraping rocks into projectile points. Also, the cold has helped keep ancient remains in stasis."

"How cold?" Katrina asked.

"On average zero degrees Celsius—right at the freezing level."

While Quinn and Katrina looked through the papers, Kritz went to her bookshelf and pulled an oversized National Geographic book of maps.

"Here's where it is," she said carting the book back. "The southern portion of the West Siberian Plain. Definitely a trek. You're not planning on going, are you? It's not the best of times to be knocking on Russia's door."

"Can't say yet," McCauley replied. "But I'm really curious about the priest's account. What else do you have?"

Kritz gave him a sheet that read in English, *Memoirs from the Altai Mountains: A Holy Mission by Father Mykhailo Emilianov.*

McCauley dove into the rest of the translation. Fr. Emilianov was a Roman Catholic who paid Dionisij visits every spring for about ten years. He described the hermit, how he provided him with whatever supplies he could carry in his sacks, their relationship and conversations, and an unusual cave Dionisij discovered.

Amazingly, some of the detail even included the dimensions of the entrance, distances between areas, and most interestingly, a description of...*nothingness*. Finally, in Emilianov's own hand, was a sketch that was virtually identical to their discovery in Montana.

McCauley sat back in awe. Katrina was equally overwhelmed. "I don't understand," she looked at Quinn bewildered. "How...?"

The word *old* came back to him, nothing more. He quickly went through Renee's material and held up a picture. "This is the entrance to the Denisova Cave?"

"Yes, from a Russian website."

The photograph showed a family walking up to the entrance along a dirt path lined with tall grass. Fauna draped over the rocks. Based on the estimated height of the people, he calculated the opening to the cave to be about fifteen feet wide and ten feet high.

McCauley looked up at the ceiling as if the answers would be there.

He re-read part of the priest's account and then found another article on the cave system.

"Here, here, here...and here," he said putting the descriptions, photographs and sketches side-by-side.

Katrina and Renee peered over his shoulder. Katrina immediately saw McCauley's point.

"The dimensions and details of the entrance…they're different. It used to be bigger."

Katrina leaned back.

"It was more than twice the size in Denis' day. Here's the priest's description." He showed them. It was remarkably different.

"What's it mean?" Kritz asked.

"Likely a different way in and it probably leads to interior areas other than the ones described by the priest. Sometime between the priest's writing and who knows when, it changed. Or, it *was* changed," McCauley assumed.

"Changed the way an airplane crash changes things?" Katrina proposed.

"Considering recent history, it makes me very curious about the fate of the priest and the hermit."

"Where's the best place to look that up?" Kritz offered knowing full well.

McCauley smiled. "The Vatican."

"Precisely."

"And we're in luck then. I got a text earlier from my teaching assistant.

"Good news, bad news?" Katrina asked.

"It's all depends on your perspective. He opened the app and read the text aloud.

Boss. I fell in lust. Will keep you posted. Heard yr guy is out of town. Returning soon. Left him yr #. Here's his.

The phone number followed.

"Can't blame him," Katrina playfully said. "It happens." She smiled warmly at McCauley.

"Suppose so." McCauley said not picking up on any signals. There was a lot that worried him right now.

SIXTY-ONE

Italy
The next morning

LUCIA HAD GOTTEN her way with Pete DeMeo the night before. Today, he talked her into joining him for a road trip. First, he explained, he had some work to do.

With a little online research, he was able to track down Father Jareth Eccleston. He was a featured speaker at a scientific conference in Prague titled Epistemological Challenges to Understanding the Cosmos—From Galileo to Hawking. The conference home page promised *Pure Eccleston.*

Next, based on what he discovered on the conference website, DeMeo made four calls and left four messages: at the Hilton Prague front desk, the concierge, the main convention office, and Eccleston's STOQ office in Vatican City. Each time he left a message to call. Not too much, but enough to seed curiosity. DeMeo also got the priest's email address from the woman at the convention and sent a more enticing tickler about a new, potentially controversial discovery. It said nothing and something at the same time.

An hour later, Pete DeMeo was on the phone with the dynamic Vatican priest. He explained in general terms what McCauley would cover in specific. It was sufficient to engage Eccleston, who said he'd be back in Rome in two days and would be open to a meeting.

DeMeo was into his goodbye just as he felt Lucia Solera's breath on his neck and her arms wrapping around him. He wondered whether she'd been listening the entire time.

SIXTY-TWO

London

KATRINA WAS FIXED on locating the French explorer. Mc-
Cauley assigned himself two calls: one to Father Eccleston,
whose number he had thanks to Pete DeMeo. When the
priest didn't answer, he left a message and dialed the second. It was eight hours earlier in California; not quite 2
A.M. He figured Robert Greene would be awake.

On the third ring, Greene answered his cell.

"Identify," he said not knowing the call ID.

"It's McCauley."

"He lives," Greene said.

"Apparently so do you."

"What can I do you for, doctor?"

"First of all, how are you?"

"Fine. Better than fine. I've never had so many hits on
my website. Immediately made bestseller status online.
Seems that attempted murder gives the conspiracy crowd
raw meat. I don't think they'll touch me again. Besides,
I came up with a great cockamamie story that gives your
friends cover and me breathing room."

"Breathing is good."

"Breathing is what I live for."

McCauley agreed. "No truer words, my friend. So who'd
you blame?"

"I mentioned a couple of shady groups working out of
Ciudad del Este, Paraguay. Shady is an understatement.

It's the Western Hemisphere home to Hamas, Hezbollah and some crazy Korean and Japanese gangs. With a little research, I stumbled on a recent CIA operation—black op stuff—that presumably brought down some major dude. So I figured, why not mention Ciudad del Este terrorists in the same sentence as the explosion. That's how it begins."

"Creepy," McCauley said.

"Oh, you have no idea," Greene added. "So I assume you need something."

"More help. We found a book. There aren't many copies around. I'll send you a screen shot of the cover, a sketch that's in it, and some translations. It'll help with a lot of what we didn't tell you."

"You didn't tell me a damn thing!"

"Right," McCauley laughed. "I forgot. Well, this will and I'd love your opinion."

"Opinion? I see we're still choosing our words carefully, Dr. McCauley. So here's the deal, if I find anything relevant, do me a favor, no more visits and keep it between us. My insurance deductible went way the hell up because of you!"

SIXTY-THREE

Southern Italy

DEMEO AND SOLERA WERE cruising along A45 heading south on a sleek six cylinder gray and black BMW K1600 GTL. Lucia held him tightly. Occasionally her fingers would wander. That was an unmistakable signal for DeMeo to pull the rented motorcycle off the road, which he did with no argument. So far they'd made three stops. He wasn't sure he could live up to another. But the vision excited him and he'd give it all he could.

A few more miles down the highway his cell phone rang. He wore an earphone and microphone in his helmet.

"So, where are you?" McCauley said on the other end of the call. It was extremely noisy.

"Apparently not out of earshot, boss. I hope the number helped."

"Thanks. I left a message."

"Where are you heading?"

"So far, on the road to debauchery. Eventually the Amalfi Coast."

"Okay. But please, Pete, be careful."

"Hang on for a sec. Too noisy. Gonna pull over."

DeMeo slowed and rolled to a stop. Cars that hadn't kept up with him, now passed at blistering speeds.

"Okay, what were you saying?"

"Waiting for a call back. Meanwhile, please be careful."

"All's fine," he said lasciviously. "Meanwhile, are you going to do what you promised?"

"Thinking about it."

"You do it! Talk to the priest, then quit this. Maybe in a few years you can write a paper on it. Whatever *it* is."

"Right."

"Do more than think. Have your conversation with your fellow traveler."

"Okay."

Lucia's hands were wandering again.

"Gotta go. I'll call you when... I," DeMeo laughed, "...recover. Bye."

DeMeo flicked the kickstand, stepped off the motor-cycle and removed his helmet.

"So who was on the phone? Seemed like work. I don't want you to think about work."

DeMeo laughed. "How'd you know?"

"Your body is like, how to explain, an echo chamber. Hellooo...helloooo."

She continued to busy her hands. "No, no, no. Let's get back on the road. I need a real hotel bed."

"What if I can't wait?" she cooed.

"You do have that problem!"

DeMeo stretched his legs and was ready to gun the bike. But Lucia kissed his neck and nuzzled up to his ear. "So, who was on the phone?"

He turned half way around. "Just my boss."

"I thought you were through."

"I am."

"Good answer, silly man," she said "But when we check in, you'll have to fill me in." Her fingers put an exclamation point where none was needed.

SIXTY-FOUR

London

McCauley quickly realized the conversation with Katrina wasn't going well. But, it was worse than that. They were circling each other in Kritz's flat, taking turns as predator.

"I've had to worry about you since you first showed up!" he said.

"You were only worried about your own standing and what I'd report," Alpert shot back.

"As a spy."

"In an open, academic, and professional evaluation."

"Bullshit. You came with a holier than thou attitude. I didn't need anyone under my feet then and I sure as hell don't want the responsibility watching over you now."

"You misogynistic, anachronistic, self-absorbed twit. Do you think for one minute that if I simply return to Cambridge, which is only thirty minutes away, I'll be any safer than I am under your supreme care? For that matter, what about you? You call *game over* and think everything will be okay back in New Haven? Jesus, McCauley, you're one of the strangest creatures I've ever dug up!"

Alpert was winning the battle of the words. McCauley exhaled slowly.

"I'm sorry, I thought it would be better for you to go home."

"Wrong. Sure I'm scared, but don't think it'll all get better sending me away. Show me what you've got inside those briefs," Alpert said hearkening back to their first conversation.

They stared at one another and then broke up.

"You were doing great until the underwear reference," he offered.

"I wasn't referring to your underwear, mister. Your balls!"

"I got it."

"Then get this. We're doing this together, just like we started."

"Why do I feel like I've known you longer?" McCauley asked.

"An argument will do that. Running for our lives will do that."

"Yes, I guess it will."

"So tomorrow we see Bovard in France. Together," Alpert affirmed. She was clearly the victor.

"Together."

SIXTY-FIVE

Lyon, France
Later the next day

McCAULEY AND ALPERT took an inexpensive ninety minute easyJet flight from London's Gatwick Airport to Lyon,
France. After another forty-five minutes, much of it uncomfortable thanks to a cabbie with a particularly heavy
foot, they gratefully arrived at Claude Bovard's home on
the outskirts of the historic town.

The French explorer invited McCauley and Alpert to
sit down and join him in a bottle of Bordeaux. They both
passed and asked for some stomach quenching Coke.
Bovard seemed to understand. "Ah, you undoubtedly had
one of our Grand Prix hopefuls," he said. "There are many.
The worst, however, are in Nice. They try to set a new
record every time they drive from the airport. Quite the
experience."

Alpert laughed. McCauley just wanted to curl up into
a ball and rest, but the soda soon refreshed him. While
Bovard casually spoke, Quinn took in the explorer's living
room, decorated with artifacts from decades of explorations representing every continent in the world. He identified fossils from a distance: a footprint of a Brachiosaurus
from the late Jurassic period, likely from Colorado, and
a backbone from a Tyrannosaurus rex that inhabited an
even older earth. Bovard noted his interest and pointed

out plaster molds of three-feet tall stalagmites and photographs of cave dweller paintings.

Quinn and Katrina appreciated his explanation, however, they hadn't come for a Cook's tour. Nor did Claude Bovard invite them there for small talk.

"Yes," the seventy-nine-year-old explorer suddenly said.

"Yes?" McCauley responded with uncertainty.

"Yes, it is now time for questions and answers. I have seen what you speak of."

Bovard settled into a leather chair as dry, worn, and craggy as the features on his face. His most notable feature—his eyes. They were completely hypnotic, maybe because of the marvels the explorer had observed through his life.

"Your principal work has been on the surface, correct?" Bovard stroked his full white beard. He looked the part of a spelunker.

"You could say that."

"The most beautiful and extraordinary discoveries are not sifted through screen meshes in the daylight, they're revealed by the narrow light from a helmet in the darkest, coldest environs. That's where true art is to be discovered—art that the earth has created.

"Based on what Dr. Alpert explained on the telephone, you search for evidence of death," the old explorer continued. "My work constantly demonstrates that the earth is truly alive."

"Both are important," McCauley said in an almost challenging tone.

"Forgive me, Dr. McCauley. Of course. I didn't mean to disparage your scholarly endeavors. Sometimes I forget myself."

McCauley nodded appreciatively. "We have the same

desire, Monsieur Bovard. To delve into the unknown, evaluate the possible, and postulate on the impossible. As academicians, we also have a hell of a lot of paperwork to do." He looked at Katrina. It was a light-hearted glance that was returned with a kick to his shin.

"Thank goodness I have only had to please the foundations who support me," Bovard replied. "But they fête me with far too many broiled chicken dinners."

"Chicken? You do realize you're eating the same protein structure that was contained in dinosaurs," McCauley noted.

"Point well taken. Perhaps there are more similarities than differences to our work."

With the mood lightened, they moved into a spirited discussion about the spelunker's explorations.

"Permit me to cover some basic ground…or *underground* as it were." Bovard laughed at his own joke.

"Please," McCauley encouraged.

"Of course, you have long learned things from the dinosaur bones that speak to you. I get my stories from the earth's bones; the vessels of which are different types of caves. As you know, limestone caves are the most common. To my mind, these are the most adventurous and challenging. I've also explored many of the world's majestic ice caves including the largest in Eisriesenwelt, Austria which is more than forty-two kilometers in length."

Next, he talked about lava and sea caves. Most were formed by volcanic rock, weakened along fault lines and carved by the action of waves. "I've been to the longest in the world, the Matainaka Cave in New Zealand."

Finally, he gave his guests a primer on how wind and rain had carved caves out of compressed sandstone, fused at the bottom of ancient oceans turned to deserts. All of this was important to Bovard. He sought to make certain that the paleontologists would see the earth's hidden spaces as he saw them. "I have been to the earth's most magnificent natural cathedrals; awe-inspiring, profound and humbling, with spires reaching through the darkness toward the heavens and light streaming through cracks that pointed to God's greatness."

"That is my world—speleothems, the cave formations that can positively leave you speechless. Like dripping icicles, but rock. Flowstones that appear to be frozen water. Stalactites that hang like curtains from the ceiling. Gypsum crystals that rise like shards from Superman's Fortress of Solitude and crystalline calcite and aragonite that resemble frost on a winter's window."

The explorer dropped his voice. "However, make no mistake, caves are dangerous places as much as irreplaceable grand museums," the explorer explained. "They're forged by the ages, shaped by wind, water, earth's movements, tsunamis, and yes, the changing climate. As permanent as we may think they are, they are not. Nothing about the earth is permanent. And," Bovard offered, "they're unpredictable. The forces that created them are the same forces that, over time, alter them. Water tables rise and fall, weakening foundations, ceilings and walls. Rain causes runoffs which can lead to rock slides. In mere seconds, earthquakes close caverns for good and open others we'd never known. And gas leaks are a true threat to deep cave explorers and casual hikers. They're volatile and flammable. You don't want to be around, near, or in one when it explodes. But many times, a human presence in a cave is the destabilizing factor to cause a major change."

The Frenchman shook his head. "And when destruction comes by man's stupidity or man's intention, it should be considered a criminal act against nature; against the earth itself."

"Monsieur, you've seen such incidences?" McCauley asked.

"Of course. When you've explored as much as I have, you've seen it all."

McCauley wondered if that was true. He'd find out soon enough.

"I've made my way through the deepest, longest, most remote, dangerous and out of the way caves in the world," Bovard further explained. "Those that others have put in their history books, and a fair share for which I can take all the credit. Among the most fascinating—the Covaciella Caves in Asturias, Spain. Tremendous finds. Upper Paleolithic age. Real evidence of how human groups helped one another survive the last glacial period. Then there's Reed Flute Cave near the Guangxi Zhuang Autonomous Region of China and Atta Cave, in Sauerland, Germany. All with remarkably different histories. I also spent a good deal of time, many years ago, exploring the Kungur Ice Cave in the Perm region of east central Russia."

"Actually, there is another cave in Russia that interested us," McCauley stated.

"Which?"

"Denisova."

"Denisova," the old explorer recalled. "Yes, Denisova. I was there when I was much younger. I know its story."

"The complete story?" Katrina wondered.

Bovard frowned. "Considering you put it that way, perhaps I'm not certain. I was referring to Saint Denis, the hermit. Is there more?"

McCauley and Alpert looked at one another for affirmation. McCauley nodded.

"There was a large cavern within the cave that contained remarkable"—McCauley thought about how to phrase his point—"out-of-place artifacts."

Bovard's mind was sharp. He responded without any hesitation. "I can assure you, there was no large cavern with any such things when I explored. What are you talking about?"

Quinn passed Father Emilianov's book to the explorer. "Look at this."

Bovard opened the memoir and turned to the page flagged with a yellow sticky. He looked troubled. He examined the book cover and the copyright. Then he leafed through other pages in the section and read the Russian quite easily. He whispered the words as his finger trailed across the sentences.

"This isn't the same cave I explored. Or at least it's a different entrance to the system.

"Exactly," McCauley said, leaning in.

SIXTY-SIX

London
The same time

"Ms. DUNBAR," KAVANAUGH SAID, breezing past his secretary's desk, "book me on a flight to Rome tomorrow morning. Non-stop. Premium class."

She didn't show her surprise. But her response surely questioned his judgment. "Mr. Kavanaugh, this week is deadline."

"I'm quite aware of my magazine's deadlines and my responsibilities."

"I understand, but sir, Mr. Gr…"

She didn't get to complete her sentence. Kavanaugh hovered over her and proclaimed, "Reservations tomorrow. Rome."

"Yes, Mr. Kavanaugh and Premium class."

Kavanaugh returned to his office and slammed the door.

SIXTY-SEVEN

Lyon, France

"DESCRIBE WHAT YOU saw at Denisova?" McCauley requested.

Bovard considered the question with multifold interest; his own and wonder over his visitors' interest.

"For accuracy sake, I would have to search my notes," the Frenchman said. "It could have been a natural cave-in. I recall tunnels that should have led somewhere, but appeared to be blocked. Remember, I am not a miner. I don't dig my way into caverns."

"So it's possible the hermit and the priest's access was closed up?"

"Yes, quite possible. Or that it collapsed. That wouldn't prevent another entrance from being discovered. But now that you raise the question, I'd like to check other incidences. It will take a while. Help yourself to some coffee in the kitchen."

Bovard excused himself for twenty minutes. He returned with a large carton of files.

"I wanted to explore so much more." He removed his glasses and cleaned the lenses with the silk scarf he wore. "Natural caves and even abandoned mines. No matter what, I was always amazed," he said nostalgically. "The real riches aren't the minerals that can be extracted and exploited. It's the history itself that remains there."

"Is there anything that relates to Denisova?" Katrina dared.

"No…and yes."

The answer was intriguing.

"No, I found nothing of an unusual, shall I say, *nature*. But taking in other reports and your cryptic suggestions, perhaps yes."

Bovard thumbed through the files in the boxes. He rejected most, but pulled a few papers. "These are principally cave-ins that I couldn't explain or didn't believe the explanations. An explosion at a cave in China. Another in South Africa, and the most interesting…let's look at this one. A site I visited almost four decades ago." He refreshed his memory with a copy of an old newspaper clipping. "In Senghenydd, Wales."

"Where?" McCaulcy couldn't quite get the Welsh name through the thick French accent.

"A mine in Wales pronounced *Sen-knee-need*." He handed McCauley a photocopy of a newspaper clipping from 1913. "Little is known about this. It was over-shadowed by another mining accident at the same location a few months later. That one still grabs all the attention, as well it should. It remains the worst mining disaster in the British Isles. Some have speculated that they are related."

Bovard explained both cave-ins were reportedly the result of coal gas explosions. He laughed. "Bull *sheet*." His accent made his expletive sound cleaner.

"The first occurred far into a mine that, according to the archival reports, was not producing any coal. The likelihood of volatile coal gas coming from nowhere? You tell me, Dr. McCauley?"

"Not likely."

"Dr. Alpert?"

"Not in my expertise."

"So, if not an explosion caused by coal gas, which, at the time, claimed the life of the site manager, then what?"

The question begged for an answer, but the old explorer held up his hand.

"Little has been reported. To this day, only a few locals gossip about it through the unreliable filter of multiple generations. Nonetheless, rumors tell a story of a mysterious find, an unscheduled visit by an unknown mining supervisor, the deadly explosion that killed the company man, and the disappearance of the supervisor soon after. Makes for a good conspiracy, wouldn't you say?"

"And we heard about you from a conspiracy theorist in America. Robert Greene." Katrina softly said.

"Ah, yes, the irrepressible young Mr. Greene. We've done some broadcasts together. How clever. He neither told you, nor me, what he wanted you to find. Maybe this is it."

"A theory? A feeling?" McCauley complained. "A rumor?"

"More than that, Dr. McCauley."

It came to Quinn. "Evidence of evidence. Maybe much like"—he tapped the cover of the priest's memoir—"what the good Father Emilianov saw."

SIXTY-EIGHT

Rome
The same day

THE PAULIST PRIEST arrived to an empty, dark apartment. *Home,* he said to himself. Five days in Prague had been quite enough. Nobody came to any conclusions. *How could we,* he thought. But that didn't prevent the member of STOQ and the Pontifical Academy of Sciences from being predictably exciting, inspiring and living up to his reputation as a renegade in the house of the Lord.

He dropped his suitcase in the kitchen, flicked on the overhead light and checked the refrigerator. The few take-out containers with leftovers didn't interest him, neither did he consider the idea of washing the sink full of dirty dishes inviting. His two roommates, also priests, were at another conference in Madrid. They'd left the mess.

Since he wasn't up for cleaning, he also didn't want to cook. So, Father Jareth Eccleston turned off the light and went for a late supper at his local haunt, De Giovanni's, for one of his favorite dishes, *tortelloni ricotta e spinaci.* Since he primarily spent alone time in deep thought, he wasn't aware of the man who had followed him in and watched him throughout his dinner.

Chicago, IL
The same time

RICH TAMBURRO HADN'T heard from Anna Chohany since he last saw her at the hospital in Glendive. He'd left so many messages on her cell that her voicemail maxed out. Considering she hadn't posted anything new on Facebook or Instagram in the days since she left Montana, he was concerned that she hadn't made it home safely. Even though there was no doubt now that she was somebody's mole, he decided to drive to Ann Arbor with the hope of finding her.

Makoshika State Park, MT
The same time

"I CAN'T EXPLAIN," Park Director Jim Kaplan told the chief on-site National Transportation Safety Board investigator, Lee Miller. "It's certainly a first for us."

"And the visiting college group? They've all left?" asked the fifty-five-year-old officer who wore a black tee shirt with the agency's NTSB letters prominently displayed on the back in bright yellow. "Rather quickly, wouldn't you say?"

"They'd packed up the day before the crash."

"A coincidence," Miller commented, suggesting just the opposite.

"No coincidence. They'd wrapped. Dr. McCauley had just returned from some meetings and he determined it was time to call it quits. He's an expert. If he felt it was time to go, it was."

"I heard they had a few more weeks."

"They did, but it wasn't a particularly successful summer and one of the team got hurt."

Miller, a former Navy F-18 pilot, was raising questions well beyond the scope of the crash. But there were unusual circumstances. Principally—no bodies in the wreck. Now three days into the investigation, the field of inquiry extended beyond the crash site. The NTSB team was scouring the badlands for a survivor who may have safely parachuted or a pilot whose parachute failed to open.

There were also other questions. Particularly interesting was why couldn't he reach Dr. Quinn McCauley… anywhere?

QUINN AND KATRINA left Bovard without anything definitive. But the intersections of the past and the present came closer together: a Russian cave and their own discovery in Montana; the priest's account from more than 225 years ago; and Scnghenydd and other mysteries the explorer couldn't explain. All *part of a something* rather than the *something* itself.

McCauley struggled with another troubling thought. He wasn't able to reach Pete DeMeo on his phone.

"He probably hasn't gotten out of bed," Katrina said suggestively.

McCauley, too concerned, didn't laugh.

SIXTY-NINE

Rome
The next morning

MCCAULEY AND ALPERT'S flight touched down at *Fiumicino Aeroporto*, better known as Leonardo da Vinci International, sixteen miles southwest of Rome. Seconds after landing, McCauley telephoned Eccleston's cell.

"Pronto."

"Good morning. Is this Father Jareth Eccleston?"

"Yes," said the groggy priest. His Welsh accent was evident.

"I'm sorry, did I wake you?"

"It's okay," the priest replied. "My stars, it's almost noon."

"I apologize. I can call back in a little while."

"Who is this?"

"My name is Quinn McCauley, from Yale University. I'm a paleontologist. You spoke with my assistant the other day."

"McCauley?"

"Yes, Father."

"Dr. Quinn McCauley? Oh yes. You had some research questions apparently."

"Yes. I've just arrived in Rome with my colleague, Dr. Katrina Alpert from Cambridge. Would you be available to meet this afternoon? I recognize it's short notice, but…"

"It depends. Can you give me a better sense of the agenda?"

"I'd rather do that in person. Let's just say that you were recommended based on your research and your willingness to think out of the box."

"Out of the box, Dr. McCauley? Or between the lines in the Bible?"

"I don't know how to answer that, Father Eccleston. All I know is that you might be very important to talk to. I think you'll agree, it won't be a waste of time."

Three hours later

KATRINA RE-EXAMINED a photograph of the priest on her cell phone. Now in the main Vatican library they looked for the same man, age fifty-five, who in the picture had a full beard and wore large tortoise-shell glasses.

After fifteen minutes, their anxiety abated. A larger-than-life character wearing the requisite garb, bounded into the Vatican Apostolic Library. He was, without a doubt, Father Jareth Eccleston, a man with an unmistakable quality and incredible vigor. The headshot on the Internet couldn't have suggested his height. At six-foot-six he could very well stand closer to God than any other priest in the Vatican.

McCauley covered half the ground toward the priest. Katrina was right behind him.

"Father Eccleston?"

"Please, Jareth works fine." His voice was as deep as his smile was wide. The priest's Welsh accent glided from a high-to-low pitch, like a lilting folk song.

"Jareth it is. Quinn McCauley. So pleased to meet you. And this is Dr. Alpert."

"Katrina," she quickly corrected.

"Well, let me show you around a bit. This library is a feast for the eyes."

Neither McCauley nor Alpert had been to the Vatican Apostolic Library before. It was a researcher's mistake. Father Eccleston explained how the library was one of the oldest in all Europe, and for centuries, the largest. The shelves covered religion, secular history, politics, philosophy and science, and a collection of Bibles from around the world. "The library houses an immense collection of Greek and Latin classics plus compendia of maps and military history. Some were claimed in bloody conquests and *found* their way to the Vatican. Speaking of conquests, we also have Henry VIII's love letters to Anne Boleyn. You know where that led!" He gave a hearty laugh. "Imagine such material being read under candlelight by, well, whomever might be into such *research*."

As they continued their walk through the venerable structure, the priest described the depth of the Renaissance collection and the thousands of volumes that chronicled the history of the Roman Catholic Church and Rome itself.

"Contrary to popular thought, it's an issue-neutral facility. You'll find books about the challenges the Church faced through the Protestant Reformation, the Catholic Counter-Reformation, and how the Vatican sided with or sidestepped dictators and despots. The resources go well beyond Catholicism. The Vatican Library is steeped in essays, letters, books and rare research covering Judaism, Islam, Hinduism and Buddhism, and likely every religion under the sun.

"This, of course, started as the pope's library, dating back to the middle of the fifteenth century, established by Nicholas V. His goal was to create a public library for the court of Rome as well as clergy and laymen. It would be a work of art itself, rivaling St. Peter's for attention," the priest added. "Nicholas and his successors collected beautiful hand-written books and the earliest of print editions, displaying them in frescoed suites, lit by huge windows. But to protect them from theft, the church brought in some of its extra iron chains and locks, anchoring the most valuable editions to wooden benches. In my estimation, a much better use of the hardware than in its dreadful prisons in the bowels of the Vatican."

McCauley and Alpert enjoyed Fr. Eccleston's engaging delivery.

"By the mid-1400s," Eccleston continued, "there were more than 3,500 volumes notated in the handwritten catalogue. Amazing for its time, even more incredible through the ages. The library soon became an obligatory destination for writers, theologians, philosophers and even scientists who visited Rome. I kind of cover both sides of the equation."

"Is that difficult?" Katrina wondered.

"Not for me. Oh, sometimes I can bend a bishop's nose out of joint. When that happens I hear about it. So far, nothing so great that it's required serious thumping. Not like what my brethren experienced years ago."

Eccleston stopped and thought. "Is this going to be one of those times, doctors?"

"Father Eccleston," McCauley said aware that he was speaking completely formally, "is there a place we can talk quietly?"

"I've half expected you to ask. Certainly. But first we have to get you admitted."

Eccleston took a few steps forward and spoke in Italian to the nearest librarian. Alpert followed as best she could. McCauley picked up a few words. It was all polite. The librarian made a call. Soon, a nun came through the door, marching toward them with the look of someone who was going to require serious convincing.

"Sister Cynthia Fernando," Eccleston said softly. "We have a number of nicknames for her."

"I can only imagine," Katrina said noting the nun's bulldog expression.

"Padre," Sister Cynthia began. The rest was only understood by expression, at first troubled, then more so. Eccleston steered the gatekeeper away from them. From a few feet away they heard their formal names. "Dr. Mc-Cauley, Yale. Dr. Alpert, Cambridge."

McCauley felt that Sister Cynthia would have made a great Inquisition jailor. It seems that's how she saw her job.

Eccleston didn't stop pitching. She listened. The worst thing he could do was pause and allow her time to curtly dismiss them.

The nun frowned, nodded *no*, and turned to McCauley and Alpert as if to evaluate their worthiness. They automatically straightened and looked as professional as possible. A suit would have helped McCauley, but he was still in an acceptable dark sports jacket. Fortunately, Katrina was wearing the proper length dress and covered up appropriately.

Another minute of selling and the nun finally nodded *yes*. Father Eccleston motioned for his guests to join him.

Sister Cynthia did not step aside. They had to walk around her.

"Gracia," McCauley said.

"Gracia, Sorella," Alpert added.

"Just walk quietly," Fr. Eccleston recommended.

"What did you tell her?" Alpert asked.

"Later."

The priest led them through the library to an open table.

When he was certain they were out of earshot of anyone else, Eccleston answered Katrina's question.

"I told Sister Cynthia that my esteemed colleagues had come all this way to compare signatures on some letters they brought from their respective colleges' collections. Very old, very rare, but if authentic, would add significantly to history of seventeenth century science." He smiled. "You did bring some letters or did I explain things incorrectly?"

"Father Eccleston," McCauley observed, "you told Sister Cynthia a bold-faced lie."

"Oh dear me. Did I misstate anything? I will surely have to apologize at some later date."

With that, they moved on. The priest took them past the public shelves, into a corridor where they settled into an empty long wooden table.

"Please, sit, but we will have to keep our voices very low. We're actually supposed to work in complete silence."

"Okay," McCauley whispered. "But I'm curious. How do you square your religious beliefs with your research?"

Father Eccleston grimaced. "That has the sting of a no-win declaration from a cardinal. And I would describe my beliefs as faith."

"I'm sorry," McCauley said, "but it's important."

"May I ask why?"

"You can see why." The professor cocked his head to Alpert. "Katrina."

Alpert picked up the backpack she'd been clutching and removed a manila envelope. She slid it across the table to Eccleston.

The priest opened it and saw the copies Kritz printed in London. Katrina waited for him to review the content. "They're pages from a book we found," she said. "An old priest's book written 150-plus years ago in…"

"In Denisova," Eccleston volunteered. "St. Denis' cave. I heard such a memoir exists. However, I've never seen it. Where did you find it?"

"Wait," McCauley said. He held up two fingers. Time for the second envelope. "Here are the translations of those pages."

The priest read them with great interest; his engagement growing with every paragraph. "Remarkable," he whispered. "Tell me where…"

"We have a friend in London to thank," Katrina said. "At Oxford."

"The Bod?"

"Yes," she added.

"That's odd. It should have come up on Google Book Search. The Oxford Library is part of their resource community."

"I can explain," McCauley replied. "After locating the book, quite by accident, I checked the catalog. It wasn't in the system. So officially, it didn't exist and as a result— full confession Father—I felt I didn't have to sign it out."

"You realize this could very well be the only edition around."

"We're checking on that."

"Perhaps the fact that it *was* on the shelves was an oversight. Maybe it was supposed to be removed or someone thought it had been. Doesn't that raise interesting possibilities?" Eccleston offered.

"Perhaps. How did you know about the book?" McCauley inquired.

"Rumors in the seminary that were told in the dark. Old tales that never went away. The things that priests whisper, mostly to scare young students. The kind of stories that you hope aren't true."

At that point, Katrina carefully removed the precious book from her backpack and handed it to Eccelston.

"Jesus, Mary, and Joseph! Is this…?"

"Yes."

"I can't believe it. May I?"

"Of course."

He held it with genuine reverence. "Father Mykhailo Emilianov's actual memoir." He slowly turned the pages, and though he couldn't read it, he felt like he was absorbing the meaning.

He stopped on the page depicting Emilianov's sketch of the cavern interior and the deep black wall. "What is this?"

McCauley removed an envelope from his sports jacket. "The same as this photo I shot." He handed Eccleston a photograph.

"You've been there," he predictably replied.

"No, as a matter of fact." McCauley smiled. "Interested in talking more?"

THEY SHARED A taxi for the three kilometer ride from the Vatican to Eccleston's neighborhood restaurant on Via Antonio Salandra.

"You'll like the food," he said pointing out the chalkboard menu of the day posted to the left of the door. The choices did look delicious. *Pasta e Lenticchie, Polenta con Salsicce, Fettuccine Agnolotti, Filetto o Lombata*, and more. Inside, they took a corner seat with Eccleston intentionally placing himself with his back to the wall so he could see everyone who entered and where they sat.

A young waiter automatically placed a bottle of the house wine at the table.

"Perfecto," he said in thanks. *"Grazie."*

It felt like a warm, welcoming, inviting family restaurant with wood-lined walls that were adorned with candlesticks, plates, photographs, and paintings; all likely meaningful to the owners.

"We'll order, then talk. Trust me, you'll be well fed."

McCauley and Katrina decided to share the *tagliolini cacio e pepe*, a pasta with pecorino cheese and black pepper. Fr. Eccleston chose the filet.

A few bites into the meal, Eccleston returned to their earlier discussion.

"The book is a treasure. But the old priest's sketch of the interior confused me. Much clearer in your photographs, but still…"

"Father, the pictures aren't from Denisova. We took them in Montana, in a cave we discovered while exploring for fossils, a half a world away and more than a century apart."

Eccleston struggled for the right response. It finally came to him. "This isn't natural."

"No, it's not," McCauley replied. "We thought you might have some sort of theory."

"We'd also like to see if you can find out anything about Father Emilianov," Katrina added.

"Like what?"

"Anything. Everything."

"Well, in the old days the kind of theory I'm working on would have seen me burned at the stake. Fortunately, no one does that anymore."

McCauley thought back on Bakersfield. "I'm not so sure."

FOR THE NEXT thirty minutes, Quinn and Katrina recounted their experiences and how they came to get in touch with Eccleston. It led the priest to what at first seemed like an intellectual discourse.

"Throughout history holy wars have been fought in the name of multiple deities and others justified by a leader proclaiming the word of a single god. Faith has been used as a tool by religious groups, not necessarily under the auspices of the religion itself. And rogue governments have equally persecuted believers they quite simply considered too dangerous to live. Territories have been claimed in the name of trade, where the spoils were measured in gold or a slave's worth. And to protect their bounty, to hold their borders and to insure their power, churches and institutions alike have relied on fear, lies, hatred, patriotism and fundamentalist principles."

"It's as true today as ever," Katrina stated.

"But with greater fragility," McCauley added. "News spreads so quickly through social media. Information is so accessible virtually anywhere in the world that words and thoughts, multiplied and amplified by hitting *send* on a cell phone can topple a regime. We've seen it in the Middle East. I'm not so sure it couldn't happen elsewhere."

"I'm afraid you're right. We tread on the thin ice of critical beliefs," Eccleston replied. "The weight of any social, political, or moral argument can do us in."

McCauley considered the issues, not just in America, but in an increasingly polarizing world. Each side espouses its positions as God-given rights, whether for or against. Without even realizing it, he started listing the extremes that fuel heated debates on any given day. "Reproduction, guns, immigration, medical insurance, gay rights, food stamps, welfare. It's all just up or down," McCauley said. "You're part of the solution or part of the problem."

And then he thought of another volatile subject, debated for centuries, more contentious than ever.

"Evolution."

"Yes," the priest agreed. He rested his hand on the envelope containing McCauley's photographs. "It's still on the table, isn't it?"

SEVENTY

"HAVE YOU EVER heard of "Gap Theory?"" Fr. Eccleston asked.

"Yes," Katrina responded. "Pseudo-science. Dismissible. An explanation that covers ancient geological ages in support of biblical belief."

"Ancient doesn't begin to describe it," the priest said.

Katrina looked confused. McCauley wasn't certain why the priest was bringing up the subject. It was hardly discussed anymore and seemingly not on point.

"If I may?"

"Go right ahead, Father. Chapter and verse," McCauley replied.

The priest poured another glass of the house wine from Castelli Romani, south of Rome. He held it to the light to examine the rich reds, drank some, and continued.

"Gap Theory proposes that a span of time existed between Genesis 1:1 and Genesis 1:2. From a strictly theological point of view, Gap Theory maintains that a cataclysmic judgment was prescribed as a result of the fall of Lucifer. For the sake of keeping you in the discussion, let's put aside the religious construal. I'll simply call it a line of reasoning."

"Appreciated," McCauley said.

"The argument can be traced to the early nineteenth century. As the science of geology gained, pardon the expression, *ground*, some theologians were at a loss how to counter the scientific claims that the formation of the earth's surfaces occurred at imperceptibly slow rates. They needed an explanation that supported the biblical record. You might call it scriptural enlightenment: a way to describe the vast geological periods before Adam. Conveniently perhaps, a place was found between the two verses of Genesis.

"It was proposed by a Scotsman, theologian Thomas Chalmers, in 1814. It was further espoused by two American ministers, Cyrus Scofield and Clarence Larkin, and evangelist Harry Rimmer in the twentieth century. Each wrote books on the subject, trying to justify the gap between ruin and reconstruction."

The priest took another satisfying sip of the wine. He saw that his guests needed more. He gave them each a liberal refill and signaled the waiter for a new bottle.

"Now to specifics. Follow me."

"We are," Alpert said.

"Genesis 1:1 expresses the creation of the universe. Then, in geological terms, five billion years presumably came and went, producing ages you're well aware of with its various life-forms. Gap Theory then seeks to explain that all life on Earth was destroyed."

"The meteor that wiped out the dinosaurs," Alpert stated.

"Yes, leaving fossils for you to uncover. This cataclysmic event, according to the theorists, is what's described in Genesis 1:2. This solved the biblical problem of *time*, and helped to square natural history with the scriptural interval, described as *days*."

McCauley interrupted. "Yes, but..."

"Wait," Father Eccleston said. "It gets better. Gap Theory rests on the need for re-creation. It holds to the paleontological record that has produced dinosaur fossil beds on every continent. It also allows for the sudden transformation of the environment. In a word, it works."

"But…"

"Not yet, Dr. Alpert," the priest chided. "I have one other point for you to consider."

She leaned back in her chair and listened.

"What if…" Eccleston paused. He wanted the full attention of his companions. "What if we dismiss the theological justification? After all, it never gained much support. Strip away the religious argument and stay with the basic idea. Can we accept a gap between life-forms? From trilobites through the dinosaurs to the evolution of man?

"Of course," Katrina replied.

McCauley remained at the table but left the conversation, thinking, *Gap.* He repeated the word to himself. Definitions rushed forward from his years of study. General usage, medical, mathematical, geographic. *An empty space; an interruption in continuity; a divergence; a difference; an interval. Disparity in attitudes, ideals and actions.*

If the priest was still talking, McCauley didn't hear him.

Etymology: gapa—a hole in a wall, a break or pass in a long mountain chain.

Impossible possibilities were coming together. Quickly. *The cave. The discovery. The conversations. The attack. The book.* And still another notion. It was a dialectic he'd had with his grad students in Montana.

"The absence of evidence is not the evidence of absence."

"What?" Katrina asked. McCauley hadn't realized he'd spoken aloud.

"What?" she repeated. "You said, 'The absence of evidence…'"

"Is not the evidence of absence. A gap."

Katrina was still confused. "The gap?"

"Not *the* gap. A gap. *Before.*"

"Before? Before what?" Katrina wondered.

"Before what is described in Genesis."

"Or part of it," Eccleston said. "We better leave." He signaled for the check. "Let's move this to my apartment."

McCauley paid the tab. On the way out, Katrina pulled him close and asked the inevitable follow-up while the priest walked a few feet ahead. "What were you talking about? It obviously scooted us out of there."

"An epiphany. Or," McCauley admitted, "a wild ass assumption. I'll explain."

Father Eccleston bounded up the three flights with Quinn and Katrina in tow. He asked forgiveness for the mess they'd face and the reason: "My roommates. I'll keep the lights down. You'll hardly notice. Even in full daylight there isn't much to see except the simple residence of three priests, two of them slobs."

He directed them to the couch. "Sit down. We're alone. Fr. Densey and Fr. Santiago left on sabbatical. So we'll be able to speak openly. I'll be right back."

As Eccleston went through his cabinets, McCauley glanced around the apartment. Eccleston's description of Spartan was completely accurate. White walls, few chairs, low wood coffee table, lamps that didn't match, an old throw rug, and no living room curtains. Apparently good enough for a trio of priests living off-site on limited Vatican stipends, right down to the three wine glasses Eccleston returned with that didn't match.

"Sabbatical. An interesting word in itself, wouldn't you say?" Eccleston noted while pouring. "From Greek *sabbatikos* and Latin *sabbaticus*. And, of course, Hebrew *Shabbat*. From Genesis 2:2-3. On the seventh day God rested after creating the universe. Described in Leviticus 25 as a commandment to cease working in the field the seventh year, reiterated in Deuteronomy 5:12-15."

"You have your numbers down," McCauley observed.

"Chalk it up to my share of sabbaticals," Eccleston laughed.

Katrina chimed in, "We live for them, too."

Once the wine was served, Eccleston proposed a simple toast. "To our finding the answers we seek."

"I'll drink to that." Quinn reached for the bottle to see what it was. "Verdicchio?"

"Yes, I think you'll like this," he said.

The priest held up his glass to the lamp light and examined its luster. "So beautiful. From a magnificent yellow-green grape. See how the final product embraces and expands upon the original hues. Much like our conversation tonight."

His guests examined it in the same way.

"Now, take in the floral aroma."

They brought their wine glasses to their nose and acknowledged the scent.

"This Verdicchio hasn't changed since the fourteenth century. It's from Le Marche region, still produced by Brothers at Verdicchio del Castelli di Jesi."

"Quite a tradition, Father," Alpert said. "I really like this."

"I'll tell you someone who enjoyed the Verdicchio in Le Marche."

The priest captivated Katrina. "Oh?"

"Galileo Galilei."

"When?" McCauley asked.

"In the early 1600s he came to Le Marche to do experiments on a new invention—the thermometer." Father Eccleston exhaled deeply.

"The thermoscope," Alpert remarked.

"Quite right, Dr. Alpert. You've studied Galileo?"

"Some. I knew he was credited with its development along with the telescope."

Eccleston nodded. "All and more. But there's probably something else you don't know. The section of Le Marche where Galileo experimented with his early thermometer is known for something other than wine."

The priest set down his wine glass. "A year before Galileo traveled to Le Marche, Giordano Bruno, a dissident thinker, was convicted of heresy by the Holy Office. He was burned at the stake. The Pope, or those who spoke for him, put reason and science on the opposing side of the religious scale that was completely weighted in the church's favor. Authority gave them that ability. Ability equaled right. Right equaled power. It wasn't merely so-called radicals like Bruno who came under scrutiny of the Holy See. It was anyone whose views challenged conventional wisdom, or as history has shown us, conventional myopia.

"Galileo confronted church doctrine, though for a time he had actually worked under Papal sponsorship. He was even honored by mathematicians at Collegio Romano."

"Mathematics," McCauley commented. "I forgot that was his principal field of study. We all think it was astronomy."

"Related. Inter-related," Eccleston said. "The basis for everything."

Eccleston's answer reminded him of the next piece of the puzzle he wanted to discuss with the priest. *Soon*, he thought.

"When Galileo published his *Letters on Sunspots*, which offered his theory that the sun rotated on its own axis, Dominican Friar Niccolo Lorini of Florence attacked him. Lorini was a professor of ecclesiastic history. And if you think you could have spoken freely in his classes, you would have done so at your own peril.

"Galileo countered, offering his views concerning the relationship between science and Scripture. Not a particularly church-friendly idea," Father Eccleston noted. "Lorini filed a complaint with the Roman Inquisition. He took issue with Galileo's disregard of Ptolemy's theory of the solar system which held that the earth was the center of all celestial bodies. This was the *geocentric* model and it fit into the strict biblical teachings. Galileo's disregard of prevailing beliefs undermined church authority."

"And led to his Inquisition," Katrina observed.

"Certainly contributed to it," the priest confirmed. "Research shows that Galileo's stubbornness and ego didn't help either. But it was an age of transition. It took radicals and radical ideas to move the needle, as it were. And Catholic scientists were the ones doing it. In fact, Copernicus, himself a clergyman, had developed his own interpretation that was in conflict with Ptolemy. Some right, some wrong. He set the sun as the focal point, with the earth and other planets in circular orbits. Where Galileo got into further trouble was when he neither accepted nor rejected all of Copernican theory, and as a result, was again criticized for not embracing geocentrism.

"When he pushed, and I mean pushed *heliocentrism* on society and the church, he raised the most ire. This thinking placed our solar system within a larger universe, with the earth and the other planets traveling around the sun in elliptical orbits. It was as far from biblical interpretation as imaginable, thus controversial and ultimately heretical."

"And the reason for his excommunication," Katrina added.

"He was never excommunicated. As a religious man, he feared he might be. It was possibly one of the reasons he recanted before the Inquisition. But who knows. Anyway, we're skipping some of the history. In 1616, the situation worsened for Galileo. A powerful cardinal named Bellarmine issued a decree that expressly prohibited teaching, discussing, writing or defending Copernican theory. Galileo thought he had tiptoed around the strictures of the edict in writing his *Discourse on Comets* and *The Assayer*. He had not. His publications further fanned the flames of the Inquisition fires.

"Seven years later, he was granted six audiences with newly elected Pope Urban VIII. The Holy See declared that Galileo could discuss Copernican theory as long as he presented it solely as theory."

"Like evolution," McCauley noted somewhat uncomfortably before the priest. "Everything old is new again. But what does all this have to do with Gap Theory?"

"I'm coming around to that," Eccleston said. "Galileo continued to explore science as he saw it, but not as discreetly as the Vatican wanted. He wrote a new work as a conversation, a debate. He called it *Dialogue Concerning the Two Chief World Systems*. Not a good idea on his part. The Pope banned its distribution.

"According to Papal history, this is what ultimately led to Galileo being summoned to appear before the Roman Inquisition."

Eccleston became more intent in his account. His eyes took on a glow. "However, it's been rumored there was another essay written by Galileo Galilei thirty years earlier. This work was given to Pope Paul V who, after reading it, ordered it destroyed. Rumors mind you, but who's to say?"

"About?"

"No one knows, but there are whispers to this day that it was so controversial, so explosive that it threatened the very fabric of the Church and its history."

Alpert and McCauley instinctively moved closer.

"In late 1632, Galileo was summoned to appear before the Inquisition. A few months later a very sick Galileo traveled to Rome for his trial. A particularly malicious opponent, Father Vincenzo Maculano da Firenzuola, utterly broke him down in the formal tribunal and again, according to whispers, in private conversations. We only have the record of some encounters, not all."

The ticking of the kitchen clock a room away was the only sound for the next few moments.

"Father Eccleston, you started a thought, but didn't complete it before," Katrina recalled. "Something else Le Marche is known for?"

"Oh, yes. Perhaps a vital detail, not to be overlooked." The priest smiled. "Le Marche is famous for its caves."

As the words settled in, McCauley's enthusiasm grew more. "Can we…"

"Ah, let's not get ahead of ourselves," Eccleston cautioned. "Tomorrow we'll delve into the Vatican Secret Archives. I've done extensive research, but never in relation to Le Marche. Perhaps there's something in Galileo's own hand. We can also see about dear Fr. Emilianov."

"And if there isn't anything?" Katrina aptly followed up. "Then what?"

The reply came naturally to McCauley; an echo, like his own voice in the Montana cave. "The absence of evidence is not the evidence of absence."

SEVENTY-ONE

June 22, 1633
Rome

THEY SAT IN JUDGMENT. The Reverend Father Vincenzo
Maculano was at the center of the table. Flanked on ei-
ther side were Fr. Cardinal de Ascoli, Fr. Cardinal Gessi,
Fr. Cardinal Bentivoglio, Fr. Cardinal Verospi, Fr. Car-
dinal Ginetti, Fr. D. Cardinal de Cremona, Fr. Cardinal
Barberini, Fr. Cardinal Borgia, Fr. Ant. s Cardinal de. S.
Onofrio, Fr. Cardinal Laudivio Zacchia and Reverend Fr.
Carlo Sinceri. Chief Inquisitor Sinceri spoke.

> *Whereas you, Galileo, son of the late Vincenzo Gali-*
> *lei, Florentine, aged seventy years, were in the year*
> *1615 denounced to this Holy Office for holding as*
> *true the false doctrine taught by some that the Sun*
> *is the center of the world and immovable and that*
> *the Earth moves, and also with a diurnal motion;*
> *for having disciples to whom you taught the same*
> *doctrine; for holding correspondence with certain*
> *mathematicians of Germany concerning the same;*
> *for having printed certain letters, entitled "On the*
> *Sunspots," wherein you developed the same doctrine*
> *as true; and for replying to the objections from the*
> *Holy Scriptures, which from time to time were urged*
> *against it, by glossing the said Scriptures according*
> *to your own meaning: and whereas there was there-*

*upon produced the copy of a document in the form of
a letter, purporting to be written by you to one for-
merly your disciple, and in this divers propositions
are set forth, following the position of Copernicus,
which are contrary to the true sense and authority
of Holy Scripture:*

*This Holy Tribunal being therefore of intention
to proceed against the disorder and mischief thence
resulting, which went on increasing to the prejudice
of the Holy Faith, by command of His Holiness and
of the Most Eminent Lords Cardinals of this supreme
and universal Inquisition, the two propositions of the
stability of the Sun and the motion of the Earth were
by the theological Qualifiers qualified as follows:*

*The proposition that the Earth is not the center
of the world and immovable but that it moves, and
also with a diurnal motion, is equally absurd and
false philosophically and theologically considered
at least erroneous in faith.*

*But whereas it was desired at that time to deal
leniently with you, it was decreed at the Holy Congregation held before His Holiness on the twenty-
fifth of February, 1616, that his Eminence the Lord
Cardinal Bellarmine should order you to abandon
altogether the said false doctrine and, in the event of
your refusal, that an injunction should be imposed
upon you by the Commissary of the Holy Office to
give up the said doctrine and not to teach it to others, not to defend it, nor even to discuss it; and your
failing your acquiescence in this injunction, that you
should be imprisoned.*

*Furthermore, in order to completely eliminate
such a pernicious doctrine, and not let it creep any
further to the great detriment of Catholic truth, the*

*Holy Congregation of the Index issued a decree
which prohibited books which treat of this and de-
claring the doctrine itself to be false and wholly contrary to the divine and Holy Scripture.*

*We condemn you to formal imprisonment in this
Holy Office at our pleasure.*

Maculano peered up from the official decree. "There
are far greater offenses against you that this learned group
has judged to be the most dangerous and heretical position
ever contemplated. However, it is so unspeakable that pos-
terity shall never be burdened by its knowledge."

With this condemnation, Galileo lost all hope.

"Galileo Galilei, do you have anything to add before
sentencing?"

"Preserve the record of my research on the stars. That
shall be my contribution. All else can be forgotten."

SEVENTY-TWO

"COULD THE LONG arm of the Inquisition reach through to today?"

"It depends. Who are you asking? The priest or the scientist?"

McCauley got his line of thinking. "*Dr.* Eccleston..."

"In that case, unmitigated power. Everything that the cardinals employed then could have made its way to the twenty-first century, disguised, no doubt—morphed, if you will. Power like that hides and survives."

"And does Father Eccleston believe there is still such a secret organization?"

"It would have to be dangerous and fearless," Eccleston added, "charged with protecting great secrets."

Quinn suddenly felt a muscle tighten in the pit of his stomach. "There's more, Father."

"There always is."

"You can't see it in the photographs. All light was absorbed, but I felt some indentations on the surface. Bumps or notches that made up a pattern of numbers. We have a drawing."

After Eccleston studied the paper, he said, "Of course you know what this represents?"

"Yes we do," McCauley admitted. "A prime pyramid."

THEY DISCUSSED THE unique quality of the numbers and their application in science and civilization This is where McCauley and Alpert learned more about Eccleston's relationship with Robert Greene and how the American investigator had more standing than they had allowed.

"Prime numbers makes you think there's a bigger picture," Eccleston proposed.

"Like a higher authority?"

"Consider it an order to the universe, Dr. Alpert. One that we can actually grasp. Numbers. Undeniable. Infinite. Easily translatable. Perhaps that's where we should leave it for tonight."

"I think you're right, Father."

"Then tomorrow we'll renew our work at the Vatican. I promise you an exciting day."

McCauley stood and stretched. He walked to the window overlooking Via Flavia.

Jareth Eccleston soon joined him. "Typical Rome. Cars maneuvering faster than they would in American cities. Tourists examining their maps. Pedestrians talking and texting on their phones."

McCauley also noticed a man standing next to a tree. He appeared to be looking up toward the priest's window.

"There," McCauley quietly observed. He tapped the window. "Look."

Moments later, the man stepped into the shadows, but not out of sight.

McCauley grabbed Eccleston's arm and inched him away from the window.

Alpert responded to what appeared to be a calculated maneuver. "What's going on?"

"Dr. McCauley believes someone's watching us," Eccleston explained.

"There is," McCauley affirmed.

Katrina tensed.

"Is there another way out, Father?" McCauley sharply demanded. "Other than the front door?"

"Well, there's the basement, but it leads to an alley that opens right up to the street next to the building. Only the rats use it. You're better off leaving quite casually. I'll go with you and stroll back to the restaurant. You return to your hotel. All very public."

"And tomorrow?"

"Like I said. An interesting day. We'll meet up at the Vatican's Secret Archives. But if you're right about surveillance, we'll be careful."

THE MAN THOUGHT he was in the shadows, successfully blending in, invisible to the threesome leaving the building. He held up a newspaper, pretending to read it. But that was impossible considering the low light. Even worse than his technique was the way he moved the paper in the direction his subjects were walking.

Not that Quinn McCauley was steeped in counterintelligence skills. But given the whirlwind ride they'd been on the past week, he was becoming adept at such things.

After saying a very public goodnight to the priest at the restaurant, Quinn turned to Katrina, and suddenly and without warning, pulled her into his arms and kissed her passionately.

Not even realizing it, she closed her eyes and gave in. When he released, which wasn't by any stretch of the imagination instantly, she managed, "What was that for?"

"Two reasons," McCauley whispered. "Because I wanted to and…"

"Yes?"

"I needed a better look at the man across the street who's obviously intent on watching us."

"You used me!" she said a little too loud for their own good.

"Shhh," he said. "Hey, I had one eye closed…some of the time."

"Well, what did you spy with that little open eye?"

"This is not his strong suit. He stared right at me."

"Okay, my turn and make it look good." She returned to his lips without waiting for permission any more than McCauley had.

At first, Katrina actually forgot to open her eyes. When she did, she slowly pivoted and saw the man looking like he was trying to read a map. He held it just below his chin but he obviously wasn't focused on the paper. Katrina sized him up. He was about six feet tall, thin, and balding. Maybe a little light gray on the sides.

A minute later, Quinn and Katrina strolled arm and arm, sharing notes, and talking about ways of losing their tail. They easily succeeded by hailing the only cab on the street.

SEVENTY-THREE

June 22, 1633
Rome, Italy

> *I, Galileo, son of the late Vincenzo Galilei, Floren-*
> *tine, aged seventy years, arraigned personally be-*
> *fore this tribunal, and kneeling before you, Most*
> *Eminent and Reverend Lord Cardinals, Inquisitors-*
> *General against heretical depravity throughout the*
> *entire Christian commonwealth, having before my*
> *eyes and touching with my hands, the Holy Gospels,*
> *swear that I have always believed, do believe, and*
> *by God's help will in the future believe, all that is*
> *held, preached, and taught by the Holy Catholic and*
> *Apostolic Church.*

GALILEO'S ADMISSION AND confession became record. Maculano then set to expunge everything else he could find
that related to what he deemed to be even more heretical
than Galileo's publications. Obliterating the past gave rise
to a vast organization that continued his legacy. *Secretum.*

SEVENTY-FOUR

The Vatican
Present Day

THE SWISS GUARDS waved the priest and his companions through St. Anne's Gate, the business entrance to Vatican City.

They swiftly walked past the throngs of tourists, around a fountain and a high wall, into a courtyard behind the papal residence, and through metal doors with portrayals of Egyptian papyrus, medieval scrolls, and monks' manuscripts.

Alpert caught her breath at the sight of the plaque which read *VATICAVM TABVLARVM,* Vatican Records Office.

"It gives reason for pause," Fr. Eccleston said.

"This is it?"

"Yes, Dr. Alpert. Welcome to *Archivum Sectretum Apostolicum Vaticanum*—the Vatican Secret Archives."

"I'm shaking," she admitted.

"If you're expecting a scene out of *Angels & Demons*, I assure you you've come to the wrong place. Dan Brown created pure fiction. Wonderful, but not what you're about to see. He played off the word *secretum* to create the sense of an archive steeped in conspiracies. It makes for great reading and fun movie-making, but the truth of it is that *secretum* doesn't denote the contemporary definition of confidentiality. It's merely Vatican-speak for private. The Vatican Secret Archives are the Pope's private archives, though quite public with the proper approval. You just have to apply and know what you're looking for."

"No bulletproof glass and secure titanium-lined rooms?" McCauley asked. "No jets taking off and helicopters bearing down?"

"Not even white gloved conspirators, although there are rooms where technicians do their painstaking restoration work. More *secretarial* than secret. It makes for a great tale, but truly, no."

"All that intrigue."

"That's part and parcel why the Vatican put some of the greatest documents on display in 2012 in celebration of the four-hundredth anniversary of the opening," Eccleston explained. "They hoped to demystify the conspiratorial concerns and shed true historical light on the archives' holdings."

"Kind of disappointing when you think about it," Katrina responded.

"Oh, you won't be disappointed, Dr. Alpert."

At that moment, they were met by a friendly middle-aged archivist who wore a black suit, a crisp white shirt, and a yellow tie. The only thing that said *Vatican* about the handsome man was a pin on his jacket lapel with the gold on red Vatican City shield.

"Good morning, Beppe."

"So good to have you back, Father. How have you been?"

"Fine. But I'm conferenced out and happy to be away from the crowds and back home."

"And this is an extension of your home, so how may I assist you today?"

"Well, first, may I present two esteemed colleagues, Dr. Quinn McCauley from Yale and Dr. Katrina Alpert from Cambridge University. I'd like to show them the Tower and then dig into the archives a bit. How's it look for un-announced guests?"

Beppe flashed a warm smile. "For you, anything." He extended his hand, first to Alpert then to McCauley. "A pleasure meeting you. I'm Beppe Poppito, senior archivist. Call me Beppe."

Quinn and Katrina introduced themselves, staying just as familiar.

"There are some procedures to go over with you, made easier considering you're with one of my favorite scholars, the reverend doctor."

"They're already impressed, Beppe. No need."

So far the access was as far from Dan Brown's plots as imaginable.

"I'll be happy to register you. I'll need identification."

"Even though they're with me?"

"Yes, Father. And everything needs to go into your electronic locker, except pads and paper. Cameras, cell phones, books, recording devices, scanners, your back-pack, Dr. McCauley, and your purse Dr. Alpert. For security purposes. I'm sure you understand."

"Absolutely," McCauley said, though he didn't want to release Emilianov's book and his cell.

"When you enter a reading room we'll electronically register you at the daily distribution desk. You'll choose a place to sit, though I know the good Father's favorite spots."

"And that's where we'll be," Eccleston confirmed.

"Splendid. So let's log in. When you're ready to leave, it's basically the same procedure in reverse. The reading rooms close at 17:15, 5:15 P.M.," Beppe concluded.

"We should be out well before."

"No problem," the archivist responded. "Take your time. Now what would you like to examine today?"

"We'll be narrowing the scope as we go. Principally we'll focus on Galileo's writings from 1601 but I may have some other thoughts. There is another area of research."

Beppe finished writing a notation on his pad about Galileo and was ready for the second request.

"We'd also like to learn about a Russian priest who lived in the late 1800s. His name was Father Mykhailo Emilianov."

"I take it, from the Russian Orthodox Church?"

"Yes," Fr. Eccleston replied.

"Can't promise much given the Vatican's history with Russian Orthodoxy." Beppe now addressed Quinn and Katrina in a whisper. "Something of a thousand year family squabble. Not a lot of Christmas cards flying back and forth."

They laughed at the archivist's droll narrative of church politics.

"Any more specifics?"

"He lived somewhere in Siberia. The Altai Mountain region. And he wrote a memoir."

"Well then, let's see what comes up."

FOLLOWING CHECK-IN, Father Eccleston led them up hundreds of steps.

"We're going to the Vatican's first observatory The Tower of the Wind, built in 1578. It's about sixty-one meters high, roughly two hundred feet. Only St. Peter's Basilica stands taller. And if you're really ready for a shock…"

"We are," McCauley said on Katrina's behalf.

"It was constructed for Pope Gregory VIII so his astronomers could track the movements of the sun and stars and plot the weather. Of course, the findings were twisted to validate the Ptolemy view of the heavens revolving around the earth."

When they reached Meridian Hall, quite out of breath, Quinn and Katrina were captivated by the beautiful frescoes that graced the thirty-foot high walls.

"What is the scene?"

"An apt question, Dr. Alpert. *The Shipwreck of St. Paul in Malta*, considered an act of divine meteorological intervention."

The vivid blues and greens of the swirling ocean were in contrast to the grey of the sinking ship. Katrina was drawn to the holy spirit hovering over the craft.

"Magnificent, isn't it?" Eccleston commented. "The work of Nicolo Cirignani, as is the fresco on the south wall, *Jesus Calms a Storm and Heals the Gerasene Demonic* and on the corner of the south and west walls, *The Angel Seals the Forehead of the Saved*."

The ceiling reinforced the purpose of the Tower. It was painted with stars. Eccleston continued his explanation noting a small opening at the top, which at noon every spring equinox shoots a ray of light directly to the center of the marble floor.

"A vaulted place from which to study the stars, even if the conclusions were false," he admitted. "Today, the Vatican has two observatories, one at the Pope's summer home at Castel Gandolfo outside of Rome and a second housed at the University of Arizona in Tucson. I've worked at both. The tradition, now different, does underscore that the Vatican remains one of the oldest astronomical research institutions in the world, though too late for poor Giordano Bruno who I told you about. He embraced the strictly heretical position that the sun was another star and that the universe contained infinite possibilities of other worlds, perhaps even some that could be inhabited. Acceptable from a poet waxing philosophical about infinite points of light; unorthodox and heretical for the Dominican friar, mathematician and astronomer that he was. Bruno was convicted of heresy and burned to a crisp in 1600. But because of his death, the Inquisition determined it might be too politically risky to put Galileo to death. They wanted to demonstrate they had the power to do so, but they'd advanced in the thirty-three years since Bruno's trial."

Katrina asked if it was leniency or political expediency.

"A bit of both. Pope Urban VIII was an early ally of Galileo's. According to some papal records, he personally agreed with the scientist, but had to uphold scripture and the beliefs held throughout the world, not just by Christians. That could explain why Galileo was permitted to write for so long."

"An amazing history," McCauley said. But he was getting eager to bring the research full circle to their own quest.

"Yes, and hopefully we'll find more today, but only if we request the right documents. You see, no browsing is allowed. Shall we get to work?"

The Vatican
Thirty minutes later

OUTSIDE, IT WAS sweltering hot and humid. Inside, it was actually chilly. Katrina shivered.

Fr. Eccleston put two bound books of Galileo's correspondences on the table; the result of his initial request. Then he removed his black blazer and covered Katrina's shoulders. "They keep it cool here. Even more so down in the subterranean vaults. They say it's cold enough there to discourage the devil from doing any research."

"Thanks. Must be the real reason they want women to wear long dresses," Katrina added lightly. "Are there any full length black blankets around in my size?"

"I'll see what I can scout up," Eccleston said. "In the meantime, start looking for anything that's dated 1601 or shortly thereafter. Keep your eyes open for words like *thermometro, caverna,* and *lo sconosciuto* or *l'ignoto.* It's Italian, not Latin. Unlike Copernicus who wrote in Latin, primarily to be read by scholars, Galileo used Italian, the language of the people."

McCauley understood the first two words, not the rest. "*Lo sconosciuto* and what?"

The Welsh priest stopped at the door of the reading room. "*Lo sconosciuto* and *l'ignoto.* The unknown."

They were humbled by the contents; collections of letters assembled in oversized scrapbooks. The documents were not glued or taped. Rice paper separated historic parchment letters and essays.

They were required to wear gloves to prevent them from getting oil on the documents. However, upon seeing Galileo's actual signature, Katrina was compelled to run her finger over his name. McCauley, too felt the impact of the moment. He gave Katrina a knowing glance. The powerful experience and the sense of bonding with the great scientist, removed them from the surroundings and transported them more than four hundred years into a cruel past.

Katrina tried to read the Italian as best she could. McCauley scanned for the recommended words and any others that might jump out.

"Sorry, no blanket," Eccleston said.

"I'm doing fine now. But sit with us. We need help."

The priest definitely speeded up the process, describing Galileo's friendly correspondence to university colleagues in Pisa, formal letters to cardinals and bishops in Rome, and simple but heartfelt notes to his wife.

Through the next hour, Quinn and Katrina swapped

volumes. When finished, they made sure Eccleston always had a pass at each.

"We're in the right time period, but nothing relevant in these. I'll get more."

Eccleston returned the first volumes to the Secret Vatican archives and brought three more to the table. Like the others, they were bound in dark brown leather with the official papal seal on the cover. Again, they found nothing.

At two hours, even the excitement of seeing Galileo's signature had faded. Two-and-a-half hours in, McCauley called Father Eccleston and Katrina to his side. "Look at this." He slowly turned the pages, all in chronological order, many day-by-day; others week-by-week through May and June, 1601. McCauley pointed to the dates on each document with his gloved hand.

"All chronological. Right?"

"Right," Fr. Eccleston replied. "One after another."

"Well, look at July 1601. The first week is here. More for the second. Then eleven pieces of rice paper, but nothing between them. The next dated page isn't until the beginning of August. Three weeks are missing."

"Do you think someone pulled them out?" Katrina asked.

"Clean, empty pages where there should have been letters?" Eccleston responded. "Yes."

He leafed through the last entries. Then forward, then back again. He read the final documents before the lapse, two enthusiastic letters to men named Luigi Pino and Roberto Santori. "Here! Right here!" the priest said excitedly. "Galileo is talking to friends, inviting them to meet him in Le Marche. There were…."

Katrina saw the phrase, *montagne con climi variabili*. "Mountains with variable climates, right?"

"Yes," the priest replied. "A perfect place to conduct

experiments on a thermometer, especially if you believe you might find locations to chart extremes."

"Like a cave." Eccleston concluded.

"Which Galileo likely found and wrote about." He tapped the blank pages.

They were suppositions. Only suppositions, but logical ones to make.

"What kind of man was Galileo, Father?" McCauley asked.

"I don't understand."

"Paint a picture for me. Methodical?"

"To a fault."

"Thorough?"

"He was a scientist in an unscientific period. So, yes."

"Guarded?"

"That's a very good question. At that point in his life, I'd say no. He had the support of the university and the Vatican. Later, well, that's where it gets interesting. I mentioned chief inquisitor Father Vincenzo Maculano last night. He was a skilled military architect and a shrewd, severe man. If anyone could bring Galileo to recant, with torture one of the means available, it was Maculano. But after conducting the first interview on April 12, 1633, Maculano concluded that Galileo was too old and frail to be subjected to such means."

"That didn't stop his trial," Katrina offered.

"No, but it did establish a tone. They sought to manipulate Galileo; beat him psychologically, if such a thing existed then, rather than physically. They succeeded, but ultimately Cardinal Francesco Barberini, the Grand Inquisitor of the Roman Inquisition and nephew of Pope Urban VIII, was one of three who *refused* to condemn Galileo."

"The Grand Inquisitor did not vote to convict?" Katrina was dismayed.

"That's right. Seven still found him guilty for the reasons described," Eccleston stated. "But most still quietly believed him."

McCauley was surprised. "I had no idea."

"Most people don't. But I've often felt there was something that got in the way of a more public review of the accusations and Galileo's defense." Eccleston rubbed his hands together, then grasped them, almost in prayer. "Maybe we'll still find that *something*."

"Not if it's in the missing pages," Katrina said with discouragement.

"Then let's see if we're smarter than Galileo's censors. Back to work. I'm going to order up more."

Katrina and Quinn sat side by side scouring for more words, phrases, or hints of Galileo's trip to Le Marche.

Katrina was the first to spot something in a November entry, a letter to a man named Alfonso Garaldi at The University of Padua. Padua was where Galileo had been appointed professor of mathematics in 1592 and chair of the department. There, Galileo taught Euclid's geometry and astronomy to medical students who needed a basic understanding of the field. Katrina was aware of the university, mostly through its highly regarded Museum of Geology and Palaeontology. She wondered if the university also had papers they should examine. That idea evaporated when she noticed a reference to Genga, the town in Le Marche where she surmised Galileo must have stayed when he conducted his temperature experiments.

"I'll need Jareth's read on this," she told Quinn. "I think Galileo is describing the mountain. He's writing about *la mia esplorazione. My exploration.* Whoever was going through the letters may have missed this."

A few minutes later, Father Eccleston walked in empty-handed. "Sorry. There are more volumes like this, but I was looking for specific diaries. Nothing relevant."

"Well, Katrina may have found something."

"May?" she objected.

"Pardon me. This amazing woman, schooled in Italian, has stumbled…"

"Stumbled?"

"I stand corrected. She's made a tremendous observation."

"Much better, Dr. McCauley."

"Let me see," the priest said. She showed Eccleston Galileo's correspondence to Garaldi.

"When did Galileo begin most of his astronomical research?" she quietly asked.

The priest knew the history. "In 1609 he made a telescope with 20x magnification modeled after a European version that had 3x power. Then he worked up to 30x power. Over time he was able to observe the moon, discover four satellites of Jupiter, confirm the phases of Venus, see a supernova, and discover sunspots. He conducted a demonstration for Venetian lawmakers in August, 1609. Oh, you'll love this. He sold them telescopes on the side."

"I had no idea," Katrina replied. "But why do you think he was writing about specific points in space eight years earlier?"

"What do you mean?" McCauley was unsure where she was going with the train of thought.

"Look. Here. In the fall of 1601, Galileo referenced it to Alfonso Garaldi, in which he discussed the Greek's fascination with Ursa Major and Ursa Minor and how a single star had pointed travelers north for ages."

"So?" McCauley asked not seeing anything particularly significant.

"He also uses the Italian word *key* in his correspondence." She pointed to the passage and read, "'*la chiave per sbloccare i misteri della paura.*'"

"I'm sorry, you have to help me," McCauley implored.

Eccleston re-read the phrases with bewilderment. There were also descriptions of terrain, wild flowers and brush.

"A translation, please?"

Katrina ignored Quinn and asked Eccleston a direct question. "He doesn't mention the trip to Le Marche specifically, but do you think it's what he's writing about?"

Eccleston looked up from Galileo's letters that few in modern history had likely seen, or at the very least, applied any real meaning. "'*La chiave per sbloccare i misteri della paura,*' now that's extremely interesting."

"Someone, please!" McCauley said louder than he should have. It immediately brought footsteps from the library archivist. "Please," he whispered.

"*La chiave* is the key, as Dr. Alpert noted. The whole thought: '*la chiave per sbloccare i misteri della paura.*' The key to unlock the mysteries of time."

A profound thought came over McCauley. He smiled. "Father, if there's a key, wouldn't that suggest there's a lock?"

"Well, arguably yes it could, but I can't say for certain," the priest replied.

"I would. And I believe I touched it."

"WHAT IF GALILEO figured it all out?" McCauley continued. "What if he discovered the same thing in Le Marche that we did in Montana and the old hermit had in Russia?"

Katrina took the possibility further. "He was a mathematician, right?"

"Right," Eccleston said.

"A mathematician who would have recognized prime

numbers and been intrigued enough to look for a solution to a mathematical problem."

"Well, absolutely."

"Then we need to figure out what's the problem and what's the solution. The lock and the key."

Eccleston nodded and rose. "I'll be right back."

"Where are you going?" McCauley asked.

"You just reminded me of something."

"What?"

"To see if there's any correspondence between Galileo and a Frenchman named Mersenne."

A HALF HOUR LATER, Beppe and Eccleston returned with more loosely bound volumes.

"How's your French?" the priest asked.

"Restaurant good," McCauley shyly admitted.

"I'm fluent," Katrina said. Then to McCauley she added, "Aren't you glad I'm here?"

"Ever more."

She smiled. "Okay, now who's Mersenne?"

"A mathematician, a writer, a philosopher, a priest. And he translated some of Galileo's writings into French. Mersenne also had a real interest in prime numbers and created a formula for determining them. They became known as Mersenne primes. The search continues to this day through an organization named GIMPS—the Great Internet Mersenne Primes Search."

"And his connection with Galileo?" Katrina wondered.

"Translating his works, but also he was a friend of Christian Huygens, who expanded on yet another principle that Galileo discovered—how the sweep of a pendulum could be used to calculate time. It was his breakthrough that led to the clock."

"The thermometer, the clock, and the telescope."

"Temperature, time, the universe, all part of Galileo's sphere of influence, with prime numbers perhaps the unifying quantifier."

"DaVinci gets all the glory," McCauley observed.

"Not in my book," the priest responded. "Now let's see if Mersenne has anything to tell us from the past."

SEVENTY-FIVE

Ann Arbor, MI
The same time

"YOU HAVE NO idea how worried I was. You left without a word. You could have been..." Rich Tamburro didn't finish the sentence. But, he was furious with his girlfriend. He had started on her the moment she opened the door to her one bedroom apartment. So far Anna Chohany hadn't given him any reason to back off.

"Why?"

Chohany, still bandaged, walked slowly to her hand-me-down recliner. She adjusted the pitch and tried her best to ignore him.

"Why?" Tamburro demanded. He stood directly in front of her, though keeping his distance. "You owe me."

"I was mad at you," she finally answered.

"At me? I didn't give you any reason. What are you talking about?"

She strained to turn around.

"No?"

"No!" he replied. "No." He walked closer.

"What about that text you sent from my phone when you thought I was sleeping?"

Tamburro's eyes widened.

"You didn't trust me."

"I'm sorry. You don't know everything that happened after your accident. We needed to find out if..."

"You didn't trust me!"

"It's only because…"

"You didn't trust me," she said again, this time quietly. "And you were right not to."

The Vatican

"LISTEN TO THIS," Katrina said. She was translating one of Mersenne's diary entries which quoted a 1629 correspondence from Galileo. "There's something to this. I won't have it completely right, but this is the essence: '*My friend gives me great pause. He wrote that I have come to realize the significance of our lives on earth is insignificant against the indeterminate nature of the universe. But, as we've discussed, we don't have to gaze upon the heavens through a glass pressed against our eyes to come to this profound realization. Answers are to be found in our midst. Answers that only raise more questions.*'"

"Feels philosophical," McCauley said.

"Yes, but then there's this word: *Premier.*"

"And?" he asked. "Premier, like leader dictator or leader?"

"Actually no. Marsenne quotes Galileo. '*La langue qui explique tout; la langue qui s'étend sur le nombre d'années, est premier.*'"

"The language, is explicit… ?" McCauley started.

Eccleston straightened in his chair. "Close. Galileo says, 'The language that explains it all; the language that spans the numbers in years, is prime.'"

McCauley broke down the translation in his head. Language, explains, numbers and prime. "Galileo *is* talking about prime numbers."

"Precisely," Fr. Eccleston said. "Very precisely."

Rich Tamburro texted a simple message to the phone number McCauley had given him. It was also precise.

However, McCauley's cell phone was in the locker at the Vatican; except when it wasn't for the few minutes that Beppe took it out and checked McCauley and Alpert's texts and the voicemail.

"Maren Marsenne was much like Galileo," Eccleston explained. "He was religious, but a pragmatist. Faithful to the church and a believer in facts. A priest and a mathematician. He studied prime numbers with the intent of discovering a formula that would represent all primes and help give greater meaning to the sum of all things.

"He studied music, also founded on mathematical theorems, and published his own findings in addition to translating Galileo. Imagine if the reason Galileo reached out to him was because he made the same deduction you have?"

"Or he cracked the code and needed more help," McCauley said. "Are there more letters?"

"I'll check and also see whether Beppe's come up with anything on Father Emilianov."

Eccleston went down the staircase and casually walked into the archivist's office. Beppe wasn't there. Eccleston stepped out and heard some activity at the lockers.

The priest approached and was ready to speak, but caught himself. Beppe's back was to him, however, Eccleston saw that the archivist was rifling through McCauley's backpack. He held Quinn's cell phone under his armpit and pulled out the old Russian priest's book.

Father Eccleston quietly backed away until he could take the Tower steps two at a time.

"We're checking out now," Eccleston explained in whispers to his guests.

SEVENTY-SIX

The next morning

MCCAULEY RENTED A Kia Rio from the Europcar rental facility on Via Sardegna. He sat next to Father Eccleston, who agreed to drive. Katrina stretched out in the backseat.

"Okay, let's see. What's the best route?" Eccleston asked in the parking lot. He looked at a map provided by the rental office and the variety of routes the GPS offered between Rome and Genga, Le Marche.

"It's pretty much a straight shot on the A24 until we hit the coast." Eccleston said peering over the map from his angle. "Then we pick up the Autostrada, A14 North. Or instead of the A14 that whole leg, we can go through some of these towns." He pointed out Orte, Narni, Todi, Perugia and Gubbio.

"That'll be slower going?" McCauley asked.

"Yes, but it's pretty," the priest recalled. "We'll cross the Apennines that way. It's an historic route."

"Pretty and historic we don't need," Katrina countered. "Quick and easy. I say let's get there today, pack in a good night's sleep and start exploring tomorrow."

"Agreed." Eccleston moved into traffic. He didn't notice the rented Fiat that pulled out behind them.

"IF YOU DISCOUNT Galileo's discovery, which of course isn't mentioned online, the caverns are actually new to the public," Quinn explained as they drove north. He was reading an Internet description of the site; the spectacular and now famous Grotte di Frasassi—the Frasassi Caves. "Geologists and cavers really began to explore the ground around Genga in 1948. That's when the entrance to the River Cave was found. The next major find came in 1966 by a speleological group that followed a branch off the initial cavern. Their exploration led to more. Little discoveries resulted in bigger ones with names like the Great Cave of the Winds and the Grotta Grande del Vento. One labyrinth is some twenty kilometers long. Apparently jaw dropping."

"And that's where we're going?" Katrina felt her pulse quicken.

"Not exactly. I think we'll be looking for something off the beaten path based on the more vague descriptions in those later letters. An entrance Galileo uncovered…"

"And the Vatican covered up," McCauley speculated.

"Not the Vatican," the priest maintained. "But someone with a purpose."

THE FIAT FOLLOWED them up the A24 to the A14 and into Genga. The driver held back as they approached the picturesque Italian town. A medieval castle was perched atop a hill overlooking the Natural Regional Park of Gola della Rossa and Frasassi, and their ultimate destination, Grotte di Frasassi—the Frasassi Caves.

One at a time the cars entered Genga through an ancient archway, the town's original defensive barriers. The Kia pulled into a space. The Fiat held back.

The priest got out of the car. The other two passengers remained. Eccleston walked from one hotel to another. All were booked. He doubled back to their Kia and drove down the hill to another hotel, a much more modern resort closer to the caves. The Fiat followed.

Here they managed to score rooms, paying more for

Hotel Le Grotte and its first class services than they would have in town. McCauley still had cash, thanks to Marli Bellamy.

Meanwhile, the driver of the Fiat hoped there would be another room available. He figured with his identification they'd be fools to turn him away. And if he liked the accommodations, he might even have one of his magazine staff writers do an article.

SEVENTY-SEVEN

Le Marche region
The next morning

THE TRIO CLIMBED up and down hills, covering hundreds of yards over three hours. They avoided cliffs they felt Galileo would not have attempted even at age thirty-seven. They tried every opening that appeared possible and dug around rocks that might be blocking the way. Mostly it was discouraging until they came across one that really looked promising. However, after fifteen minutes of grueling work the team hit solid rock.

It was now midday. They were tired, hungry, and searching separately. McCauley was about to call a break when, from a distance, the priest shouted, "Hey, give me a hand."

Quinn and Katrina both converged from different directions about thirty feet apart.

"Remember Galileo's general descriptions in his letter to Garaldi? It feels pretty similar," Eccleston explained as they closed in. "But we have to deal with this." A four-by-five foot boulder was wedged in the way of what might be a point of access. "Looks like it could have been rolled into place."

"Or just fallen," McCauley said taking the more pessimistic view.

"Either way, it goes or we move on. I think it's worth a try."

McCauley shook his head—not at the challenge now, but at the sight of the surroundings. It was close to Galileo's description of the white asphodel, orchids, and cyclamen growing wild on the hillside. Below was the valley he wrote about, formed by glaciers and towering limestone gorges. In his mind, McCauley adjusted for some general geological shifts, fauna and flora growth, and the changes that weather brings to land over centuries. Father Eccleston was right. It was worth a try.

"I like it," McCauley said enthusiastically. "And we're still close to town. Galileo could have easily walked it."

"So, who's up for a hernia?" Eccleston asked.

McCauley stood next to the priest. They quickly observed that the rock wasn't going to budge without some serious muscle. There was too much fill around it, a true measure of how things really worked on the face of the earth, how history covered its tracks. Or, as McCauley speculated, how humans could have covered it up.

"Gentlemen, a little science in honor of Signor Galileo. Perhaps you can come up with a lever and a fulcrum?" Katrina proposed.

The paleontologist and the Vatican scientist looked at one another.

"Right," they said simultaneously.

McCauley thought. A simple tree branch would break under the strain. "Find some rocks we could use for the fulcrum. I'll go to check the car for a tire iron. That might work. And break out the sandwiches. We'll need the energy."

McCauley walked back down to the flats where they'd parked their Kia. Going down was assuredly easier. He made it in twelve minutes.

Inside the trunk was a good enough tire iron to change a tire. But it was barely two feet long, which meant they'd have to dig down more to get an effective angle to move the boulder—if it were even possible. On his way back, but before he hit the hill, he saw something better: the international *Do Not Enter* traffic sign atop a long metal pole. "Perfect!"

The bit of vandalism would not be easy until he decided what he couldn't do by hand, he could do with a ton-and-a-half car.

He backed into the pole, uprooting it to the cost of the rental car deductible. McCauley laughed to himself. This was becoming a habit.

KATRINA AND FR. Eccleston had finished their sandwiches. "What took you so…"

Katrina caught herself. "Ah, good thinking, Dr. McCauley."

"Thank you, Dr. Alpert."

"We'll start digging around the boulder. But history can wait," she implored. "Grab a bite first."

McCauley couldn't argue with that. He ate the remaining prosciutto, lettuce and tomato sandwich and polished off the quart water bottle that Katrina had left for him.

While he relaxed, the priest got to work scrapping, digging and scooping out the dirt on one side of the boulder while Katrina cleared a path in front. Once dislodged, they hoped the obstacle would roll down the hill. Even a few feet would make the difference, enough for them to squeeze past to see if they had come to the right place.

It was slow going. The rock had stood in one place for decades if not centuries. The effort hardly speeded up with McCauley's help. However, after ninety minutes they believed they'd dug enough.

The priest had picked out a triangular rock, just the

right size and shape for the fulcrum. Now for a practical test of the physics.

All three of them grabbed hold of the pole wedged under the boulder and over the fulcrum. In success, their full weight would start it moving. McCauley calculated they'd exert a combined 560 pounds against the load.

Back to the science of it all, he knew the standard equation that calculated the effort and the load in relation to the fulcrum. McCauley's real problem was over the force it would really take since they didn't know the weight of the load—the boulder.

"On the count of three," McCauley announced. They were ready to move part of the mountain. However, three came and went five times. "Back to digging."

"This better be the place," Katrina said with real hope.

"We won't know unless we get this mother, sorry Father, Mother Earth out of the way."

"Clever, my love," Katrina added. "It's still staggering to think that we may be standing within Galileo's own footsteps."

"I can take you to a few dozen places I know for sure where you can accurately say that," the priest responded.

After digging deeper and adjusting the placement of the fulcrum, they were ready to try again.

"Okay—on three?"

"Okay."

This time, one-two-three brought results. The boulder slowly inched forward, enough to put it on a downward course. It gained speed and rolled for nearly fifteen feet before hitting an olive tree that shook but did not break.

"Roots win!" Katrina proclaimed.

The team let out grateful cheers. However, their work was not yet done.

"Now let's see if we hit pay dirt," McCauley joked. He

dropped to his knees and started scooping away the soft soil that had been behind the huge rock.

Katrina and Fr. Eccleston joined in. The dirt flew between their legs. Two feet in, McCauley, leading the pack, felt a rush of cooler air. "Here! Right here!" he exclaimed. "Faster!"

Minutes later, they broke through, refreshed by the cooler temperature.

"Amen!" the priest said.

WITH THE WAY CLEARED, they cautiously moved forward on their knees, pushing their backpacks. Each held powerful flashlights, illuminating the narrow corridor, defining the size of the space and the safety of proceeding.

"So far, so good," McCauley headed the single file. Katrina was behind him, Father Eccleston, last.

So far didn't last long. Soon they were reduced to crawling.

As the ceiling dropped, their angst heightened. "If this gets too dicey, we're turning back," McCauley said. He recalled saying the exact same thing not long ago in Montana.

Katrina allowed herself a momentary joke. "No room to turn."

"Onward it is, then." But, McCauley was apprehensive. So much could have changed in four-plus centuries.

One thing would tell them if they were taking the right step back into history, McCauley thought. *The electrical anomalies.*

He felt another dip in temperature. "Cooling more." As he told Alpert and Eccleston, he heard his voice echo. "Hold it for a second."

McCauley shined his flashlight above and beyond. The

roof was rising and further on he could see that the cave was widening.

He turned his head back to his cohorts. "Looking okay, We'll be able to walk again, soon."

Another twenty meters they were upright and gazing upon a sight more magnificent than any of them had witnessed: magical colors enhanced and embellished by their flashlights; brilliant hues that defied description in any language; indescribable geological shapes that would inspire any artist's imagination; a slowly flowing subterranean river that mirrored the wonders and reflected the experience. All of this was part of the Grotte di Frasassi cave system. None of it was in any tour guides.

"This has to be it," McCauley stated. "The earth at its grandest."

"Oh, so much more," Fr. Eccleston said sharing his true beliefs. "God at his best."

They had all seen awe-inspiring caverns. Nothing on this level. Katrina was the first to take pictures with her disposable mechanical camera, one of three they bought along the way. They had also purchased basic match-lit carbide lamps.

"Use the cam on your cell for now. You might not be able to later."

"Got it."

Katrina lingered a few minutes. No one could fault her. Before they continued, they put on sweaters, lightening their load and warming their bodies.

PUSHING ON, THEY entered another cavern, which fed into tighter quarters again. They weren't worried now. Their sense of discovery, more accurately rediscovery, drove them until....

"There's a damned fork. Two tunnels. Galileo probably described it in his July letters. But they're missing."

Eccleston stepped forward. He shined his light down both passageways. Nothing ahead gave him a clue. Then he laughed. "We're going left."

"How do you know?" Katrina asked.

"Well, let me rephrase that. I have faith in the direction Galileo took." Then he corrected himself. "No, I'm convinced. This way." He pointed to the left.

"Why there?" she still wondered.

"It would have been natural for Galileo. He was left-handed."

"You know he was left-handed?" McCauley was amazed.

"I do."

"But in those days," Quinn recalled, "wasn't a dominant left hand considered the mark of the devil? A negative trait the church knuckle-thwacked out of people?"

"More schools than the Catholic Church. Okay, some of them religious schools. But the pejorative connotation really goes back to the Greek word, meaning weak and the Latin synonym for left which is sinister, *sinistra/sinistrum.* Right-handed in Latin is *dexter,* like in dexterity or skill. So you can see how language led to habitual thinking."

"But you're convinced he would have unconsciously veered left?"

"Completely convinced, Katrina."

"What if left didn't lead anywhere and he came back to this point and went down the right fork?"

"Well then, we'll be doing the same thing. But first, left it is."

And left it was. At the fourth narrow passageway, McCauley's flashlight flickered. It was the signal he had anticipated.

He twisted around in the cramped space. Katrina's light

was also fluttering. The last thing she saw before it went out was McCauley smiling.

"What's the matter?" Eccleston asked.

"This is it," she replied.

"How do you know?"

"Come a few feet closer. Watch your flashlight."

"What?"

"The electronics," she explained. "Galileo didn't have that problem. We do. But it means we're close. Really close. Time for the lamps. I'll do mine. Just follow until we get more room to work in, then light yours."

The passageway brightened and widened. Soon they were able to stand side-by-side. Now all three lamps were illuminated and focused forward, revealing the opening to another more remarkable cavern.

The entrance expanded into a space too large for their lights to fully flood, more magnificent than imaginable.

"In my Father's house there are many dwelling places," Eccleston said.

"What's that from?" McCauley said raising his torch.

The priest explained as McCauley examined the ceiling. "John 14:2. From *The Holy Gospel According to John. 'In my Father's house there are many dwelling places. If it were not so, would I have told you that I go to prepare a place for you? And if I go and prepare a place for you, I will come again and will take you to myself, so that where I am, there you may also be.'*"

"Well, if this is God's house, Father, he's a phenomenal architect."

"None more creative, Quinn."

The lamp lights revealed a ceiling that appeared to be two stories high with glistening crystals and colors that had no names.

McCauley strained to get a sense of the true size. He took a few steps to the side. "More light."

Katrina and Eccleston lifted their torches.

"Higher."

The priest had the height advantage. Alpert did the best she could.

"Come closer."

Combined, the lights brightened the ceiling enough to detect a curvature. "Higher than I thought. Thirty feet? Forty?" He wasn't sure. "Let's keep walking. Looks like the cavern closes in again up ahead," he said.

They took twenty cautious steps around golden formations of stalagmites. Then darkness.

"Watch your head. The ceiling's dropping fast," McCauley warned. "And the passage looks narrower. Can't see much."

But it wasn't that the ceiling was lower or the walkway was narrowing. No matter how McCauley held his lamp or focused the beam, the approaching section of the cavern was in pitch black.

He held his hand out in front, groping for obstructions, yet touching nothing. "Stop."

Alpert and Eccleston huddled close. They could see one another, but nothing ahead, to the sides or above.

"Like Montana," Katrina whispered, almost afraid to speak louder.

"And Denisova," Father Eccleston added.

"This is it. But if there are more spurs, we could get lost," McCauley realized.

"Galileo was inquisitive, but he wasn't crazy," Eccleston explained. "I'm sure he found something otherwise he would have turned back with the same worry."

"So one step at a time?" McCauley proposed.

"Yes, but together," Katrina said.

McCauley took the lead. "I'll cover the front. Katrina, you keep feeling for the sides. Father, you're the tallest. Make sure the ceiling's not closing in on us."

They proceeded. Three walking as one. A minute later McCauley called a halt.

"Dead end." He felt a surface, but it wasn't rock, not even igneous It was smooth to the touch; polished. Neither hot nor cold. It was just there.

"Amazing," Father Eccleston said reaching out. "It's…" he searched for the right word. "Perfection."

SEVENTY-EIGHT

KATRINA TOUCHED THE smooth surface and held the light to her hand. There wasn't a speck of dust.

"The properties are amazing. It repels dirt and disrupts electrical pulses in its realm. How, Father?"

Eccleston affirmed Katrina's observation. "Science I can't explain. But rest assured, it's surely science. No matter what Denisova or the old priest thought, this isn't the devil's work. Galileo recognized it." He paused. "No, he understood it. He got inside. Now we have to."

McCauley began to feel along the wall he couldn't see. So did Alpert and Eccleston. They gradually spread out, McCauley to the left touching middle-to-high; Katrina below him, the priest to their right. It was the left that brought results.

"Got it," McCauley said. The base of the prime pyramid was embedded at roughly waist level, angling upwards into a triangle, meeting at a point marked by one indentation.

"Okay, okay. So prime numbers are the universal standard that can reach across all space and time, right?"

"Correct," Eccleston said.

"And although we don't know *who* inserted the prime pyramids or *why*, I suspect the *what* begins right here. This is it. This is the lock. We need to figure out the key."

"Galileo wrote about *la chiave*, the key," Eccleston exclaimed.

"Yes, but he didn't leave it," Katrina added.

"Perhaps so it wouldn't be so easy for others," the Vatican scientist deduced. "But there are some number games related to primes that a mathematician would know. And Galileo was a mathematician."

"My God," McCauley said, "I used to do them in grad school. One of them dealt with squaring any prime bigger than five. Then add—"

"Seventeen," Eccleston interrupted, "and divide by twelve."

"And?" Katrina asked not knowing the trick, and not being able to work the problem so quickly in her head.

"There's always a remainder of .6," McCauley said.

"Or .5 on a calculator," Eccleston added. He went through a few easy examples. Each time the remainder turned out the same.

"Okay, so what do we do with that?" she continued.

They couldn't come up with any solutions. Everything in the pyramid was representative of whole numbers, not fractions.

"All this way and we can't get any further" Katrina was disappointed. "What did Galileo know that we don't know."

"Not *know*. What did he *try* that we haven't tried?" Eccleston thought for a moment. "I remember another prime number brain teaser," he said. "Even easier. Square any prime number larger than three. Subtract one. See what happens."

McCauley tried it once with five, then again with seven and eleven. He smiled. Katrina was doing the same with numbers of her choosing. This time she got the formula. "It's always divisible by twenty-four!"

"Right. The remainder is twenty-four. So back to the pyramid. Where can we find twenty-four?"

McCauley removed the prime pyramid cheat sheet from under his sweater He shined his light on it. "Whoops, twenty-four isn't a prime number."

"No," Eccleston said looking over his shoulder. "But there are twos and fours. Fourth row there's both. I'll try them." Eccleston pressed the indentations. Nothing happened.

"Maybe we add up numbers to get twenty-four." Katrina suggested. "I'll show you."

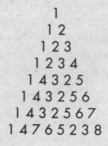

```
           1
          1 2
         1 2 3
        1 2 3 4
       1 4 3 2 5
      1 4 3 2 5 6
     1 4 3 2 5 6 7
    1 4 7 6 5 2 3 8
```

She pointed to the number one at the apex, then another one on the second row. "One plus one equals two," she explained. Then add the next two on the second row. That's four. So, twenty-four?"

"We're here, let's try," Eccleston said lightly.

The priest started at the top, pressing each of the perfectly imprinted notches in the unknown metal. Finishing on the second row, he stood back and waited.

Again, nothing.

"Too simple and too complicated at the same time," McCauley offered. But the key has to be hiding in plain sight. Galileo got it."

McCauley scanned his sheet one more time. "We can add up the numbers, but do the numbers add up to anything?"

"In the prime pyramid they always do," Eccleston explained.

"Right, but what if the answer is already *in* the prime pyramid. Back to what we were trying before. If it's related to the mathematical equation let's just go to the answer in its most simplest form."

"Alright, here and here," Eccleston said, pointing to the number two on the second row and the four on the fourth row. "That's where they first appear."

"My thought exactly," McCauley said.

The Yale professor returned to the black wall, felt for the correct orientation and began to count as he touched the first two depressions followed by the four on the row two down. "One, two and one, two, three, four."

Quinn McCauley was filled with anticipation, but once more, the supposition failed.

"It's a dead end," Katrina reluctantly admitted.

McCauley stared straight ahead silently. He couldn't see a thing, which suddenly made the answer all the more clear to him. He smiled.

"Take my light, Katrina." With self-assurance he asked, "Twenty-four, right?"

"Well…" Now, Eccleston wasn't any more confident than Katrina. "Twenty-four if…."

"Good, just checking. He flexed his fingers. "Twenty-four it is."

Extending two fingers on his left hand and four fingers on his right, he felt for all of the notches he had just touched one at a time. Finding them, he eased back. "Here goes." With another deep breath, he gently pressed them *simultaneously*. "Twenty-four," he whispered.

Five seconds of disappointment. Five seconds of wondering if he had found *le chiave*, or ever would. Then their ears suddenly began to ache as air pressure in the cave changed. They heard a muffled sound beyond the wall, like hydraulics or a motor. Then they felt air flowing towards them, first at foot level, then gradually higher to above their heads. Though they couldn't yet see, a large section of the wall containing the prime pyramid rose.

Compelled by curiosity, and in the priest's mind, probably some faith, the trio ventured forward. Without realizing it, they held hands and entered...*somewhere*.

Moments later, the perfect black began to lighten. First to an appreciable black, then a dark gray through increasing lighter tones, and ultimately to the whitest white they'd ever perceived. The change occurred over more than a minute, allowing their eyes to adjust. Soon they realized they were within a vast environment, but they could no better judge it by height, width, or depth than the black that had preceded it. It had no visible light source, yet everything— the ceiling, the walls, the floor— were illuminated to the same bright white level.

"Amazing," Katrina said.

"Extraordinary," Eccleston exclaimed.

"Where are we?" McCauley managed.

"*When* are we?" Eccleston proposed. He didn't have the chance to explain himself.

"Turn around slowly! Very slowly!"

It was a sharp order from a voice at the entrance to the chamber. Demanding, insistent. Most of all, threatening.

SEVENTY-NINE

"Dr. McCauley, Dr. Alpert and Fr. Eccleston. I commend the three of you on your quest. Thank you for lighting the way."

A man stepped forward. He held a semi-automatic pistol in his right hand and a flashlight that wasn't working in his left.

"Would you describe it as holy or scientific? Or wholly scientific?" he asked.

McCauley judged him to be about six feet, bald and thin, maybe forty or forty-five. He wasn't dressed for the job at hand, whether it was cave exploring or murder. He wore tan pants, now filthy, and a light blue pullover sweater. McCauley recognized him: the man who had stood outside Eccleston's apartment.

McCauley held his left arm out and waved Katrina behind. "Who are you?"

"An unimportant question."

Katrina now also recognized him. She started to speak, but McCauley squeezed her hand and whispered, "I know."

"I think you can put the gun away," the priest implored.

"Not likely, Father."

"Look, if we're not supposed to be here, we can all just leave. No problem," McCauley said.

"My dear Dr. McCauley, the problem exists precisely *because* you are here. And you have cost me sleep for weeks. Your exhaustive pursuit of things you have no concept of. Your inability to stop."

"Before or after the bombing or the plane crash? I take it that was your work," McCauley declared.

"You are quite the sleuth."

"… And what about my assistant? I haven't been able to reach him," McCauley said hoping to hear something about Pete DeMeo.

"I wouldn't worry about anyone else right now," the man with the gun said.

"You're going to…" Katrina couldn't complete the thought.

"Well, not right at this rather remarkable spot. Far too pristine. Besides, thanks to you I now know how to re-enter. But I see you understand the gravity of the situation, Dr. Alpert."

Father Eccleston took a step forward. "You don't have to do this. You…"

"Oh, but I do. It's my job."

"This is absurd," Katrina argued. She tried to step around McCauley who held her back.

"As absurd as what you've come across?" the man asked impassively.

The point was ironic.

"You can live with three murders including a priest?" McCauley asked.

The man looked like he considered the point.

"We're not here to exploit anything. Hell, we don't even know what *this* is. We're merely academicians, invisible in the long run. Father Eccleston is a Vatican scientist. Assuredly, the Vatican knows how to contain him. So why don't we all leave none the worse and as ill-informed as when we arrived. We go our way, you go yours."

"Perhaps," the man volunteered.

McCauley didn't believe him for a second, but thought it might buy them some time or opportunity.

"But we haven't begun to understand anything about…"

"Not your job, Father."

"And what is your job?" Eccleston decried. "You mentioned your job."

"Right now, cleaning house. Okay. Everyone out. One at a time. Father Eccleston first, then you, Dr. McCauley. Dr. Alpert comes up third, close to me. She will be the first to die if you attempt to run."

"Run?" Katrina complained "Through here?"

"Out," the gunman ordered. "Out!"

THEY LEFT THE expanse and its mysteries. As they passed through the opening, the white dissolved quickly to black and the wall began to close behind them as silently as it had opened. They walked, then crawled where necessary.

"I think the flashlights will work about here," McCauley soon said. Katrina started to douse her lamp.

"No!" the man shouted. "Flashlights on first. I need to see you!"

They did as they were told, but McCauley lost an opportunity he hoped he'd get.

While still on all fours, McCauley found a small rock; not quite round, but something he could palm. It might be the only weapon available.

Their footsteps began to echo again, indicating the tunnel was opening up. The lights lit the pathway and the walls. Soon they were fully upright re-entering the expansive cavern with the extraordinary geological shapes and the underground river.

There was a moment, only a moment when McCauley could tell Katrina and Eccleston what he planned. With his back to the gunman he whispered, "Get ready to shut off your flashlights and hit the ground when I say, *Now*."

"But?"

Katrina was about to argue that the man was going to let them go. McCauley knew better.

"Okay, stop," the captor ordered. It surely wasn't a conversational tone. He panned his flashlight from McCauley, to Alpert and lastly over to the priest.

They stood about fifteen feet in front. McCauley was ready to give the signal, but the gunman acted first. He fired at his target with no warning.

Father Eccleston heard the shot, which was enough to surprise him. Then he felt growing warmth in his stomach. All of this was within the initial second. He looked down, then up, confused. The next shot ended all his surprise and eliminated the pain. Father Jareth Eccleston dropped to his knees, then toppled into the water.

McCauley had the wits to yell, "Now!"

He dropped his flashlight. Katrina did the same and fell flat on the floor just as another shot rang out. Both of their lights broke.

McCauley stepped to his left and turned his body sideways.

The man fired again, but had no true target. However, the gunman's flashlight gave McCauley his. He pulled his right arm back and aimed for the man's head.

His throwing arm didn't fail him.

The man dropped. The flashlight fell from his hand which plunged the cavern into complete darkness.

"Katrina!"

She didn't answer.

"Katrina!"

"Over here." She struggled with her reply.

"Where?"

"A few feet away."

Katrina groped for her flashlight. She found it, but it didn't work.

McCauley pulled another from his backpack and turned it on. He was grateful to see she wasn't hurt. McCauley helped Katrina up.

McCauley panned his new flashlight along the floor. The man was down.

"Is he…" Katrina hesitated. "…dead?"

"I don't know, but get out now!"

"Father Eccleston?"

"Out now! I'll be right behind you." He gave her another flashlight.

Alpert started toward the pathway, but turned when she heard a splash. She rushed to the water's edge.

"Quinn!" She shined her light into the water.

After twenty seconds McCauley's head popped up for air. He filled his lungs and went back under. Another thirty seconds, he returned, took a deep breath, and dove again. After the third attempt, he swam to Katrina.

"He's gone. But you should have…."

"Shut up and let me help you."

She reached out, bracing her legs against a stalagmite. "Grab hold." McCauley took her hand and struggled onto the cavern floor.

"Okay?" she asked.

"Yes, yes. Okay. Thank you," he said shivering.

McCauley took her flashlight and shined it on the downed man. He was groggy and disoriented.

"Can you make it?" she asked.

"Yes."

They quickly retraced their steps. Adrenaline kept them going. When they could, they held hands. When that wasn't possible, McCauley made sure she went first.

For an instant, McCauley thought he heard breathing or wheezing behind them. "Faster!" he exclaimed.

"Is he…?"

"Just go!"

Soon, they saw welcomed daylight. The late afternoon sun would warm McCauley and the open road would provide escape. Ahead, more unknown. For now they were grateful to be free and alive.

As they emerged from the cave and their eyes adjusted, they abruptly realized that that option had disappeared.

EIGHTY

Inside the cave

COLIN KAVANAUGH GRADUALLY regained awareness. McCauley's rock had only dazed him.

He groped for a flashlight. First forward, then side-to-side. Without it he feared he'd never find his way out. Suddenly, he heard something roll toward him. Metal on rock. He struck his hand out as the flashlight reached him. He turned it on and scanned about for his gun.

"Looking for this?"

The voice came from the side. It was as cold as the cavern, but more chilling because he recognized it.

He turned to the direction of the voice. All he saw was a flashlight beam shining on a handgun aimed directly at him.

"I believe this is yours." The gunman tilted the flashlight up to his face—a sneering, angry face; the last man in the world Colin Kavanaugh ever imagined he'd see again: the man with the umbrella.

Outside the cave
The same time

QUINN AND KATRINA stood ten feet from a row of gunmen armed with semi-automatics. The afternoon sun created something of a halo around them. Given their weapons McCauley determined it was totally undeserved.

"You're to stay right where you are," a man in the middle of some twenty others emphatically ordered.

Quinn thought the instruction sounded secondhand, delivered by someone awaiting final instructions. The breathing he heard in the cave?

"Mind if we sit down?" Katrina was serious. She was exhausted.

"Be my guest."

Inside the cave

"MR. GRUBER, APPARENTLY your death preceded you."

Gruber shined the light onto his prey.

"I had to be certain you were ready," Gruber said.

"So this has all been another test?"

"Oh no, young man. Not just another test. Your final, as it were." The voice behind the light sounded all the more cruel. "You failed."

"Mr. Gruber," Kavanaugh pleaded, "I was only following protocol. Find, research, review, contain. Just as you always instructed."

"You bungled your research. You let emotion rule your decisions. You ordered an attack on an individual when none was warranted, thus raising increased suspicion. You brought chaos to our organization and created opportunity for disunity, which is not permitted."

"But!"

"*Secretum!* Did you not understand anything I taught? Obviously not. You ultimately risked it all by killing a priest, no less. You. With your own hand. It's sure to bring an investigation from the church, potentially exposing *Autem Semita*. I cannot recall such ineptitude in our history. You, Mr. Kavanaugh, shall be a brand-new lesson for all future candidates."

Of all the words he could have used, *candidates* was the most damning. *Candidates,* not *successor.* Kavanaugh read it like a death sentence. He struggled to find a way to defend himself.

"It's a new day, Mr. Gruber. Social media spreads word in seconds. A tweet from an explorer's cell can produce viral recognition for his discovery and trouble for us. Try to contain that. Impossible. So we must intervene at the earliest possible opportunity. That's what I did. I acted in time; appropriate for this new age. Swiftly, efficiently."

Kavanaugh was gaining strength and a renewed sense of his own purpose.

"We can no longer merely hide behind a research publication. We must be more aggressive; more proactive. Ours is a holy mission. A priest who digs too deeply is as much a threat as a teacher."

"Right now, you, Mr. Kavanaugh, you are the biggest threat to our ongoing success."

"No, I am the future."

"You failed to understand the past. How can you possibly see the future?"

Kavanaugh wondered if Gruber would actually pull the trigger. *No, not like I did, without prejudice. He loves talking. Time to talk.*

"Mr. Gruber, we can fix this. I can make it better. Obviously I have more to learn."

"Appealing to my paternal side? Remember, I have no children."

"Sir, I am deferring to the man I most admire and have obviously disappointed." *Keep this going.* "I'm happy that you're alive." *What a lie.* "I wasn't ready to take over." *Bullshit.* "This test has proven that to me as well. You were correct to do it." *Lower the fucking gun.*

"You are a danger to all that we have built. If you had

truly understood our purpose over the power you sought, you could have been a deserving leader. I had hope, even though I harbored doubt. Yet, you disappointed me and I'm troubled I misjudged you so."

Kavanaugh could no longer contain himself. "Damn you and your endless lectures. Your incessant rants, your antiquated approaches. All so formal and so meaningless. I listened until I heard enough. Do you want to know the truth?"

"Ah, the truth. That would be enlightening."

"I perfected the art of tuning you out while fully being in your presence."

"And thus, your true self. A charlatan posing as a believer," Gruber declared as he took a wide berth around Kavanaugh. He finished by tapping his umbrella on the cavern floor. First slowly, then faster. It was an unnerving sound. Suddenly he stopped.

"How could I have so misjudged you?"

"I *am* a believer!" Kavanaugh rubbed his scalp, the unconscious sign of his anxiety that Gruber read all too well. "But I finally had to see for myself if the secrets were real."

"They are!" Gruber shouted. He paused and lowered his voice. "My boy, my impertinent boy. If you had any doubt, you had merely to ask."

The response startled Kavanaugh. He looked up at his mentor, who didn't seem like a sickly old man in the partial light and shadows.

"You would have shown me?"

Gruber simply smiled.

"You would have?" Kavanaugh asked again, struggling with his words, trying to get to his knees…to beg.

"Had you asked and had you proven yourself. In time, yes."

Outside the cave
The same time

McCAULEY SIZED UP the guards flanked in front of them and now to the sides. He gauged they were all roughly age 40. Ex-military or certainly with military training. They wore khaki pants and shirts with no insignias or identification, matching tan caps and boots. Besides handguns they were equipped with an array of rifles, some with scopes, others that looked like they'd be ready for a full-on assault.

McCauley sat next to Katrina to hold her, believing the worst was yet to come.

"Move apart!"

"Come on," McCauley complained.

"Apart now!" The man backed his demand with the a steely-eyed look and his gun coming up, first aiming at McCauley, then shifting to Katrina. "Farther!"

McCauley moved to the side but held Katrina's hand. They waited in the sun, perspiring as much out of fear as the heat.

Inside the cave
The same time

"YOU FAKED YOUR DEATH!"

"Only to lessen my misgivings," Gruber admitted. "After all, I think we can both now agree they were well-founded."

"You spent all those years investing in me. All your lessons. Now take a look at yourself. Go ahead look at your reflection in the water. You're a failure as a teacher. It's you who haven't passed the test your own mentors set for you. Without me, you have no one to take over. There is no one else!" He defiantly stared at the old man.

Gruber took the three steps closer. He used the tip of his umbrella to lift up the young man's chin, so he would not only hear, but see him more clearly.

"There was always someone else."

The heartless answer echoed against the cavern walls. Gruber stepped back.

"There always is," he said softly.

Enraged, Kavanaugh finally lunged at Martin Gruber who stood very close.

He was wrong about Gruber's commitment to pull the trigger. Gruber shot the younger man in his right kneecap.

Colin Kavanaugh dropped his flashlight and grabbed his wound. "Damn you," he said writhing in pain. "I was only trying to live up to you."

"You didn't come close."

Gruber shot Kavanaugh's other kneecap.

Kavanaugh shrieked, "Please!"

"Our discussions are over. Just as you wanted." Gruber kicked Kavanaugh's flashlight into the water.

"Good-bye, my boy. You have much to think about, but little time. I suggest you get to it."

Martin Gruber left.

"Don't leave me," the dying man screamed. "I just wanted to succeed, to follow *The Path*. Please!"

Gruber disappeared into the darkness leaving his former protégé alone.

"Please!" Kavanaugh yelled in agony. "Please, Mr. Gruber! Please!" His cries echoed through the chamber.

Gruber recovered a package he'd left against the rocks and quietly said, "Too late." He reached inside, adjusted the contents, and carefully stepped away.

EIGHTY-ONE

Outside the cave
The same time

"WHO ARE YOU PEOPLE?" McCauley finally braved.

The only man tasked to speak remained silent.

"Government? No." McCauley answered the question himself. "You're on your own, aren't you? This is all ideological, not political."

McCauley wanted to engage them, but he also wondered why they were waiting or whom they were waiting for.

"You're part of some organization. You believe in what you're doing. You're committed. But, hell, you're not holding high value assets. We're just…"

At that moment, an out of breath voice from behind interrupted with a polite, but urgent instruction.

"I suggest everyone move away from the cave as quickly as possible."

McCauley and Alpert looked over their shoulders. They saw an old man carrying an umbrella. He stepped around them and repeated the warning. "I must insist, now!"

They hustled as a group.

"Faster," he implored.

"Why?" Katrina shouted as they raced downhill.

The answer came with a deafening explosion. If the blast weren't convincing enough, the accelerating force and debris field that funneled out of the cave certainly was. Katrina and Quinn were bowled over. Martin Gruber was able to stay upright only because one of his men steadied him.

Katrina wasn't sure how long it took to recover. Her ears ached and she felt dust in every pore. She reached for Quinn. His fingers grasped hers.

They slowly helped one another find footing. Quinn steadied Katrina with his arm as they stood.

"Ah, Dr. McCauley. For the present, it's good to see that you and Dr. Alpert appear no worse for the wear."

"For Christ's sake, how can you say that? Father Eccleston is dead. And who are you? What's this all about?"

"I'm sorry, no climactic admissions except that this is all about *you*. Who I am is of no matter. Simply consider me someone who holds the upper hand. And despite my advanced years and obvious ill health, I remain in good company. You've met my associates. Trust me, there are many more."

"What about the man inside?" Katrina asked.

"Dead or dying. With a great deal of regret. His, not mine. What's more, I have no qualms adding to the death toll today." He looked smug and satisfied. "Tell me, what did you find inside before all the commotion began?"

Katrina was appalled by the comment. "He killed Father Eccleston and you call it commotion?"

"My sincere apologies, Dr. Alpert. Admittedly a poor choice of words," Gruber said. "However, the answer remains important. How far in did you get? What did you see?"

McCauley interrupted before Katrina could say anything. "We were on our way when we were confronted."

"Oh is that so? Should I believe you?" He turned to his troop. The officer who had spoken only shrugged his shoulders.

"Quite the dilemma, wouldn't you agree? You could

be telling the truth. If that's the case, then I should feel a modicum of guilt. Conversely? Well, then I will have no remorse. But for clarity's sake, back to my question. How far…?"

"Where Father Eccleston was shot," Katrina stated. "Quinn threw a rock at the guy and then he dove into the water to try to save the priest. It was too late. I helped Quinn out and we left."

Gruber applauded while resting the handle of his umbrella on his arm. "A very nice recital."

"What did we miss?" Katrina asked without flinching.

"Oh, Dr. Alpert, you do us a disservice. As I said before, no climactic admissions. Let the explosive charge we all felt finally close that chapter. Of course this should have been properly taken care of *in the day*. Such secrets potentially exposed. But now it's done."

"In the day?" Katrina knew what he meant. "Galileo's day?" she boldly proclaimed.

"Ah, before my time," Gruber stated. "But I see you know your history."

"We're actually pretty much in the dark," McCauley admitted. "…and were when we were interrupted by the assassin you've since sealed in." That much was true.

Gruber studied McCauley. "Well, this is the very thing that leads to my dilemma." Gruber aimed his gun at McCauley. "What to do with you?"

"Dr. Alpert," McCauley started again. "Katrina and I are grateful to be alive right now." He held her tighter. "That makes us very eager to listen."

Gruber nodded. He looked around for someplace to sit. The boulder that they'd moved was a few steps away. He rested himself against the rock. "Impressive feat. Dislodging this boulder couldn't have been easy."

"It wasn't."

"You mentioned secrets," McCauley said.

"Observant, Dr. McCauley. No doubt in academics you believe you have a responsibility to report what you have found. I am in the business of doing the opposite. As such, I'm methodical to a fault.

"That underlying character trait makes me believe that you understand more than you admit. After all, your travels took you beyond your own discovery to a researcher, an academician, an explorer, and lastly a priest. Have I missed anyone?"

McCauley did not volunteer Marli Bellamy's name.

"California, London, France and quite deep, as I understand, within the Vatican library," Gruber continued. "Very impressive. With some extremely intuitive and focused requests. Isn't that so?"

It didn't require a response or confession. Gruber clearly knew what he was talking about.

"Considering what you have likely seen here, your own exploration as well, and your association with a recently departed Galileo scholar, I'd say your emergent conclusions and my avowed duty are in direct conflict."

"We followed clues to Le Marche, but they haven't led to any understanding," Katrina admitted quite honestly.

"Yet, you may have a theory. And that alone can lead to risks civilization can ill afford."

"I don't understand," McCauley said.

"Keeping it strictly philosophical?"

"Of course." McCauley felt their only hope was to string out the conversation long enough for the police to come—if, on the chance, anyone heard and reported the explosion.

"You seek a different truth than I do," Gruber explained. "You may call it reality. I would argue that you know nothing of what is really real. However, you both have surprised me. You've traveled far in your quest. Perhaps farther than I believed possible. However, no matter what you might think you saw, would you be prepared to live with the knowledge that your discovery could become the catalyst for sweeping revolutions…that you, Dr. McCauley and Dr. Alpert could cause a rise in fanaticism on a scale the world has never known? I've ordered deaths to keep the secrets. What I've done would not compare to the devastation that you would cause."

Katrina looked at Quinn, confused.

"You're scientists. Your stock in trade are facts. You are also members of, as we used to say, the family of man. As such, I recognize you have responsibilities. To put it in a metaphor relevant to your life's work, the earth is solid, but we walk on eggshells. Civilization itself is fragile, held together by political parties, organized religion, and disparate sects. It's been that way for millennia."

"And wars have been fought defending religious dogma and keeping dictators in power," Alpert interrupted. "Millions upon millions killed."

"Yes, Dr. Alpert. And also billions of people clothed and fed, sheltered, and protected. There has been goodness. Yet, all of that would be gone come next Sunday if faith fails in the world's largest religion. And what do you suppose would fill the vacuum?"

They had no answer for such a direct question.

"To put it in your pedagogy, seismic change. Another religion feared by the West, misunderstood by the world, and often misrepresented by its own congregation would take over, more swiftly than imagined. Or a fanaticism we haven't even known. Call it ISIS today or something else entirely new tomorrow, it surely wouldn't end in undeveloped or third-world countries. The ultimate impact on western civilization would be immeasurable, redefining life and society as we know it."

Gruber stood and stretched his arms and legs. "Too much sitting. I have to walk a bit." Gruber strolled and took deep breaths. His age was showing. He checked his watch. "It's always about time, isn't it? We'll have to wrap this up soon, though I'm sure you want our talk to continue with the hope that you'll be rescued by the local authorities. Sadly, for you, I've taken care of them."

Gruber haughtily took in the fresh country air and straightened. "You wouldn't know it, but doctors pronounced me dead a number of months ago. Personally, I felt it was not a good time to die and so here I am."

Now he paced, using his umbrella as a crutch.

"The foundation of my mission is maintaining the social fabric of the world. And still, I'm reminded by events as recent as minutes ago, we're only human. My would-be successor, whom you had the misfortune of meeting, was guilty of avarice."

"That sounds as if it's a distinctly religious condemnation," Quinn remarked.

"Perhaps it is both religious and personal. While the organization I represent is not theologically based, we are an order that cannot allow self-worth to be placed above the greater good."

"And murder," Katrina said pointedly. "You people kill priests."

Gruber did not answer.

"And next? You have no ethical issues about killing us?"

"None, Dr. Alpert. But admittedly, the job gets harder."

"The job?"

"Containing potential exposure. Eliminating threats. In past years, we could destroy evidence with little notice. We could buy off investigators, intimidate and even blackmail. Today, there are more and more people like you who explore anywhere on the face of the earth and others who map from satellites. It's increasingly difficult. Ours is a duty to maintain order, long ago decided, for the betterment of all. But we live in the age of Google Earth."

Gruber stepped closer. As he did so, his associates brought their guns up into firing position.

"Governments come and go," Gruber continued. "Wars move national boundaries and establish temporary alliances. The rule of normality is the only constant, driven by doctrinal faith."

"But...."

Gruber shot his hand up. "No!" He acted perturbed for the first time. "In fact, there are many religions. Each preaching its own version of things. And truth be told, I believe that all of them would be doing the same thing if they knew."

"If they knew what?" McCauley exclaimed.

"The secrets."

"So the Vatican continues its Inquisition five hundred years later because it wants to?" McCauley demanded.

"Oh, no. I haven't made myself clear. We're not the Vatican," Gruber stated. "Beyond Galileo we never were. I'm not a clergyman. We have no affiliation. None. Individually, we may have our own beliefs, but there is much more at stake."

"What are you then?"

"In simple terms, Dr. Alpert, I am the man who can put an end to your questions with merely a nod to my left or my right. No guilt. You die. I walk away and have an early dinner."

Gruber wasn't completely satisfied with what he was saying. He gathered his thoughts.

"I have to admit, I'm not used to being out of the office. I've had a difficult time finding a successor. As you've seen, my primary choice did not live up to expectations. So all things considered, I've had a lot on my plate recently. Normally, we've been able to deal with things in a cleaner manner, but we are in a bit of transition."

"You fucked up."

"Dr. McCauley, can we keep this at a respectable level? If it's any consolation, I think you're criticizing me much too harshly. Here I am admitting mistakes. I also acknowledge that fulfilling our charge is becoming increasingly difficult. A new pope brings new leadership. The nonstop hunger for news gives muckrakers and blowhards louder voices than journalists and intellectuals. Things will change in time. Ultimately, we may be unable to contain our secrets. I pray it will not be because of my shortcomings or unwillingness to act. I fear for the world if and when that happens."

Gruber pointed his umbrella at Katrina, then McCauley.

"There is an expression," Gruber continued. "It's Latin. Have you heard it? *Cui bono?*"

"Yes," Katrina said. "To whose benefit."

"Very good. It's attributed to the wise Roman judge, Lucius Cassius, who was known for asking, *'Cui bono?'* It often suggests that a person who's guilty of committing a crime may be someone who has something to gain.

"*Cui bono*, Dr. McCauley? Let's be truthful. *You* believed you would benefit. Research. Publication. Dr. Alpert's positive review. Yes, I know these things. Tenure. Lectures. Fame. None of it possible if you truly knew. The cost to civilization is far too great."

McCauley remained silent.

"Your site in Montana has been destroyed. The same here. There is nothing for you to report. No reason to light the fuse. We've contained that which would surely affect the present and change the future. *Cui bono?* The world benefits."

The old man took another cleansing breath. His expression changed. "There was a man, a cardinal, Francesco Barberini. Are you familiar with him?"

"Yes," McCauley acknowledged. "Why?"

"Just a footnote in history. It's of no matter."

Gruber checked his watch again. "I must admit, this was a most engaging discussion. One of the best in quite some time. But now I have other things to do. And you must take a walk with my colleagues while I begin down the hill."

Katrina gasped.

"We won't be seeing one another again."

Gruber motioned with his umbrella for Quinn and Katrina to head toward the edge of the cliff they'd seen hours before.

"Good-bye Dr. McCauley, Dr. Alpert."

As they were marched off, they heard the old man repeat the single, simple word. *"Secretum."*

EIGHTY-TWO

"DO NOT TURN AROUND. Keep walking. No talking."

The paramilitary soldier's command was sharp and direct, uncompromising, non-negotiable.

Quinn and Katrina stepped through overgrowth that reached up to their thighs. The swooshing of their feet was the loudest sound, but boots rhythmically filled in behind them.

After two minutes, the weeds gave way to rocks. Now they only heard their own breathing and footsteps. Quinn figured the mercenaries had taken up their final positions. He squeezed Katrina's hand as they approached the ledge.

"They're going to make it look like we jumped off," she whispered.

McCauley glanced left and right, trying to scope escape routes, at least one for Katrina. The landscape was too open for any successful run. "Maybe we can angle toward a soft landing."

In another minute they were at the shelf. They stopped and faced a two hundred foot drop. Below, sharp boulders and dead trees. Katrina and Quinn looked deeply into one another's eyes and dared a kiss. A deep, loving kiss.

Quinn didn't know when or how it would come, but if the kiss was the last thing he'd know, he wanted it to last.

And it lasted. For ten seconds. For twenty. For thirty.

McCauley slowly released Katrina, turned toward his captors and opened his eyes.

They were gone.

EIGHTY-THREE

Makoshika State Park, MT
Five weeks later

THE EARLY MORNING sun cast long shadows westward. The ground was wet from a late night thunderstorm. A family of turkey vultures squawked overhead. Aside from the birds, the only other sounds that cut across the landscape were the footsteps of four curious explorers.

They walked single file. Each carried a heavy backpack. Two knew where they were going. Two didn't. Only one of them knew why McCauley was playing Kinks hits on his iPhone—Katrina Alpert.

Quinn McCauley was a great deal more careful now. McCauley was also attentive to a word that had echoed in his mind for more than a month. *Secretum.*

Katrina was second in line. Like the others, she wore a long sleeved shirt with a hoodie, jeans, and work boots. Her backpack contained even warmer clothes.

Behind Katrina was Peter DeMeo. He was alive, and quite amazingly in love with the Italian woman he'd met at the Vatican. McCauley's concerns were apparently unfounded.

Last in the line, Al Jaffe, the only member of the summer class McCauley had invited back for this venture.

After trudging through the mud, McCauley brought them to a halt in the middle of the flats. Directly ahead— the hillside. The base was strewn with splintered rocks from the Cessna's impact. Every piece of the plane had been painstakingly recovered and removed by the NTSB investigators. Remaining strands of police tape that had cordoned off the area fluttered in the light breeze. Soon all traces would be gone.

"The wind and weather are already taking their toll," Jaffe said softly. "Like you said when we met, Dr. McCauley, we're just visitors here."

"No, Al, I was wrong. We're more than visitors. We're partners. We have been for a long time." He pointed at the challenge that faced them. "Let's see what we can learn about the earth."

McCauley started walking in the direction he'd indicated.

"Wrong way, Quinn," Katrina quickly corrected him. "To your right."

McCauley stopped and smiled mischievously.

"What?"

He didn't say anything.

"What?" she demanded.

Jaffe walked to her side and also smiled broadly.

"What?" she said for the third time. "The plane crashed there!" She pointed to a slightly different position, off axis of where Quinn was heading.

He walked back to her. "You're absolutely right, sweetheart. That *is* where the plane hit, but I gave Al an assignment while we were driving to LA. Research a man named Maskelyne. Jasper Maskelyne. I think you were asleep at the time. My oversight for not mentioning it to you." He laughed. He hadn't intended on telling Katrina.

"Dr. McCauley had me look up what Maskelyne accomplished at the Port of Alexandria during World War II," Jaffe added.

"So?" DeMeo was equally confused.

"Jasper Maskelyne was a vaudeville performer who enlisted in World War II," McCauley explained. "A countryman of yours, Katrina. He believed his special talents would translate from the stage to the theater of war."

"A clever turn of phrase. But what talents?" she asked.

"He was a magician," Jaffe noted.

"A master magician. Masterful in fact," McCauley continued. "He wanted to demonstrate that trickery had value to the Allies. He believed his illusions could help defeat the Germans."

"I don't get it," DeMeo said.

"Well, neither did the British commanders at first. However, Maskelyne knew how to divert the eye. Deflect attention. Make his audiences focus on something they thought was real, but wasn't. He was an expert in the art of deception. So to convince the officers, he created the illusion of a large German warship floating on the Thames. He used only a model and mirrors. From a distance and the correct angle it looked real. Absolutely real. Having proven his point, they gave Maskelyne a commission in the Royal Engineers. Soon he deployed to North Africa. For some time he simply entertained the troops. But in January, 1941, Maskelyne was allowed to pull together a team which he called 'The Magic Gang.' They consisted of a carpenter and painters, an architect, chemist and electrical engineer, and, this is vital—a stage set builder, all the people he'd need to put on a spectacular show.

"You've heard of Erwin Rommel?"

"Of course. He was the German general who rolled across North Africa," DeMeo answered.

"Well, Maskelyne slowed him down. Rommel was poised to take out a British desert division. Surveillance told him the enemy's strength and where they would be. Reports were based on aerial observations. Rommel prepared for a strategic and lethal strike, especially because the British tanks were advancing without support. Their supply trucks were heading in another direction rather than sticking with the tanks. As a result, the tanks were exposed; an easy target for Rommel.

"But that was what Maskelyne wanted the Germans to believe. At night, he and his Magic Gang painted and re-framed the tanks, disguising them as trucks and transports. They also added cardboard, wood siding and tubing to the actual trucks, masquerading them as tanks. Diversion. Deception. Distraction. Rommel's spotters saw what they thought were tanks. They went after them, only to leave their flank exposed to the real British firepower bearing down from another direction."

"Unbelievable," Katrina remarked.

"Yes, but his masterpiece was Alexandria, Egypt." Mc-Cauley now cued Jaffe to explain.

"His greatest illusion of all: the Port of Alexandria. German bombers were prepared to destroy the target. So, Maskelyne moved it."

"Moved it?" Katrina said incredulously. "How?"

Al Jaffe continued. "The city's ancient collections were priceless. The libraries and museums were too important to lose. It was the main British base in the region and Alexandria, in particular, held great strategic value for re-supplying oil to the Allies. Jasper Maskelyne did what only a magician could achieve in a short period of time. He moved the Port of Alexandria."

"The whole city? Everything?" DeMeo was completely bewildered.

"Depends on your perspective," McCauley replied.

"Actually he created a grand distraction," Jaffe explained. "The British calculated that the German bombers would head over the Mediterranean at night. The pilots had their compasses and charts. However on cloudless nights they'd rely on the port's lighthouse to guide them in. They'd trust their eyes on the bombing run. Except for the fact that Jasper Maskelyne and his Magic Gang had been at work. As the lead German bomber approached the target, he observed that the lighthouse beam and the city lights were just a few degrees off compass. Not much, but enough to question his German mapmakers. So he banked his plane slightly, lining up for a straight-in visual attack. All the bombers similarly adjusted their flight plans and simply, unquestionably followed the leader. When they flew over ground zero they dropped their bombs and left. They did it night after night. The city was in ruins. A total success."

"But I thought?" Katrina interjected.

"A total success for Maskelyne. Not the Germans. He'd successfully moved the Port of Alexandria."

"But you just said the Germans destroyed what they saw," she exclaimed.

"Absolutely. They destroyed what they saw. It wasn't the real lighthouse or the city. The true objective was completely in the dark. The Germans obliterated a wooden replica—a model of Alexandria, geographically close enough to the real city, structured on the same urban plan, but on a much smaller scale. They bombed the living daylights out of a fake wooden target built by set designers. They trusted their eyes over their compasses. Maskelyne saved Alexandria."

"Brilliant!" DeMeo exclaimed.

McCauley corrected him. "Magic."

Now it was time to take his team behind the curtain he'd created. "How'd you like to see the tunnel we discovered and not what Al set up as the target?"

EIGHTY-FOUR

Minutes later

AL JAFFE HAD camouflaged the entrance to the actual cave as perfectly as he had fashioned the false one—the airplane's target. He'd replicated Maskelyne's magic.

They removed the brush and the rocks he had piled up. Once clear, McCauley led the team through the passages. He stopped and commented on the Native American cave drawings, now more meaningful.

DeMeo was awestruck.

"Stay together," McCauley instructed as they advanced. "I'll need everyone to…" McCauley's voice suddenly echoed into darkness. "Okay, slowly take out the propane lamps. Time to light them…carefully."

He'd had five weeks to think about returning. Ultimately nothing could dissuade him from seeking answers. In some way, he believed the old man in Italy wanted him to understand why the secret was too great to share. McCauley had invited the others, explaining they didn't have to come. It might not be safe. The trio never objected.

Katrina, Pete DeMeo, and Al Jaffe pulled up behind McCauley. They continued until there was utter darkness ahead. Zero black darkness.

"Oh my God!" DeMeo exclaimed. "More incredible than you described."

"Amazing, isn't it," McCauley stated. "No light reflects back. It's all absorbed."

"So where are we?" DeMeo asked.

McCauley recalled Father Eccleston's comment. *When?*

He moved forward and groped around the black wall. McCauley exhaled when his fingers touched the depressions that made up the prime pyramid.

"We're here," he quietly said.

"Are you sure you want to go further?" Katrina replied with a warning tone. She knew what might come next, but not why.

McCauley smiled. "Yes. Yes, I am." As he reached for the apex of the pyramid he said, "Turn your lamps off now."

The lamps dimmed and went out. The darkness and the quiet was enveloping.

McCauley gently slid his fingers across the wall and located the sequence of notches within the prime pyramid. Just as he had done in Italy, he pressed the two indentations on the second row and the four in the fourth row exactly together.

The same five seconds passed and then the pressure changed, followed by the wall slowly rising.

"Now watch," he said.

The scene that unfolded didn't disappoint. Darkness slowly morphed to white as if programmed on a slow rheostat.

"Incredible!" DeMeo exclaimed. "There's no actual light source."

There wasn't. Yet light now engulfed the environment. From the floors. The walls. The ceilings. Everywhere. It defied reason. It operated under its own physical laws.

DeMeo barged forward with youthful enthusiasm.

The others advanced more cautiously, enthralled by the perfection of the technology.

"This can't be man-made," DeMeo said. His voice should have echoed, but it was actually muted.

McCauley had his own thoughts, but no way to confirm them. Not until…

"Damn!"

DeMeo, well ahead of him, doubled over.

"What?" McCauley asked. "Are you okay?"

"I bumped into something. It's right in front of me, but I can't see it. Damned thing blends into the rest of the whiteness. I'm holding onto it, but that's the only reason I know it's here."

"Don't move." McCauley walked straight toward DeMeo, but more carefully now, not knowing whether there were more obstructions.

"Okay, right here, boss. Feel," DeMeo offered.

McCauley extended his hand across what felt like a desk or tabletop. It was as smooth as the wall and likely made from the same material. But the surface cast no shadows since it was illuminated with the pure white light that bathed, or more correctly emanated from within everything and everywhere.

He continued to feel around the edges to the sides, noting the size was roughly four feet square. The width was approximately two inches. The entire top was supported by a single post that was anchored without seams to the ground.

"Everyone stand around the sides. Let's try to visualize some definition to this."

They took positions. Katrina to his left, Jaffe opposite him and DeMeo on his right.

It helped give them perspective. Next McCauley ran his hand along the top. Suddenly he stopped.

"What?" Jaffe asked.

"Another dent." It was closest to Katrina. "Put your finger on it."

Katrina placed her hand over McCauley's. He guided her finger to the spot. Then, with palms flat and his fingers extended, he slowly swept across the surface, finding another dent higher up near Jaffe. "Here, Al."

McCauley continued and came to another also within Jaffe's reach. He tapped the spot and Jaffe automatically put his index finger on it.

The Yale professor looked at where the hands were and made an assumption that another might likely complete the shape. It was there. "Pete, this one's yours."

"So what is it?" Jaffe wondered.

"A square?" Katrina noted. "No, more like a rectangle, but slightly askew."

"Another puzzle. Another lock," McCauley ventured.

Katrina's left hand was free. She rested it on the surface and another depression.

"Whoa. Here!" She tapped the point. From McCauley's perspective it was slightly left of her corner.

"What's in your pockets?" McCauley asked excitedly.

"Car keys, wallet, cell phone," DeMeo said.

"Pretty much the same, Coins." Jaffe added.

"Same here," Katrina replied.

"Coins. Let's go with coins. Easiest to see. Place one on each of the spots."

With their nickels, dimes and quarters they were able to see an off-center box with one coin to the left.

"Feel for more," McCauley continued.

Katrina found another close to the last. Jaffe added one more beyond it near the end of the surface.

"More coins?" McCauley stated.

"Here," DeMeo said.

They marked them.

"Any more? Feel all around."

There were no more.

"Okay, what is it?" DeMeo wondered. From his perspective it looked like a shovel.

"I don't know, a pot? A crooked broom?" Jaffe proposed.

"A bent flag?" was Katrina's first thought.

"Interesting how we tend to look for relatable images within even the most rudimentary shapes," McCauley said. "It's been something people have done since, I suppose, the dawn of time."

"You sound like you've figured it out?" Katrina said.

"Oh, yes. It's right in front of me. The most recognizable design ever known. The one that guided travelers and quite likely pointed Galileo to the stars. He was fascinated by it. So of course he recognized it. Father Eccleston would have, too. Ursa Major. The Big Dipper."

EIGHTY-FIVE

"WHAT'S THE BIG Dipper got to do with anything?" DeMeo asked.

"Back to *'La chiave.'* It's more than just the key to the lock. The whole sentence," Katrina explained. "Galileo's complete thought was *'La chiave per sbloccare i misteri della paura.'* The key to the mysteries of time."

"That helps a lot," DeMeo said facetiously.

"It's a signpost, a guiding way. The Big Dipper points to Polaris, the North Star, the most identifiable star in the sky," McCauley explained. "The star that doesn't rise or set, but remains relatively in the same position above the northern horizon while other stars circle it. It's all because the axis of the earth is pointed toward it. We're being pointed toward it."

"But where?" Katrina wasn't sure of the position.

"I know." Jaffe, the army veteran volunteered. "It's a straight shot up from lower right to the upper right." Jaffe came around to McCauley's side. "From the two stars, Merak to Dubhe," he continued, "and onward. At least that's what it is in the night sky."

McCauley thought more about the design. The position of the stars, the meaning Galileo or even Father Eccleston would have recognized.

"The number!" he said aloud. He counted the stars represented by the coins. "Seven. Another prime number." He looked at the layout, this time as a path. "If I start at the far end of the dipper's handle and end at, what's the name of the last star?"

"Dubhe," Jaffe replied.

"Ending at Dubhe…then? Well, let's find out."

Quinn McCauley removed the coin on the last star point and pressed the space. Then he moved in toward the corner, repeating the action. He was pressing on representations of Alkaid, Mizar, Alioth, then Megrez at the upper left of the bucket, down to Phecda, over the base to Merak and up to Dubhe. One after another, all in order. All seven.

Instantly the environment darkened, but not to the deep black. Now a warm blue-black enveloped them. It was punctuated by a bright point of light straight ahead on the wall and in line with the last two stars.

"Polaris," Katrina gasped.

"Walk toward it," McCauley implored.

They did, side by side. Without a sense of space, they weren't sure how far they walked, but soon other areas began to illuminate. Not with a pinpoint of light, but blurry images.

"Like it's dialing through filters," Jaffe said.

"Video projections?" DeMeo articulated.

"Right, but I can't tell what they are," Katrina replied.

McCauley couldn't either. The resolution and focus were still adjusting. McCauley stepped forward from the team and looked directly at the Polaris star projecting his own desire for answers. Suddenly a beam of light shot directly into his eyes.

"Quinn!" Katrina screamed.

McCauley was frozen in place for nearly thirty seconds, breathing, but not able to speak. Then it was over. The beam faded but Polaris remained.

"Are you all right?"

"Yes." McCauley shook his head to gather his thoughts.

"I felt like my eyes were being examined. Like an oph-thalmologist trying out different corrective lenses on me. And I *felt* things."

"Felt? What kind of..." Katrina didn't finish her question. Images suddenly exploded throughout the chamber with the sounds of wind and water.

Now they sharpened, popped up above, below and all around them, expanded in size and then merged into one moving conceptual display which surrounded them. It was an astounding sight—colorful, emotional, overpowering—as beautiful as it was mystifying.

They rotated, looking up, around and down. Katrina was the first to put impressions to words.

"A, a planet forming," Katrina exclaimed.

"Yes, but not...." McCauley stopped short.

The image now began to spin quickly, form and re-form over and over until it slowed and merged again, but this time into one huge landmass surrounded by water. It looked like an inverted L, but thicker on the side than on top.

"Not just a planet," McCauley proclaimed. He recognized what it was. More than that, he sensed it.

"Pangaea. Or what we know as Pangea. The super continent. Earth from three hundred million years ago. Early Paleozoic." He spoke with authority, with knowledge, not speculation. Like the idea was implanted within him. "When all the continents were fused as one. Before the continental shifts."

They continued to pivot, watching the single image morph again into dozens, if not hundreds of different displays.

"Look there and there," Katrina exclaimed. She pointed to specific moving images. "Those plants and animals; fossils to us. But..."

"Old Earth," McCauley declared. "We're seeing Earth as it was."

"How?" Jaffe asked the question for everyone.

"We're in a library, an archive. These pictures were recorded for earth's heirs and pre-programmed for discovery. Somehow the intelligence behind this had the technology to make sure it survived."

"But, humans didn't evolve until hundreds of millions of years later," DeMeo declared.

Katrina watched as the pictures revealed emerging life-forms, changing landscapes, undersea organisms and soon animals moving across the land. Then they saw upright creatures, not completely familiar, but not unfamiliar either.

"Quinn, what are they?"

McCauley reached for a memory now ingrained.

"This is what his Inquisitors must have feared. It's the secret guarded for centuries."

They watched in awe as lanky people-like bipeds established communities in clans, then families and cities. Cities that were transformed through inventions, and technology unknown today.

They stared at the images trying to make sense of the ancient history that unfolded before them; a virtual other-world that preceded modern times.

Beings. Families. Communities. Births. Children growing into adults. Institutional buildings and even houses of worship. Teachers and students. Scientists and doctors. Heroes and villains. All accompanied by a cacophony of sounds.

"We're witnessing life that came before us…civilization that existed and flourished…and died." McCauley now embraced the ultimate realization. "And we're the reboot."

Just as the images had subdivided, they now reassembled into one shocking faster moving master video revealing a staggering saga.

"Oh my God," Katrina sighed.

Massive earthquakes unhinged the plates. Volcanoes spewed toxins into the air. The giant continent broke apart.

McCauley exhaled. Katrina wrapped her arms around him.

"This is the last record of a prior version of humankind," McCauley solemnly said. "As the forces acted on the earth, it also changed what was breathable. The air was on its way to becoming ours. They couldn't evolve quickly enough. It ended up being a false start, with their archives surviving beyond them."

"I don't know a lot about the constellations, but wouldn't the Big Dipper have appeared completely differently back then?" DeMeo asked.

McCauley again subconsciously sensed the answer. "Yes. It was still forming in their time out of a cluster of scattered stars. But the beings projected that movement into the future for when they believed—or hoped—intelligent life would return. Our time. Us."

"It's the greatest discovery of all time." Katrina gasped.

"It is," McCauley agreed. "Like Greene said, when the continents formed, conditions gave life an opportunity to exist. Intelligent life emerged. And we've looked back some three hundred million years or more to see it."

"What should we do?" DeMeo asked.

The decision was being made for them. The images began to fade from brilliant colors to shades of gray. The sharp focus dissolved into the soft blurs. The sound returned to ocean waves and then nothing. Soon the only light was the North Star. Then that faded and the chamber began to darken.

"We have to leave," McCauley urged. "The old man was right."

Katrina Alpert understood. They all really did.

"The world isn't ready. Religions, governments, people," McCauley proffered. "Not ready. Initially other scientists will feel excited, as we are. But how can civilization possibly reframe guiding belief systems, rewrite histories already in stone, or replace principles and laws that hold society together. Here's proof that there's so little we know or can possibly understand. Our fields of science are just that. Vast open fields. We plow through facts. We plant seeds of interest in students' minds. We cultivate their thinking process. And we hope our study will bear fruit. And yet, sometimes we harvest an apple we just shouldn't bite."

"And who's to say it won't happen again," Katrina said. "What kind of record will we leave behind?"

"I hope it's not one filled with failure," McCauley offered. *Failure?* he thought. *Not today.*

"I understand why the old man asked us about Cardinal Francesco Barberini," he said. "Why he let us live."

He took Katrina's hands in his. "Remember, what Eccleston told us? Barberini was on the Inquisition panel. He headed it. All that responsibility. All that knowledge and yet he abstained when it came time to convict Galileo of heresy even though he knew about these secrets. And so they allowed Galileo to live. The old man did the same for us."

"Why?" Katrina asked Quinn.

"A dying man's gift. He might have seen in us, what we see in each other—stewardship."

"And now?" she continued.

"Now?" McCauley replied. "We have our duty."

They retreated from the cave, climbed down the ladder

and silently walked one hundred yards more. Jaffe attached wires they had strung from inside the cave to a generator. The former corporal had had real experience with such things in Afghanistan before going to graduate school.

There was one more thing to do.

"You want the honors, Dr. McCauley?"

It had been his discovery. Now it was his path.

"Yes."

The Yale professor placed his right hand on a detonator cobbled together from electronic supplies bought at the local hardware store. He shook his head. "Too much responsibility," he quietly offered. "It's better this way."

McCauley took a deep breath and pressed the button. The explosion rumbled across the valley floor. Tons of earth, representing millions of years of history billowed up, then slowly drifted down making a new layer of strata at Makoshika State Park.

What the Cessna had not done, the team of paleontologists accomplished. They covered up history of Old Earth.

PAST IS PROLOGUE

BY THE ORDER of Inquisition, Galileo was placed under house arrest at his villa in Arcetri, near Florence, Italy. For the rest of his life, his writing and his movements were restricted by the Pope and the Vatican courts.

By 1638, he wasn't even able to gaze at the stars any more. He went completely blind. The result of looking at the sun through his telescope. Some in the Church called it God's punishment.

Galileo died in 1642.

It wasn't until 1992, 359 years after he was wrongly convicted, that the Roman Catholic Church formally admitted its mistake in condemning Galileo's assertion about the earth's relationship to the sun. Pope John Paul II expressed regret and issued a declaration acknowledging errors made by the tribunal.

In 2008, the head of the Pontifical Academy of Sciences announced that the Church would honor the work of Galileo by erecting a statue within the walls of the Vatican. A month later, the plans were suspended.

Venice, Italy
Winter Break

PETE DeMEO WAS vacationing with Lucia Solera. She'd managed to seduce him in every shape and manner, including finding out about the discovery in Montana and what they had done to keep it a secret. Of course she passed along what she learned in a detailed report. That was her job. Falling in love wouldn't change anything.

The following Spring

THE NEWS WAS hardly reported. Two research spelunkers escaped with minor injuries after a catastrophic collapse within a two mile section of Western Kentucky's remarkable Mammoth Caves. They'd been mapping the one thousand mile cave system for National Geographic. Some six hundred miles had remained unexplored. Now it appeared a good section would be inaccessible forever because of the massive internal rock slide, perhaps triggered by unstable earth.

The Associated Press gave it two paragraphs. *USA Today*, the fifth page. The cable news channels didn't cover it at all. But in London, Simon Volker, Martin Gruber's successor, considered it business as usual.

Yale University
One year later

MCCAULEY'S PHONE RANG. "Jesus, who the hell… ?"

He picked up his cell phone from the nightstand and answered in a whisper, hoping not to wake Katrina. "Hello."

"Hey there, Dr. McCauley, it's Robert Greene."

"Oh man, do you have any idea what time it is?"

"Sorry. I never do. Anyway. I finally got great info for you. Don't ask how I tracked it down, but the book you were asking about led to a…."

"Stop! Bury it!" McCauley said. "Trust me. Bury it now and forget you ever saw it."

"You're serious?" Greene asked.

"Beyond serious."

"But you've got my juices going."

"Turn them off. Not this."

"Okay, if you say so. Consider it buried, deleted, erased, and expunged from the record."

"Thank you," Quinn said. "Now may I please go back to sleep?"

"Wait! I have to tell you about something else I'm onto. Ever hear of *mokele-mbembe*?"

"Sure. It's rumored to be a living dinosaur stalking somewhere in west central Africa. About as real as the Loch Ness Monster."

"Maybe you'll think differently after I tell you what I have. Up for an exploration, Dr. McCauley?"

* * * * *

ACKNOWLEDGMENTS

I HAVE SO many people to thank for their help and support through the research, writing, editorial, and marketing stages of *Old Earth*. I'll start with Bruce Coons, my oldest friend and retired Army Officer with a distinguished 40 year military career. Once again, he gave me true guidance on technical detail. Special thanks also go to Brian Aubrey for his attention to earthly issues. Where I bent geological history for the sake of suspending disbelief, he helped me maintain a sense of reality and, dare I say, grounding.

To Jan Greenhawt, Barbara Schwartz, and Chuck Barquist for their assistance reviewing the manuscript. To Debbie and Mark Masuoka and Stan and Debbie Deutsch. To Susan Mitnick and all my friends from Hudson, NY, for their unending support for my latest work.

Of course, thanks to my family. To Helene for her help and excitement in the project, Sasha for her infinite curiosity that always inspires, Zach for our fossil hunting some years back where the idea for *Old Earth* began to gestate, and Jake for introducing me to a key element in the novel, which by now you've read: Vantablack.

Additional thanks to the executives, members, and the community of writers and fans of the International Thriller Writers Association, the great Michael Palmer who launched me in the mystery and thriller genre, and Kimberly Howe for her ongoing attention at ITW convention time. Added thanks to friends and colleagues Jeffrey Davis, Dick Taylor, Robb Weller, along with researcher/

investigator/producer John Greenewald, Jr., KTLA Entertainment Anchor/Reporter Sam Rubin, WBZ Radio talk show host Jordan Rich, and thriller author WG Griffiths. To esteemed PBS television host Barry Kibrick for booking me again and again on his remarkable Emmy Award winning series *Between the Lines*, and to Adam Cushman at Red14Films for his company's creative approach to my book trailers. Thanks as well to Lake Arrowhead Jurassic Fossils, Lake Arrowhead, CA.

Of course, special thanks go to the wonderful team at Diversion Books in New York, led by Publisher Scott Waxman, Editorial Director, Mary Cummings, Editor Randall Klein, the Marketing team of Hannah Black and Brielle Benton, Production Manager Sarah Masterson Hally, and Caroline Teagle for her inspired cover design. Thank you. You're all amazing!

Finally, my interest in the area goes back to my parents, Stanley and Evelyn Grossman, who encouraged me to be a rock hound. I dug and scraped for fossils in limestone quarries left behind by the Columbia County, NY cement factories and chiseled great finds out of the cliffs that overlooked my high school athletic field. I'm sure this will resonate, too: I have to point to those classic Random House *All About Books* and *Landmark Books* on earth sciences, dinosaurs, and history. They were fascinating reads as a kid that definitely created a through-line to my writing today.

ABOUT THE AUTHOR

GARY GROSSMAN'S FIRST NOVEL, *Executive Actions*, propelled him into the world of political thrillers. *Executive Treason*, the sequel, further tapped Grossman's experience as a journalist, newspaper columnist, documentary television producer, reporter and playwright. The third book in the series, *Executive Command*, brought his trilogy to a conclusion...or has it? He has written for the *New York Times*, *Boston Globe*, and *Boston Herald American*. He covered presidential campaigns for WBZ-TV in Boston, and has produced television series for NBC News, CNN, NBC, ABC, CBS, FOX and 40 cable networks. He is a multiple Emmy Award winning producer, served as chair of the Government Affairs Committee for the Caucus for Television, Producers, Writers and Directors, and is a member of the International Thriller Writers Association. Grossman has taught at Emerson College (where he is a member of the Board of Trustees), Boston University, USC, and Loyola Marymount University, and is a contributing editor to *Media Ethics Magazine*.

For more information on Old Earth and other works by Gary Grossman visit www.garygrossman.com.

Follow Gary Grossman on Twitter@garygrossman1.

REQUEST YOUR FREE BOOKS!
2 FREE NOVELS PLUS 2 FREE GIFTS!

 HARLEQUIN®

INTRIGUE

BREATHTAKING ROMANTIC SUSPENSE

REQUEST YOUR FREE BOOKS!

2 FREE NOVELS PLUS 2 FREE GIFTS!

H HARLEQUIN®

ROMANTIC suspense

Sparked by danger, fueled by passion

YES! Please send me 2 FREE Harlequin® Romantic Suspense novels and my 2 FREE gifts (gifts are worth about $10). After receiving them, if I don't wish to receive any more books, I can return the shipping statement marked "cancel." If I don't cancel, I will receive 4 brand-new novels every month and be billed just $4.74 per book in the U.S. or $5.49 per book in Canada. That's a savings of at least 12% off the cover price! It's quite a bargain! Shipping and handling is just 50¢ per book in the U.S. and 75¢ per book in Canada.* I understand that accepting the 2 free books and gifts places me under no obligation to buy anything. I can always return a shipment and cancel at any time. Even if I never buy another book, the two free books and gifts are mine to keep forever.

240/340 HDN GH3P

Name _____ (PLEASE PRINT) _____

Address _____ Apt. # _____

City _____ State/Prov. _____ Zip/Postal Code _____

Signature (if under 18, a parent or guardian must sign) _____

Mail to the **Reader Service:**

IN U.S.A.: P.O. Box 1867, Buffalo, NY 14240-1867
IN CANADA: P.O. Box 609, Fort Erie, Ontario L2A 5X3

**Want to try two free books from another line?
Call 1-800-873-8635 or visit www.ReaderService.com.**

* Terms and prices subject to change without notice. Prices do not include applicable taxes. Sales tax applicable in N.Y. Canadian residents will be charged applicable taxes. Offer not valid in Quebec. This offer is limited to one order per household. Not valid for current subscribers to Harlequin Romantic Suspense books. All orders subject to credit approval. Credit or debit balances in a customer's account(s) may be offset by any other outstanding balance owed by or to the customer. Please allow 4 to 6 weeks for delivery. Offer available while quantities last.

Your Privacy—The Reader Service is committed to protecting your privacy. Our Privacy Policy is available online at www.ReaderService.com or upon request from the Reader Service.

We make a portion of our mailing list available to reputable third parties that offer products we believe may interest you. If you prefer that we not exchange your name with third parties, or if you wish to clarify or modify your communication preferences, please visit us at www.ReaderService.com/consumerschoice or write to us at Reader Service Preference Service, P.O. Box 9062, Buffalo, NY 14240-9062. Include your complete name and address.

HRS15

REQUEST YOUR FREE BOOKS!

2 FREE NOVELS
FROM THE SUSPENSE COLLECTION
PLUS 2 FREE GIFTS!

YES! Please send me 2 FREE novels from the Suspense Collection and my 2 FREE gifts (gifts are worth about $10). After receiving them, if I don't wish to receive any more books, I can return the shipping statement marked "cancel." If I don't cancel, I will receive 4 brand-new novels every month and be billed just $6.49 per book in the U.S. or $6.99 per book in Canada. That's a savings of at least 19% off the cover price. It's quite a bargain! Shipping and handling is just 50¢ per book in the U.S. and 75¢ per book in Canada.* I understand that accepting the 2 free books and gifts places me under no obligation to buy anything. I can always return a shipment and cancel at any time. Even if I never buy another book, the two free books and gifts are mine to keep forever.

191/391 MDN GH4Z

Name	(PLEASE PRINT)	
Address		Apt. #
City	State/Prov.	Zip/Postal Code

Signature (if under 18, a parent or guardian must sign)

Mail to the **Reader Service**:
IN U.S.A.: P.O. Box 1867, Buffalo, NY 14240-1867
IN CANADA: P.O. Box 609, Fort Erie, Ontario L2A 5X3

Want to try two free books from another line?
Call 1-800-873-8635 or visit www.ReaderService.com.

* Terms and prices subject to change without notice. Prices do not include applicable taxes. Sales tax applicable in N.Y. Canadian residents will be charged applicable taxes. Offer not valid in Quebec. This offer is limited to one order per household. Not valid for current subscribers to the Suspense Collection or the Romance/Suspense Collection. All orders subject to credit approval. Credit or debit balances in a customer's account(s) may be offset by any other outstanding balance owed by or to the customer. Please allow 4 to 6 weeks for delivery. Offer available while quantities last.

Your Privacy—The Reader Service is committed to protecting your privacy. Our Privacy Policy is available online at www.ReaderService.com or upon request from the Reader Service.

We make a portion of our mailing list available to reputable third parties that offer products we believe may interest you. If you prefer that we not exchange your name with third parties, or if you wish to clarify or modify your communication preferences, please visit us at www.ReaderService.com/consumerchoice or write to us at Reader Service Preference Service, P.O. Box 9062, Buffalo, NY 14240-9062. Include your complete name and address.

READERSERVICE.COM

Manage your account online!

- Review your order history
- Manage your payments
- Update your address

> ## We've designed the Reader Service website just for you.

Enjoy all the features!

- Discover new series available to you, and read excerpts from any series.
- Respond to mailings and special monthly offers.
- Connect with favorite authors at the blog.
- Browse the Bonus Bucks catalog and online-only exculsives.
- Share your feedback.

Visit us at:

ReaderService.com

RS15